# THE
# TRUTH
# ABOUT
# WHITE
# LIES

BY OLIVIA A. COLE

*The Truth About White Lies*

A CONSPIRACY OF STARS

*A Conspiracy of Stars*
*An Anatomy of Beasts*

# THE TRUTH ABOUT WHITE LIES

OLIVIA A. COLE

LITTLE, BROWN AND COMPANY

New York · Boston

*For Jess and Starkisha*

---

Little, Brown and Company
Hachette Book Group
1290 Avenue of the Americas, New York, NY 10104
Visit us at LBYR.com

First Edition: March 2022

Little, Brown and Company is a division of Hachette Book Group, Inc. The Little, Brown name and logo are trademarks of Hachette Book Group, Inc.

The publisher is not responsible for websites (or their content) that are not owned by the publisher.

Library of Congress Cataloging-in-Publication Data
Names: Cole, Olivia A., author.
Title: The truth about white lies / Olivia A. Cole.
Description: First edition. | New York : Little, Brown and Company, 2022 |
Audience: Ages 14 & up. | Summary: "An unflinching story about Shania, a white girl who, after moving to a gentrifying city, reckons with her role in racism there, the historical and present day effects of white supremacy, and the danger in silence"—Provided by publisher.
Identifiers: LCCN 2021010569 | ISBN 9780759554122 (hardcover) |
ISBN 9780759554115 (ebook)
Subjects: CYAC: Racism—Fiction. | White supremacy movements—Fiction.
Classification: LCC PZ7.1.C6429 Tr 2022 | DDC [Fic]—dc23
LC record available at https://lccn.loc.gov/2021010569

ISBNs: 978-0-7595-5412-2 (hardcover), 978-0-7595-5411-5 (ebook)

Printed in the United States of America

LSC-C

Printing 1, 2021

"The opposite of love's indifference." —The Lumineers

"In maintaining the pretense of its invisibility, Whiteness maintains the pretense of its inevitability, and its innocence." —Dr. Eve L. Ewing

Dear Reader,

This story contains discussions of racism and white supremacy in subtle and not-so-subtle terms. There are no outright racial slurs in this book, but their absence may not make its contents less painful. In addition, there are discussions of fatphobia and Islamophobia. Please read with caution.

# PROLOGUE

*February*

With her grandmother's heart and arms too weak to lift the soil, Shania had come to help bury the dog.

"I think under the sycamore is best," Gram said. "Or maybe by the willow. What do you think?"

Shania surveyed the wide green yard, the chipping white fence that contained it. There were only the two trees, as scrubby and stunted as the rest of her hometown of Morrisville, and Simon had spent enough hours under them, it was true. But like his person, Simon's true love had been the shade of the garden, and Shania's eyes fell on the neat rows at the center of the yard. This was where he had often settled his smooth, spotted body while Gram tended the vegetables.

"What about by the tomatoes?" Shania asked. "Is that bad for the garden, to put a dead dog in it? He took so many naps there. Maybe right next to it?"

And if Shania hadn't been thinking of one kind of grief, she may not have missed the other—the cloud that passed over her grandmother's face as she considered the garden, the only thing Gram really called her own. Medicine and doctors' bills took the rest, Gram's efforts to fix the heart in her chest that didn't quite know how to be a heart without some help. Gram looked at the tomatoes, and Shania might have seen the remembering, but she was picking up the shovel, testing it against stiff earth.

"Why not?" her grandmother said softly. "Nothing helps growth like death."

Shania dug while her grandmother watched, both shivering a little in the wind. The sycamore shuddered. At their feet was the bundle of yellow blanket, Simon inside, once a beagle but now just another seed. The wind shifted the fringe of the blanket he had claimed as his own. "Chenille!" Gram had always exclaimed, but she never took it from him. Now it was going in the ground.

"I don't think I can keep it up," her grandmother said, but Shania kept digging.

"I'll help you," Shania said. "Anything you can't do, you can teach me, and I'll do it."

Shania was busy with the soil, the sharp tooth of the shovel, thinking about how this garden in the middle of Morrisville sometimes felt like the only place with life. Gram saw the whole town as an oasis she would never abandon, and Shania felt a duty to love it a little out of loyalty, but the way the garden looked in February was the way Morrisville felt to her year-round. School was school—her handful of half-friends, theater kids who didn't mind that she sat silent most of the time. They needed an audience, and Shania needed to watch—at least at first. But first impressions always turned into expectations, especially in Morrisville, where you were cast as the role you auditioned for. In first grade, Shania had been a swaying daisy in the background of the *Alice in Wonderland* musical, and a swaying daisy she had remained. In Morrisville, a daisy could never become Alice. At least in her grandmother's garden, Shania was where a daisy belonged.

"There's something I always wanted to tell you," Gram said, and Shania looked. At some point while she'd been digging, Gram had crouched down next to the still form that had been Simon. "Something I think you need to know."

Shania thought it was about her father—a feeling Gram had always had, an omen on Shania's parents' wedding night that predicted his eventual departure with a rich woman eighteen years his senior, floating out of Morrisville the way Shania's mother always wished she herself would. Shania went back to digging. The shovel sounded like a hatchet.

"If it's about Dad," Shania said, "I don't really need to know, okay? He's a liar."

And if Shania hadn't been so focused on the cracking in her heart, she might have noticed the way Gram's hand had risen to cover her own.

"We all are, sweet pea," Gram said. A few strands of silver hair had escaped from her hat and fluttered as the breeze picked up.

"We're all what?" Shania said.

"Liars."

At the moment Shania's shovel cut through pale roots, her grandmother slumped over in the garden, lips fluttering. Her hat rolled on its brim and came to a rest beneath the tomatoes. Gram and the beagle were two bright, still things under a dishwater sky, and Shania's scream rose into it, startling the crows, sending them spinning toward the sun, as her mother sprinted from the house.

By the time the ambulance took her grandmother away—Shania's mother in the back, her eyes dry and grim—the birds had settled back onto their branches. Shania had nothing else to do but put the dog in the hole she'd dug and smooth soil over the top like gauze over a wound.

# CHAPTER 1

*September*

After the drab blue and gray of the bus's interior—the color of a public bathroom, the same lingering smell—the blood on the concrete seems impossibly red. Comic book red. A deep, important scarlet. Shania doesn't notice until it's already on her shoes.

"Shit," she whispers, staring down, trying to convince herself it's paint. She looks up and scans the brick wall beyond the sidewalk. Graffiti, but none of it red. None of it new. She assumes graffiti artists use spray paint, not a bucket that might be tipped. She glances around, but there's no one near enough to see, and certainly no one she knows. She's still learning the names of all this new city's parts, and this is South Blue Rock, or as most people call it, SoBR.

At night SoBR's streets swarm with bar hoppers, cars with Lyft signs in the windshields. At eight o'clock in the morning, however, just Paulie's and Goddess are open: doughnuts and cold-pressed organic juice. SoBR has only been a trendy part of town for a few years. Graffiti is starting to peel in places, men with no homes fade in and out of sight like specters, and across the street two thin white women wearing leggings leave Goddess clutching cups of juice and laughing nasally laughs. Shania had applied to Goddess before Paulie's but didn't know what wheatgrass was. She knew what doughnuts were. Mr. Ahmed hired her immediately.

She steps inside Paulie's, where Mr. Ahmed himself stands behind the counter. He's tall and narrow as a phone pole, with only a slight paunch at his waist to indicate he owns the oldest doughnut shop in Blue Rock. When the door closes behind her, Shania is sealed into the yeasty aroma that only old-fashioned bakeries can emit. She has to swallow then, as she does every time she walks in. The smell is like her grandmother's house, and as happens often since the funeral, the memories are so loud in her head they threaten to scream.

"You've come for your riches," calls Mr. Ahmed, not taking his eyes off the TV hanging in the corner.

"My minimum-wage treasure, please," Shania says, but he ignores her, gesturing instead at the TV in outrage.

"A new Dunking Donuts," he enunciates. "By the airport. Bastards!"

"But the airport is like eight miles from here," Shania says.

He narrows his eyes at her.

"You think people will not drive eight miles for this? Their cheap coffee? We must have a special now. We will call it Commuter Coupon. You come Monday through Thursday, and then Friday you get free coffee. Eh?"

He opens his arms wide, a demand for feedback.

"That's pretty good," Shania says. "Maybe let them choose whether they get a free coffee or a free doughnut. People like doughnuts on Fridays."

"They do?"

"Yeah, sure. The weekend. You know? I don't know."

"Yes," he says solemnly. "TGIF."

"Right."

"Everything is good, working at night?"

"Yeah, it's good, Mr. Ahmed. Thanks for working with my school schedule."

He nods, rubbing his short beard.

"You work late. You are a young woman. You have someone taking you home at night?"

"I take the bus," she says. "It's no big deal."

"Your parents are happy with this?" he asks. She thinks he doesn't really mean *happy*; he means *okay*. It's not okay, but she lies.

"Sure," she says. "SoBR is really busy at night. It's not like anything's going to happen with all those people around."

"Yes, yes, but this neighborhood...it is changing. Can cause bumps."

"Huh?"

"You know. Like an earthquake." He places his hands palm down, side by side, then rubs the sides of them against each other. His fingers overlap, then move apart, then overlap again. "When the plates in the earth shift, everything shakes. There is shaking here sometimes. Watch where you put your feet."

Outside, check in hand, she feels the temporary surge of "having." A few feet away, two more white women, one carrying a rolled-up yoga mat, prepare to cross the street. The one carrying the mat wears a shirt that reads NAMA-STAY IN BED. She discusses her imminent juice order, and Shania's eyes flit toward Goddess. The woman is pretty, and Shania considers spending six dollars of her newly acquired money on the bright-green juice, just to have something in common with her. But then she sees the woman's teeth: impossibly white, all obeying the rules of geometry, a mouthful of blank dominoes. Shania's tongue finds her top-right canine, which sticks out slightly like a bent spoke on a bicycle. It's her reminder: Every penny is already claimed. She imagines fixing her teeth will somehow fix all her other problems. But right now she needs to catch the bus.

The Blue Rock Transit Authority app tells her she has four minutes as she trots down the street toward the corner, eyeing the cracked soil on either edge of the sidewalk. Here and there is bindweed, which perhaps someone encouraged to grow, not recognizing a weed when they saw one. The roots, she knows, are nests of pallid snakes beneath the ground—the same plants are outside the dumpy apartment she and her mother now call home, their own roots dug out of Morrisville after her grandmother's death. First her parents' divorce and then Gram's funeral—Shania doesn't blame her mother for fleeing.

This new state is concave and humid, but it's green—at least, once you get to the edges of Blue Rock. Gram never visited this city (or any city) and would've preferred, if they'd had to leave Morrisville, that they live in the country as she did. "Closer to God," she always said, and even crocheted it on a pillow. But the countryside doesn't have the most expensive high school in the region, and that's why Shania and her mother are really here—a parting gift from her father, financed by "the woman," as Shania's mother calls her: *If the woman wants to try to buy us off by paying for your school, we'll let her. But we won't make it cheap.*

Shania pulls out her student ID as she walks. In it, her face smiles out uncertainly, the pastel pink and blue in her hair still fresh from when she had it done over the summer, her eyes the same cerulean. They'd spelled her name wrong: SHANIA GESTER. It's Hester. But she's grateful that they at least hadn't spelled it with an *F*. The hair had been a "new school" gift from her mother when they decided she'd be going to Bard Academy for Excellence—a bribe for leaving Morrisville. Her life there has faded like the colors in her hair, and she's glad of the latter, at least. She realized quickly that Bard isn't the kind of school for unicorn hair. At the edge of SoBR, Bard is something like a hidden fortress in *Lord of the Rings*, surrounded by (urban) wildlife, populated by the children of the oldest, wealthiest families in Blue Rock. Highlights are always Legolas-blonde at Bard, one of their many codes.

Her phone vibrates—a text from Hallie, the one person from Morrisville who has tried to keep in touch.

**Miss you! Guess who just found out she's on the event planning committee? PROM SHALL BE MINE.**

Shania smiles. Hallie is a theater kid but also a big activity girl. Whoever gave her the reins would realize very soon that they may have created a monster. Shania replies with a long string of hearts and a Cinderella GIF. It feels a little strange texting her— like Gram's death turned Morrisville into a cemetery. Texting Hallie is like communing with the dead.

At the bus stop she almost steps in blood again. The sun has moved just in these few minutes and falls differently on the puddle now. It coats the pavement ahead of her in a wet, crimson splash, an undefined shape like a red cloud or a puff of smoke.

And there she is, appearing as she so often does. Her grandmother—the blood is hers for the instant Shania lets her mind wander. It's a strange thing, because Gram's death wasn't the bloody kind. It was the slow kind, the kind with tubes and shrugging doctors. So perhaps, Shania thinks, the blood on the pavement feels like her own—as if the ripping of her grandmother from her life left a gaping hole, as red and raw as fresh meat.

"Breakfast," a voice says, and Shania jerks. It comes from a man leaning in the corner of the bus shelter, his dingy gray shirt hanging off his body like a shroud. Shania hadn't even noticed him.

"What?" she says.

He clears his throat.

"Puts you off your breakfast." His gums are the bright pink of a kitten's tongue.

"Yeah," Shania mutters, looking again at the blood. Her mind reels back from the day in the garden, from the following days in the Morrisville hospital. Now a stab of different unease aches between her ribs, her mind beginning to run away with itself. The man's proximity, the rasp of his voice, the hole in his shoe with the sock exposed like fuzzy organs through a wound. He, too, is staring at the blood.

"Called the police," he says. "By the time they came, the thing was gone. Should've called animal control. Maybe they could've helped it."

"Helped what?"

"The cat," he says, blinking at her. "Somebody knifed it up. Started down there." He points, and Shania follows his finger with her eyes, back the way she had come. She sees the blood now, a trail down the concrete that she hadn't noticed.

"In front of the hat shop," he says. "That's where it happened."

"You saw it happen?"

"Cops weren't interested," he says, nodding. "I told 'em you gotta be a monster to kill an animal like that. No reason. No defense. What's a cat going to do about a knife? I thought it came here to die." His eyes are back on the blood at Shania's feet. "But it ended up somewhere else."

"Oh," Shania says. She wants to be on the bus, to be departing.

"Watch yourself out here," he says, and she thinks it sounds like he's talking to himself now. "There's monsters in Southtown. The light is always above them, so they don't cast a shadow."

She steps off the bus in front of Bard Academy, and the morning air curls around her ankles like uncut grass. The *Farmers' Almanac*, a slim bound book with dates and predictions for the year ahead, says it will be an early fall. Shania carries her own edition, a sad replacement for the one she'd grown up watching her grandmother leaf through. Gram's copy was out of date—from 1999—but Gram always swore, without explanation, that it was the only year that mattered. It's been almost seven months since her death, and where some people might get closer to the Bible, Shania has turned to the almanac. She and her mother had emptied Gram's house after the funeral, Shania searching every inch for the 1999 copy. But like her grandmother, it was a ghost. Shania's current version is an imitational comfort, and she peeks in her bag to ensure it's there, tucked in with her book of Anne Stanton's poetry. Gram had liked Anne Stanton, a woman who wrote about the earth and its creatures. So Shania carries them both: talismans.

Shania climbs the steps, moving between classmates who ignore her. If she had dreams of leaving the role of swaying daisy behind, she has now become a different sort of Alice. The student body of Bard regards her like the talking flowers did on the girl's first foray into Wonderland: *Is she one of us? No, not quite. Her dress is like petals but there's something that's off. She must be a weed.*

She drops off her bag at her locker. Two girls brush past her, all spray-tanned legs and white, white teeth. They carry over-priced coffee from Rhino. Before she moved here, Shania had no idea people her age drank coffee. In Morrisville, if you were tired before class, you drank Red Bull. Bard is like a movie-set version of a school, and nothing about it feels like home. Except the greenhouse.

It's nestled in the heart of the building, a humid core of flowers and vines and rows of work planters where every semester the class raises a variety of plants, experimenting with soil toxicity, different pesticides, hydroponics. Shania's careful little family of hollyhocks and spiderwort are the only relationships she's been able to cultivate since school began; her tiny crop of green babies is a mere two feet long, but she looks forward to seeing it, like a dog at the end of a long day. Except this day is just beginning. Just sixty-two more until winter break.

Michelle is already there, at the neighboring planter, the only person who might like the greenhouse more than Shania.

"Hey," Shania says. They usually say hey. Michelle doesn't hear her today: She has earbuds in, and rap music drifts faintly to Shania's ears, a small surprise. Michelle looks like a beauty queen, a Black girl with straight hair to her shoulders and a wide, warm smile that belongs at the door of a church. She doesn't seem like the rap-music type, Shania thinks. When Michelle asked Shania's name at the beginning of the year, she'd said, "Oh, like the singer?" and Shania had reserved some small hope that perhaps they had some secret common interests. But Michelle mostly keeps to herself, and Shania hasn't quite mastered the trick of being a normal person in a world without Gram. It's a little like relearning how to walk.

She almost tries greeting Michelle again, but Adam and JP are blundering in, laughing. Michelle looks up, one hand plucking an earbud out. The music is gone.

"Those are my garden gloves, bro," JP says, snatching a pair from Adam's grasp. "You've got little, tiny baby-hands. You can't fit these."

"Better than your little, tiny baby—"

"Oh, bro, shut the fuck up!"

"What even is that?" JP grunts, pointing at Adam's planter. "Did you plant poison ivy?"

"No, but that would be an epic prank."

"Better if you planted some weed."

Catherine Tane sweeps in, her blonde dreadlocks tied into a thick bushel at her neck. She doesn't wear the short shorts and sandals that the rest of the girls wear: She swishes around in a long white peasant skirt, three inches of golden belly showing above it before the rest of her is concealed in what appears to be a hand-knit halter top. She's fond of calling herself a sexy hippie.

"Who's talking about weed?" Catherine says.

"Michelle," JP says, pointing.

Michelle rolls her eyes. "Please."

"I bet you Ms. Hassoon is a total weedhead," JP says.

"Obviously." Catherine nods.

"Didn't she move here from Cali? I'm going to ask her if she knows anybody who owns a dispensary. That's what I'm going to do with this botany shit."

"You and a thousand other people," says Catherine. "By the time you graduate, there's going to be so many."

"It's not even legal here yet! Maybe I'll be the first fucking one."

"You need to sell munchies too," Adam offers. "What are those chips your brother's always eating, Catherine? The square ones."

"I don't keep tabs on Prescott's snack habits," she says, staring at her phone. Shania's heart flips a small, irrational somersault at the mention of Prescott Tane. Catherine's brother is a Bard golden boy despite missing so much school that the teachers applaud when he actually shows up. He plays lacrosse and has Captain America hair and the same catalog smile as Catherine, though he uses it much less. Shania has never spoken to Prescott, but she sees him and has spent a lot of time thinking about what she would say to him if they did speak.

"Well, whatever they are, I'm going to need them," JP says. "If I'm going to corner the market, then I need all your support."

"Too much competition," Catherine says, still looking at her phone.

JP laughs. "All my competition is in jail," he says.

"This is the perfect time to become a weed expert," Adam says with a nod. "You're going to be rich!"

*Richer*, Shania thinks, annoyance sprouting in her like a sapling. JP's car keys are sitting on his work table—she can see the

Jaguar emblem from where she sits. If the keys were hers, her tooth would already be in line.

"It's not really fair that they have to be in jail if it's legal now," Shania says. She surprises herself. But there's no going back now.

"What?" JP's smirk is the expression one makes at an ant before it is squashed.

"If they're legalizing weed everywhere," Shania says, making it up as she goes along, "then, I don't know, they should let out all the people that are in jail for it from before."

If Shania's mother were here, she'd stare at her daughter as if she had grown a second head. She's worked in jails for the last twelve years, and Shania knows she would disagree with this speech. Shania doesn't even know if she herself believes it, but the need to be contrary is like a sudden twitch of limbs. This is who Gram had been—tough as a walnut, mouthful of opinions. Shania steps into her shadow.

Adam shrugs on behalf of JP.

"I mean, they broke a law, though. It was illegal before. They need to do their time."

"That seems like—like bullshit," Shania says, stammering a little now that it's settled in that she's actually talking to these people. "People are making tons of money doing the same thing other people used to get arrested for? That's...I mean, that's bullshit."

"Oh my God," Catherine says, finally putting down her phone. "You are so fucking *woke*."

On her other side, Shania hears the slightest scoff from Michelle, sees the smallest twist of her mouth. Michelle's eyes dart in Catherine's direction, then she puts her earbuds back in.

"You hear that?" Catherine says, curling her lip at the boys. "Woke Girl says your dispensary plans are nardshark."

"What does that even mean?" Shania says. This is part of the Bard lexicon. *Nardshark. Quayloo. Tomrom.* Nonsense words mostly invented by Catherine that the rest of the student body snaps up like piranhas.

"It means JP is an idiot," Catherine says happily.

Ms. Hassoon glides in then, the hijab she wears a soft lavender. She's paired it with a matching gardening apron.

"I'm having a party later," Catherine says, addressing JP and Adam. "Bring some of your future stock."

She winks, and then Shania is surprised when those shiny blue eyes are turned on her.

"You should come too. It'll be fun. I need somebody to tag team JP with when he gets drunk and starts talking about how great *Game of Thrones* is. Do you hate *Game of Thrones*? You have the look of someone who hates *Game of Thrones*."

"I do." Shania nods, slipping on the lie like velvet gloves. She's never seen the show.

"Tomrom," says Catherine. "I knew it."

"Pesticides," Ms. Hassoon calls. "Who did the homework?"

Beside Shania, Michelle strokes the leaves of her roses. Shania looks down at the strong green shoots weaving their way up the trellis of her own planter. She makes plans to read the *Game of Thrones* wiki. She's already planning what she will wear. *Growth,* she thinks. *Good.*

# CHAPTER 2

She shouldn't have worn a dress.

Shania had envisioned entering the party and the music slowing, the fabric of her dress a swinging red lantern that lights up the room. But home mirrors are traitors—she had thought she looked retro-movie-star pale, moonrock pale. Now, stepping off the bus that the BRTA app said would take her to Catherine Tane's house, her skin looks splotchy, bluish. She's on the sidewalk, hesitating, considering catching a bus home, when someone calls her name. She looks around, startled, and finds a Black girl standing near the corner, looking at her curiously. It takes Shania a moment to recognize her.

"Michelle," Shania says finally, surprised. Michelle waves, and Shania notices the person beside her, Willa Langford, a white girl from Bard who Shania had seen on Catherine Tane's Instagram when she'd lurked her long-ago posts. Willa's hair is different, Shania decides: dyed a deep red now instead of the blonde featured in Catherine's feed.

"What are you doing over here?" Michelle says. "Are you going to Catherine's too?"

"Yeah."

"You're about to cross the wrong way," Willa says.

They walk through the residential area that has emerged near the SoBR neighborhood. Shania follows Michelle and Willa, almost breathless from trying to keep up in her cursed wedges, but to ask them to slow down would be too close to acknowledging the ridiculousness of her chosen attire, so she just trudges along. She distracts herself by gaping at the outlandish houses. Most of them hug the street closely, ornate gates guarding their meticulously landscaped front yards.

"None of this used to be here," Michelle says. "I remember when this was all warehouses and shotgun homes. We would drive through on the way to my aunt's church."

"No wonder these look so new," Shania says.

"My uncle lived over here when I was a kid," Willa says, texting as she walks. "There used to be a lady who sold cookies on that corner every Sunday. Wish she still did. I'm hungry as shit."

"Catherine will have something," Michelle says.

"Of course she will," Willa says, and Shania thinks she hears something in her voice, but by the time she gets a glimpse of Willa's face, any trace of it is swallowed up.

Michelle looks at Shania out of the corner of her eye, a subtle up and down.

"First party?" she asks, a hint of a smile in her voice.

"Is it that obvious?"

Shania looks down at herself once more. Her legs don't look as violently white now that she's off the bus. She prays Catherine's house is dim.

"It's a cute dress, though," Michelle says, generous.

Shania is about to reply when a man appears before them, hanging out the window of a green car, mouth wide open. He's already passed by the time she catches the words he spews.

"ONE HAS TITS, TWO HAVE ASS! I'LL TAKE ALL THREE!"

The girls stare after him silently.

"Who the fuck drives a green car," Michelle says finally, and Shania bursts out laughing. Michelle smiles a grim smile and Willa chuckles. The crosswalk pings to WALK, and the three of them cross the street, making the rest of their way to Catherine's in silence.

Catherine Tane's home is a three-story outrage on a hill, at the end of a winding driveway surrounded by a crush of leafy trees. The entire ground level is made of glass and metal, wood and crystal, and Willa opens the door without knocking. Music bursts out. She walks right in, Michelle on her heels. They seem to be on a mission. Shania hesitates and then follows them inside, where Bard kids sprawl on couches and plush rugs. There are no cardboard boxes crowding the edges of the room; the baseboards aren't gray with several tenants' worth of dust. The house and the people in it seem to shine.

"Look who's here," Willa says next to her, nodding at a chestnut-haired boy coming out of what must be the kitchen. He has a slice of pizza on a plate and edges along the perimeter of the party with the look of someone who wants to go unnoticed.

"Who's that?" Shania says.

"Benjamin Tane. Prescott and Catherine's brother."

"Wait, there's a third Tane? Does he go to Bard?"

"There's actually a fourth Tane too," Willa says. "Older,

though. Dad's first marriage. But no, Ben opted for public school. Catherine and Prescott unofficially hate him. The redheaded sheep."

"He doesn't have red hair," Shania says, peering.

"No, but like, you know, the 'redheaded stepchild' but with 'black sheep.' Like, he's not actually a stepchild, but...ugh, never mind. You ruined my joke."

"Sorry," Shania says, shrugging.

"I haven't seen him since last year," Michelle says. "He got cute."

"He was always cute," Willa counters.

"Says the gay girl."

"Which makes my taste even more trustworthy. He's cool too, though. Comes to the library sometimes. We've been talking more."

They drift off, and Shania is too shy to follow, which leaves her weaving her way through people whose faces she knows but who don't know her. Parties, and especially this one, make her feel like an alien zipped into flesh. She drifts outside, trying to look human.

"You came!" Catherine's voice rises over the music and party chatter, and Shania turns to find Catherine beelining toward her through the crowd, drink in hand. Catherine pauses, assessing Shania's dress. "You're so...fancy."

"I, uh, I'm coming from a dinner," Shania says.

If Catherine hears the lie in Shania's voice, she plows right past it, handing her a drink.

"No bigs! Feel free to take your shoes off. They look like they hurt. I can't wear heels anymore. I have bunions. My mom says I'll need surgery at some point, but if I did it now, then I'd have to be in a cast or whatever, and I'd be out of field hockey. So quayloo. Fuck that. I'll wait."

"I didn't know you played field hockey," Shania says. She did, in fact. But this was a conversational tool of her grandmother's. Be polite. Be curious. Shania remembers Gram smiling in her garden. Then she was slumping on the ground.

Shania shakes her head, returning to the conversation. But Catherine has already moved on from field hockey, leading Shania toward the table where the drinks are stacked.

"There's food in the kitchen too," Catherine says, flapping her hand toward her beast of a home. "Pizza and shit."

"I saw your brother with some. Ben."

"Oh, Ben made an appearance? Shocking. Honestly, Shania, my family is the worst. I have two brothers considered hot by people not related to them, and both are different versions of annoying. Why couldn't I have sisters? We could have been like the sexier version of the Bennets."

"Who?"

"*Pride and Prejudice*, Shania. I'd be Elizabeth. If Elizabeth smoked weed."

Having Catherine talk directly to you, Shania realizes, is sort of like standing in the path of a grinning hurricane. Catherine passes her a drink.

"Where's that dress from?" Catherine says, changing gears.

Shania tells her, and Catherine nods several times.

"I always see that account on Instagram, but I don't think my boobs are big enough to make anything they have look good. You don't really have that problem, so that's cool. Good for you. Good for your boobs."

"Thanks, I guess." Shania laughs. She can feel her spine

loosening. She slips her wedges off, bends down, and clutches them in her drinkless hand. *I can be normal*, she insists to herself. A new normal. Someone whose throat doesn't close around a sob when she smells bread or sees a beagle. Someone who goes to parties and laughs. Morrisville is in the past. This is now.

Someone cranks the music, and a pop song Shania vaguely recognizes booms out over the pool, jerking her back into the moment—she swears the water ripples. Catherine points at someone Shania can't see near the house and yells *yeahhhh* in approval of the musical selection. Turning and shimmying her shoulders playfully, her blonde dreadlocks *thwip* left and right as she swings her head in time to the beat. Her smile is infectious, her tan convincing, and her teeth white as a puppy's. *She's the right kind of friend*, Shania thinks. *The kind of friend who's like confetti over your life.* Shania lets her shoulders loosen and sways a little to the music, trying to look as carefree as Catherine Tane absolutely is.

The song transitions into a bass-heavy rap song, and Catherine grabs a drink off the table, holding it aloft and wiggling her hips.

"*Michelllllle*," she cries, throwing her head back like a wolf. "Dance with me!"

Michelle looks up from where she's sitting by the pool with Willa. She sits cross-legged at the edge rather than putting her feet in. She smiles at Catherine, but it's a guarded smile, delicate like a cathedral window. She waves Catherine off and doesn't move.

"Michelle! Teach me how to twerk," Catherine says, galloping over to the pool and reaching down to tug on Michelle's wrist. "Come on, I love this song! Teach me!"

Michelle's church smile tightens, like the glass it's made of has encountered a pebble, a hairline crack spreading across it. Beside her, Willa's back has stiffened. She'd been twirling her hair around her wrist, but now she lets it flop free, a curtain of fire over her shoulders. Her eyes dart over to the house, then back at Catherine.

"I don't know how," Shania sees Michelle's mouth say, but she can't hear her.

"Come on, of course you know how! Teach me to twerk, Michelle!"

Willa leans in and whispers something to Michelle, her mouth twisted to an angle that communicates *pissed*. Having no luck pulling Michelle to her feet, Catherine backs away, dropping her hands to her knees and jerking her hips left and right. Her smile is star bright, the drink in her cup spilling onto her bare feet. Willa and Michelle maneuver to the edge of the party. Catherine's laughter carries over the music, and then Blake and Amy and other people laugh too, at the absurdity of it—at the welcome feeling of shared shame transforming into pride.

Shania knows one must be careful in moments like these. Laugh too much or stand too close, and the lens can shift quickly. Then it'll be "Shania, can you twerk? Let's see!" and Shania is not a girl like Catherine, to whom a blush is a tool or a trick. A blush for Shania is a fallen domino, which will then lead to her entire chest turning strawberry, her voice squeaky, her armpits sweaty. While the song booms on, she edges carefully sideways, making her way around the water to a balcony.

The air is chillier at the balcony rail, away from the heat of intoxicated bodies and the pool. But the view. She remembers what the homeless man at the bus stop had said about monsters lurking in SoBR, but from here the area is fangless and sparkling.

If there are monsters below, they've retreated to their caves. Still, Shania can think only of her grandmother, the way she spurned cities, even pretty ones, and again finds herself longing for the almanac that Gram had kept so close, always on her bedside table. Shania supposes that a book, like a person, can be there one moment and then gone the next. She pulls out her phone. It's ten—her mother should be on break.

**Can we go to the storage unit this weekend?** Shania texts her. **I want to check that box with Gram's photo albums one more time to make sure we didn't miss her almanac.**

Her mother's reply is quick—just as Shania expects. Knowing her schedule has been key in getting away with working nights at Paulie's.

**We've checked ten times, Shane. It'll turn up.**

"You dropped a shoe," a boy's voice says, and she jumps. Her grip slips, and she juggles her beer for a long second before it ultimately falls with a pop, hissing out onto the concrete.

"Whoa." He laughs, jumping back. "Relax. I'm not going to rob you."

Between her shoe in his outstretched hand and the liquid just beyond her bare toes, it takes her half a breath to realize the boy she almost spilled beer on is Prescott Tane.

"I—I—sorry," she stammers, reaching for her wedge. The beer snakes closer to him in a slow golden swell. "Look out... Those look like really nice shoes."

"Shoes," he says, touching the approaching beer flood with a toe. "That's what they're for."

"Yeah," she says, still flustered. "Yeah, I guess so."

His eyes sweep down over her, and it's as if her blush has grown massive red hands that encircle her throat in a chokehold.

"That's a really nice dress," he says, and his eyes mean it. "No one dresses up for parties anymore."

His hair is short on the sides and long on top, a golden-brown flop hanging down near one eye. It's jock with maybe a little punk, grown out from a floppy swoop into something gelled and purposeful. If this were a movie, she would have a clever comeback, something about why he's just wearing a white T-shirt if he wishes people would dress up. But the T-shirt looks like a tux on Prescott Tane, so all she can say is, "Thank you."

This princely boy puts her shoe into her hand like a cork-soled glass slipper, and when she finally looks up into his eyes, gray-blue in the Tiki torches set up to keep the bugs away, she thinks maybe she could be Cinderella.

He steps over the sea of beer and leans on the rail.

"This is my favorite spot," he says. "Being able to see the whole city...I can't decide if it makes me feel small or big."

"We're kind of both at any given moment, right?" she says, another of her grandmother's sayings.

Prescott looks at her with his eyebrows raised.

"Deep," he says.

"Not really," she mutters, and looks out at the city again. She can feel him staring.

"I didn't know Catherine was having a party tonight," he says. "Makes it hard to enjoy my solitude out here."

"Sorry." She makes to move, but he reaches out and lays a hand gently on her wrist—not encircling it, but resting there like a butterfly.

"No, no," he says. "Stay. I usually just sit here and pretend I'm Batman looking down at Gotham City, so it's not like you're interrupting anything really important here."

She's so surprised that she laughs a real laugh, forgetting about her tooth. Her hand flies to her mouth, shocked by her own off-guardedness. He laughs too, and might even be blushing a little, and the possibility that there's something about her that's warm enough to put heat in his cheeks fills her with a glow between sunshine and lightning.

"Where's your cape?" she teases. She's teasing Prescott Tane.

"Well, I mostly focus on the brooding part. Batman's a brooder."

Catherine charges up, the music thumping behind her almost like the *Jaws* soundtrack.

"You're back!" she says, punching her brother.

"I never left," he says.

"Yes, you did." She rolls her eyes, then turns to Shania. "My brother thinks he has an invisibility cloak. He doesn't. Come on, Shania."

The hostess has summoned her. Shania mumbles goodbye to Prescott—the blush is in her tongue too—and follows his sister back to the pool, where other white girls are doing the thing where they writhe-dance with hands in hair. But something has shifted, Shania thinks: a subtle changing of view, a camera's lens widening to include her in the frame. People look at her, maybe for the first time since she arrived at Bard. And for the rest of the night, when she lets her eyes wander from whatever conversation she's part of, Catherine at her elbow, she finds Prescott's eyes on her. They're so blue she could drink them.

The buzz of the party takes a long time to leak from Shania's veins. She's still awake, her phone long abandoned, and she's staring at the ceiling when her mother comes in from work. It's two thirty in the morning.

She watches as her mother hangs her keys on the hook by the door, quiets them with her palm, and glances toward the couch that serves as Shania's bed. Her mother silently creeps through the living room before pausing in the hall, and Shania wonders if she does this every night Shania is already asleep. Or perhaps she can somehow sense her daughter's wakefulness, can recognize versions of her breath that Shania isn't even aware of.

She turns away a moment later and heads down the short hall to her bedroom, where Shania can hear her taking off the uniform she wears for her job at the prison. The muted clatter of her badge on the dresser. The sink and sigh of her body onto the bed. Other soft sounds that Shania takes in silently, her eyes fluttering closed. It's almost a lullaby, until a new sound finds its way to her ears, a sound that nudges her awake.

Her mother is crying.

There's still a slice of light in the hallway, cutting through the narrow opening of her mother's door, and Shania swings her legs off the couch. Her feet carry her across the tired brown carpet, past the bathroom. She sees her mother's legs perched at the edge of her bed. Shania raises her hand to knock, when she sees what her mother holds in her lap.

A shoebox, full of an assortment of things Shania immediately recognizes as Gram's.

Between her mother's fingertips is a red feather, and she twists it for a moment before carefully returning it to the box. It joins a round flash of silver—a windup toy, a monkey crashing cymbals. A cloud of warm yellow—a spool of mustard-colored yarn left over from the blanket Gram knit, which Simon the beagle eventually claimed as his own. Useless things, things that did nothing but sit in the house that was once Gram's home. Shania's mother's private stash of memories, things she had deemed precious as they packed the rest of the house for donation. But then Shania sees it. The faded yellow cover, the cracked black and red letters.

Gram's almanac.

The night feels suddenly tight and hot around her, and she isn't sure what makes her turn quickly from the door and go back to her couch, away from the sound of her mother's tears. She's asked about the almanac a dozen times since they watched Gram's coffin be swallowed by soil. Her mother has said, "It will turn up" a dozen times in return. Now it *has* turned up. It was never lost. The part of Shania that wants to shove open her mother's door and point at the evidence in her lap is overwhelmed by the part that remembers her grandmother's voice the day she died, the last thing she said.

"We're all what?" Shania whispers in the dark.

*Liars.*

# CHAPTER 3

On Saturday, Shania is late to work for the first time. The neon OPEN sign isn't illuminated and it's eight o'clock in the evening, which means she's scheduled to work with Jai. He always turns it off. Proof, he says, that no one respects signage. And he's right. Paulie's, Shania has been told, has been in SoBR since before it was SoBR. Everyone knows it doesn't close until after midnight.

"Should I roll out the red carpet?" Jai says when she rushes in. He's helping a crowd of already-tipsy bar goers. "You left me to the wolves!"

The drunkards titter as though they're not the wolves he's speaking of.

"Relax," she says. "I'm ten minutes late, not ten hours."

"If you were ten hours late, my ass would already be at home in bed, so don't even!"

She grabs a pair of tongs. A usual Saturday night—all the SoBR wanderers looking to get carbohydrates in their stomachs to soak up some of the alcohol. In the corner of the shop sits the slumped form of a man who comes in regularly: short and dark skinned, with tangled hair and a jacket that might once have been orange underneath the layers of stains.

"Didn't you say you were going to scale back your shifts when school started?" Jai says when the shop has cleared out. They relax before the next rush.

"I need the money," she says, plucking a doughnut hole from the display bin behind the glass and popping it in her mouth.

Jai looks at her over the top of his nonprescription nerd glasses.

"Your mama hasn't found out you're working night shifts, then?"

"Nope."

"One of these days you're gonna get home and she's gonna be in a swivel chair, waiting on your ass like Dr. Evil."

"We don't have a cat."

"She's gonna have bought a cat."

Shania laughs.

"Why do you even work so much? Your mom make you pay rent or something?" he pries.

"No," she says. "Just my phone."

"So why, then?"

Answering with "teeth" is a surefire way to have him staring at her mouth. She could name the other things she secretly wants: boots like the Bard girls, a tan. She imagines transforming, an inch at a time.

"I just need money," she says, removing her gloves and grabbing the broom. "Saving for college. Stuff."

"And your mom doesn't notice that you're sneaking out of the house to sell doughnuts?"

"Nope. That's why it's the perfect arrangement. She works nights, I work nights."

The bell above the door jingles, and a familiar face enters the shop—a Black woman wearing a shiny purple bonnet, silver hair just visible in the front. Shania has learned that the woman's name is Mrs. Rudolph. She always gets a jelly doughnut, and Shania moves to bag it for her while Mrs. Rudolph chats with Jai.

"You see that Dina's is closing?" she says.

"Across the street?" Jai says. "Yeah, I saw that today."

Shania glances over Mrs. Rudolph's shoulder at the shop. Dina's, the hat shop with the same fossilized feeling as Paulie's, where yesterday a blood trail had begun. It looks clean now. Shania has seen the hats in the window since she started at Paulie's: bold, garish to Shania's eyes. Feathers sticking out at loud angles. Cheetah-patterned ribbon.

"Pushing everybody out," Mrs. Rudolph says. Shania hands her the doughnut, and the old woman nods her thanks. Shania hangs back while Jai counts out a dollar in change from his own pocket and waves Mrs. Rudolph's hand away when she reaches for her purse.

"Thank you, baby," she says. "I hope Paulie's can hang on. Somebody said something about some kinda *designer* doughnuts today. Green-tea doughnuts and bourbon this and that. Paulie's keeps it simple, and there ain't nothing wrong with it."

"That sounds nasty as f—That sounds nasty, Mrs. Rudolph. They're doing too much."

"We don't need all that," she agrees. "But you see the way the neighborhood is changing. All these new types."

Shania thinks that Mrs. Rudolph casts the smallest sideways

look at her, just a slice of a glance. If Jai notices, he doesn't show it, and he and Mrs. Rudolph go on lamenting the changes in the neighborhood. Shania has lived in Blue Rock for only four months, but the changes Mrs. Rudolph and Jai are discussing feel suddenly personal.

"Change is good, I thought," Shania says. Jai doesn't look at her, but Mrs. Rudolph does, her eyes made owlish by her glasses. Shania plows on: "Nothing stays the same forever."

"Change is good when it doesn't hurt people," the old woman says sternly.

The bell clangs as the door opens wide, admitting a pack of college guys. The young white men cram into the shop, taking up more space than one would think four people could. Their voices, full of football and alcohol, bounce off the glass.

"I'm gonna need all your doughnuts," a guy in a red shirt says, pointing finger guns at Shania and Jai. "Put 'em in the bag and nobody gets hurt."

"Sir, I will call the cops," says Jai in a supremely bored voice.

Red Shirt pauses, finger guns still drawn, and Shania prepares for him to be angry, but then the young man cracks up, his face flushed with buzz.

"Okay, dude, relax. I'm not actually going to rob you!"

Jai picks up a box and puts on food-service gloves, then stares at the group of men apathetically. Sometimes Shania is put off by Jai's complete lack of customer service, but it works for him. Mrs. Rudolph plucks a couple of napkins from the dispenser and waves goodbye, giving the college boys the same berth she would give a pack of hyenas.

"Bye, Mrs. Rudolph," Jai calls, and they beam at each other, some secret message passing between their smiles, a code Shania can't quite crack.

"Give me all the cinnamon ones," Red Shirt says. "Like, *all* of them."

Jai squints at him.

"There are twenty-four cinnamon out," he says. "Do you for real want all of them?"

"I said *all!*" Red Shirt says as he laughs, fake-pounding his fist on the glass.

Jai turns to Shania and extends the box.

"You can take this one. These are your people."

"What? What's that mean?"

"You owe me," Jai says. "You were late, and I was alone while we got slammed."

Shania rolls her eyes and accepts the box.

"Fine. Give me the tongs."

Jai beams and sashays over to the single stool behind the counter, perches on it, and pulls out his phone. He takes a selfie, tilting his work visor to a jaunty angle and winking. He's effortlessly cute. Shania thinks she'd look like a peeled potato if she took a selfie in this light.

"Okay, so twenty-four doughnuts?" she says.

"Are you going to eat them with us?" one of the other bros calls.

He's not really flirting. This is the thing men do when they're dealing with a girl behind a counter. A waitress. A concierge. The expectation of compliance. The older men do it by pinning her down with "polite" conversation. She's behind the counter: She can't exactly go anywhere, and they know it. And she—in theory—has to be nice to them because she's at work.

"No," Shania says, blushing against her will.

"Why? Does your boyfriend have rules about not eating doughnuts with other dudes?"

She involuntarily thinks of Prescott. The Cinderella moment of the night before.

"No," she says. "Do you want twenty-four doughnuts?"

The guy in the red shirt fishes around in his pocket and then slams a bill on the counter, grinning at her, his eyes as glazed as the doughnuts.

"How many will that get me?"

She peers down at the bill. A five.

"Five," she says.

"FIVE IT IS," he crows.

Behind her, she hears Jai suck his teeth.

She returns the dozen box to the shelf and gets a bag instead. The bell jingles again, and a group of girls in very short dresses comes in. Just like that, Shania is forgotten.

Shania puts the cash in the register and sets the doughnuts on the counter, slinking back to lean against the wall by Jai while the frat boys and made-up girls perform a mating dance.

"One of the last warm nights," Jai says, still staring at his phone. "And people know it. It's going to be busy as hell the next couple weekends."

"How long have you worked here?"

"Since I was sixteen."

"How long is that?" she asks with a laugh.

He looks up.

"Three years," he says.

"Is that how you know Mrs. Rudolph?"

"Psh. Everybody knows Mrs. Rudolph."

"I don't."

"Everybody *Black* knows Mrs. Rudolph. Plus she goes to my church."

She gets another glimpse of the secret code that had passed between them. It makes her cagey, like a coyote just beyond the glow of a campfire.

"Why does it have to be a Black-white thing?" she says.

"Because it *is* a Black-white thing," he says neutrally, his eyes back on his phone.

"I don't see color," she says. She hears her grandmother's voice—*I don't care if you're Black, white, or polka-dotted.*

"It sees you," Jai says, laughing.

"Um, excuse me!" says a girl with a shrill voice. "Are you even listening?"

Shania looks up to see one of the girls tapping long fingernails on the countertop.

"Did you need something?" says Jai.

"I want a custard doughnut and someone to get rid of the dead cat outside your door."

"Okay. Wait, what?"

"That's what we were saying when we came in!" she cries. "There's a dead cat on the fucking sidewalk outside your door!"

"Are you . . . are you serious?" Shania says.

"Yes," says a nearby voice, deeper and not blurred with alcohol. It's a guy Shania's age, waiting to order. He must have come in behind the girls. "It's out there to the left."

Chestnut hair, wavy around his face. Eyes murky blue. His eyelashes sweep down once or twice, away and back. Shy.

"You're Prescott's brother," she blurts. He looks startled.

"Uh, yeah," he says.

"I...um, I was at your house on Friday. At the party. Willa Langford pointed you out."

"Oh, you're friends with Willa?" He perks up.

"Uh, kinda. I just met her."

"Are you going to get the cat?" the girl behind him whines. "It's so gross."

Shania looks at Jai, but he holds his hands up, surrendering all dead-cat duty.

"Absolutely not," he says. "Ab. So. Lute. Ly. Not."

"Let me guess," she says. "I owe you because I was late."

"That's right."

"Do you need, um, help?" Benjamin Tane says as she grabs the broom and dustpan. He looks concerned.

"Oh," she says. She sees Prescott in his face, but not much. She thinks one of them must look like their father, and the other like their mother. "Sure. Thanks."

They step out into the evening air. Here, the sidewalks are crowded with people milling from bar to bar, the air heavy with the unmistakable scent of fall's first breath. At the thought of autumn, Shania's mind is dragged toward the sight of Gram's almanac on her mother's lap—Shania has been carrying around her own to fill the void, and all this time the 1999 copy has been sleeping under the same roof. Shania looks up at the stars, fighting the prickly feeling of tears. She knows right then that as soon as the gets the chance, she's going to take the book.

"Full moon," Ben says, and she goes on looking up. It only makes her think of Gram more, so all she does is nod.

Before it was SoBR, this street might have gotten dark, but not anymore, not now that it's a strip: Flashing lights encase what little of Shania's shadow exists, splashing down from the nightclub to the left, the burger joint to the right. It's the neon that shows her the mauled form of the cat, all of its nine lives pooling under the still, black body.

"Jesus," she mutters when they see it.

"Yeah."

She may not have known it was a cat if the girl hadn't said so—Shania wouldn't have wanted to look that closely. She sucks in a ragged breath, remembering the morning before, the blood at the bus stop shockingly red. Is this *that* cat? Had it waited this long to die? She can't see its face, but she can see three holes in its body, jagged and wrong.

"People are sick," Ben says.

Shania stares at it, unmoving. She'd been told to expect a dead cat, but this cat seems more dead than she had prepared for. Not a cartoon cat with Xs for eyes. This is a dead animal, its fur shifting in the wind, its eyes open and soft looking. She has seen eyes like this—the white ceiling of the hospital. Pale tubes. The jumble of the intercom in the hall. She sucks in her breath.

"You okay?" Ben says, frowning.

"I need to put it in the trash," she says slowly, drawing herself back from February.

"I'll hold the dustpan still."

Together they manage to get the cat's body onto the dustpan without touching it. Feeling its weight, her arm sagging, makes her eyes sting. Ben reaches to take it, but she shakes her head.

"I've got it," she says. Then, to distract herself as she carries the corpse toward the dumpster, she says, "So, you know Willa."

"Yeah. I see her at the library sometimes. We're cool."

"But you don't go to Bard."

"Nope. Bedlington."

"Public school."

"Uh-huh."

"What's that about?"

He shrugs and the shyness returns. He doesn't answer until she tips the cat into the rust-brown dumpster. They talk over the sound the body makes falling in.

"Bard isn't for me," he says. "I started there as a freshman and didn't . . . fit in."

"I could see that. Especially with the shoes of a brother like Prescott to fill. I'm assuming you're younger, right? You don't look like twins."

"I'm a junior," he says, nodding. "But I'm not worried about Prescott's shoes."

He says it in an offhand way, and she laughs. His smile is like a flutter of wings.

"I like your hair," he says.

"Thanks," she says. "That makes two of us, at least. Wish someone had told me blonde highlights were a prereq at Bard."

She's surprised by his snort of laughter. She's never thought of herself as funny, but maybe she is. Maybe she can be. She slides the dumpster closed, a definitive sound. She really needs to wash her hands.

"Who stabs a cat?" Jai says when Shania and Ben are back inside, up to their elbows in soap.

"I mean, maybe it was something else that killed it." Shania frowns. "I didn't want to look too close."

"I'm glad I didn't see that shit," Jai says, wrinkling his nose.

Shania wishes she hadn't. It's the kind of thing that sticks in the cracks of the mind, peering back at you when you try to look through at something else.

"Did you come for a doughnut or just to help out?" Shania says to Ben while he dries his hands.

"A glazed," he says, and smiles. She gives it to him, waving his hand away when he tries to pay. He toasts her with the bag and moves to the door.

"Tell your..." She catches him with her voice. She almost says *brother.* Wishes she were that bold. "...sister I said hey."

"Will do," he says, and pauses as though he, too, wants to add something. But he takes a bite out of the doughnut, gives a shadow of a grin, and leaves.

"Somebody else found a dead cat around here a while back," Jai says. "Dorothy. She works day shift most of the time. She was telling me she saw it out back when she opened up. She used to work at the police station. Doing transcription back in the day or something. Said the cops always said when you find animals mutilated, somebody's serial killer ain't far behind."

"What's that supposed to mean?"

"Apparently serial killers practice on animals and then they escalate or whatever."

Shania just stares at him. He eventually glances up, sees her face, and shakes his head.

"Chill, princess. You're not a cat."

"Okay, but you don't think it's a little fucked up that somebody's out there butchering cats?"

"Until he moves on to nineteen-year-old Black dudes named Jai that work at Paulie's, I've got other shit to worry about."

She folds her arms around her, cold but not cold. She eyes the hunched back of the homeless man, still hunkered in the corner.

"We should tell him to leave," she says, keeping her voice low.

Jai lifts his eyes and follows hers.

"Earl? Earl ain't bothering nobody."

"What if he did it?"

"You think Earl is out here murdering cats?"

"I mean, maybe? What if he is?"

"Earl ain't out here murdering cats, Shania."

"How do you know?"

Jai slips his phone into his pocket. His face is neutral but she senses something tight in him, something that she's unknowingly wound up.

"Shania, I been working at this shop for three years. And Earl been coming in here for all three of them and probably the three before that. Earl wants a place to get some coffee and maybe pour a little liquor in it and maybe a day-old doughnut to eat while he drinks. And when it starts to get cold outside he wants a table in the corner where he can stay out the wind for a while. That's it. You work here for a couple months—only lived in the damn city for four—and now you want to kick Earl out on one of the first cold nights of the year? Fuck outta here. Earl ain't bothering you and he sure the fuck ain't bothering no cats."

The strawberry patch that grew on Shania's face when she talked to Prescott bears a different kind of fruit now. Prickly, fast, like a sparkler on the Fourth of July. They stare at each other and if Jai notices the spread of red, he doesn't follow it with his eyes: He keeps them on hers. His face isn't hostile: It's annoyed, dismissive. It makes her feel like a fly at a barbecue. But more customers clang through the door and the tension is mostly broken—they work in silence, passing the time until every sweet thing is gone.

# CHAPTER 4

Shania wakes up and swears Gram is in the kitchen humming before she realizes it's the buzz of the bathroom light. It's too early to be awake—she knows because she smells her mother's coffee and she's usually gone by the time Shania is up. Shania extracts herself from the couch and drifts toward the closet-sized kitchen.

She finds her mother at the counter, holding but not drinking from a chipped mug she presses against her chin. She stares at a spot somewhere above the faucet, and Shania notes the subtle slump in her mother's shoulders. Her hair is dyed honey blonde, cut short and choppy. She doesn't look like Gram, but their faces make the same expressions. Like Gram, her mother isn't much for crying, but her face creases in on itself these days, a closed envelope.

"Are you okay?" Shania says softly.

Her mother doesn't even jump, just looks up slowly.

"I'm fine," she says. "Just thinking. Did I wake you up?"

Shania studies her, this liar's face. Part of her thought that the next time they were face-to-face, her mother would admit it. But the only thing that makes this lie special is that Shania knows about it, and the realization that her mother has done this before, is good at it, makes Shania's throat tighten.

"No, I'm just up," she answers. "I wanted to get to school early."

"Letting it grow on you?" her mother says, smiling.

Shania makes a face. Yesterday she would have told her about Catherine, about her cute brother—brothers—who are as mysterious and charming as a boy from a romcom. But her mother's lies make her want to have lies of her own.

"I guess so" is all Shania says.

"It has to be better than Morrisville," her mother presses. She sips her coffee now, eyes brightening. "Give it a chance. We have a shot at something new here. I'm sorry it means being without your dad, but this is a fresh start for both of us."

She sighs as though she doesn't really believe it but wants to. Her mother must sense her skepticism because she smiles again.

"I'm just saying, Shane," she says. "I always wanted to get out of Morrisville. But I got pregnant when I was seventeen, and that limits your options in a lot of ways."

She's told Shania this before. Gram was an older mother—old enough to raise eyebrows at the time—but Shania's mother got pregnant at seventeen, she and Shania's dad living in Gram's spare room when they couldn't keep up with the rent at an apartment. Morrisville was like a waiting room they never checked out of. All the things Shania has been told bump up against the invisible bulk of what she hasn't. *Liars*, she hears in Gram's voice.

"Gram never talked about that," Shania says, looking at the counter, avoiding her mother's eyes. "When you were younger.

Or I mean, when she was younger either, now that I think about it."

"Your grandmother didn't see the point in thinking about the past," her mother says. She stirs her coffee fast. "You know how she was. She kept so busy. Charities, church. She didn't have time to think about what was. She took care of me—of us—and that's all that matters."

She turns away, and Shania knows she's right: that this was Gram, always moving forward. Shania's mother is the same way. Only able to look at the pieces of the past that can be contained in a shoebox under the bed. Shania's questions don't fit in that shoebox.

"Tomorrow's her birthday," Shania says quickly. "Gram's."

Her mother pauses.

"I know. Want to get breakfast to celebrate?"

She means biscuits and gravy, the thing neither of them can make because Gram always did the making. Here is one more part of the past her mother can bear to look at. She doesn't understand that the past is where her daughter wants to live; rather than tell her mother this, Shania says, "I want a tattoo. Of a lilac."

Her mother's eyebrows drop like sandbags. She knows what the lilac means. Neither of them can see the buds without remembering the crowds of them on either side of Gram's door.

"Your grandmother hated tattoos," she says.

"Maybe she wouldn't if it was her favorite flower."

"Or maybe she would hate it even more."

Shania smiles at that, because her mother might be right. But she thinks maybe if she could see those blossoms all the time, maybe the hole Gram left in their lives would be bearable.

Her mother sees that her daughter is really asking—the smile softens, then fades.

"You're almost eighteen," she says. "Next year you can do whatever you want."

Next year feels like a foreign land to which Shania has no passport. She shrugs and watches her mother pour more coffee, then waits until she says goodbye, until the car rattles away, before going into her mother's room. She lifts the almanac out of the box, replaces it with her own. Taking the book feels like pushing through a layer of cobwebs that wall off the past, emerging on the other side in shadow. Her mother has been keeping it from her, and Shania doesn't know why. But she has it now, even if she can't bear to open it. She can hardly bear to look at it. But she tucks it into her bag like precious contraband and peeks at it the entire way to school.

There are still six minutes left before class actually begins when Shania enters the greenhouse. It's empty, and she's grateful. She settles onto her work stool, guilt pooling in her stomach after the theft of the almanac, and when her phone vibrates, her shoulders seize; she expects a text from her mother, psychically aware of what Shania has done. But it's only Hallie.

**Check this out! My first event of the year!**

She's included a photo that she snapped of a flyer, big green letters proclaiming that Morrisville High School is running a food drive. FOR DETAILS, CONTACT HALLIE FLYNN OR MONICA MAJORS.

**Cool! You're partnered with Monica?** Shania texts. She had nearly forgotten about Monica, Morrisville High's sole Black student. She, like Shania, was a listener. Shania sat next to her in Chemistry and sometimes in the cafeteria. They spoke occasionally, sharing memes or eyerolls. But Monica was quiet, and seeing her name associated with event planning is unexpected.

**Yeah**, Hallie writes. **She's really coming out of her shell!**

Shania considers this, wondering about the shell she, too, hopes to emerge from. What kind of creature had she been in Morrisville, and what kind would she be in the light?

She reaches into her bag and draws out her grandmother's almanac, newly liberated. For a long moment, she considers actually looking inside. A *Farmers' Almanac* predicts meteor showers. Full moons. Some give a range of days for these events. Shania wishes life could have its own almanac. *Sometime between January 8 and January 15, your father will file for divorce, with an older woman holding his hand. In the second week of February, expect your grandmother to die unexpectedly. Full moon. Falling star. You will go to the hospital once she's in a room and be told she's already gone. You will walk into the hospital room, and there will be tubes climbing out of her dead mouth like vines. There will be a faint trail of blood from her right nostril. She will never tell you the thing she thought you needed to know.*

Shania has spent a lot of time wondering what her grandmother had intended to say that last day, a door half open and dark on the other side. It must be about her father. What else besides his lies could be painful enough to put that look in Gram's eyes? If Shania opens this book, she'll either find the secret or she won't, and she's not ready for either. The creature that emerges from the shell depends on what is or isn't in this book.

The door to the greenhouse makes the slightly squishy opening sound and a group of lacrosse boys troop in. Adam. Paul. JP. Shania swallows her grandmother's garden, feels the tubes from her memories in her own throat. She remembers where she is. Here, in the greenhouse. She doesn't know why she hopes to see Prescott, because she knows very well that he's not in this class, so when he steps through the door, her heart doesn't know what kind of balloon it wants to be: water or hot air. Either way it might burst.

"Feeling like doing a little digging, Pres?" JP says, and Shania wonders if JP is here on partial scholarship like she is. He's too eager.

Prescott carries a camera. Shania has seen him with it before, a boxy black film camera that makes a thick sound like a typewriter when it takes a photo. He aims it at one of the planters nearest the door. *Snap*. He sweeps his eyes across the humid space, taking in the rows of green, the vines and stalks all seeking sun they won't find. Prescott seems to be seeking something else. His eyes land on Shania's.

"You could say that," he replies.

He's a little like Edward Cullen, she decides. Not that he's particularly pale, but he's cool and distant in a Washingtonian vampire sort of way. He's still holding her gaze when she realizes he's walking over to her workstation.

"Good morning," he says. He leans against her table.

"That table is dirty," she warns. "I've been working with Russula."

One corner of his mouth twists up into a smile.

"What the hell is Russula?"

"It's, um, a fungus actually." She's already smiling. He has that effect. He raises his camera, aiming its black eye at the flowers to her right. *Snap*.

"These idiots said you guys were in here growing weed," he says, lifting his chin to indicate JP and the other lacrosse boys who loiter nearby.

"Well, they are idiots, after all," she says.

He grins at that and she keeps her smile small to hide her pointy tooth.

"What else are you planting? Aside from your fungus."

"Chiffons, among other things."

"Why those?"

"Um...well, the *Farmers' Almanac* says it's a good year for them."

"I'm sorry, the what?"

"*Farmers' Almanac.* It's like, uh, a calendar. But it has dates for planting and stars and full moons..."

She trails off, realizing that she probably sounds like either a witch or a country bumpkin.

"Is that it?" he says, nodding at the book in her hand.

Her stomach tightens.

"Yeah. Well, kind of. This was my grandmother's. It's...out of date."

He extends his hand in the same princely way he'd given back her shoe on Friday night, and as if under a spell, she slowly hands him the almanac. Seeing her grandmother's book in his hands brings the cobwebby feeling back—something from the past brushing fingers with the future.

"Please don't open it," she says suddenly, and his eyes flash up, catching hers. She stares, he merely nods, and she's grateful. He turns it over and reads the back instead.

"If you're concerned about the coming of a hurricane, you need only watch your persimmon tree," Prescott reads. He raises his eyes to Shania's and arches one eyebrow. "Interesting."

"Fun facts," she says with a straight face, but even in seriousness, their eyes shine on each other.

"Are you particularly worried about hurricanes, Shania Hester?"

He knows her last name. Which means he's been asking questions. Which makes something inside her inflate a little, the balloon closer to bursting.

"One can never be too prepared," she says. "I think Batman would agree."

His grin is the sunrise. She sets her ship's course due east.

"I heard you met my brother," he says. "I didn't know you worked in SoBR."

"Oh. Yeah. Paulie's."

"Figures you'd work somewhere sweet."

"Pesticides," Ms. Hassoon says, sweeping into the room. Her hijab is a buttery yellow today. "Hopefully you all have done more reading than you did last week."

Prescott hands the almanac to Shania. When she takes it, she imagines it's warm from his fingers, that her grandmother sighs her approval.

"Does the almanac say you'll you be hungry tomorrow?" he says.

Next to Shania, Michelle slides onto her stool. Shania can feel her staring. Prescott ignores her entirely.

"I'd have to check the forecast," Shania says.

He smiles.

"Let me take you out. I can pick you up."

"Mr. Tane, should you be in here?" Ms. Hassoon calls. He ignores her and extends his phone to Shania.

"Put your number in here."

She glances up at Ms. Hassoon before taking the phone. Their teacher's attention is fixed on them, her thick eyebrows low, with a mixture of incredulity and irritation. Shania's fingers tremble a little as she takes the phone from his hand.

"Mr. Tane?"

Shania types in her name and number in a rush and then hands the phone back. He stares at the screen for a moment before adding a flower emoji to the end of her name. Only then does he turn and move back toward the greenhouse door, his step unhurried.

"Mr. Tane, what are you doing in here?" Ms. Hassoon says, impatient.

"Admiring the flowers," he says.

He doesn't look at Shania when he says it, but her cheeks bloom anyway.

# CHAPTER 5

Morrisville had made Shania feel like a fossil—the shape of something left in rock for an eon, flat and unchangeable. But even if that's the way it worked—that eventually who you are is set in stone—in Blue Rock, she might eventually be the igneous variety. With her name in Prescott's mouth—and in his phone—she feels hot and liquid, as though she could become anything if only poured into the proper mold.

This feeling carries her through the rest of the school day, buoying her all the way to the bus stop, where she stands watching the Bard student body roll one by one out of the parking garage. Land Rover after Range Rover after BMW, a glittery train that slowly inserts a needle through the bubble of her day, a gradual deflation. But then a white Mercedes pauses, holding up traffic to a cacophony of honks, and the window hums downward to reveal the grinning face of Catherine Tane. She flips an enthusiastic bird in Shania's direction, sunglasses like the eyes of a fabulous martian, and Shania barely has time to raise a grateful hand in return when the window is up again, Catherine weaving down Broadway.

"The only time I wish cops were around is when Catherine Tane is behind the wheel of a car," someone says, and Michelle steps under the shade of the bus shelter, Willa by her side.

"A danger to society," Willa says, shading her eyes to gaze after the Mercedes, which zooms through a red light before disappearing from view. Shania can't tell if they're kidding.

"She does kinda march to the beat of her own drum," Shania says. It's something Gram would say.

"And what tune does it play, I wonder?" Willa says, tapping her chin.

"I don't know, but it's probably offbeat." Michelle grins. Shania decides they're joking.

"What are you doing on this side?" Shania says, aiming this at Michelle. "I've only seen you catching it going the other way."

"Little art show," Michelle says. "In Round Hill. Wanna come?"

Being invited to something is unexpected, and Shania flushes.

"Oh," she says. "I would. But I have to work."

"At Paulie's?" Willa says, eyeing the visor Velcroed around the strap of Shania's bag.

"Yeah."

"Excellent choice of employment."

"Thanks."

Michelle returns her attention to Willa.

"Is Ben still coming?"

"He says he's getting on at Monroe to meet us."

"Skipping soccer practice for art," Michelle says, impressed.

"Man cannot survive on athleticism alone."

Their laughter is a force field that makes a glowing circle around them, Shania at its edge. As the bus squeals to a stop, she realizes with finality that she's no longer in Morrisville: Going to a party at Catherine's, her name in Prescott's phone with the promise of a text later—it's all proof enough. If she wants things to be different, she thinks, *she* will have to be different.

"Are you talking about Ben Tane?" she says as they all board the bus.

"Yep." Willa scans her bus pass and moves to the back without another word. Michelle glances at Shania with a look she can't quite decipher.

"He's a cool guy," Michelle says.

Shania follows them to where they flop along the bus's back wall. She has the distinct feeling that she's not altogether welcome—particularly by Willa—but she takes a seat anyway.

"He came into Paulie's the other night," Shania says. "Ben, I mean. If I didn't know he and Prescott were brothers I would never guess."

Michelle and Willa exchange a glance.

"Yeah, they definitely don't look like brothers," Michelle says. Willa looks out the window.

Just a few hours ago, Prescott was obtaining Shania's phone number in the middle of the greenhouse, and it occurs to Shania that Michelle absolutely overheard. She wonders if mentioning Ben makes her sound like the kind of girl who would flirt with both brothers, and imagines the self she's trying to create bending and twisting through the filter of Michelle's eyes. Shania pivots.

"So," Shania says to the girls, hearing her voice go up an

octave. It brings Willa's eyes back from the window. "When did you two become friends?"

They toss another look at each other, but the meaning is different this time; the thing being exchanged is something Shania is allowed to witness. The bus growls on.

"We met in kindergarten," Michelle says. "And were friends until fifth grade. And then middle school happened."

"Middle school," Willa sighs. "The plague years."

Michelle laughs, shoves her lightly.

"Oh, you had a friendship breakup?" Shania says. "Middle school is the worst for that."

"I knew she'd come back to me," Michelle laughs. "I hoped, anyway."

Willa just scoffs. "I'm lucky you let me come back at all."

The bus stops, and a few people climb on, the sound of their coins echoing to the back. Boarding last is Ben Tane. He scans his bus pass and speaks to the driver—they both laugh. Seeing his smile from the back of the bus is like stargazing. Shania directs her eyes to the floor.

"Benjo!" Willa calls, but he's already spotted them and heads their way in stuttered steps as the bus cruises back into motion.

"Why do you call me that," he groans, sinking down next to her. He waves at Michelle and then his eyes shift over to Shania. "Oh. Hi."

"This is Shania," Michelle says.

"We've met actually," he says. And there's the smile again. Shania's conscious of her breath shallowing. "At her job. I helped her with a dead cat."

"A what now?" Michelle says. "You know what, never mind. I don't want to know."

"Is Paulie's selling dead cats now?" Willa cries. "Is that part of gentrification?"

"Not enough to kick out the people—gotta kick out the cats too," Michelle says, joking but not.

Shania only listens. She feels like a swaying daisy again, or maybe she truly is Alice after all, she thinks—entering a strange land where everyone speaks a language she can't quite grasp. It was easy enough to argue with Jai about SoBR—the stakes felt lower outside the Bard orbit.

"I don't know what they're doing down there," Ben says, shaking his head wearily. "The business association is trying to put up a statue in the Sparkle Park, did you know that? Something symbolizing unity. Nobody asked for a statue. There are so many better things that money could be used for. And, like, nobody uses the Sparkle Park but drunk teenagers. Who's the audience? It's just to say they did it."

Michelle leans forward to look around Ben at Shania.

"The Sparkle Park," she says with the tone of a tour guide, "is this little park with benches just outside the South Blue Rock area where people our age hang out sometimes. Somebody hung up fairy lights a couple years ago and no one ever took them down. So it's the Sparkle Park."

"Oh, cool," Shania says. Willa ignores her but Michelle smiles a small encouraging smile.

"It's cool that you guys are friends," Ben says, indicating Shania as a limb of the body that is Michelle and Willa. His eyes are as clear and genuine as a well-kept aquarium. Shania can't help but make the silent comparison between him and his siblings, how conversations with Catherine are like wading through algae, Prescott's eyes like dark water. But in this moment, Shania mostly notices the soft puff of air Willa breathes through her nose after Ben speaks.

"I mean, we're not really," Shania says, embarrassed. *Sometimes better to quit before you're fired*, her mother always says. "Not yet, anyway. We just kind of happened to be on the same bus and were talking. They're just being nice."

"Girl, you're fine," Michelle says, but she doesn't disagree, and Shania hates the blush she can feel creeping across her cheeks like a weed.

"They *are* nice," Ben agrees. That freshwater grin. "But you are too. Good people tend to gravitate toward each other, you know?"

Willa looks out the window.

"Isn't this your stop?" she says, pointing. "You said you work at Paulie's, right?"

"Shit, yes," Shania says, and grabs the cord to yank it. But the bus has already passed the stop, swinging around the corner off Broadway and sending Shania's bag spinning to the floor. Everything inside scatters. "Crap!"

"I've got it!" Ben says. "Don't worry, the next stop is only two blocks."

He and Willa are closest and reach down to gather pens and notebooks, Willa stacking schoolbooks on her lap. Gram's almanac ends up on top.

"*Farmers' Almanac*," she reads. "Is this for school?"

And then Willa opens it.

As the pages crack apart, something inside Shania does too. Her hand is faster, even, than the sudden jackrabbit of her pulse, snatching for the book—the cover tears, a jagged lightning bolt that surprises her almost as much as the look on Willa's face. A look like someone at a haunted house, Willa seeing a ghost's mask slip to reveal only another ghost beneath it.

"Give me that," Shania says quietly, and Willa silently releases the book into her grasp, passes her the other things she dropped.

"Sorry," Willa says, and she is. "I didn't mean to tear it."

Shania can only shrug. Ever since Gram died there's been something in her throat, and in this moment she realizes it's a scream.

"Are you okay?" Michelle says. Ben is silent.

"I'm fine. Thanks," Shania finally says around the thing lodged just behind her tongue. She makes her way to the back door of the bus, fumbling with all the things that had been set loose from her bag. Ben and Willa and Michelle all murmur goodbye and she nods, hands full.

When Shania stands in the open air and the bus is gone, she lets everything drop but the almanac, a small landslide of cardboard and paper that draws glances of distant concern from passersby. Before today, she felt that opening the almanac would be like opening Gram's coffin. Now, through the crack of the torn cover, she sees that she was right. Blue ink sprawls on the first page, the loose loops of her grandmother's hand.

*Do better, Shania*, it reads.

Shania stares until another bus passes, not daring to fully open the book. She goes on staring until she's late for work, at which point she slowly conceals the jagged page within the refuge of the others and pretends she never saw it.

# CHAPTER 6

There's a taco place in SoBR that was once a truck, El Jefe, now parked permanently alongside a concrete court of seating. On Friday, Prescott slides his silver Audi into a spot out front and opens Shania's door. She steps onto the sidewalk, which dances with red and purple flashing chili peppers that adorn the cross-hatched terraces. His car and the lights and the way the crowd seems to part for them makes Shania dizzy. She marvels at this development in her life at Bard—she doesn't want to look too closely. She thinks of a video she once saw of a raccoon being given a piece of pink cotton candy to eat, waddling over to a puddle to wash its prize. The thing had dissolved in his little paw-like hands. She doesn't want to be the raccoon. She will accept this gift without washing it.

"How many can you eat?" Prescott asks. There's a place to order at the truck's window, with a selection of tables bearing a variety of salsas. Surrounding and scattered among the entire area are heat lamps that breathe down a haze of warm air.

This question paralyzes her. It's not about eating in front of

Prescott but how complicated everything seems. Morrisville's Taco Bell is the only experience she's had with tacos and burritos, but the menu she's staring at now feels overwhelming. Carne asada. Oaxaca.

"Hmm I don't know," she says.

"What do you like?"

"I'm good with anything." Anything but mushrooms and sour cream. She doesn't say it.

"Okay, I'm going to get some of my favorite ones and you can tell me what you think."

He doesn't seem to notice the insecurity oozing from her, just walks up to the window where a guy a little older than them is taking orders on an iPad. He has brown skin and close-cropped hair, a tattoo of a tiger crawling up from his wrist to his elbow. He slouches sideways on the stool behind the window, speaking Spanish to an older guy wearing an apron. They both laugh and then the young guy turns his eyes on Prescott and smiles warmly.

"Two number fours, two number sixes, two number threes," Prescott says. "Two lemonades." Shania glances sideways at him, the sudden tightness in his voice like the snap of a campfire. The tightness is in his jaw too. But the young man taking orders doesn't seem to notice.

"Any chips?" he asks.

"No," says Prescott, and Shania flinches a little at his tone. She hates when people talk to her like this at Paulie's.

"Thirty-two fifty-two," the guy says, and Prescott hands over his debit card without a word. When the entire transaction is finished, he and Shania sit at one of the long tables sipping lemonade, watching a young dad wrangle three little kids who seem to have been submerged in guacamole.

"My nieces won't eat guacamole," Prescott says, watching them. "At least those kids tried."

"I've never actually had it," Shania says, and Prescott careens theatrically in his seat.

"Never?"

"Nope. I mean, I think I've had it on a burrito..." She almost adds *at Taco Bell* but doesn't think guys like Prescott eat at Taco Bell unless they're drunk or on a road trip. "But that's it."

"If I didn't want to avoid that dipshit taking orders I'd go back up there and get us some."

"Do you know that guy?"

"No, I don't know him," he says distastefully. "But I don't like his attitude and I'm pretty sure he was talking to his buddy about you."

She feels her eyes widen, replaying the interaction in her head. She chances a glance back over her shoulder at the order window. The guy relaxes in the chair, chatting with his aproned coworker. They don't look up, but Shania has the feeling of staring at an empty backyard on a summer night, knowing as soon as no one's looking there will be fireflies.

"Wow, you don't miss anything," she says.

He shrugs, but finally smiles a little.

"I just try to be observant. Anyway. Guacamole next time. You're missing out, trust me."

"How'd you know about this place? I assume you've been here before since you have favorite things on the menu."

"Catherine actually," he says and rolls his eyes a little. "She knows all the good places. Even if it is Mexican food."

The way he says it makes her think of her grandmother. Gram never stopped pronouncing the *l*'s in quesadilla, turning it into a word like *piccadilly* or *chinchilla*, transforming it into a concept that fit into her life. Her life was a lunchbox for foods like egg salad and frozen fish sticks.

Today is Gram's birthday. *Do better, Shania.*

"That's the face you were making at the party," he says, and Shania snaps out of her thoughts, darting her eyes up at him. "What are you so sad about?"

"Nothing," she says quickly. "I'm just thinking."

"About guacamole?" he says, and pokes her wrist.

"No, not about guacamole." She grins. "Just...everything. Anyway. You and Catherine are both seniors. How does that work? You're not twins, obviously."

He shakes his head.

"No, not twins. Thank God. I can't even share a class with her, let alone a brain."

"You know twins don't actually share brains."

"Okay, not literally," he says, flashing those perfect teeth at her. Invisalign at one point for sure. "You know, twins are supposed to be on the same wavelength or whatever. We definitely don't have that. But she's two years younger. Skipped two grades."

Shania's eyes widen.

"Catherine? Quayloo-tomrom-whatever Catherine?" She realizes too late that she just implied his sister is a dumbass. "I mean..."

But he waves her off, nodding and laughing.

"No, I know. Cathy and all that ridiculous shit. She seems like an idiot half the time. Always wants to party. Doesn't give a shit about college."

"What about your brother?"

"Ben?" he scoffs. "Oh, he'll go to college for sure. He thinks he's proving a point by going to public schools and by not driving the car our parents got him. But he'll end up at Yale. Environmental law or some shit. He's like you. Green thumb. Animals and nature."

"And you are the opposite?"

"Is this an incognito interview? You find out stuff about me by asking about my siblings?"

"Just making conversation." She smiles in a way that covers her tooth.

The young man who took their order approaches, an arrangement of tacos balancing on a round metal tray. He places it between their lemonades and stands back.

"Everything look good?" he says.

"It looks amazing," Shania says, staring at the food in awe. It's not like anything she's ever ordered. The tortillas are different, not smooth and white but grainier looking. The meat and vibrantly colored vegetables: peppers, tomatoes, drizzled lines of salsa.

"Fine," Prescott says gruffly, and she glances up to see the waiter's reaction. He merely sends the briefest glance skyward and leaves.

"The food is great," Prescott says apologetically. "The service not so much."

He's pushing the tray in her direction before she can reply, indicating each one.

"This is fried cod, this one is steak, and this one is braised chicken. I don't really like spicy food, but you can add more salsa if you want."

"I'll try them as is first," she says, and picks up the one he says is chicken, eyeing the other two. She doesn't want to tell him she's suspicious of fish on a taco. It's not that she thinks he won't like her—her fear isn't that they'll disagree, but rather that her answer will reveal something she's not aware she's hiding. What kind of tortillas are these? Who puts fish on a taco? She doesn't drink coffee. She doesn't have a car. None of these things felt like secrets before she started at Bard.

"Are you sure?" Prescott says when she's eaten two and is too full for the third. "You're not doing that girl thing where you pretend you're full but you go home and eat a bowl of cereal and text your friends about what a terrible date I was?"

"Does that happen to you often?" she says, trying to ignore the swarming feeling in her stomach when he says the word *date*. He laughs, unconcerned about his teeth.

The tattooed guy is back for their tray and the little red baskets the tacos came in.

"Need anything else?" he says.

"No," says Prescott, staring at his lemonade with a frown. His smile from a moment before left a buzz in Shania's skin, but behind it she feels the flutter of anxiety like bat wings. When the waiter leaves, Prescott stares at his back.

"You really don't like that guy." She tries to laugh. This is how she has always dealt with conflict. Half jokes, distractions.

"That's giving him too much credit," he says, snorting. "I think he's nothing."

Something behind her catches his eye. He's smiling again, nods over her shoulder.

"Look who it is!"

She turns, expecting one of his lacrosse buddies, or maybe even Catherine, but instead finds a massive bloodhound, leash clutched by a little white girl no more than ten. Walking a few paces behind her is Ben Tane.

62

"Hey, girly, how's the goalie life?" Prescott says, standing up from the table.

"I can get the tip," Shania says, standing too, casting a glance back.

"He doesn't get a tip," Prescott says with a scowl. He's moving away, holding her hand, pulling her along, approaching the girl and her dog. Shania allows herself to be pulled. The dog rolls out a fat pink tongue and wags its heavy tail.

"She's not a puppy anymore, huh?" Prescott says to the girl, who giggles and says no. "This is Allie," he says to Shania. "She's on our cousin's soccer team. Ben babysits sometimes."

"And this is Bruna," Allie says, holding up the leash.

"Allie loves bloodhounds," Prescott says.

"They're the Sherlock Holmes of dogs," Allie says, as if reciting from a book, and Shania smiles at her, reaching out to pet Bruna, who, smelling tacos, covers her hand in slobber.

"Oh man," Prescott says, grabbing a few napkins from the nearest table.

"It's okay," Shania says. "I love dogs. My grandma had a beagle. Simon."

Her skin stings with phantom ice as she remembers the way the ground had resisted the shovel burying Simon that day. Bruna reminds her of Simon, the way his eyes drooped as he'd gotten older and older, he and her grandmother sharing the creaking shotgun house. Shania buries her fingers in Bruna's warm, biscuit-brown wrinkles.

"Babysitting?" Prescott says to Ben.

Ben nods. "She wanted tacos. Didn't expect to see you here." His eyes shift to Shania and drift away, then dart back when he actually sees her for the first time. "Oh. I didn't recognize you with your hair up. I didn't know you would...be here."

"It would be kinda weird if you did," Prescott says, and Ben smiles stiffly. He's still looking at Shania, and looking back, she thinks something shifts behind his eyes. Ben glances away and then doesn't look at her again.

"A beautiful girl who can eat and doesn't mind getting messy," Prescott says, extending another napkin for her dog-slobbered hands. "Did your almanac predict my luck?"

His eyes are filled with sunshine for a moment, and then he's staring at the street, at a car rolling slowly by in the thick SoBR traffic. A girl whose face Shania can't see is in the passenger side, bobbing her head to music. A young Black guy drives, his smile wide and clear, saying something that makes the girl throw her head back and laugh. The taco restaurant employees are turning on the heat lamps, but the air around Prescott feels suddenly cold.

"What's wrong?" Shania says, before she can wonder if she should ask.

"That was Eric Young," Ben says flatly, and Shania glances at Prescott again just in time to see the poison in his eyes oozing from the car to his brother. She almost flinches at the sight of it, but then he's reaching out for her hand, leading her to his car. As they walk, something flashes over his head, and she glances up, expecting a spark from the heat lamps. But it's a firefly, illuminating once, lazily, and then disappearing into the dark.

# CHAPTER 7

The almanac has been whispering to her. When she sleeps, it wakes her. When she brushes her teeth, it seems to hiss: *Do better, Shania.* It's not until a Wednesday, while waiting for the bus, when from a distant window she hears the unmistakable bellow of a hound, that she decides it might be time. Whatever secret or curse her grandmother had tried to tell her in the garden the day she died might be in these pages. She won't know until she knows. When she finds a seat on the bus, passengers nodding sleepily around her, she slips the slender book out of her bag and holds it on her lap, staring down at its worn cover.

This feels dangerous. She's trying to remember her grandmother as she was—blue sun hat over her neck in the yard; sweet tea sweating on the low brick wall—but all she sees is Gram's pale fist clenched against her chest, the tubes snaking from her mouth. Shania traces the number 1999 with her bitten fingernail, all the text on the cover faded and blurry—the only thing unyellowed is the piece of tape she'd gently bandaged its recent tear with. She swallows, opens the book, and swears the scent of her grandmother's house wafts out of its tattered pages, soft and sweet and a little like soil.

There, on the title page: *Do better, Shania.* She doesn't stare at these words long. Maybe this is the only thing in the book. She rushes past it, praying it isn't. Praying it is.

*Stinkbugs are a risk this year for your house and your garden alike. Ventilate your planters properly and wipe away excess moisture where possible.*

Her grandmother had made a little arrow here, doodled in blue pen. Shania presses her finger to this before flipping through the pages. Another note, written in Gram's hand: *Use cornmeal to sew tiny seeds.*

And another: *Never coddle tomatoes.*

Shania swallows here, thinking of Simon's body planted near the tomatoes. Someone else lived in that house now. Had they kept the garden?

*Store your tools in sand.*

Gram wrote her *a*'s the same way Shania does. She's starting to breathe a little easier. She studies the writing, looking for something that might connect them, granddaughter to grandmother, in a way that crosses time. Maybe this is all there is: knowledge. A reminder to follow her green thumb.

The Bard stop is coming up. She's about to close the almanac, turning one last page, when another note catches her eye. The page is an article about green manure and cover crops. But it's the blue pen in the corner Shania's interested in: an address, scrawled in a hurry. *18 W Chestnut, Blue Rock.* And beside it, written small: *I'm sorry.*

Shania stares at it so long she misses her stop again. Blue Rock. Her grandmother always said she never set foot in the city, and yet here's an address, in the very city Shania now lives. The cursive apology is just as perplexing. When she finally pulls the string, she gently closes the book and slides it back inside her bag. But when she closes her eyes, she still sees the blue ink.

She's only walked a block when she hears someone calling her name. It's Michelle. She's across the street, having just stepped off her bus coming from the opposite direction. She looks both ways and then dodges across.

"Hi," she says. "Do you always come this way?"

"I missed my stop," Shania says. "I just had to walk back."

"Daydreaming?" Michelle asks, smiling.

"Yeah, I guess you could say that."

They walk together in silence for a moment, Shania's head still inside the book.

"Are you from Blue Rock?" Shania asks as they wait for the crosswalk sign.

"Mm-hmm. Well, I was born in Richmond," Michelle says. "But we moved here when I was just a baby."

"Oh, okay. So you know the city pretty well?"

"Most of it." Michelle shrugs as they cross. "It's small enough to know pretty well but big enough to not know everything."

"Do you know where Chestnut is?"

"Sure. It's in Pocket."

"Pocket?"

"Well, I guess if you heard it on the news, they'd call it the Western Pocket of Blue Rock. Everybody who lives there calls it Pocket."

"Like they call South Blue Rock SoBR?"

"Um, no, not like that at *all*," Michelle laughs. "*Hipsters* call Southtown SoBR. The people who actually live in Pocket call it Pocket."

"Which is who?"

"Black people," Michelle says, nonchalant.

"So, Pocket is a Black neighborhood, and Chestnut is in Pocket?" Shania blushes when the word *Black* leaves her lips. It's like sitting down at a corner table beside the elephant in the room.

"Yup," says Michelle.

Shania wants to ask why her grandmother, who had never set foot in Blue Rock, had an address from a random Black neighborhood in her *Farmers' Almanac*. But if it's a mystery, it's one she thinks she needs to solve alone. So all she says is "okay."

"So. You went out with Prescott," Michelle says.

"How'd you know?"

"You know how it is. Grapevine."

"Oh. Okay. Well, yeah."

"Has he or Catherine or anybody told you about Eric?" Michelle says. Her tone carries something careful.

"Who's Erica?" Shania says quickly.

"No, *Eric*."

"Oh." The phantom girlfriend that erected her shadow so quickly in Shania's brain disappears as swiftly as she rose. Eric. "Who's that?"

"A guy that used to go to Bard."

"No, I don't think so. Why? Who is he?"

A 22 bus screeches to a halt beside them, startling them both. The doors are thrown wide.

"This is the stop," the bus driver, a middle-aged Black man, shouts at someone behind him, staring at the person in the rear-view. "Get off."

A woman's voice, screechy, rises and carries out onto the street.

"You're trying to strand me in the ghetto!" she says. "Don't think I don't know!"

"You said you needed to get to the new library," he says. "This is your stop. You need to walk three blocks north."

A blonde-silver white woman comes into view. She wears a string of pearls and a track jacket, and pulls one of the little backpacks on wheels that old ladies always have.

"I'm not getting off! Your job is to take me where I want to go!"

"Lady, my job is to drive this bus on the route I'm assigned and tell you what stop to get off on. *This* is that stop."

Michelle laughs and so does Shania. They bond over the pleasant absurdity of a woman wearing pearls on BRTA and screeching like she's ordered a private limousine.

"I don't see the library!" the woman snaps.

"Of course you don't," the driver says, and points. "It's three blocks that way."

Michelle cracks up, shaking her head as she and Shania move on.

"It's your job to help me!" the woman says.

"It ain't my job to *do* shit for you," the bus driver cries, his frustration mounting.

"I'm calling the police," the woman announces, pulling her phone from her purse. She struggles with unlocking it, looking up to stare daggers at the driver. "Using that kind of language! I'm a paying customer and now I don't feel safe!"

Shania continues on toward Bard but beside her, Michelle pauses, her Nikes making a squeaking sound as she doubles back.

"Hey, where—" Shania starts, but Michelle is back at the bus, lingering in its doorway.

"Ma'am," she says softly. "Do you need help? I can help you find the library if you want. I go there all the time and I can tell you exactly where it is."

The woman pauses, phone halfway to her ear. She looks back and forth between the driver and Michelle, a look of lasered distrust on her features as if scanning the air for a trick being played.

"This is the stop for the library?" she says hesitantly, squinting.

"One of them, ma'am," Michelle says. "We go to school right there. This isn't the ghetto."

At the sound of "we," the woman scans the sidewalk and her eyes land on Shania. The muscles around her eyebrows relax. The screw of her mouth comes undone.

"There's a school here?"

"Yes, ma'am, Bard Academy for Excellence."

The woman slowly steps off the bus, not looking back at the driver. Shania sees him catch Michelle's eye and they share a long blink. He shakes his head and then slides the doors closed. The bus growls away. Michelle stands with the woman for a moment, explaining with her hands how to find the library. When the woman finally walks away, smiling and waving, Shania is still watching, stuck to the spot.

"That was nice of you," she says as they resume the walk to Bard.

"Not really," Michelle says. She seems deflated, as if the interaction had sucked some vital bit of energy from her that needs to be replenished.

"What an old bitch," Shania offers, and Michelle smiles a little at that.

"You should've told her that," Michelle says.

"You want me to tell some old lady she's a bitch?" Shania laughs.

"Yeah, something like that."

Michelle sighs and rolls her shoulders, as if to shift an anvil that's settled around her neck.

"We're going to be late," she says, and her smile seems strained. "We're talking about fungus with Hassoon today. Can't miss that!"

Asking her if she's okay would be so easy. But it's even easier for Shania to latch onto the smile and the sarcasm she offers like a pacifier. Shania gets the feeling she's being sheltered in some way and she's embarrassed, then relieved. The relief is an embarrassment.

"You know how she is about her fungus," Shania says in the end. Her smile feels as forced as Michelle's but built on different ground.

They don't go to Ms. Hassoon's after all. There's a soccer game after school and the administration has decided to hold a surprise pep rally of sorts for the student body. The teachers have all committed: They wear face paint and jerseys, the kind of blatant pandering to the student body that will always work, even on high schoolers, fed by the thrill that comes from a deviation from the norm.

"Are you going to the game?" Michelle says when the entire student body is in the auditorium eating cookies donated from Rhino. She and Shania have ended up beside each other again somehow and it feels nice, Shania thinks—like what having an actual friend would be like.

"I wasn't going to," she answers.

"I used to go to all the games," Michelle says. "I kind of miss it. Have you seen the field?"

"Nope."

"It's really nice," she says. "Makes you feel like you're already in college."

Something about the way she says it draws Shania's eye.

"Do you already know what you want to study?" Shania asks.

"Conservation biology."

"Wow. That's...specific. Do you know where you want to go?"

"Harvard," Michelle says immediately, then her mouth snaps shut like the word was a smoke ring escaping in a nonsmoking section.

"Wow, you aim high," Shania laughs.

"Should she aim low instead?" Willa Langford says, appearing between them with a pair of cookies. Michelle takes one when offered, smiling, her eyes fastened somewhere across the room, or maybe farther.

"No," Shania says, flustered. Willa has a way of saying things like she's kidding but there's something like a broken bottle in her eyes. "I'm just glad we have another year to think about it. If I had to pick a college right now I'd probably just...not."

"Yeah," Michelle says, but her mind is elsewhere, maybe on the teachers, who have now formed a conga line at the front of the auditorium.

"Where do you want to go?" Shania asks Willa.

"Somewhere far away," Willa says.

"Willa wants to be an artist." Michelle smiles a sly sideways smile.

"Oh, really? We're doing that? Wow," Willa says, chomping the cookie.

"What? You need to own it, okay?" Michelle shrugs. "Speak it into existence!"

Willa rolls her eyes but grins.

"Okay, well, yes. I'd like to go to LA or New York maybe. Art school."

"She's had some pieces on exhibit here," Michelle says proudly. "And one in Savannah."

"Wow," Shania says, and studies her with new eyes. "What kind of art?"

"Sculpture," Willa says.

"Oh," Shania says, surprised. "I guess I thought you meant painting."

"I do a little bit of that too," she says. "But there's something special about the hard stuff."

"What do you want to do?" Michelle says, turning her eyes on Shania. "You're obviously good with plants, based on your stuff in Ms. Hassoon's class. Agriscience?"

It's a question Shania has been asked before and one she never knows how to answer. Even before her grandmother died, her parents had desperately sought a wind that would fill the sails of Shania's aimless boat. No sports or school accolades, no cheerleading or marching band. Just poking around in the garden. Reading poetry. And when she's sure no one is around, writing a little too.

"Yeah, maybe agriscience," she says. "Have you gone to Bard all through high school?"

"Yep. And their middle school."

"I didn't even know there was a middle school."

"Yep. All the way down through kindergarten. My family couldn't afford to pay for all that, but middle school and high school they made sure to afford. Plus scholarships or whatever."

Shania glances at Willa.

"Yeah, me too," she says.

"You two really have known each other a long time," Shania says, assessing.

"We've been through a lot," Michelle says, a little ruefully.

"Your friendship breakup?" Shania says, trying to tease, trying to show that she remembers, that she knows.

"Just Bard," Michelle says quickly. "That pretty much sums it up."

"Scholarship kids unite," Willa says, smiling a thin smile.

"Are you applying for aid for college?" Shania says, addressing both of them. She wonders what their families are like, if they're poor, or like Shania's family: poor enough not to be rich.

"Hell yes," Michelle says. "Praying for scholarships."

"You mean you're not planning on spending $100,000 on a degree you probably won't use?" Willa says, feigning surprise.

"If I have it my way, I'm going to use the fuck out of it," Michelle says, and though she's still smiling Shania can see the grit in her, the doggedness of a soldier.

A Black girl whose name Shania doesn't know appears in front of them, skinny as one of the stakes Gram placed for tomato plants to climb. The girl is decked out in Bard athletic wear.

"Really feeling the school spirit," Michelle says, eyeing her with a grin.

"Rah-rah, bitch," the girl says, a megawatt smile illuminating her face.

"This is Tierra," Michelle says. "My cousin. She runs track."

"I didn't know your cousin went here," Shania says, giving Tierra a little wave.

"Yep. They legit have a scholarship—a discount, they should call it—for family members of current students. My auntie and uncle thought, 'Hey, why the fuck not?'"

"If only they had asked 'why the fuck?'" Tierra says, shaking her head.

"You don't like it here?" Shania laughs.

"It's fine. It's school. It's just..." She looks at Michelle. "Dumb homogeneous."

"Homogeneous as in...?"

"As in *white*," Willa says, and produces a bottle of water from her bag. She laughs and takes a sip. "Look around."

"I thought you meant rich," Shania says, embarrassed. In conversations like these the word *white* is a giant pair of eyes in the sky that shift onto her and her entire life.

"That too," Tierra chuckles.

"Remember when Essence Arnold got into it with JP Byers?" Michelle says.

"*Classism is the new racism*," says Willa, pulling her chin into her neck and using a toad voice. "*You're the real racist!*"

"Essence ate him up," Michelle says, sighing happily. Tierra giggles.

"Who is Essence?" Shania says, desperate to contribute something.

"She graduated last year," Willa says. "Debate team captain. State champ. JP...well, he chose the wrong girl to fuck with."

"They didn't give her any peace after that." Michelle shakes her head, her smile fading.

Something sinks down between the small group, silent and heavy as wet snow.

Tierra shakes her head and turns her eyes to Michelle. "Anyway, were you still gonna twist up my hair before the game? It's looking like they're gonna cancel classes for the day and have everybody go out to the field straight from here for the game, so you can do it now if you want."

"Do you have a big comb? I don't think I have mine."

"I'll go get it. Come with me?"

They march off, Tierra chattering about the game and track conditioning. She looks like she could run a hundred miles and not break a sweat, and then step onto a runway straight after. Shania watches them go, the athlete supermodel and her beauty queen Harvard-aspirant cousin, and a shuddering egg of envy cracks open in the nest of her stomach. She looks around the room for a distraction, for some place to put the egg down, but everyone seems to already be engaged, so she stands awkwardly next to Willa, hoping she talks to her.

"I never asked you how you ended up at Catherine's party," Willa says.

Catherine is far across the room with her posse. Shania hadn't even attempted entrance into the circle of designer shorts. Catherine catches Shania looking and grins at her.

"She invited me," Shania says. "In class that day."

Willa takes a loud slurp of her water, staring at her over the top of the bottle.

"Did you have fun?"

"I mean, I guess? I'm not really a party person."

"And yet you attended said party," says Willa.

"So did you," Shania says. "Did *you* have fun?"

"I was there for Michelle," Willa says, raising an eyebrow. "She needed my help."

"Help?"

"You saw how Catherine 'Nardshark' Tane gets when she's drunk." Willa shrugs.

"Why even go to the party, then?"

"We were looking for something," says Willa.

Then Catherine appears beside them like a periscope breaking through water.

"Shania," Catherine says. "Greetings. Good to see you. Aloha. I've never met anyone named Shania. Just curious. No shade."

She's backed by Julia, who Shania has English with and only knows as the girl who has reminded Mr. Foster twice that she is Korean, not Chinese. Then there's Hannah, Catherine's right hand and near clone, plus a gaggle of other girls Shania has class with who never speak to her. They all wear pep rally face paint.

"Um, I'm named after Shania Twain," Shania says. "The singer."

"Oh?" Catherine says. "What does she sing?"

"She's not really super famous anymore," Shania says. A blush begins. The eyes of Catherine and her posse are like stage lights. "But 'Man! I Feel Like a Woman!'? Or 'You're Still the One'?"

"Sing one," Catherine says, waving her hand. It's evident that ordinarily people do exactly what she says. Shania wishes she were the sort of person who didn't succumb to this kind of thing, but she is. She glances at Willa, who watches passively; Catherine's piercing gaze reveals nothing. Shania gets the feeling that Catherine already knows who Shania Twain is. The Tane sister is a shiny-eyed scientist in a lab coat, presenting a mouse with a needle and a wheel of cheese.

"You'd know it if you heard it," Shania says slowly. "'Man! I Feel Like a Woman!' starts with guitar...."

She pauses, deciding. She sighs, then mimes holding a small guitar and makes the unforgettable twanging sounds of the opening notes. "Baow baow baow baow-baow..."

Shania raises her eyebrows, waiting for recognition.

"Oh, wait! I know this song," Hannah crows. Catherine just grins, but not in a cruel way. *"Baow baow... Let's go girls!"*

"Yes, that one," Shania laughs, relieved.

"It's a country song, right? She's a country singer."

"Yeah."

"Oh, okay, now it makes sense," Catherine says. She's back on her phone. "Shania. It just sounds kind of ghetto when you first hear it, right? *Shania.* It's like, I don't know, like a Black girl. *Shanequa.*"

Shania starts to say that she has been told this before, back in Morrisville, but Willa jumps in.

"Why does it sound like you think *ghetto* and *Black* are synonyms?" Willa says, staring in that piercing, broken-bottle way. Michelle returns with Tierra in that moment, a purple wide-toothed comb and a bag of other hair accessories in her hand. It feels like a face-off, but Catherine is smiling.

"Michelle!" Catherine says brightly. "Are you going to the game?"

"Yes," Michelle says. "To pass out flyers."

Tierra waves a stack of papers, studying Catherine the way a zookeeper might regard a cobra through glass.

"Well, I don't have one! Give me a few," Catherine orders, smile glowing.

Michelle and Tierra exchange a look without actually looking at each other. It passes between them like a flicker of telepathy. Michelle extends a small stack of flyers to Catherine, who passes them around blindly while reading out loud.

"Join Us for the Twentieth Annual Western Pocket Community Garden Fundraiser and Community Event," she says, her gaze slithering across the page. "Raffles, food, and family fun."

She raises her eyes to Michelle.

"Cute."

"Come and donate some of your parents' money," Tierra says from her cousin's shoulder, fast and fluid. Michelle elbows her.

"I would," Catherine says. "Truly. But Western Pocket is... Western Pocket. I might get robbed."

"Who the fuck has a fundraiser in Western Pocket," Prescott says, seeming to materialize at Shania's side. Like his sister, he appears out of the deep blue nothing. He doesn't look at Michelle or anyone else, instead drapes his arm around Shania's shoulders.

"A community garden that's been there for twenty years," Tierra snaps, then looks at Shania. "Are you going to come?" she says pointedly. Shania senses she's being asked about something more than just the fundraiser.

"Yeah, maybe," she says quickly. She tucks the flyer into her bag alongside the almanac and book of poems as a way of avoiding Tierra's eyes.

"Other parties to attend?" Willa says, smiling into Shania's face while applying shiny red lipstick, mirror-less.

"You know, Willa," Catherine says, finally acknowledging her, "I'm always surprised you're still with us."

Catherine's eyes are wide and shining and would be deer-like if Bambi had been rabid. The corners of Willa's flawless mouth rise in a mirthless smile.

"As long as your parents are still pouring those bucks into the scholarship fund," Willa says in a syrupy voice. "Hope that isn't cutting into your allowance, sweetie."

"Do you want to skip the game? Drive around with me?" Prescott says, close to Shania's ear. "I'm going to go get my car. Meet me out front?"

"Yeah, okay," she says.

She watches him go, clothed in yet another plain white T-shirt, the material thin and heathered. By the shoulder she can make out the indistinct shape of a tattoo showing through the light fabric—a faint green triangle, perhaps, pointing downward. Shania looks back at Catherine. Michelle, Willa, and Tierra have gone.

"Tomrom," Hannah says, her words curling like cat whiskers. "Someone has a crush."

"I don't—" Shania begins, but Catherine cuts her off.

"Not you. Him," she says matter-of-factly. She's pulled an aluminum bottle from her bag and clanks it open. It has stickers adorning every inch of its surface: *Nevertheless she purr-sisted* with a pink cartoon cat. "I saw when he came into the greenhouse to get your number. Very cute."

Asking "Why me?" feels deeply uncool.

"We're kind of just friends," Shania says instead.

"I'm feeling a gardening joke here," Catherine says. "Something about going to *garden bed* together. *Plant husbandry.* But that would be if you were dating the other shithead known as my brother. You and Ben and your green thumbs."

"Speaking of Ben, did you know we're playing Bedlington today?" Julia says.

"What?" Catherine snaps. "Seriously?"

"What's wrong?" says Shania.

"Eric plays for Bedlington," Julia says.

"Who *is* this Eric guy?" Shania asks, the name like a firefly in her head now.

"We'll just have to sit right down in front," Catherine says, ignoring her.

"What about Prescott?" says Julia, frowning.

"Thanks to Shania he's not going." Catherine beams.

"I'm lost," says Shania.

"A human trait," Catherine says. She's buried in her phone now—brand-new, Shania notices: Catherine's programming the language—and Shania feels herself fading from sight. She feels like she's been shipwrecked until her phone buzzes, and Prescott's name appears.

**PT: Outside. Where do you want to go?**

She leaves Catherine and the others without saying goodbye, texting as she walks.

**SH: To the moon.**

# CHAPTER 8

Ever since she picked up her check, Shania has arrived at the bus stop in SoBR expecting blood—the appearance of the dead cat outside Paulie's only makes the possibility loom larger in her mind. But when she steps off the bus on Friday night, instead of blood, she finds the warm smile of Ben Tane, bordered on either side by Willa and Michelle.

"Wow, hey!" he says. "You're like a genie popping out of a lamp. First there's just a bus and then . . . poof, Shania!"

"I guess this is *your* block," Michelle jokes. "If we're near Paulie's, we should know you won't be far away."

Shania puts her phone away—she'd been mid-conversation with Prescott and unprepared for other human interaction before work. She tugs at her work shirt, sneaking glances at Ben. He'd acted strange outside the taco place, but the warmth is back now.

"I guess I'm just a doughnut gangster," she says, and then feels stupid, but they laugh anyway.

"Want us to walk you?" Ben says. "We're on our way to

the movies, but our bus isn't going to be here for like fifteen minutes."

They walk, Shania at the center of the small herd they create. They jostle pleasantly.

"All I'm saying," says Willa, continuing their conversation from before Shania stumbled into their midst, "is that *small-dog people* aren't really *dog people* at all."

"I think your definition of *dog people* needs some solidifying," Michelle chuckles.

"Sorry, Michelle, I might be with Willa on this," Ben says. "And as a person who works at a dog rescue, I think I'm an *authority*." They laugh, and Michelle fake punches him. "Sometimes people come in only wanting small dogs because they're convinced they're *nicer*, but if they knew anything they'd know that dachshunds and Chihuahuas are the most likely to bite."

"I don't know about everything else, but that last part is definitely true," Shania says. "There was a dachshund in my hometown that bit everybody from the postman to the principal. They never put it down, though."

"Don't let it be a pit bull, though!" Michelle cries. "If a pit bull so much as growls..."

"Always the double standard," Willa says. She glances at Shania. "Do you have a dog?"

Shania shakes her head.

"Just my grandma's dog, Simon. He was a beagle and he was perfect."

"Funny," Willa says. "I would have taken you for the Chihuahua type."

"Those aren't real dogs," Shania says passionately. They all laugh, even Willa, and even though they've entered the cloudy territory of her grief, Shania doesn't flinch.

"They're not even cats," Michelle agrees. "They're like vicious little weasels with bell collars."

"Speaking of cats," Ben says, and he looks at Shania meaningfully. "Any more...?"

"No," Shania says quickly, and now she does flinch. "Not since that night."

"They need to give you a raise for dealing with that," Michelle says. "Minimum wage already asks for too much."

"Just tell me you didn't use the tongs to move it," Willa says. They're standing outside Paulie's now—inside, Jai is tonging doughnuts into a box.

"No!" Shania cries, then laughs. "Tongs are for doughnuts only. But Jai is going to turn them into a weapon if I don't hurry up, so I'll see you guys later?"

It comes out as more of a question than she had hoped, but Michelle only smiles.

"Later," Michelle says, and Willa waves.

"I hope so," Ben adds. He opens the door for her and she hopes he doesn't see her blush as she ducks under his arm.

Inside, the first person to greet her is Earl.

"Good evening," he says, eyes bleary. He's seated at his usual table in the corner, his orange coat like a caution cone glowing in her eyes.

"Uh, hey," she says. One of his hands curls around a cup of coffee; the other rests near his chest. Shania glances down, away, and then back again, startled. Tucked into the fold of his coat is a cat, small and blue-gray. She wouldn't have noticed it except for the patch of bright white on its sleeping head. When she looks at

Earl, he merely stares back, expressionless, and into her stomach drops a feeling of dread.

Jai pops up from behind the counter, a stack of to-go boxes in his hand. He looks up at the doughnut-shaped clock on the wall.

"You're late again. This is the third time."

She's glad to move away from Earl, glad to be distracted from the story that builds in her head about him and what will become of the cat in his coat. She crosses to the counter, frowning at the clock.

"Oh, please. It's only one minute."

"Late is late!"

"It's *almost* on time."

"In the great words of Brandy, my personal idol: Almost doesn't count."

She stares at him blankly, the reference lost, and after a moment of silence he tosses the boxes on the counter and smacks his lips.

"The youth."

"You're like nineteen!" she cries.

"THE YOUTH, I said!"

They both laugh and she raises the section of the counter that acts as a gate and ducks into the work space, closing it behind her. Next door, the bass thumps through the wall.

"What's that club called now?" Jai says. "Inferno? They've changed the name like fifty-leven times."

"Lantern," she laughs. "It's called Lantern. Except they spell it L-N-T-R-N."

"That's only missing two letters."

"Yeah."

"So what's the point?"

She shrugs. "Maybe they hate vowels."

"Lord Jesus," he says, squeezing his eyes shut and then gazing at the ceiling. "By the time white people are finished with Southtown, then it'll be on to Pocket. Then that'll be P-C-K-T. Paulie's is gonna be P-L-S. Do you want a C-F-F with your D-G-H-N-T?"

"So Southtown is...here?" she says. "I've heard somebody else call it that."

"Southtown is what SoBR used to be," he says. "What, you thought it was always SoBR?"

Time passes, and the thump of bass next door at LNTRN has intensified, a signal that the hours have ticked by and the evening has deepened. Jai and Shania hustle to wait on everyone, and by the time they get a lull they're both slightly sweaty.

"These damn drunk people love doughnuts!"

"You don't?"

"I love doughnuts, but I don't drink," he sniffs.

"Not at all?"

"I'm nineteen, Shania! I'm not of legal age!" he cries, but he's kidding too and they laugh.

"Seriously though, I don't meet too many people who don't drink," Shania says.

"Not my thing," he says.

"Not even at parties?"

"Right now I'm just trying to set a good example for my son."

She pauses, studying him.

"You have a son? I didn't know that."

He pulls his phone out and clicks the home screen, holding it up to show her the photo saved as his wallpaper. Staring back at her is the silky white face and shining nose of a teacup poodle.

He maintains a look of utmost seriousness for another beat and then cracks up laughing. It's contagious, and they both stand giggling for a moment. He looks lovingly at the phone.

"Nah, he's my baby, though," he laughs.

"What's his name?"

"Chester."

*"Chester?"*

"Don't hate on my dog's name!"

"I'm not! It's funny, people just usually name their tiny dogs stuff like Killer and Bruno."

"Nah, he's a Chester."

"He's cute. Not super manly, though."

Jai shrugs, smiling fondly at the photo again before putting his phone away.

"Ahh, manly's boring," he says.

The door tinkles open, and she turns and pulls on a pair of prep gloves, expecting the next rush of customers. Instead she finds Julia and Hannah, headed by Catherine Tane.

"There she is," Catherine says, her smile like a chandelier, shimmering and a little bit precarious. She's been drinking, Shania can tell—they all have.

"*Tomrom*," Julia says, and does a sort of dance with her hips, jerky and awkward. Next to Shania, Jai scoffs softly then politely retreats into his phone.

"How'd you find me?" Shania says, and then regrets how wrong it sounds.

"My brother," Catherine says simply.

"Oh," Shania says. "Yeah, I saw him with Willa and Michelle earlier."

Catherine freezes, her gaze becoming razor sharp for a half second.

"You're talking about Ben," she says. "I meant the other one. The tall one."

"*Prescott* told you to come to my job?"

"No," says Catherine. "He just told me you work here. He'd probably be pissed if he knew I was here, actually. Worried that I'll rub off on you. But no, we came to rescue you."

"Rescue me?"

Hannah snorts. "Who the fuck wants to sell doughnuts on a Friday night?" she says.

Catherine leans on the glass, leaving a trail of fingerprints between her and the glazed.

"These aren't the most stunning confections," Catherine says, peering. "There's this place in Chicago called Mooncakes, and all the doughnuts sparkle. Like, some of them have glitter sprinkles and some of them have like sugar cubes that look like diamonds. Designer doughnuts. That's what SoBR needs. *Designer. Doughnuts.*"

"Mooncakes sounds like Moonpies, though," Julia says thoughtfully. "Isn't that taken?"

Grief tilts the floor under Shania's feet, the way it often does. Her grandmother always had Moonpies in a box by the fridge— Shania would eat them on the back porch and share pieces with Simon while watching the birds in the garden. She pushes this away. She wants to replace it all with something else.

"Moonpies are fucking gross," Catherine laughs. "That's gas station food. Only poor people eat those fucking things. Anyway, it's Moon*cakes.*"

"A doughnut isn't really a cake," Shania says to say something, her cheeks burning.

"And thank God for that," Catherine says. Shania lets herself laugh. "Now, are you coming with us or what?"

"Coming with you...?"

"To LNTRN."

"The nightclub?"

"No, the lamp store," Catherine says brightly. "The nightclub, Shania, yes. Or do we need to find an establishment with a country-western theme?"

It's half mean and half friendly. Shania thinks of the movies that characterize rich girls as rattlesnakes with manicures. But if Catherine is a rattlesnake, her rattle plays a pop song.

"I don't get off for another hour," Shania says.

"Come *onnn*," Catherine begs. She smacks the display twice and stands up straight. "Will the doughnut gods striketh you down? Will they forgive this one transgression?"

Jai is listening now—he looks amused but doesn't exactly smile.

"First you come in late, and then you leave early," he says to Shania.

"I was *one-minute* late!" Shania protests.

"Yeah, yeah. Well, look, feel free. Go on and skate. But you owe me thirteen dollars if you do."

"Thirteen dollars?"

"That's how much I make an hour. So if you gonna have me on the clock by myself, then I'm gonna need a wage."

"You're serious," she says.

"I put it on my son," he says, and laughs.

"I don't have any cash."

"For you, good sir," Catherine says, producing money. She

gives him a ten and a five. "For your service. And one of those cinnamon thingies."

Catherine's Mercedes is parked three blocks away, where Shania and the others stand watching while Catherine digs through her trunk, searching for something for Shania to wear.

"You're so skinny," she says. "My stuff is going to be baggy on you."

"You're skinny too, shut the fuck up," Julia says. "You just have a big ass."

"Not big enough," Catherine says, and makes a triumphant sound as she produces what appears to be a green sequined scarf.

"Is that a dress?" Shania says, eyeing it skeptically.

"Well spotted," Catherine says in a British accent.

"Is there ... more of it?"

"How dare you slut-shame my dress." Catherine thrusts the dress in Shania's face. "On."

A moment later Shania is crunched in the back seat of Catherine Tane's car, wrestling herself into the stretchy green fabric. It's reptilian in the glow of the streetlights that angle into the car.

"Chip chop, Twain! My connect at LNTRN gets off at twelve thirty—if we miss him we don't get in."

"So *that's* your secret!" Hannah says from near the front of the car. She's smoking a joint: The smell of it drifts into the back seat, where Shania is trying to figure out how to hide her bra straps. At the bottom of her pale legs are the black flats she'd worn to work, and she hopes they pass inspection. When she climbs out of the car, Catherine attacks her face with green eyeshadow.

"Very lizardy," Catherine says, nodding. The nod includes the shoes. "Maybe we should take you to a herpetarium instead."

"Why does that sound like herpes," Hannah says slowly, high.

"Because you're a nardshark," Catherine says affectionately, and then throws her arm forward like a general before her army. "Onward!"

The street is much more crowded than when Shania clocked in at work, and she feels like a block of cheese being pressed through a grater. She thinks of the dead cat outside Paulie's, the way Earl rested his hand on the one inside his coat. Inside the shop it was bright, but what happened when Earl stepped out into the dark? Every alley she passes feels like one of too many shadows lacing through SoBR like veins. With that in mind she's grateful for the push and chatter that fills the street with light and noise. She thinks of Jai and Mrs. Rudolph, the way the change in SoBR makes them feel as if something is being taken, but as she walks, insulated by Catherine and Julia and Hannah on all sides, she allows Jai and Mrs. Rudolph to blur in her mind, allows herself to feel safer among the bars and the craft breweries. These things are familiar sights in a territory of the gritty unfamiliar. She settles into it like worn slippers and suddenly walking down the street between Catherine and her friends feels good, like she's somewhere that belongs to her. She allows that feeling to fill her up.

"Guess who texted me today," Catherine says.

"Who?" Hannah says. She still has a joint in her hand, but it's no longer lit.

"Willa."

"What'd she say?" Julia asks.

"She did what Willa does best," Catherine says. "She was cunty."

"Did you reply?" Julia asks.

"And say what? *Greetings, you backstabbing bitch! Have a lovely weekend!*"

"What did Willa do?" Shania says, nearly shoulder to shoulder with Catherine.

Catherine waves her hand from the wrist, an indolent queen.

"We used to be best friends. Did you know that? You probably haven't been at Bard long enough to know that. But yes, she and I used to be besties, until someone sprinkled cunty fairy dust on her and she turned into the beast that we all know as Willa Langford."

"Wow," Shania says, not knowing what else to say.

"Willa basically took *when they go low, we go high* way too far," Catherine says.

"Willa went to the dark side." Hannah laughs through her nose.

Catherine rolls her eyes.

"Get it? The *dark* s—"

"Yes, thank you, Hannah!" Catherine says loudly. "Fuckity fuck, am I ready to drink. Oh, look! My brother-ren! Ben! BEN!"

The girls all pause as Catherine stands partly in the street, waving manically. On the other side of the slow traffic a group of people pause, and among them stands the sturdy frame of Benjamin Tane. Shania sizes him up without meaning to, noticing that even from across the road, his shoulders are square against the chilly breeze.

He peers across at his sister, then gives one stiff wave with his free hand. He's carrying a large bag under the other arm.

"Is that a body?" Catherine screams. Strangers look, laugh, unconcerned.

"Mulch," he calls. "Winter-proofing garden beds at Sunset Homes."

"Vote for Ben Tane!" his sister yells. "A friend to flowers and geriatrics alike!"

Shania watches him shake his head and start to turn away. Then she feels him see her, his eyes catching. The road isn't too wide for her to notice his gaze, the way it clears then clouds. She raises her hand to wave. One of the people standing with Ben nudges him, and he turns away without waving back. Shania's ribs feel bruised.

"Sayonara, Mr. President!" Catherine calls after him, beaming.

But Catherine's electric smile falters when they arrive at LNTRN.

"We missed him!" she cries, indicating the doors, where a man that Shania guesses is not Catherine's connect checks IDs. She checks her phone. "Twelve thirty-five. That little bitch probably left early. Despair!" She shouts this. The people dressed in club clothes around her barely notice.

"Can't win them all," Julia says. Shania thinks she looks tired, and that the absence of Catherine's club connection isn't a disappointment at all.

"Plan B," Catherine announces, already moving down the sidewalk. Hurricane Catherine has been downgraded to a tropical storm, but she crashes onward.

"Sparkle Park?" Hannah says.

"Sparkle Park."

"What about drinks?" Julia calls.

Catherine pivots mid-step, jacket held open to reveal the glint of a flask poking out of an inside pocket. Shania laughs, feeling free, and has the sudden impulse to take a photo. She takes out her phone, turns to walk backward, tilts her face toward the moon. She snaps a selfie, the blonde head of Catherine like the North

Star in the frame behind her. She pauses, then sends the photo to Hallie. What would she think, to see Shania sparkling on a busy street after midnight, gold and green and glitter? Her desire for Hallie to see that she's not just the quiet watcher from Morrisville is as strong as her desire for it to be true.

The Sparkle Park is like a burrow on the edge of SoBR, closed on three sides with trees still clinging to summer, their crush of leaves blocking out the lights from the strip and most of the moon. But the fairy lights Michelle described are there, and Shania hadn't envisioned just how sparkly the Sparkle Park actually is. Dozens, if not hundreds, of strings are draped across tree branches and over the backs of the benches lining the park's perimeter; they make the silent, empty fountain at the center glitter and dance.

Other groups of people their age are already here—white boys smoking cigarettes in the back, laughing and kicking a Hacky Sack, and across the fountain at the center are three or four Black kids playing music from the speaker of one of their phones. One girl is trying to teach the others a dance and laughs uproariously every time they mess it up.

"Cool," Shania says, wandering in after Catherine, who has her sights set on a bench across from the fountain.

"We haven't been here in forever," Hannah says, sighing happily.

"If I ever become a vampire," Catherine says, and crosses her fingers dramatically for luck, "this is where I want my coffin. Just make me a cozy little crypt under the fountain and this will become my lair."

"I'd much rather have my coffin at your house," Hannah says.

"How cute would that be if we were all vampires? It could be, like, a sorority."

Shania laughs along, sitting at the edge of the bench. She finds that she's relieved they hadn't ended up at the club—she doesn't really like to dance and the music at LNTRN would have required it. Now they just pass Catherine's flask back and forth, Shania taking tiny sips. She's only ever had beer, and whatever Catherine has them drinking is clear and sharp and burns her nose worse than McDonald's Sprite.

"Plan B isn't so bad," Catherine says, as if reading her mind. She pulls her feet up on the bench, sitting sideways and leaning her back against Shania. "No boys, but whatever. Boys are fucking overrated anyway."

"Somebody still hasn't moved on," Hannah says in a singsong voice, and like a kangaroo being released from a box, Catherine's feet shoot out, connecting with Hannah's hips and shoving her off the bench. Hannah lands hard on her butt with a surprised squeak.

"You whore!" she shrieks.

"Oops!" Catherine cackles, letting her head loll back on Shania's shoulder. Shania isn't sure if she's drunk or if this is just what it's like being friends with Catherine Tane, boundaries obliterated by the bomb of her affection.

"If you broke my tailbone, you're paying for my new ass," Hannah says, climbing back on the bench while trying to look dignified.

"Fine. Why not! We can *all* get surgery," Catherine announces, throwing her hands skyward. "I'll get my nose job; Hannah, you can get Kardashian buns; and Julia, we'll get you some eyelids."

The "fuck you" that flies out of Julia's mouth is like an arrow, but Catherine plows on.

"What about you, Shania? What do you need? Let's see . . ."

She's just turning to provide analysis when Hannah snatches the flask from her hand.

"Cops," she says, and sits on it.

Shania's heart feels like a cat by a freeway, having narrowly avoided Catherine's dissection. Now she follows Hannah's gaze to the entrance of the Sparkle Park, where two uniformed police officers sway in, the glitter from the fairy lights illuminating their hands, which are resting on their belts, their chests square with armor. White men shaped like her father, tall and blocky, heads revolving to take in the benches along the park's perimeter. For a flash of a moment, Shania thinks they're here about the blood on SoBR's sidewalks, the dead cat she and Ben Tane picked up. She imagines them asking if anyone has seen a man in an orange coat. Instead, the officers stand talking, surveying the clusters of teenagers. The white boys with cigarettes go on laughing, a few of them turning their backs to conceal their jokes, or maybe their bloodshot eyes. The group of Black kids' music plays on, tinny from the phone's tiny speaker, but their conversation has hushed.

"Getting late, kids," one of the officers calls. "What's everybody doing?"

No one answers. Shania is suddenly very aware of how shimmery the green sequins she's wearing are. She feels like a lighthouse. How many sips has she taken? What if they give her a Breathalyzer? Shania feels the familiar stab of panic she has always felt when on the edge of getting in trouble—her mother works for the same system as these cops, and she imagines a telepathic connection formed by blue uniforms, her mother seeing her daughter out in a park after midnight wearing a green dress that isn't hers.

"Mind turning that music off?" the other officer says. This time he's looking directly at the girl who'd been trying to teach a dance to her friends.

"Why?" she says.

"It's a little late for loud music."

"Is it really loud, though?" she says. "We don't even have a speaker."

"Do you have some identification?" the cop says, taking a few steps toward her and her friends.

"Not on me," she says.

"Why not? What's your name?"

The officer's partner trails after him, hands still clutched around his belt. From the back of the Sparkle Park, one of the white boys mutters something and his friends burst out laughing.

"Are those cigarettes?" the second officer calls in their direction.

"Yes, sir!"

"Better be," the cop says, and continues on his path toward the girl with the music. Shania can just barely make out the tune from where she sits—she knows the song. It's new: It came on the radio when she was at Paulie's, and Jai hummed along.

With both cops' backs turned, Catherine reaches under Hannah's butt and yanks out the flask—Hannah squeals as Catherine takes a sip, winking hugely at Shania.

"I'm going to escort you out of the park," the officer is saying loudly. He has the Black girl's phone in one hand, points at the entrance with the other.

"Why? For what?" the girls says, reaching for her phone.

"Are you giving me lip? Get the fuck out of the park, kid, you can have this back once you're outside and I see that you're on your way home."

One of the girl's friends murmurs something and the cop shouts now.

"I said I don't want any fucking back talk, do you hear me? You're lucky I'm not in the mood for paperwork or I'd take your ass for a ride."

They all shuffle toward the entrance, everyone watching and not watching. The second cop trails behind, keeping an eye on everything, giving the white boys with cigarettes one last glance. As he sweeps his eyes over the rest of the benches, his gaze lands on Shania and the other girls. He seems to see them for the first time, studies them. Shania is again hyper aware of the sequins. The officer takes them in, something sweet and hungry in his eyes.

"You ladies be careful out here," he calls. He looks at each of them—Shania feels herself being seen. But still Shania glances at Catherine, their leader.

"Oh, we will, Officer," Catherine says, her face made pink by the chill and the lights. "Thank you."

Shania's head spins like a carnival game. She wonders, watching Catherine and Hannah giggle and sip again from the flask, if this is luck, if luck is what Catherine's made of, if it rubs off and is carried like pollen. Shania had left Paulie's feeling like it was two evenings, two worlds, twisted into one. But she thinks there's another world that she and Catherine exist in together that overlaps, the Venn diagram of their lives putting them in the same fairy-lit bubble. Whatever it is, this luck, it made the cop stare, noting no difference between them. In his eyes they were two of the same perfect something—wrong tooth or not.

Shania could give this thought. She could stop and consider what code is functioning that allows them to win game after game in this arcade of an evening. But not caring feels good. Oblivious feels good. When Catherine offers her the flask, Shania looks her in her eyes and takes it.

# CHAPTER 9

Shania and Michelle are two of four people who bring their lunch to school. Shania stands in the door of the common room, watching Michelle, hunched over a book on one of the ancient, misshapen couches, eating a panini she'd warmed up in the common-room kitchen. A school with a kitchen: It's still weird to Shania. She considers avoiding Michelle, thinking of the tension at the pep rally. In the end, the prospect of sitting alone is more daunting. Shania sinks down in an armchair across from her.

"Smells good," Shania says, venturing.

"Really?" Michelle eyes her sandwich.

"You don't think so?" Shania laughs.

"I don't have a sense of smell."

"Seriously?"

"Well, I do. But it's not very good. I can taste things. I guess if I didn't have a sense of smell I wouldn't be able to taste stuff. They use the same receptors or something. Tierra and I were just talking about this actually."

"Tierra's a freshman, right?"

"Yeah, but she shouldn't be. She's kind of a prodigy, honestly."

"In piano or something?"

"Definitely not," Michelle laughs. "She can't carry a tune in any capacity. No rhythm either. But biology and stuff. She's known the periodic table since she was like three."

"Wow," Shania says, impressed. She opens the lid of her Tupperware—leftover casserole. "You're just a sciency family, I guess."

Michelle laughs lightly and closes her book. The cover says *Sing, Unburied, Sing.*

"Yeah, I guess we are. Are you? I mean, you seem to love botany."

"Kinda. I really just love gardening," Shania admits, casting her eyes down to her food. She feels like a chameleon trying to blend in beside a pair of dragons.

"Nothing wrong with that," Michelle says. "Did you grow up doing it?"

"Yeah, with my grandma. It was what we did together." Shania swallows. "She was just, like, the sweetest lady. I know everyone probably says that about their grandma. But she was the best person I knew. She really was."

"She passed?"

"Yeah."

"I'm sorry."

"It's okay." It's not, of course. But this is one of those things she must say. Most people know someone who has died, but Shania never knows how they feel about death, if they believe in heaven, or if, like Shania, they're still trying to get the blood out of the back of their mind.

"Speaking of gardening," Michelle says, graciously changing the subject. "Are you going to come to the event I was telling you about? The fundraiser?"

The flyer is still in Shania's bag and she hasn't given it a second glance. She reaches for it now, avoiding the almanac like hot coals. She unfolds the flyer and really looks at it for the first time.

"This Saturday?" she says, scanning the blue page.

"Yup. Even if you don't have money to donate, you should come. The weather is supposed to be amazing, and there'll be food and shit."

Shania nods, feeling nervous and hopeful at once.

"Eleven a.m.," she says. "I should be able to. I don't work until later. Is the address on here?"

"At the bottom."

Shania checks to confirm, but her eye catches on the line of text: *18 W Chestnut, Blue Rock*. She stares until it clicks, then reaches back down into her bag. She'd hoped to leave the almanac closed for a while, sitting with her grandmother's mysterious notes. But it was like the world was calling the book from her bag.

"Eighteen West Chestnut," she says, flipping through the faded pages, frowning.

"What's the deal?" Michelle says, chewing but curious.

"I could have sworn...," Shania says. Then she finds it: the blue ink, her grandmother's scratchy note in the margins. She's so shocked to be correct that her head pops up and she looks Michelle right in the eyes. "What the hell is 18 West Chestnut?"

Michelle looks momentarily pissed.

"Are you serious?" she says slowly, lowering her panini. "You already asked me where Chestnut is. And 18 West is the community garden."

"No, sorry," Shania says, covering her face with her palm. "I know. I mean, I just don't know why it's in my grandma's almanac from 1999!"

Michelle stares, then puts the sandwich down.

"Girl, what?"

Shania brandishes the almanac, holding it up for her to see. Michelle squints.

"Well, damn," she says, raising her eyebrows. "You sure that's from 1999?"

"Positive," Shania says, closing the book and peering at the cover. "Nineteen ninety-nine was, like, her lucky year or something. But she hated cities."

Michelle shrugs. "Maybe she was planning a trip. What does 'I'm sorry' mean, though? Did she know someone here?"

"I have no idea," Shania says. She almost adds that her grandmother had never been to Blue Rock, let alone the part that Michelle calls a Black neighborhood. But she doesn't, because Prescott is walking toward them, a cup in each hand.

"Hey," he says, looking straight in Shania's eyes. She blinks away, down at her lunch, at all the things that could be lodged in her teeth.

"Hi…hey," Shania says. Michelle picks up her book and stares hard at its pages.

"I brought you a coffee," he says, extending one of the cups. "I was at Rhino and I hadn't seen you all day. I don't have a free period until after lunch."

"Yeah, me neither," she says. She accepts the coffee because it's right in front of her face. She's surprised by how hot it is, surprised by this whole interaction. She's never had coffee in her life. But she leaves her casserole balanced precariously on her thighs, holds the cup with both hands. She feels like a ten-year-old pinching a cigarette.

"So, did you have fun Friday?" He grins, sipping his coffee.

She laughs, switches the coffee to one hand, and tucks the flyer and almanac back in her bag.

"I guess you got the story from Catherine," she says.

"Parts of it. I'm sorry if she overwhelmed you. She has a way of doing that."

"I mean, it was kind of was overwhelming, yeah. But not entirely in a bad way? It got me out of my head."

"I don't know," he says. "I feel like inside your head would be a pretty cool place to be."

They just smile at each other, her heart half mouse.

"Do you even like coffee?" Willa says. She stands just behind Michelle, carrying an orange recyclable bag. Her eyes on Shania are like two spotlights, then she turns them on Michelle without waiting for an answer. "Hi. You okay?"

"Yes," Michelle says, and Shania is surprised by the relief in her voice. Michelle pulls herself up from the couch. "Do you want to go somewhere and eat?"

"You bet your ass I do," Willa says, and she picks up Michelle's backpack while Michelle packs her panini. They're gone before Shania can say anything, and when she looks at Prescott to gauge whether he's surprised by their sudden exit, she finds him sipping his coffee with a look of amusement on his face.

"I guess I scared them off," he says. Through the glass wall, Shania can see Michelle and Willa climbing the stairs, headed for the second floor. Shania feels a twinge of regret: She and Michelle had actually been having a conversation, and the potential of friendship glitters like Christmas lights. But then Catherine Tane sails into the room, backed by Hannah.

"*Shaniaaaa*," she sings. "Sorry, I don't remember any of the songs you named by her or I'd sing them. What are you doing right now?"

"Um…"

"Talking to me, obviously," Prescott says.

"So nothing. Good. Come on, I want to show you something."

The thing about Catherine, Shania realizes, is that no one says no, even when she seems to be setting a trap. So Shania gets up, shooting Prescott a smile. She is carrying coffee. She is walking toward Catherine Tane. She feels good about this.

"Thanks again," she says to Prescott. He smiles a little before looking up through the glass at Willa and Michelle just as they disappear around the corner.

"Chip chop," Catherine says when Shania reaches her, and then they're hustling toward a side door that leads outside. Catherine casts a quick glance around, then withdraws a key from her pocket. She fits it into the tiny hole on the door's lock, and with a muted click, it swings open. She grins like a devil, and Shania and Hannah follow her outside.

Shania finds herself behind the school in the alley that connects to the student garage filled with shining vehicles. One of them is Prescott's, and Shania is so focused on looking for the silver Audi that she barely notices Catherine leading them to her own car, opening the door, getting in.

"Quayloo, can you bitches hurry?" she says. "We have a very small window, Shania Twain."

Shania knows not to say no. She gets in the car. Hannah has

claim to the front seat and Shania slides into the back, barely putting on her seat belt before Catherine is steering them out.

"What are we doing?" Shania asks when they're snaking down Main.

"Going to Taco Bell, obviously."

"Taco Bell...?"

"Surely you've heard of Taco Bell," Catherine says in her occasional British accent.

"I mean, yeah, but—"

"It's too far to walk and my soul requires a chalupa, Shania. Don't argue."

"I didn't think people were supposed to drive during the school day."

"We're not. But Mr. Foster is on the desk today."

"So?"

"So Catherine caught him smoking weed in his van before school this morning," Hannah giggles. "She's got a trump card till at least the end of the semester."

"Oh." Shania allows this to sink in, and she feels a smirk growing. "Of course he's a pothead. How else could he tolerate working at Bard?"

Catherine laughs heartily at this, and Shania feels a thrill skitter like a lizard in her skin. In Morrisville she had never been funny. She thinks of Hallie, always on a stage, always something to say. Shania could be like that.

"JP just posted a video from school," Hannah says. She has her phone out in the front seat. "Julia was in the background talking to Willa and Michelle."

"Way to make me lose my appetite," Catherine says brightly.

"Still hate her, huh," Hannah says, smiling.

"Hate who exactly?" Shania asks.

"Everyone," Catherine says, and in the rearview mirror Shania sees her shoot Hannah a warning look but Hannah is staring at her phone and doesn't catch it.

"Willa," Hannah says. "The Great Stabsy."

"That's not even good," Catherine says, but she grins anyway.

"Why *do* you hate Willa?" Shania presses. Knowing who to hate at Bard seems suddenly very important.

"Hate is a strong word," Catherine says. "Except for when it's not strong enough. I do not hate Willa Langford. I despise Willa Langford."

"But why?"

"Because she's a thief. That party of mine? Willa showed up and stole my phone."

"She stole from you?" Shania says. She suddenly remembers what Willa had said—that she had gone to Catherine's party to look for something.

"I shouldn't be surprised," says Catherine. "She leeched off my friendship and then stabbed me in the back."

"I wonder if she hangs out with Eric," Hannah says, still staring at her phone. In the rearview mirror Catherine's eyes go icy. "That would be weird, right? If he told—"

"There's nothing to tell," Catherine says sharply. "Willa knows nothing and neither does Eric. He hangs with shitty little bitches like Michelle now. Fuck all three of them."

"I thought you and Michelle were cool," Shania says, surprised.

"Yeah, well," says Catherine. She hangs a sharp turn into the Taco Bell on Proctor Boulevard, the pearly car rattling against the curb. "Things change."

# CHAPTER 10

Shania has never ventured past Bard on Main Street, but when Saturday arrives, she finds herself doing just that on the 4 bus headed west, the almanac clutched in her lap like the talisman she half believes it to be. When she had first gotten on the bus downtown, she felt brave—embarking on an adventure, tracking down the address written in Gram's hand—but the farther the bus goes from familiar, the less the city feels like hers. Which is why, when Ben Tane gets on just past downtown, she's surprised by the hopeful leap she feels in her chest. She pushes it guiltily away, thinking of Prescott, but mostly she's glad for a familiar face. He sees her and a shadow passes through his eyes. He doesn't sit in the empty seat next to her, choosing to sit across the aisle instead. He's carrying a soccer ball and rests it on his lap.

"Hi...?" she says cautiously when he doesn't speak.

"Hi."

"Are you going to the thing?"

"What?"

"The event."

"I'm on my way to play soccer at Sage Park."

"Oh." She looks down at the ball. "Oh. That makes sense. I just thought this bus went to Western Pocket, and I didn't know why you'd be..."

She trails off, embarrassed. He looks back at her unflinchingly. Something about him has turned cold again.

"A white guy on a bus headed west?" he offers.

"Uh, yeah, I guess so."

"The best games are at Sage," he says. "There's a big Liberian community in that area and a lot of the guys play."

"Oh. I...didn't know that."

He shrugs. Three younger kids board at Twenty-Second Street and sit nearby, a single phone out between them blaring a slightly distorted song from the small speaker. Shania glances around to see if anyone cares, but the adults sitting nearby ignore them, reading or napping. One elderly woman smiles fondly at them as if they were her own grandchildren.

When Shania's phone buzzes, she's grateful for the excuse to look down.

It's Catherine.

> **CT:** I just went to Paulie's & somehow you weren't there. I thought you lived there?

Shania smiles, feeling affirmed. Catherine going out of her way to text on a Saturday makes Shania feel as if she's moving toward the distant and mysterious land of friendship.

> **SH:** I don't work until later. I'm going there after I leave this event.

CT: What event?

SH: Michelle's garden thing.

CT: I wish you could see my face right now.

Shania feels a twinge of something like regret: Maybe she shouldn't have told her. After all, Catherine made it clear that Michelle was no longer someone she considered worthy of pretending to like, and Shania isn't sure about the terms of friendship with a girl like Catherine.

"Is that my brother?" Ben says, nodding at her phone.

"Um, your sister actually."

"How nice," he says, and she's surprised by the bite of sarcasm. He'd been so friendly at Paulie's the night of the dead cat. Even more so on the bus stop that day with Willa and Michelle—she can still remember the glow of his smile.

"Um," she says, unsure how to proceed.

"So, what *thing* are you going to?" he says, staring out the window.

"The fundraiser. Michelle's thing."

He blinks over at her.

"Wait, you're going to *Michelle Broadus's* fundraiser? At Mrs. Walker's garden?"

"I don't know about a Mrs. Walker, but yes, Michelle. I just assumed you knew about it since you two are friends."

"I helped her set up the banners yesterday," he says, squinting. "I told her I'd be over later."

He pauses, staring for a moment, gears turning behind his eyes. In the end he just squints, then reaches for the bus string, yanking with a ding as the automated voice calls *Sage Park*.

"I really don't get you," he says, then stands, shaking his head.

"Huh?"

"I don't get you," he repeats. "I saw you in SoBR with Catherine and her friends on Friday, you know? I know you're dating my brother. So how does being cool with Michelle make sense in your head?"

"Excuse me?"

"Tell Michelle I said I'll see her after soccer," he says. And then he's moving down the aisle, string backpack swinging across his shoulders, leaving her baffled. He's a little shorter than Prescott, she notes. Stockier. She thinks of the curl of hair under Prescott's navel she's seen when he stretches, when his shirt pulls up, and wonders if Ben has it too, then swipes the thought away, embarrassed. When he gets off, she forces her eyes not to follow him down the sidewalk.

*What a dick*, she thinks.

A middle-aged Black woman sits down next to Shania. She's wearing an Arby's shirt and cap, both of which fit loosely and bear the stains of fast food. Shania puts her phone away. The woman looks at her sideways, sighs deeply, and they continue on down Main Street together until Shania pulls the cord at Forty-Second Street. When she stands, the woman doesn't make way, and Shania feels a rush of blood to her cheeks, trying to squeeze past.

"You can't say excuse me?" the woman says, and Shania's blush is now lava. She isn't sure why she's embarrassed, and it embarrasses her further. She has always expected the world to see her intentions and make way for her. She feels her set of expectations and the woman's rubbing up against each other, rumbling tectonic plates. *Earthquake*, Mr. Ahmed had said.

"Excuse me," Shania mutters, and the woman's legs swing out

into the aisle, allowing her passage. Shania moves past, hurries down the aisle, and escapes out into the sunshine.

She feels as if she's stepped off the bus and into another city. In Morrisville, she only knew Monica, and Monica didn't live in a Black neighborhood because there was no Black neighborhood. But Shania had never been to her house, and so she had no comparison. Still, she doesn't allow herself to stare directly at the assumptions her mind had conjured—her imaginings of broken-down apartment buildings and graffiti seem to sprout from nowhere and everywhere. The thoughts feel like they belong to someone else, as if they live in the house of another's brain and have only come to visit—it makes it easier to push them away. Either way, Western Pocket is a surprise.

There is no graffiti. The neighborhood is rough around the edges; there are a few windows with plywood, front yards with grass that needs cutting. But the houses are huge. She feels like she's stepped onto a historic street in a city like Brooklyn or Philadelphia. The houses have columns, double balconies, ivy. The verandas have sweeping windows, French doors. Many of the houses need paint, but where Shania had expected graying cubes that were even more cramped than the apartment she and her mother had settled on, she found something like mansions.

The sunny day has drawn everyone out of their homes. People sit on the verandas with small barbecue grills, occasionally shouting from porch to porch or at the teenagers and kids who move down the walkways in clusters. Most wear light jackets, laugh in melodies. Shania smells both weed and cigarette smoke; the warm, full smell of barbecue. Jazz drifts into one ear, hip-hop into the other. She has never felt so overwhelmed in her life.

She keeps her eyes straight ahead, expecting to be questioned.

She feels and looks like an outsider, because for everything she does see, she doesn't see any other white people. Her whiteness feels suddenly neon, a sign flickering to life whose presence she's generally unaware of. The realization forms into a single, lonely butterfly. The decision to call her mother is as sudden as if the butterfly had flitted through a spiderweb.

"Shania?" her mother says, low. "I'm not on break. Are you okay?"

"I thought your phone would be in your locker. Sorry," Shania says. She'd wanted the phone against her ear to busy her hands, to somehow look more casual than the racket of emotions in her chest enables her to actually be.

"Oh...so, what, you're just saying hi, or...?"

They don't do this—emotions. They had emptied Gram's house in silence. Their discussions of Shania's father leaving were limited to facts: *He left. We're leaving.* They tend not to just "say hi."

"I was just thinking about Gram," Shania says as she passes a yard where little kids run around chasing bubbles a big kid blows. That's all she can say. She can't tell her mother where she is. It would be like plucking a thread that would unravel a sweater. She can see the garden up ahead, can hear the swell of voices. Saying she's at this address mainly because she saw it in the almanac she stole from under her mother's bed isn't an option.

"What are you thinking about?" her mother asks.

"Wondering if she would have come with us for a fresh start," Shania says. She's stopped on the sidewalk, frozen in place. "I mean, if she hadn't—if she was here, would she have come with us?"

"No, because we would have stayed," her mother says.

113

"But you wanted a fresh start."

"After what your father did to us, leaving?" her mother says, impatient. "Yes. I wanted a fresh start from that."

"But only if Gram passed?" says Shania. She's genuinely confused.

"Gram wouldn't have wanted to come with us to Blue Rock," her mother says. Her voice is still low, talking to her daughter from somewhere in the prison she shouldn't be talking, but her tone snaps like oil from a skillet.

"Why?" Shania says. Two people maneuver around her on the sidewalk she blocks with her indecision. Two Black girls Shania's age. They look back at her curiously, and she sees herself, her whiteness, her in-the-way-ness, through their eyes in a flash like a sunburn across the back of her neck. Though no one else approaches, she moves hastily off the sidewalk, just in case, staring ahead at the garden. Eighteen West Chestnut. The phone is pressed hard against her face. "Why not?"

"Because Mom couldn't go—" her mother starts, then Shania hears the smack of her lips. "Because, Shania. *Because.* Gram didn't like the city. She stayed where she was. And I know this is hard and I'm sorry. But this is a fresh start. Remember? I miss your grandmother. I know you do too. But we're doing something new. You and me. We're stepping into the future. Now, I have to go. We can talk later."

Then she's gone, and the only sound in Shania's ears is the jazz, the children, the bass of a passing car that rattles her teeth. And the sound of Michelle's voice echoing down the street.

A crowd gathers just within the gates of the Western Pocket Community Garden, which are large and shiny and meticulously clean. There's an air of celebration, and little kids dart this way and that. Someone is passing out more canisters of bubble mix; bubbles rise into the sky all around like galaxies of tiny, transparent planets. Shania skirts around the edge of the crowd, following the one voice she knows, and finds Michelle balancing on the edge of a raised garden bed and speaking into a megaphone.

"Everybody knows Mrs. Walker is traveling for a funeral today; otherwise she'd be here to thank everybody for coming out," Michelle says. She's wearing a bright-yellow blazer that makes her skin glow. "Mrs. Walker has been tending this garden for twenty years now, and a lot of us have grown up in it, myself included."

"Probably got dirt under your fingernails right now," someone calls from the crowd, and Shania snaps around to see who said it, but everyone laughs, loving, and so does Michelle.

"Like I was saying! Mrs. Walker has not just tended but *owned* the Western Pocket Community Garden for twenty years, and if you've lived here as long as my family has, you know that Pocket has been victim to food apartheid for just as long. Most people have come to the garden at least once to get the fruits and vegetables that you can't get nowhere west of Twelfth Street. And not only that, Mrs. Walker has been the person who would watch your kids if you picked up an extra shift at work and wanted to make sure they weren't running the streets. Some of my earliest memories are helping her weed out tomato patches or planting garlic before the ground froze."

Around Shania, heads nod and a few soft claps ring out. Shania wishes Mrs. Walker weren't traveling so she could get a look at her, this gardener, babysitter, hungry-mouth feeder. Shania also notices the subtle way Michelle's voice has changed: a rounder, rolling sound to her speech than the tight, clipped voice she uses in the halls at Bard. Her hair is different too: Usually bone straight, it's now a soft bubble of curls, corn-rowed in the front and poofing out in back.

"I'll keep this short," Michelle says into the megaphone. "Y'all know why we're here. Mrs. Walker offers up this garden to the community of Pocket, and the least we can do is all put in on keeping it running.

"Also, Destiny's here"—she points, and a girl around fourteen with box braids smiles and waves—"and she has information about her upcoming trip to DC to advocate for clean air in Pocket. You know Pocket has the worst air pollution in Blue Rock? The city won't let them build the factories in white neighborhoods, but they give them the green light to build down here. I wonder why? She's raised money at her school to take other folks from Pocket, so if you're interested, go talk to her. Also, we've got food donated from Nafizah's—"

"One of the few Black-owned businesses left in Pocket!" someone shouts to cheers, and Michelle smiles.

"Not for long!" Destiny shouts back. She's smiling but her eyes are determined. "This will all be ours again. They're trying to start doing in Pocket what they did in Southtown—trying to look for ways to kick us out, more and more police—but we're not having it."

People murmur in the crowd, and at the front, Michelle nods fiercely.

"That's right. Today is just one step. And we're all here together. We've got face painters and activities for the kids, and the band is setting up now. So have a good time and donate what you can. There's a raffle at noon. Have fun!"

Cheers go up and Michelle waves, smiling that beauty queen

smile. Shania feels a surge of envy. Michelle holds the mic so easily, smiles without reserve—in Shania's mind, Michelle is able to move weightlessly through the world.

More people have filtered in through the gates, forcing Shania in farther, back toward the garden itself: long neat rows, some in elevated planters and some in the ground, all with stones of various shapes and sizes hand-painted in bright colors to resemble the crop they demark. Shania ends up by the squash, the unmistakable smell of sun on tomatoes filling her nose.

And there she is. Her grandmother lies at her feet, Simon's body still and cold beside her. Shania stares down at the rows of tomatoes, her grandmother's hat loose beneath them. Shania can feel the scream unfurling in her throat. She frantically imagines angels. She replaces the hospital bed with wings. She tries to snatch at all the things that have come unglued and nail them back down.

"Are you okay?" Michelle appears beside her, puffy hair shifting a little in the breeze.

Shania is jerked back into the garden, stares at Michelle breathlessly.

"I feel—"

"Like you might throw up?" Michelle asks, concerned. "Cuz that's how you look."

"I'm fine. I'm fine. Your hair is different," Shania blurts. It gives her something to focus on. She's accustomed to the straight black curtain that frames Michelle's face at school, and for a reason Shania can't explain, this change jars her. Michelle's whole face seems different now, her features rounder. She looks like a Disney princess but real.

Something about Michelle's smile changes, still bright as a chandelier, but like a piece of the crystal chipped.

"Girl, I'm just not wearing a wig," Michelle says, and laughs lightly.

"A wig? You wear a wig?"

"Sometimes." Michelle shrugs and seems to make a decision. She keeps talking. "So, what do you think of the garden?"

"It's amazing," Shania says, using the opportunity to fully take in the whole of it. At the gate, behind the crowd of attendees, she couldn't see the expanse of it. Back by the beds she can see that the rows extend much farther. "It almost takes up the whole block. It must have taken forever."

"Mrs. Walker has a lot of help," Michelle says as she smiles. "Everybody kinda pitches in."

Shania sniffs.

"I love the way it smells."

"We just laid new mulch over there. Most people think it stinks!"

"I mean, I guess it does. It kinda reminds me of my grandma's house. She would get manure from some of the nearby farms for her garden."

"Oh," Michelle says, with her eyebrows raised a little, like this bit of personal information was more than she wanted in this casual interaction. "That's sweet. That you remember that."

"Yeah. Sorry. I just think about her a lot."

"Don't be sorry," Michelle says, and shrugs, grinning again, softer this time. "My nana passed two years ago, and for like six months I couldn't go anywhere without smelling banana pudding. It was so weird. It wasn't even the best thing she made, but the smell of it just stuck with me."

"I get that!" Shania nods hard. "I really get that."

Michelle's cousin pops up at her shoulder and waves.

"Oh shit, someone from Bard actually came," Tierra says. "I told Tink not a single soul would come since Willa had to work."

"Tink?"

"It's just what my family calls me," Michelle laughs.

"She wanted to be Tinkerbell when we were little," Tierra says, fluffing her hair.

"I like your hair," Shania says to Tierra. Tierra looks amused.

"Thanks," she says. "Weekend tings."

"Huh?" Shania says.

"Gotta let the curls be cute on the days we don't have school."

"You don't like having an Afro at school?"

"Check the handbook," Tierra says, laughing, but the sound is bitter. "I get written up for this 'fro all the time."

A bit behind Michelle and Tierra, a few people have begun to congregate. It's clear Michelle is the captain of this event's ship, and people need her attention. One is a boy.

"Ay, Tink, they need help with the food!" he calls. He looks familiar but there are only three Black male students at Bard and he's not one of them.

"You see me talking," Michelle shouts, twisting around to look at him and laughing. "Big hungry, always tryna find some food, dang!"

Her voice changes like the gear shift of a Porsche, smooth, steering up a steep mountain and then humming down again, shifting back into the voice that sounds like Bard—clipped and hollow, a gourd cut from the vine.

"Anyway," Michelle says, looking back at Shania.

"Is that your brother?" Shania asks.

"That's my boyfriend," Michelle says with a snort.

"Oh," Shania says. "What's his name?"

"Eric," she says. "How's your project in botany coming?"

"Good, I guess." Shania shoots one more glance at Eric, wondering if it's the same Eric whose name exists behind a veil at Bard. "I haven't killed anything yet."

"Not killing things is a good start," Michelle says, and grins.

"*Tiiiiiiink*," Eric calls. "Come on!"

Michelle turns and puts her hands on her hips.

"Lookin' like a Muppet," he teases.

"I got your Muppet," she laughs, then turns back to Shania. "Aight, they need help getting the food line going, so I need to take care of that. Get you a plate when we get things set up!"

Shania feels a stab of irrational panic, the notion of being safe within a lifesaver and then watching a knife cut the cord to the boat. She watches the eager crowd absorb Michelle and Tierra, two shining beacons who move with the self-assuredness that comes with knowing where they belong. Even from far away, Michelle seems taller somehow, taking up more space with her brassy cousin and her secret boyfriend than she does in botany.

Shania shrinks back to the edge of the garden. Three boys loop through the party with a cooler: one on each end and the third fishing out bottles of water. They offer her one and she's grateful to have something to do with her hands. She stands against the fence under the sole tree, watching children get their faces painted with Black Panther and Shuri designs, eating barbecue and grilled corn. An elderly woman appears next to Shania and fans herself.

"Where'd you find that water, young lady?" she says, nodding at the bottle in Shania's hand.

"Um, they were passing it out. A couple kids."

"You found a good shady spot," the woman says. "That's the

thing about a garden. It needs all this damn sun! Not supposed to be so hot this time of year."

"Yeah, um. Climate change and stuff."

The woman eyes Shania.

"You ever been down to the Pocket garden before? I don't think I've seen you."

Shania flinches, wondering if she's referring to Shania being white. She thinks of Ben, how he had sat on a bus as one of two white people and hadn't even seemed to notice.

"This is my first time. I actually came—" She pauses, the story about her grandmother on the tip of her tongue. She changes her mind. "I came for Michelle. We go to school together."

"Oh, Michelle!" the woman says, her face breaking into a wide smile. "Now that is a diamond child, you hear me? She is just so bright and talented. Pocket's angel. Her cousin is wild but they're good girls. Mrs. Walker wouldn't have 'em here helping out so much if they weren't."

"I wish I could've met Mrs. Walker," Shania says. "She sounds really cool."

"Oh, baby, you don't know the half of it. That woman been through hell and back, and that would turn some people into a devil of their own kind. Not Mrs. Walker. She made lemonade out of lemons and made enough for the whole neighborhood. They were going to turn this block into liquor stores and gun stores if Mrs. Walker hadn't done what she did."

"Wow," Shania says. In her head the picture of Mrs. Walker grows, expands, becomes a winged legend. "What'd she do?"

"She won the lottery for starters," the woman says with a grin. "But then she put that law degree she got to good use. Put her money down and went to court to contest the construction, and six months later she was turning soil. Smart too, because that old white man had already broken ground, demolishing the houses. He thought he was just going to"—she makes a swooping motion with her hand—"slide right in."

She chuckles and then turns to look at Shania straight on.

"That's one thing about Pocket," she says. "It's been shifting for as long as I've been alive. I was born here, but my parents were one of the first Black families to move in, back when Western Pocket was full of people who looked like you. If my family was the first, Mrs. Walker's was the second. I've known her since we were kids, when our parents first tried to make their way. You can guess what happened next."

She drops her chin expectantly, as if waiting for an answer. Shania feels like a deer watching a semi speeding toward her, frozen.

"All those white folks packed up and left," the woman says, laughing mirthlessly. "Happened all over the country, but Blue Rock was real bad with it. Black folks moved in and white folks suddenly grew wings. Before you knew it, Pocket was all Black. It took time. And a lot of pain." The smile fades. "Now, nothing too bad happened to me and mine. But Mrs. Walker...well, like I said. She went through it. But here we are!" she says, and throws her hands out, gesturing at the garden beyond. "Here we are. And we are growing, honey! Sprouting like weeds. The best kind."

Deep in Shania's stomach, her grandmother's almanac burrows into a dark hole. Everything this woman is saying seems to be growing legs and forming a trail of ants that snake toward the book.

The three boys wander near, lugging the cooler, which sloshes now with melting ice.

"Where y'all been? Watering the plants? What about old ladies? Give me one of those bottles, and I'll give you each a dollar."

She ambles off after patting Shania on the shoulder, leaving her silent and speechless, staring at the garden, at all the people it has sprouted. Shania almost jumps when her phone vibrates. A text from Prescott.

> **PT:** Catherine says you're in Western Pocket.
> **SH:** Yes, at that garden event thing.
> **PT:** In Western Pocket??

She hesitates before responding.

> **SH:** Yes. The community garden.
> **PT:** I'm coming to get you right now.
> **SH:** ???
> **PT:** What's the address?
> **SH:** 18 W Chestnut?
> **PT:** Stay there. I'll see you in 10 minutes.

# CHAPTER 11

They drive around the city, into parts of Blue Rock Shania has never seen before. Prescott drives wordlessly for a long time, and she sneaks looks at him, silently comparing him to Ben. Ben was first warm and then cold, but something in Prescott runs hot. There always seems to be something burning and it thrills her in small, inexplicable ways.

"I can't believe you went all the way down there," he says as they enter SoBR. "Jesus Christ. You're sure you're okay?"

His concern had overwhelmed her at first, but now, settled into the front seat of his expensive car, it feels like a compliment.

"I'm fine," she says, looking out the window. "It was mostly a bunch of kids."

"I know you don't know Blue Rock very well yet," he says. "Next time you want to go somewhere, just call me. You don't have to take the bus. Let alone to fucking Western Pocket."

"Okay," she says. She starts to say something else—about how this reaction from him makes her feel both safe and scared. But she doesn't. By the time Prescott's car ends up downtown—the windows down, music from his speakers a warm lull—she feels like they've been on a road trip and have landed in a new city.

It's old downtown, not the center of the city that SoBR is transforming into. The buildings are more uniform, red brick and large windows. Prescott parallel parks outside a building with stained glass, and at first Shania thinks he's taken her to a church.

"How do you feel about art?" he says.

She realizes then that it's a museum.

"What can anyone say to that question?" she says. *"Hi, no, thanks. I hate art, actually."*

He laughs and turns off the ignition.

"I'll rephrase. How do you feel about walking around a building with me and also coincidentally looking at art?"

"Now that's a better offer."

For Shania, entering a museum is always like putting on a jacket and pretending it fits. Whenever she glances at Prescott, he seems distracted. She wonders if she should be commenting on the art, but that would only leave her open to saying the wrong thing. And so neither of them speak until they move into a room full of statues, most of them planted in the center of the room under a skylight. The white marble is like a vortex, drawing the eye and pulling museum goers toward the velvet ropes surrounding them.

"This is my favorite part," Prescott says, leaving her side and drifting to the statues. When she joins him, he's staring up at the face of a Roman-looking huntress, one hand raised with a bow, face tilted toward the sun.

"They're beautiful," she says.

He nods.

"Do you ever wish you could time travel?" he says. Now she's not sure if he's looking at the statues or something beyond, up in the clear blue sky that's become a ceiling through the skylight.

Shania gazes up at it too. Her mother had told her that Gram wouldn't have come with them to Blue Rock—somehow it makes the pain of her loss more acute, as if Shania has traveled somewhere her grandmother's memory can't reach. She would willingly step into a time machine if it meant being with Gram again. Her mother would rather not look back.

"All the time," she says.

"Me too," he says. "Sometimes I think I was born in the wrong time. The wrong place. Things used to be so much simpler."

"Simpler how? Like no indoor plumbing simple, or...?"

His lips twist in a half smile but his eyes stay fixed skyward.

"Like these statues," he says. He looks like he wants to reach out and lay a palm across the huntress. "They're perfect, right? Smooth, white marble. Nothing complicated. But they're so beautiful and make you feel like you're standing in the presence of something... angelic."

She looks up at the sightless white eyes and the symmetrically hooded lids. She tries to see them as he does. The marble shines.

"They do look like angels," she says. It makes her want to write a poem.

His smile widens.

"Exactly. You know these were originally based on women from the Caucasus mountains? They were considered the most beautiful women in the world."

"She's gorgeous," Shania says, staring at the huntress.

"This is where beauty came from," Prescott says. He's moved

closer to Shania now, farther away from the huntress, and together they stand gazing up at her, at the direction the arrow notched on her bow points. "This is where it all began."

"That's actually bullshit," chirps a voice too loud for the hushed museum atmosphere, so loud that Shania jumps. It's Willa Langford, on the other side of the huntress, side-stepping into view and then approaching them. She wears a crimson sweater and crisp blue pants. "Here's a free history lesson. The dude who studied these white statues back in the day, Winckelmann? He was kind of a dumbass. They call him the father of art history but what an *idiot*, seriously. The white statues were actually copies. He saw all these white statues in his travels and chose to believe they depicted the most beautiful people in the world and all this crap and the whole idea that white skin was the most beautiful basically started with him and people like him. Turns out his dumb ass didn't even travel to Greece to see the originals— which had lots of paint and stuff depicting lots of different colors of people—he just saw the white copies and made a bunch of assumptions. Classic."

"Classic what?" Shania says, looking to fill the space Willa's declaration has created.

"Classic white dude," Willa says.

"Is crashing dates something you enjoy spending your Saturdays doing?" Prescott says.

Willa taps her chest, where Shania notices a badge: Blue Rock Museum of Art & History. She remembers Tierra saying Willa had to work today...and here she is.

"Just doing my job," Willa says, her teeth not as white as the marble but still glowing. "Are you guys taking notes?"

Shania notices two other employees—interns, a boy and a girl, both with notebooks. Willa gestures them closer and then points at the huntress.

"See, y'all, this is how art influences life. You name some dumbass the father of art history and then just because he knows a thing or two about composition he shapes centuries of attitudes about what beauty is. This dude said, and I quote, 'The whiter the body is, the more beautiful it is.' And from there we have all this sculpture that literally erases melanin from the canon of beauty. Is that not the most twisted shit you've ever heard?"

The interns eagerly take notes on their twin pads of yellow paper.

"Exhibit number billion in the history of lies white people tell ourselves to feel superior," she says. "If you can't beat 'em, rewrite history!"

"It's a shame you and Catherine aren't BFFs anymore," Prescott says coldly. "You're both so full of shit I thought you'd be friends for life."

Willa smiles a steely smile, leans against one of the silver poles supporting the velvet ropes.

"I guess blood is thicker than water," she says coolly. "You two can sort that out in family counseling. Maybe eventually you'll get to Catherine's dreadlocks and your ridiculous little tattoo."

She turns on her heel and the interns follow enthusiastically, pencils scratching. Shania stares after her, wondering what her job is. Willa is a sculptor, Shania remembers, and the inertia of the other girl's life feels suddenly dazzling: perpetually moving forward, knowing things. Shania perpetually at rest. Willa and Michelle are thinking of college, art school, scholarships. What is

Shania doing? Selling doughnuts. What might her grandmother have been doing at this age? Probably already running a charity.

Prescott's fingers on her elbow jerk her out of her thoughts, and when she looks at him she expects the distant gaze he's been wearing all day. She's surprised by his intensity, his eyes like two ship's lights piercing through fog.

"I'm glad you're not friends with her," he says. "She's fucked every guy at Bard except for the gay ones. Fucking bitch."

Shania isn't sure if it's the intensity that shocks her or the words themselves, and she goes on staring after he has returned to gazing at the huntress and her posse of white-skinned maidens.

"Did she do something to you?" Shania says. She almost doesn't want to ask, wants to leave this particular root buried in the ground. But he's angry in a way that feels specific.

"You ever meet someone that just grates you? Like their entire existence irks you so fundamentally that you can't even look at them without feeling pissed off?"

"You mean besides myself?" she says, trying to laugh.

"I'm serious," he says, frowning. "Willa is twisted. Like her ideas about the world and the way it should be are just so far off base."

"She seems really smart," Shania says slowly.

"She *is* smart! That's what makes it so fucking annoying."

In the next room, Shania can hear the echo of Willa's voice explaining things to her two charges, and she tamps down the faint itch that scratches in her belly, a microscopic twinge that wants to follow Willa and carry a yellow pad of paper herself. Then Prescott's hand is on her back—he turns back to her abruptly. She almost jumps.

"I think you're really special, you know?" he says quickly. It melts into her ears. Her bones feel suddenly soft. "I don't want you to get lost in the bullshit of Bard. It's a black hole. Me and my sister have issues but she at least can be reasoned with. She puts the right people first in her life."

"So what, are you trying to set me up with your sister?" she says.

The hand that has been resting on her back tightens, drawing her closer. She allows herself to be pulled in, allows herself to stop hearing Willa's voice in the next room and press into his side.

"I just want you to be okay," he says into her hair. The inexplicable hole in her heart made wider by her grandmother's departure from this world feels suddenly smaller, or that it might be capable of eventually being filled. The white clouds over the garden that day transform seamlessly into white marble. *To be loved*, she thinks, *maybe that's what's missing, the question that needs answering.* Before he kisses her mouth, he presses his lips against her forehead. Her eyes flutter closed, and above, the huntress and her maidens look on.

# CHAPTER 12

When Shania's grandmother was still living, Shania would go to her house on Sunday mornings and help her pick vegetables, gather tomatoes, and pull weeds, Gram in her sun hat, wrists obscured by gardening gloves, Kroger muffins on a plate. After she died, Sunday mornings didn't take on new meaning. They remain like a dead tooth in the mouth of the week, gray and hollow. Since the funeral, Shania has tried to make a new ritual: farmers' markets. Sometimes she even buys a muffin.

"Next time I get a Sunday off, I'm coming with you," her mother says as she always does, drinking her smoky-smelling coffee. She doesn't actually want to come. The farmers' market would remind her too much of Gram, the smell of soil and small, lumpy apples. There it is again, Shania thinks—grief. It's like staring at a cloud: She and her mother both gaze at the overwhelming loss of her grandmother, but Shania sees a bear where her mother sees a sailboat. Shania doesn't understand how putting so much distance between herself and the memory of the person she loved can make things hurt less. Part of her thinks this is why her mother hid the almanac. The other part knows it's the mouth of a volcano.

"You're still dropping me off, right?" Shania asks. She's tired from the late shift her mother doesn't know she worked but tries to look rested to keep the questions away, folds the comforter on her couch.

"Yes," her mother says. "Turn on the TV for me. I want to hear the weather."

"I can just look on my phone," Shania says.

"Data," warns her mother, and she sticks her head out of the kitchen. She points at the television with a slice of untoasted bread.

On TV, the anchorwoman speaks in the usual anchorwoman voice. Shania checks her phone anyway and sees a post from Hallie as she scrolls. The thing about social media is that it's a version of time travel—like Dr. Strange, living in many realities at once. One glance and Shania is plunged back into Morrisville, watching Hallie and Monica painting a sign for an upcoming fall festival at the high school. Their smiles are brilliant. The trees around the parking lot are a deeper orange than the ones in Blue Rock. It's already fall where home had been, and it makes Shania feel that she left a version of herself in Morrisville and she's going on living there, a quiet life where grandmothers can slip into a grave and the doctors just shrug.

"...a man found beaten in the SoBR neighborhood, after he was apparently attacked by an unknown assailant. The victim was confirmed to be homeless by an individual at Pine Street Baptist Church, which often houses Blue Rock's homeless population."

Shania is drawn out of her phone and stares at the screen.

"Whoa," she says.

"Someone got hurt?" her mother calls.

"Yeah," Shania says. "A homeless guy in SoBR."

"That's down there by your job," her mother says, stepping out of the kitchen.

"...the attack occurred overnight," the anchorwoman says, "and is believed to have been carried out by another person living in the homeless encampment. Law enforcement officials say they'll be canvassing the area for the next few days looking for any information in the attack. The victim is in stable condition at Methodist West."

Shania's breath catches in her throat. Overnight. She'd left Paulie's at midnight.

"They need to clear them all out of there," her mother says. "They should be in a shelter or looking for jobs, not hanging out under a bridge! It's no surprise this happened!"

Another face appears onscreen, a Black woman with reddish dreadlocks.

"The attacks on South Blue Rock's homeless population are just the latest symptoms of the greater disease attacking this area. The dehumanization of Southtown residents, from the media to town hall, tells us exactly whose lives matter in Blue Rock, and I'm wondering just what the mayor and BRPD plan to say about this latest assault on some of this city's most vulnerable."

"That was local activist Mika Barry speaking in SoBR early this morning. She and other activists have harsh words for the mayor and the police, saying last night's attack is part of a greater problem in Blue Rock that needs to be addressed. We obtained a brief statement from Detective Rana Omar, who is on the team investigating the case."

The screen flips to a video clip of a woman wearing a blazer and a navy-blue hijab, walking toward an official-looking building.

"We are investigating a number of angles in regard to this case." She's answering a question asked offscreen. "But we don't have a lot of information about this attack, and we are actively encouraging anyone with information to come forward."

The anchorwoman moves on to another story, her tone brightening as she changes gears to talk about an elementary school's walk to raise money for cancer research. Shania stares at the screen, knowing what's coming.

"I don't like you working down there, Shane," her mother says.

"Mom—"

"I mean it, Shane! I thought it was sketchy to begin with."

"Mom, it's fine," Shania says, but as a teenager reassuring her mother, it's the kind of thing she *must* say. Honesty isn't an option, because honestly, nervousness spiders through her veins, thinking of Earl.

"What time do your shifts end?" her mother says, turning on her.

"Eight." The lie comes out smooth.

"That's too late. Morning shifts *only* now," her mother says, shaking her head. "You shouldn't be working so much anyway, Shania. How many times have I told you to focus on school? If I had better grades when I was your age, I wouldn't have gotten..."

She makes a sound of disgust instead of finishing her sentence. Shania knows the next word: *stuck*. She's never quite sure if she's part of what's sticky, so she glides over this back to the argument at hand.

"Mom, I'm not going to get any hours working morning shifts."

"I don't care. Your safety comes first."

"I *am* safe," she says. She tongues her tooth—only money can force it into submission.

"Shane, I know you want to be responsible, and I admire that about you, but—"

"Mom, they need me," she says. "And I need to stay busy. If I sit around too much I just keep thinking about..."

She trails off. Her mind is on the almanac her mother doesn't know she has.

"Afternoons, then," her mother says quickly. "No more evenings."

Shania bites the inside of her cheek, wondering what her mother would say if she knew the truth. The truths. Her mother checks her watch.

"Let's go," she says, and stuffs her toast in her mouth.

The market is crowded with people carrying coffee and chasing kids and groping fruit. Shania runs her fingers over the lacy greens of carrots, the tops left on like in cartoons. This is her favorite part of markets. Here, she receives things in their full form, the dangling roots, the messy ends. She wishes it was like this with people.

She's drifting, eating a cranberry muffin, when she sees dogs ahead. A booth of them. She finishes her muffin quickly, speed-walking toward them. It's a new table at the market: B-Rock Dog Rescue. The logo has a dog wearing a space helmet. A breath later she's on her knees with her hands buried in the ruff of a Saint Bernard mix.

"Oh, you're so pretty," she mutters into one of its big floppy ears. "You're so, so pretty."

When she finally looks up from the perfect canine face, she finds a human face staring down at her from the rescue table— Ben Tane's.

"Hey," he says. She can tell by the twist of his mouth that he's deciding whether to be warm or cold.

"We meet again," she says.

"Are you looking to adopt?" he says as if reading from a script, extending a business card.

"I can't," she says, standing reluctantly. Her place at the altar of Saint Bernard is immediately taken by a little girl wearing a bicycle helmet.

"You can always volunteer," he says, still on script. He seems reluctant to look at her. She approaches the table.

"Why are you so weird with me?" she says, finding his gaze and holding it. She doesn't know why she feels bold around Ben Tane. She never seems to know what to say around his brother.

"I'm not," he says. "I'm just working."

"Reeling in another volunteer?" A redheaded white woman swoops in with a clipboard. "You can always spot a dog lover!"

"We don't deserve dogs," the guy next to her says. He's a Latino man with a big smile. "I've yet to find a human anywhere near as pure-hearted as my mastiff. But dog people are close."

"Don't forget cats!" A white girl with a tattoo on her neck flops down at the table and passes out muffins from the booth Shania just visited. "They need love too! Especially in SoBR. Have you heard people talking about these dead cats turning up?"

"She actually found one," Ben says, nodding at Shania.

A table of widened eyes turns to her.

"What? Seriously?" the girl with the tattoo says.

"I work in SoBR," Shania says. "Nights and stuff. A little while ago there was a dead cat outside the shop and it—it seemed like someone, you know. Killed it."

"That is fucking sick," the girl spits, her face flushing with anger. "Who would want to kill a defenseless animal?"

"Have you found any more?" Ben asks her when the attention of the others has shifted.

"No. But this morning on TV they said a homeless man got attacked in SoBR. My mom freaked."

"I mean, it is pretty concerning," he says.

"Yeah, except she thinks it means someone's going to murder me on my way to work. But I love doughnuts as much as I love money, so my mom will have to pry me out of there when I'm cold, dead, and covered in powdered sugar."

He laughs, the warmth of it filling his eyes. She feels a moment of satisfaction, like she's won him back from wherever (and however) she'd pushed him. She wants to ask about what he'd said on the bus, but she doesn't want that smile to fade.

"Did you see this guy?" he says, gesturing to a dog on his side of the table. She leans forward, peeking over, and finds a tan hound dog gazing up at her with mournful eyes. Her heart leaps as she thinks of Simon. "He doesn't like anybody but me but he's sweet."

"Hey, good boy," Shania croons.

It's at that moment the dog decides to lunge. He leaps up from where he sits by Ben's feet and rushes under the table, the green leash clipped to his collar yanking taut and jerking Ben's arm down painfully. Shania gasps, fully prepared to be bitten, and Ben makes a sound of warning. A woman nearby jumps back with a shrill cry.

But the tan hound leans hard against Shania's leg, ears drooping and docile, heavy round head on her thigh. The mournful eyes gaze up, begging, until she overcomes her shock and pets him, his fur warm from the sun.

"Wow," Ben says, eyebrows high. "Wow. What a betrayal."

"Witchcraft!" a volunteer exclaims. "Sunny doesn't like *anybody!*"

"He's...he's...so sweet," Shania says, and feels suddenly, absurdly, like crying. The vegetables. The muffin. The dog with bottomless eyes. She finds herself backing away, away from the dog and the boy. "Excuse me."

She walks off and lets the crowd swallow her. The smell of produce and sunshine fills her hair, wafts off her like baked wheat. She thinks she needs to eat something right now. Another muffin. An entire box of macaroni and cheese. She wants to eat the memory of her grandmother—chew it up and swallow it. She wonders who she is with Gram gone. Gram's last words to Shania are like a brand on her skin: *There's something I think you need to know. We're all liars.* What did it all mean?

Shania takes a seat under a row of trees, pulls the almanac out of her bag, and sighs as if over a holy text. With the book on her lap, she rests her hands on top, closing her eyes momentarily. She can almost hear Gram's voice guiding her hands as a child, as they relocated slugs to the grass outside the garden. *They may come back, but we'll just move them again. Killing is ugly, and God don't like ugly.*

Shania opens the almanac and thumbs through until she finds the page where the address had been penned in blue ink. *18 W Chestnut.* The unknown of it is a question that burns on her heart. She had gone to Michelle's event yesterday with the hope of finding something that would explain why her grandmother had a Western Pocket address written in her almanac from 1999, but the only thing she could hypothesize was that her grandmother, a gardener, had somehow heard about the community garden and stopped by to see it. But Shania rubs her thumb over the other words—*I'm sorry*—and the hypothesis loses air. She half expects the pen to smear, but it was written before Shania was born and remains there, faded and cryptic.

"Are you okay?" It's Ben, standing nearby and looking cautious, as if she's one of the rescue dogs and she might bite, or howl.

"I'm fine," she says. "I'm fine. I'm just having a weird time. This all just reminds me of my grandmother and...she..."

"She died?" he says.

She hates always having to answer this question, admit it over and over. She nods instead.

"I'm sorry." He sits down next to her on the curb, averting his eyes. "When?"

"February."

"Was she sick?"

She feels cold, the scream in her throat like jagged ice.

"Kind of. She had a heart condition and..." Shania pauses, wondering if she'll actually say it out loud. "No one could help her."

He doesn't reply right away. People mosey by, laughing. It doesn't even grate her. By now she's used to feeling trapped by other people's joy.

"I'm sorry. That's hard," he says after a moment. "That had to have been terrible."

"We were in the garden together," Shania says. "A Sunday

like this. And I think she felt it before she could say it. Or maybe she tried to tell me and I didn't hear her. They took her to the hospital, but by the time I got there . . . she was gone."

She sits beside Ben and is standing in the room, the light above Gram's bed white and humming. Tubes like snakes from her mouth.

"I'm so sorry," Ben says quietly.

She nods in agreement, not trusting her voice. The scream in her throat feels itchy. She can't tell if that means it's settling lower or moving upward toward the light—she doesn't want to find out. Ben glances at her then, and perhaps it's the way she cradles the almanac, but somehow he knows, and nods at it.

"That was hers?"

"Yeah, it was."

He looks at it, and his eyes—so like Prescott's, but somehow so different—flicker up at her.

"Um, I hate to be the one to tell you, but you know the predictions and things change year to year," he says. It's a joke. She sees the tinge of it in his eyes, testing stormy water.

She laughs and doesn't scream. Not now.

"I know, I know. I'm just . . . keeping it."

"Did you used to come to this market with her?"

"No," she says. "No, she had never been to Blue Rock. At least, that's what she said . . ."

She trails off, looking down at the words in blue ink. He peers at her.

"You don't sound so sure."

She feels strangely protective over the small mystery written in the pages of the almanac. Somehow discussing it out loud feels like admitting perhaps she wasn't as close to her grandmother as she believed. That the whispered word "liars" ran deeper than the garden's roots.

"It's just...," she says, hesitating. "She wrote an address in here. A Blue Rock address. This almanac is twenty years old. I'm just wondering what it means, that's all."

"Did you already google it?"

"Google what exactly?" she says, amused. *"Has my grandma ever been to Blue Rock?"*

"Her name." He shrugs. "The city with her name. Things like that. You never know what you'll turn up. If you use quotes and parentheses and all that you get better results. If all else fails, there's the library."

"The library?" she says, skeptical.

"Archives. Old newspapers. Stuff. I don't know where you'd start, but librarians are like magicians."

"Thanks," she says. "Really, thanks." She pauses, thinking. "Why are you being so nice?"

He fixes her with a stare and a smirk, his eyes like those of the puppies at the table.

"I mean, if Sunny likes you..."

They smile at each other until he turns to the sound of someone calling his name, the redheaded woman from the rescue.

"Ben, we need you! Sunny just tried to bite Amanda!"

"Speaking of..." He grins, turning to walk away. Then he pauses. "Hey...do you...want to give me your number? I could text you dog pics whenever you're having a rough day. If you want."

She hears "sure" coming out of her mouth before she even realizes it's her tongue forming the word. A moment later she's reciting her number to Prescott Tane's brother, and he's grinning in a way that makes the twinge of guilt in her belly feel like a butterfly.

He gives a wave before turning back, picking his way through the crowd. When she can't see him anymore, she picks up her phone, ready to google "Helen Rutherford Blue Rock."

But there's a text waiting from a number she doesn't know.

**You kissed my brother didn't you**

For a brief, panicked moment she thinks it's Prescott, that she and Ben have been somehow witnessed. But no, Prescott's number is saved in her phone. It can only be Catherine.

> **SH:** Catherine?
> **CT:** Affirmative. So . . . ? DID YOU KISS PRESCOTT
> **SH:** Maybe?
> **CT:** I knew it.

The three little dots hover for a moment.

> **CT:** He was in such a good mood when he left town. I
> figured it had to be that.
> **SH:** Prescott left town?
> **CT:** He didn't tell you?
> **SH:** No . . .
> **CT:** Had to go on a last-minute trip with our dad. He'll be
> back.

Shania doesn't reply, a leaf of disappointment uncurling.

> **CT:** Don't tell me you're over there moping.
> **SH:** Maybe.

CT: Well stop moping and get dressed. Me and Hannah are 10 minutes away.

SH: I AM dressed. You're 10 minutes from where?

CT: From Russia. From your house, Shania. I'm texting while driving and everything.

SH: Stop! I'm not home.

CT: Paulie's?

SH: Farmers' market.

CT: Quayloo, Shania Twain, your mother really nailed it with your name. Send me a pin of your location. WE SHALL BRUNCH.

SH: I have to go to work!

CT: You're going to be late.

Somehow it feels good to be commanded away from duty. No almanac. No blue ink. No hounds calling from the past. She stands, moves toward the street to watch for the Mercedes.

# CHAPTER 13

The woman who drives the night bus looks like she was carved out of a redwood tree. Hard-faced, scratchy features, a burnt red. It's the color Shania's grandmother might have been if she had lived a little longer. Tonight Shania boards without a word, pays her fare, and moves to the middle of the bus as usual. Sometimes there are other passengers: people dressed in uniforms, either coming or going to work. Occasionally a guy asleep in the back, his snores adding to the rattle and shake.

But Shania is alert, made of eyes. In truth, the night bus isn't so different from the day bus—the same kinds of people, just working the late shift. But the dark makes it all different, and ever since the man was attacked in SoBR, every crack in the sidewalk has turned into a machete slice. Every doodle of graffiti takes on a sinister connotation—it could be a mark left by a killer, working his way from cats to people. She could avoid the anxiety by doing as her mother told her and switching off night shift. But having this secret from her mother feels somehow like justice.

When Shania's phone lights up, she lights up too, expecting Prescott. Instead it's a number she doesn't have saved, and when she opens the text she finds a photo of a greyhound smiling out at her, pink tongue as long and skinny as the dog itself.

**As promised. Sylvia hopes you had a good day.**

Ben.

She stares at the screen, wondering what to say. If she should even answer at all. Prescott isn't her boyfriend—he hasn't texted her today, after all, their museum date like a semicolon holding an unfinished sentence in limbo.

> **SH: My day was good but not as good as this good girl. Thanks.**

He responds a moment later with a smiley, and she can feel possibility stretching there. She had told him about Gram, even if she had stopped before the confession: *My grandma said we're all liars and it turns out my mom actually is. I feel like there's always something in my periphery, but when I look, nothing is there.* But she had talked and he had listened, was kind. But then she thinks of his coldness on the bus, his smiles like a crapshoot. And most importantly, his brother.

> **SH: How's Prescott?**

She blushes even asking, but asking feels like an alibi.

> **BT: Still out of town.**
> **SH: Where did he actually go? Catherine didn't say when we were at brunch.**

It feels a little like bait—part of her wants him to ask about her friendship with Catherine, if only so she can confirm it is indeed a real friendship. But he doesn't answer, and after a few blocks of silence she puts her phone away and withdraws her grandmother's almanac from her bag, Ben's name and the memory of their conversation at the farmers' market turning her reluctantly toward its pages.

She could ask her mother about it, point blank. But Gram's last words are like a tattoo in her mind, paired with the words on the title page: *Do better, Shania.* This is a mystery for her alone. She flips it open now, skimming to the page where the address in Pocket is printed. Does she want to know more? Ben had suggested the library—so simple for him. He doesn't understand that, for Shania, the past feels like a box of snakes. Just a crack, and out they'll slither. She could choose not to know. But that thing in the corner of her eye hisses, and she turns the page.

She flips single page by single page, slowly, resolutely. Her heart pounds. She flips and flips, each blank margin a relief.

And then the blue letters fill the entire page.

She almost gasps at it: the words and numbers starting at the top and repeating over and over until they reach the bottom, where they crowd, written smaller and smaller to fit it all in.

*May 1, 1959. May 1, 1959. May 1, 1959. May 1, 1959. May 1, 1959. May 1, 1959.*

Over and over and over. Some of the letters look skewed, some slanted and rushing, others square and solid. But all in her grandmother's hand. Shania stares until her eyes feel dry. She glances up, sees her stop is next, and then snaps the book shut gratefully. Back into the bag, hidden beneath her scarf. Even there it scratches at her. It muscles into her world of Gram's voice, Simon's yellow blanket. She can't quite let it go—or maybe the other way around. The only time she feels soothed is talking about Gram—to Michelle, to Ben, even the occasional text with Prescott. Not Catherine yet.

As she walks up to the stoop, the creaking door and its chipped paint, she thinks about Catherine. She's a ball of cotton: fluffy, pure, a wad stuffed in the hole Shania is trying to fill. Does she fill the empty space better than the almanac? Does a hole like the one inside her change shape, filled by different things at different times? *This is why people have dogs*, Shania thinks as she climbs the stairs to her apartment. Dogs dig holes in your yard to distract you from the holes in your heart. They feed a hunger. In lieu of a dog, Shania needs a burrito.

She opens the door and drops her bag to the side. She beelines to the kitchen and opens the freezer, where there is, blessedly, a stack of frozen burritos. It's not until she slams the microwave door that she realizes someone is sitting in the dark beyond the kitchen door, half hidden by shadow.

"Jesus Christ!" she screeches. "Mom!"

"Yeah, creeping around sucks, doesn't it?" her mother says, her voice shrill.

She uncrosses her legs, stands abruptly, anger pinking her cheeks as she steps into the light.

"I work seven nights a week, Shania. Every night, and double shifts half the time too. And the only reason I'm able to do it without losing my goddamn mind is because I tell myself, *Shania is home and safe, and I can trust her to stay home and safe while I am at the jail working my ass off.* Imagine my surprise when I get off a little early and come home to hang out with my daughter and find that she's not here. Where she's supposed to be. So where have you *been*, Shania?"

Her mother is only five four, but she seems tall in her anger, standing up straight in it like she's hoping to be measured. She still wears her uniform pants, but on top she wears a Disney T-shirt, a souvenir from the one time they had gone on vacation as a family.

"I was—" Shania begins, but her mother pounces on the words, ripping them out of the air.

"I don't even want to hear it!" she shouts, and Shania winces. "How can I even believe you? For months since we moved to this city, I've been texting you good night and you've been saying good night back, and now I'm wondering how many of those texts were lies, Shania! Sent from somewhere you weren't supposed to be!"

She pauses, one hand pressed to her mouth. Her eyes begin to shine, and like a reflex they prickle in Shania's as well.

"Mom," she starts again.

"Don't you lie to me, Shania!" she shouts.

They've become the neighbors that shout. Her mother pauses, swallows.

"Shane," she begins, and Shania can't tell whether her tone is the calm before the storm or after. This is what her mother's anger is like: rising quickly, falling even quicker. She's right in front of Shania now, and Shania can smell the jail on her: stale cigarette smoke, the driest dust. Even the fluorescent lights seem to leave an odor. The microwave beeps—Shania can hear the sound of the cheese in her burrito popping. Her mother's gaze wanders from her daughter's eyes up to the Paulie's visor that she still wears.

"Why are you wearing your work hat?" she says, surprised.

"Because I just got off work."

148

Her mother stares, confusion battling back the wave of her anger.

"That's where you've been?"

Shania points down at her shirt, the Paulie's logo blurred by powdered sugar.

"I was trying to tell you."

It's like watching the needle on a car edge slowly out of the red.

"You weren't out with a boy."

Shania turns away to the microwave, pulls the burrito out with two fingers, and hot-potatoes it onto a waiting plate.

"Don't sound so disappointed," Shania says. She moves around her mother into the cramped dining room, plopping down. Her mother spins and follows her.

"Watch your mouth, Shania Marie," she snaps. "I've told you a thousand times that the shit I did when I was your age took my life off the rails. So no, I'm not *disappointed*. Am I *relieved*? Yes, yes, I am relieved that my daughter isn't sneaking around with some boy I've never met."

"Okay, well, then what's the big deal?"

"You're not off the hook," her mother says, pointing. "I told you no more night shift! And what the hell shift is *this* anyway? It's one thirty in the goddamn morning, Shane!"

"I know what time it is, Mom," she says with a sigh.

"Shania..." Her tone a red flag snapping in the tsunami of her dying rage, warning that the storm could whip up again at any moment.

"Mom, look. I'm sorry. It's the main shift they need somebody for. And I need money, so who cares? It's a job."

"School is your job, Shane," her mother says. *"School!"*

Shania chews aggressively in reply.

"You went out with those girls," her mother says. "You told me you went on a date. What's his name? Preston? I thought... I don't know, I thought you were out somewhere. You know..."

"We don't all repeat our parents' mistakes," Shania says, and her mother looks up sharply.

"The past has a way of creeping up on you if you don't keep an eye on it," she says.

"Like Dad," Shania says around the burrito.

"What?"

"Like Dad. You snuck around with Dad when you were seventeen, and then he snuck around on you with some old lady."

"Jesus," her mother mutters. She slumps down in the chair and runs her fingers through her hair, sighing. "This is my fault, isn't it?"

Shania stares at her, chewing. The storm has passed for sure. At her house in Morrisville, Gram had a cellar, all cement and wooden shelves, mason jars filled with tomatoes and peppers. The summer Shania was eight they had to go down into it until the whine of tornadoes had moved on, when the thick silence passed into birdsong. There isn't birdsong in Shania's mother's voice, but it's as if she's cupping a robin in her palms, ready to release it when the time comes. Shania just chews.

"I mean, look at this situation," her mother says. "Some people's kids are out buying meth from their babysitters, and my kid rebels by working late."

"Do babysitters really sell meth?" Shania says around her burrito. They stare at each other, almost laughing, and when things were good, this is when her father would fake roll his eyes and say they were just alike, they looked just alike, it was two against one. Gram made three.

"Oh, Shane," her mother starts again.

"And I'm not rebelling," Shania says quickly. "I'm not thirteen. Jesus."

"Do seventeen-year-olds not rebel?"

Shania just takes another bite, shaking her head.

"Christ," her mother says, flicking her fingernails against each other, *click click click*, the way she does when she's wishing she hadn't quit smoking. "I told you I can cover the goddamn bills, Shane. You don't need to work so much."

"I'm not worried about the bills," Shania blurts.

Her mother raises her eyebrows. Shania's face feels like the burrito, hot and splotchy.

"Look," she says finally, desperate. "Did you think sending me to that stupid rich school was just going to be normal?"

"Excuse me?"

"You just had to send me to Bard," Shania says, ugly. "You could have sent me to a normal school with normal people, but you had to get back at Dad—"

"Shania! It wasn't just about your dad and that woman paying for it. You got a scholarship too! It's the oldest school in Blue Rock—the best school! It's about...about...history."

"Who cares?" Shania cries. "What was the point? You send me to this school in this city with these *people* and don't care what happens."

"What has happened?" her mother says, a red line appearing in the air somewhere, fear that she has missed something serious.

"Nothing! I just wish I was different. I'm trying so hard,

and Bard is just...Bard. And you didn't even think about how I would feel like I needed more."

"More what, Shane?"

"More," she snaps. "Just more!"

"Honey, *what*?"

"I don't know! Highlights! A car! Fucking brunch!"

Her mother's finger pops up.

"Watch your goddamn mouth, Shania Marie!" she says, her tone a switchblade springing from the guarded handle of her mouth. Shania can hear the wall clock in the kitchen.

And then her mother is laughing.

"I'm so bad at this!" she cries, giggling but still angry, still sad. "Everything is shit since we lost Gram. I tell you not to curse and I've got a mouth like a goddamn sailor."

"Like a pirate," Shania corrects automatically, which is what her grandmother always said, because her papaw was a sailor in the Navy and the worst curse he ever spoke was "dag nab." The long rows of the garden spring up behind Shania's eyes as she remembers her last day with Gram, but her mother is laughing now and it pulls her back. They're both laughing and then crying and somehow Shania's chair ends up by her mother's, her head on her shoulder, and she cries even harder then, because as much as she loves her mother, she hid the almanac from her daughter, and her shoulder isn't soft like Gram's.

"I don't know how to fix it. I'm trying," her mother says. "Honey, I'm trying."

"I know. I know you are."

They're quiet for what feels like a long time. Shania is thinking about Gram. The chairs they sit on were hers, unmatching from different rooms.

"Did Gram ever come to Blue Rock?" Shania says quietly.

"What?"

"Did Gram ever come to Blue Rock? Did she ever live here?"

"You know your grandmother hated the city," her mother says, shaking her head. Something in her voice sounds heavy. Shania knows then that she hid the almanac for a reason.

"How do I fix it?" her mother sighs into her hair. "I can't bring Gram back."

"You could buy me a Lexus," Shania says after a while, perhaps as a joke, and under her cheek her mother's shoulder starts to shake. Shania can't tell if she's laughing or crying and she doesn't dare lift her head to see.

# CHAPTER 14

Shania's grandmother isn't googleable. Shania has tried all the tricks Ben mentioned: parentheses, closed quotes, her married name. She came across one promising listing—a scan of a newspaper from 1949 in which a Helen Rutherford won a blue ribbon in a contest for the biggest pumpkin—but it was only a fragment and required a subscription to the *Blue Rock Times* to view its entirety. Shania doesn't think paying $9.99 would magically solve the mystery of her grandmother's connection to Blue Rock or the Western Pocket Community Garden, especially when the library is free, so she looks up the route and catches the bus after school.

The building resembles a church, gray and serious. But one of the front windows looks into the children's area, a mural of Clifford the Big Red Dog smiling out onto the street, and the warmth of it draws her up the stairs. Halfway up, her phone buzzes, Ben's name flashing onto the screen. She smiles before she can remind herself to feel guilty for texting Prescott's brother, the message a looping video of a stubby wagging tail. She watches it again, but sees she missed a message from Hallie and swipes it open before she can tell Ben where she is.

It's a screenshot of a tweet by an account with a blue check: *Proud of these young people.* She's included a photo, and the young people in question are Hallie and Monica, standing next to a statue in Morrisville. They each hold signs. Shania knows the statue well: a man on a horse situated on a small rise in the land next to the courthouse. Hallie's sign reads KEEP THE HORSE—and Monica's—LOSE THE DUDE. Shania texts back:

**Wait, what is this?**

**A protest!** Hallie replies. **Did you see whose tweet it was? She was in that movie! We're lobbying them to take down that Confederate statue everybody hates—I guess she saw online!**

**Who is everybody?** Shania types. She doesn't even know who the statue is of. It has never occurred to her to find out.

Hallie replies with a short video, she and Monica at the front, smiling in selfie mode, and several dozen people behind them, all with signs, all chanting words Shania can't make out.

**At least all of us** ☺, Hallie replies.

Shania watches the video one more time, seeking and finding faces she knows. As she always does with anything related to Morrisville, she finds herself looking for Gram. When Shania remembers she's gone, she puts the phone away.

The library doors make the yawning sound of old buildings, and inside it feels round, curving around her with shelves and shelves of books, magazines, and DVDs. The not-quite-silence seems to bloom upward into the domed ceiling. Shania hears typing, pages turning, the occasional cough and, from the distant kingdom of the children's section, shrieks of little kids. In the center of it all is the circulation desk, two librarians busy at work with stacks of books between them.

"Hi," one says brightly, noticing her. Shania glances at the name tag. HEATHER CONTI: THEY/THEM. They have curly blue hair cut asymmetrically, a realistic tattoo of a bluebird on their wrist. Shania likes them immediately. "Can I help you find something?"

"Um, maybe," Shania says. "I don't even know if you have this kind of thing. My friend told me to try the library."

"I find that anyone who recommends the library for anything has excellent judgment," the other librarian says. Her skin is light brown and her eyeliner is immaculately winged. NORMA GONZA-LEZ: SHE/HER. "As a rule."

"Try me," Heather says to Shania.

"Okay, well, I was wondering if you had records? Of, like, the city. Old newspapers or anything? I don't know exactly what I'm looking for. I mean," she says, unsure. "I'm just looking for stuff about my grandma."

Heather brightens further.

"Like archives?" they say. "Of course! If you had gone to another branch you would've been out of luck, but you've come to the right place! This is the oldest library in Blue Rock, so we house lots of scans of old newspapers, city history, and all kinds of stuff like that."

"Really?" Shania says, perking up. "I googled a little bit but didn't find much."

Heather starts to leave the desk, waves for Shania to follow.

"Google is good, but not the be-all end-all." They gesture

down at their shirt: LIBRARIANS MAKE SHHH HAPPEN is printed across their chest. Shania laughs.

"That's a great shirt."

"I have it in three colors."

Heather leads the way, past study rooms and rows of computers and long tables littered with magazines. Shania has the sensation of entering a secret world that's only a secret from her. She scans the faces around her as Heather leads her through: studious, amused, daydreamy. She passes the poetry section, thinks about Anne Stanton. Some small part of Shania feels at peace, at least for the moment. Then her eye lands on the profile of a familiar face: sloping nose, full cheeks, glistening red hair.

Willa.

She's reading in one of the glass-enclosed study rooms, her eyebrows furrowed. Shania quickens her pace to keep up with Heather, hoping Willa doesn't look up in time to spot her. When Heather speaks again, they're leading Shania into a subsection of the library, glass walls and a door separating it from the rest.

"The machines are kind of loud sometimes," Heather explains, holding the door for Shania. "We're getting a 3D printer soon too! So we try to keep things separate."

"Cool," Shania says, taking in the room. Only one long window along the back wall, which is lined with a half-dozen tables. The rest of the room is full of long tables with work lamps on each, computers and other machines dotting their surfaces. Some of the machines look like desktop computers but bulkier, square and clumsy. Old.

"This is how you look at microfilm," Hannah explains, seeing her looking. "Those file cabinets have hundreds and thousands of documents stored on microfilm. I can help you load it into the machines."

"Wow," Shania says, a little taken aback. "It's more complicated than I thought it would be."

"A labor of love." Heather shrugs. "There's more involved than googling, but you find stuff you wouldn't otherwise. Not too many people use these anymore but it's nice when they get some attention. So much history is in this room. Now, what are you looking for?"

"I'm not sure," Shania admits. "All I have is a date."

"A date is better than nothing. It gives us a starting point. What is it?"

In Shania's head, the blue numbers and letters conjure themselves, filling the page of the almanac, getting smeary and shaky the farther down they go.

"May 1, 1959."

Heather nods.

"All righty, let's dig in."

They stride over to a section of the file cabinets, Shania on their heels. Heather runs a hand over the top of the cabinets, eyeing the tiny labels expertly. At one point they stop and peer a little closer, then scoot over to the next cabinet before opening a drawer.

"Here we are," they say, peering into the drawer. Shania peeks inside.

Rows and rows of neat white boxes, each with their own labels, shine up at her. Heather pulls one and loads a set of microfilm into the machine, and a moment later the image of a newspaper leaps onto the dimly lit screen.

"Ta-da!"

Shania joins them at the screen, taking it in.

# BLUE ROCK BALL CROWNS
# 50TH ANNUAL CASINO QUEEN

"Not exactly breaking news." Heather presses the button that slides along the next section of film. They handle the machine expertly and with fondness. Shania feels as if she has stepped into a detective movie.

"I'm probably not looking for breaking news, honestly," she says. There's a low seat in front of the machine, and she sinks down into it. "It may not be news at all. It's just, my grandmother wrote the date down in, um, a significant way. But for all I know it was just to remember a haircut. It could be nothing."

Heather looks at her, eyebrow raised. They have a small dot under its arch where a piercing used to be.

"But *you* think it's something," they say. "Otherwise you wouldn't be here."

"Kinda," Shania says, averting her eyes. "Something like that. I don't know."

"Well, let's keep clicking!"

They slide through another few frames, Heather at the helm. Shania gets the feeling that they don't quite trust her to operate the machine herself, that her indecision will make her clumsy. She finds herself wishing she could be alone. Something about this hunt feels private, and despite Heather's friendliness, Shania wishes they would leave. She had given Heather the date, but all Shania can see are the words *I'm sorry* scrawled under the address to the Western Pocket Community Garden. Her bones seem to shiver. *All these somethings are related*, she thinks. She doesn't tell Heather this. She also doesn't tell them that staring at this *something* so directly fills the backs of her eyelids with the shape of her grandmother's lips forming the word *liars*. Shania is desperate to replace it.

Behind them, the door creaks open and they both turn to look. The library had felt hushed before they entered this room, even quieter, and now the light sounds spill in with the person standing there in the door. The person is Willa.

"*Heyyy*, Heather," Willa says in a teasing voice, her smile wide and bright. It fades a little when she sees Shania sitting next to them. "Oh. Hey, Shania."

Heather looks pleased.

"Oh, you two know each other?"

"Kinda," Willa says quickly. "From school. Shania's new at Bard this year."

"You go to Bard?" Heather says, and laughs. "I'm sorry."

"Heather's not a fan of the bourgeoisie," Willa smirks.

"Only the bourgeoisie are fans of the bourgeoisie," Heather says.

"False. Why else do white people all think we're destined to be millionaires?"

"Do you *need* something, Willa?" Heather laughs.

"Not me," says Willa. "Norma. The computer locked her out."

"It likes me better," Heather says, grinning, and rises. They pause halfway to the door, glancing over their shoulder.

"Willa can help with the microfilms if you need it," they say. "There's not much in this library that she doesn't know about."

"Do you work here *and* at the museum?" Shania says. She wonders if either of them can hear how sharp her tongue feels.

"No, my mom used to work here, though. Retired. I pretty much grew up in here. I literally had a cradle behind the desk when I was two."

"Let me know if you need me," Heather says, and slips out of the room. The door makes a soft thud behind them.

"Doing some research?" Willa says, nodding at the machines.

Shania's anxiety, at a low simmer with Heather, bubbles up. She doesn't really know Willa, who both Prescott and Catherine seem to hate. Shania thinks of Prescott's disapproval of and rescuing her from Western Pocket. Now she imagines him swooping in to save her from Willa Langford. Shania might welcome it to avoid the awkwardness that surely lies ahead. She turns back to the microfilm.

"Kind of," she says, and presses the button Heather has pressed. The machine makes a thunking sound, but the slide doesn't switch.

"Here, let me show you," Willa says, approaching with a hand outstretched. She holds down a small lever to the side and then presses the button. The slide clicks away, a new one replacing it. Shania mumbles her thanks. Willa Langford is not the partner she had expected or desired for this project. She doesn't know how to ask her to leave and so the microfilm clicks on and on, slide by slide, Shania's eyes traveling over the endless black type and occasional photo, and often traveling sideways to sneak looks at Willa, who stays silent, staring too.

"What are you looking for?"

"Something to do with May 1, 1959," Shania says, stubbornly refusing to be more specific. Willa must sense the mule in her voice because she doesn't reply.

"Wait," Shania says, and points, her eyes flying over the slide on the glowing screen.

"You said May 1," Willa says, frowning. "This says May 13."

"Yes, but..."

She reads. It's a subhead about halfway down the page:

# WESTERN POCKET EMPTIES

Willa leans forward, reading the headline, but Shania has already started skimming the article.

> **The Western Pocket neighborhood of Blue Rock has seen continuous departures of its residents as the East End grows in appeal. The departure of long-time residents, including many families, illustrates the changing face of Blue Rock. More homes went up for sale following an incident on May 1, and families affected harbor growing concern about the declining promise of real estate value.**

Willa makes a scoffing noise and Shania looks at her sharply. "What is it?"

"They're talking about white flight," she says.

"What?"

"White flight. When neighborhoods that were previously white start seeing an influx of not-white people. In the case of Western Pocket, Black people. Black people started moving in and white people literally picked up and ran as fast as we could."

"You say *we* like you were there," Shania says, unnerved. She remembers what the older Black woman at the garden fundraiser had said. This sounds like that.

"I wasn't," Willa says with a shrug. "But I'm white and I'm

from Blue Rock, so I kinda was. I wonder what May 1 event they're talking about. You've already been through all the May 1 papers and didn't see anything, right?"

"Right," Shania says reluctantly. "Nothing that would have had anything to do with my grandmother."

"So, you're looking for something about your family?" Willa says, squinting.

"She didn't even live here," Shania says quickly. "I don't know what I'm looking for."

She continues reading the article, and she can feel Willa watching her.

> Former Western Blue Rock homeowners are settling in to the East End with ease, often among previous neighbors. One new East Ender, Thomas Renfroe, says the new shops and trolley on the East End make it easy to adapt to the move. Others see it as an opportunity.
>
> "I own the whole block back in Western Pocket," said William Rutherford II. "I didn't sell. If Negroes want to live in Blue Rock, that's all right with me, even if I don't want my wife and daughter rubbing elbows with them. I'll rent to them just the same. Might open a business or two down that way as well."

Shania stares at the screen for a long time. So long that everything starts to blur and warp, and eventually Willa nudges her.

"You okay?" she says.

"That's my great-grandfather," Shania says, too stunned to lie.

"Huh?" Willa looks back and forth between Shania and the screen, as if searching for the man's face. "Who?"

"William Rutherford II. That's...that's my grandma's dad."

Willa's eyebrows scrunch toward each other, her frown deepening.

"So, he owned a block in Western Pocket? And the daughter he's referring to was your grandma?"

"I...I guess so. This makes no sense."

"Because your grandma said she never lived in Blue Rock?"

"Yes, and...and this makes him sound...I don't know. Like an asshole."

"Like a racist," Willa corrects, and Shania jerks her head to look at her. Willa is staring back, her expression one of frankness. "I mean, Shania, it was 1959. The likelihood of your white great-granddad being a racist is high."

"My grandmother never said anything about that," Shania insists. "Neither did my mom. My mom loved her grandfather. She called him Pop-Pop. They were nice people..." She trails off.

"I think you're looking at this the wrong way," Willa says gently. "Nice doesn't cancel out racist. Besides, I mean, not to be harsh, but do you not think this is something your grandma and mom might, you know, not tell you? White people are sort of experts in rewriting history, both literally and, like, in our own minds. There's like a full mythology of the lies we tell ourselves. *About* ourselves."

It's the gentleness that makes Shania want to slap her. The

gentleness implies that what she's saying is true and that Shania need only accept it. Shania pivots.

"Why are you always talking about *white* people?" Shania demands. "It's like every time I'm around you, you're talking about someone being white, something being white."

Willa has the audacity to look slightly amused.

"I mean, there's a lot of stuff that's white, Shania. You, for example. Me, for example. Our parents, for example—"

Shania waves her hand to shut her up, but Willa laughs lightly and keeps talking.

"You know the only reason it makes you uncomfortable is because whiteness is supposed to be invisible, right? We're not conditioned to think of ourselves as *white* people—just as *people*. We're the default and everyone else is different colors of *us*." She snorts. "What a crock of shit."

Her words are like a fingernail prying under a bandage that's not ready to come off.

"It's like this club we're members of but we're supposed to pretend the club doesn't exist," Willa goes on. "It's the lie that's like—what was that creature? The hydra? All the heads? The lies we tell about ourselves—our white selves—are like that. Except like a *hundred* different heads. *Oh, not my family. My grandpa was nice. That's how Uncle Jimmy jokes. We worked hard too. We suffered too. But weren't the Irish slaves?* Blah blah blah. Mythology, like I said."

"You must be fun at parties," Shania snarls.

"Oh, do you go to a lot of those?" Willa smirks. "Look, all I'm saying is that there's nothing wrong with talking about what it means to be white. Most people don't even *know* what it means."

"And what does it mean?" Shania demands. "Since you're so fucking smart."

Willa shrugs. "Different things to different people, probably. On a very basic level it means I'm part of a system I didn't ask to be part of, but that I benefit from. And so do you."

"You don't know what you're talking about," Shania says, averting her eyes back to the screen and staring at it as hard as she can. Willa says nothing, but her eyes are on the screen too. Shania reads more, hating every word, hating that Willa is there to see it.

> **"The Western Pocket increasingly appears to be a Negro neighborhood now," Rutherford says. "That's okay with me. As long as I'm on the East End of things." He laughs.**

In the silence of the room, the buzz of Willa's phone against the table is jarring. Shania jumps, watches Willa pick it up, pause, and then grin.

"Michelle is forcing me to try sushi tonight," she groans, but she's laughing. "I don't know why anyone would want to eat raw fish, but it's her birthday, so I'm beholden."

She shakes her head, tapping out a reply.

"I've never had it either," Shania says, just to say something. She's gone back to staring at the screen.

"You could come with," Willa says, shooting her a quick glance as she texts. "I know Michelle wouldn't mind."

The implication, Shania thinks, is that Willa, however, would. She feels herself prickle.

"It's fine, I have plans," she says quickly.

"With the Tanes?" Willa says. She doesn't look up, but Shania still feels watched.

"Maybe?" Shania fires back. "So?"

Willa sighs deeply, from the very bottom of her rib cage.

"*What?*" Shania says. "Weren't you friends? I saw you on her page once."

Willa looks uncomfortable, an expression Shania is unaccustomed to on her face.

"Yeah, we used to be friends."

"What happened?"

"She didn't tell you?"

"She says you stole something from her," Shania says.

Willa barks out a laugh. It startles Shania, amplified in the small room.

"Is that what she said?" Willa chuckles. "Typical rich shit. Only thinking about what I might have taken from her."

"So you didn't steal anything."

"Not exactly."

"Um, *okay*. Then why aren't you friends anymore?"

"Oh, come on," Willa snorts. "You've hung out with her, right? You've been to her house. You're telling me you can't fathom a single reason someone might not want to be friends with Catherine Tane?"

Shania shakes her head, looks back at the screen. Her grandfather's name and words are still there. It makes her frown. She refuses to say anything against Catherine. This feels like pledging allegiance to something. Catherine has offered her friendship, has tucked Shania under her wing.

"That's okay," Willa says. "I was you at one point. Shit, so was Ben."

"What does *that* mean?"

"It means you can't choose your family, but you can choose who you're going to be." Willa scoots her chair back then, rising from the table. She gestures to the screen. "I hope you find what you're looking for."

A moment later Shania is alone, the only sound the buzz of the microfilm. It's too loud. She switches off the machine, but even when the screen has gone dark, she can still see her great-grandfather's name lighting up behind her eyelids, glowing like white marble, and brighter still than that, one other word.

*Daughter.*

# CHAPTER 15

After Gram died, Shania had a blister between her thumb and forefinger for a week, the consequence of burying Simon in the semi-frozen ground. After what Shania saw in the library, it's almost as if a new blister has formed, a pocket of pain lodged in her chest that she doesn't dare touch. As she'd feared, a box of snakes has opened, and all she can hear is hissing. Worst of all, Willa had been there to witness it. This is the first time since she moved to Blue Rock that she wishes she were back in Morrisville, and she slumps on a couch in the Bard common room conjuring invisibility. But she's only been there for a few minutes when Julia and Hannah appear, draping themselves on either side of her. They have the look of mischievous elves.

"We have a plan," Julia chirps.

It's been a strange week for all of them. On Monday Catherine had entered the greenhouse, speaking to no one, and sat silently on her stool studying her plants. It set the tone for the rest of the week. She said neither hello nor goodbye to Shania—or anyone else for that matter, the one fact that built a small dam between

Shania and the flood of paranoia that Catherine's silence might have otherwise induced. Neither Julia nor Hannah had spoken to Shania either, the body of the snake cut off from the head and unsure of where to slither. But today they seem to have decided something, and it makes Shania nervous. On some level she knows that Catherine is the ambassador who allows her friendship with the other two to persist, that they patiently follow suit.

"We're going to kidnap Catherine," Hannah says happily.

"Kidnap?"

"She's been a bitch all week, in case you haven't noticed," Hannah says, then pauses, glancing at Shania. It feels like a trap, but Shania gives one quick nod and Hannah continues. "This requires a girls' night. I went to Costco already with my mom and got like six humongous containers of snacks. We're going to kidnap her, go to her house, and watch movies and eat snacks."

"She needs this." Julia nods solemnly. "She's so on edge."

"We're going to kidnap her and take her to her own house?" Shania says, laughing.

"Have you seen her TV?" Julia says, dropping her chin.

"No."

"Well, there you go."

In the end, Shania calls into work and tells Mr. Ahmed that she's sick. He accepts this without question, as she's never called off before, and she tries not to think about the money she's missing, the things she wants still just out of reach.

As it turns out, kidnapping Catherine just means showing up at her house, and it's easy for Shania to be distracted from the box of snakes once she gets there. She thought Prescott was still out of town with their father, but as Catherine walks the group of girls into her kitchen, she explains that the housekeeper has made spaghetti and meatballs and a thick loaf of garlic bread while her parents are out overseeing a local charity event. She wonders if Prescott is at the event as well, as he's supposed to be with his father. She doesn't text him. His silence since their museum date feels like a chasm only he can cross.

Catherine shovels spaghetti into her mouth, dreadlocks pulled into a bundle of blonde ropes.

"You brought sour straws," she says through half-chewed noodles. "You lovable bitches."

"We knew you needed some cheering up," Hannah beams. "You've been sad this week."

Catherine looks away, and Shania wonders for the first time if there's a cloud somewhere in the perfect blue sky of her life.

"Not sad, just—" she starts, and then she looks at Shania. "What about you, Shania? Did you bring me any doughnuts?"

"I called into work," Shania offers, shrugging.

"Good enough," Catherine says and chomps a meatball.

The housekeeper comes in from one of the three entrances to the kitchen. A plate of spaghetti is in Shania's hand, heavy with thick sauce, and she considers thanking the woman. She glances at the other girls, who have not even acknowledged her presence. Shania has never eaten spaghetti that wasn't at an Olive Garden or from a jar, and it barely tastes like the same dish. White chunks of garlic shine out like dice. She decides to agree to the woman's invisibility, until she speaks, and they all look up.

"Will your brothers be eating tonight?" the housekeeper says to Catherine.

"Prescott is still out of town," Catherine says, her tone flat. "He'll be back Tuesday."

"And Benjamin?"

"I think we both know that Ben only comes into this house when he absolutely has to."

"I'll clean up," the woman says, and her bustle suddenly seems to contain even more bustle.

"Let's go upstairs." Catherine heaps another pile of spaghetti onto her plate, bites onto a piece of bread, and grabs the bag of snacks that Hannah brought with her. Catherine leads the way up a winding staircase.

There are no family photos on the walls. Shania has seen this in movies, the way rich people's walls are bare except for actual art, art that was purchased at a gallery and not from Target or TJ Maxx. Shania's grandmother's house was full of photos, every surface stacked with frames. One had to push past new ones in the front to reach the embarrassing ones in the back. When Shania and her mother cleaned out Gram's house after the funeral, one of the few things her mother could bear to keep was the photos; all the tables in their home are now full of faces. Catherine's house is faceless, but it doesn't feel sinister. It feels clean. A dustless void. Shania wonders if this is how they feel about their dead, if letting go is easier when you have other things to cling to.

"I call the pink one," Julia says, and Shania sees that she's referring to a beanbag, one of four in Catherine's room, vibrant and fuzzy against white carpet. Her room is what Shania would imagine a rich girl's room looking like, but dirtier. There are nail polish stains on the carpet, clothes slung over the backs of chairs and over the top of the closet door, and clumps of hair in front of the mattress-sized full-length mirror. There are pictures and posters and a school calendar that's still on April of last year. Field hockey team photos. The room would be normal if it wasn't massive.

"I told you she has a nice TV," Julia says.

The screen is the size of Shania's couch and so crystal clear she had mistaken it for a window: a screensaver of sorts rotates between a photo of a dewy field and a misty wood. If Shania didn't know better she would think the room contained that too.

"Netflix or Hulu?" Julia says, remote in hand.

"Netflix. Let's watch something with aliens so I can fantasize about leaving this fucking planet," Catherine says.

"One alien abduction coming right up," Julia says, and starts clicking, tossing a massive bag of Cheetos Catherine's way.

"Are you going to tell us what's wrong now?" Hannah says after Catherine's fingers and tongue turn orange with Cheeto dust. "Or are you going to keep being a moody bitch?"

"I haven't been moody," Catherine protests.

Julia and Hannah roll their eyes at each other. They eventually roll them toward Shania too, who tries to make a face that she thinks is neutral: Shania has noticed she's been a moody bitch, yes, but she doesn't think their friendship has reached the stage where it's acceptable to say so. Shania thinks it would probably sound forced, anyway.

"Just my dad being a dick," Catherine concedes after the ceremony of eye rolling. "And my mom being a dick. And my brothers being a pair of dicks. Just everybody being a dick. I am part of a family of phalluses."

"What did Prescott do?" Shania says before she can stop herself. She knows immediately that she's annoying. She can feel the display of it like the tiny lamp in a fish tank. Catherine doesn't look at her, her eyes on the screen as Julia sifts through alien movies.

"He's just like my dad," she says. "And everybody always thinks he's so fucking perfect no matter what he does."

"What about Ben?"

"Ben actually *is* perfect, so that's even worse."

"My family is like that with my brother too," Hannah says. She's opened a carton of rainbow Goldfish and is color-coding them in one palm. "They didn't give a shit about his grades when he was in high school but they freaked when I got a B- in Chem. He wrecked two cars his junior year at Bard and they didn't even care. I dented Muhammed last week and they had a conniption fit."

"Muhammed?" Shania says.

Without meaning to, she catches a look that Julia has slid her way. Something on her face is unstill, a stirred pot.

"Muhammed is Hannah's car," Catherine drawls.

"You named your car Muhammed?" Shania says, confused. Julia says nothing, a silence that might be wedge-shaped if anyone but Shania notices it.

"Cuz it's a convertible," Hannah explains.

Shania hopes her face doesn't look too blank. It must— Hannah looks at her and laughs.

"You know, like a cloth top?" she giggles. "Like a turban. Muhammed."

Shania pauses, and on either side of her, Catherine and Hannah go on giggling. Julia flips determinedly through movies, looking at no one. She is opting out, refusing to find it funny, and Shania could too, but Catherine is staring right at her, eyes bright, and it feels somewhere between permission and command. Shania giggles too, then, and it feels a little forbidden, a little free. A thing said in private, a safely dirty joke. In the city of Shania's head, Hannah and Catherine belong in her neighborhood.

"Bingo," Julia says loudly. She points at the screen. "*Romeo and Juliet* but in space."

"Exactly what my soul desires," Catherine says. She flips backward, her butt on the carpet and her back on a beanbag. The other girls lounge into soft positions of familiarity. Shania doesn't look at Julia.

"Quayloo, Shania, get comfortable," Catherine says. "You guys are on duty to cheer me up and this could be a long night."

She smiles in her irresistible way and Shania wonders how girls skip being awkward and become Catherine Tane. She doesn't think it's ever occurred to Catherine to be awkward. Julia, on the other hand, shows the signs: always in motion, always the first to speak—until tonight. But silences are usually short-lived with her in the room; they're a risk she's not willing to take. Shania recognizes this and is determined not to replicate it. She eyes Catherine's bookshelves, which, behind the various photos and medals on display, actually contain books. A few familiar spines catch Shania's eye.

"You read Anne Stanton?" she says, surprised.

"RIP ancient-ish white lady," Catherine says without taking her eyes off the screen. But a moment later she flicks her eyes at Shania. "You like poetry?"

"Yes," Shania says, and starts to say she writes it too, but thinks it would be too much all at once. "I love Anne Stanton. So did my grandma."

"You know that poem 'The Bluff'?" Catherine says. Her voice sounds different, quieter.

"Yes."

"I love that poem."

The movie starts. Shania squishes into the green beanbag chair and watches the movie unfold. It's terrible but the four of them decide that the guy playing Romeo is hot. He doesn't look much like an alien other than blue paint and some eye makeup. They're just getting to the point where the alien lovers spend the night together when Julia's phone makes a squawking sound.

"What in the quayloovian Christ is that?" Catherine demands.

Julia snatches her phone up, rolling her eyes as she silences the alert.

"Some Crime Snap app my mom made me install," she says. "She was so freaked out about me going to school in SoBR. This is like the Amber Alert thingies that everybody gets sometimes, except it gives alerts based on your GPS or phone location or whatever. I don't know."

"So you're telling me someone has just been killed in my house," Catherine says.

"Not yet." Julia smirks. She squints at her screen. "It says someone got beat up on Market. That's in SoBR."

"That's what it says? *Someone got beat up on Market?*"

"Alert: Assault at Third and Market, Blue Rock. 5:15 p.m."

Catherine snorts. "That was like an hour ago," she says.

"Yeah."

"So, not super helpful as far as avoiding the attacker. Thanks a lot, Crime Snap. More like Crime..." Catherine pauses. "I can't think of anything clever."

Julia shrugs and puts her phone away right as Catherine's rings. She groans.

"Mother," Catherine says, curt and British, when she answers. She listens, the distant blur of her mother's voice reaching Shania's ears, no actual words. "No, I have friends over. I'm fine."

More listening.

"Yeah, actually Julia's phone just got an alert. It was on Third and Market. It's like three miles from here. No biggie."

More listening.

"Elena made us spaghetti and meatballs. We're fine. Everybody is probably going to spend the night. Because. Because I hate being alone, Mom. It's Friday night, I don't want to just sit here by myself. Okay. Okay. I mean, thanks? Okay. Bye."

She tosses the phone to the carpet.

"Your mom's never home," Hannah says, a bassline of envy in her voice. "Where are your parents all the time?"

"Working and donating and schmoozing so they can avoid their children at all costs," Catherine says, upbeat as always. "Anyway, your app just beat the evening news, Julz. Apparently another homeless guy got beat up in SoBR."

"Jesus Christ," Julia says.

"Also, my mother would like to inform everyone that there are ice cream bars in the freezer," Catherine says.

"Ooh," says Hannah, perking up.

"Not it," Catherine snaps, then reclines on her beanbag.

"NOT IT," Hannah and Julia say simultaneously. They turn to Shania, grinning.

"All you, Shania!"

"Me?"

"You are the bringer of ice cream bars," Catherine says. "Gotta be fast if you wanna be lazy. I know: counterintuitive."

Shania allows herself to laugh.

"In the freezer? I'm not going to find a body in there, am I?"

Catherine laughs, but Hannah and Julia do the critical throat chuckle that indicates they find Shania strange and awkward.

Shania inwardly slaps her forehead. She was trying to be someone who fits into this little arrangement—she has now tried too hard.

"No corpses—just dessert. Want us to pause the movie?" Catherine says.

"I . . . think I'm okay."

"You mean you *don't* want to see alien Romeo get it on with alien Juliet? You prude."

"I'll be right back."

The house feels even bigger with the sound of three girls' laughter echoing farther and farther behind as Shania winds her way back downstairs. In the kitchen, Elena is gone and all traces of the spaghetti are cleared away, the granite countertop bare except for a bowl of perfect oranges that Shania prods with her finger to ascertain whether they're wax. They're not. She wonders where one buys oranges like that, so perfectly round they could be from a still life.

She opens the freezer door. There's vodka and individually packaged chicken breasts and other things in freezer bags. Quinoa and red pepper ready-made meals. Ravioli. A box of ice cream sandwiches that are almost certainly fancy—the green-and-brown box suggests the cows whose milk made this ice cream are the kind that are allowed to wander; cows that know what clover smells like. She pulls out four bars and gently closes the freezer door. She has to make herself tear a paper towel off the dowel—taking something she wasn't specifically asked to take makes her cheeks flush absurdly, as if there's a camera that will catch her, freeze-frame her for a later meeting in which she will be interrogated. It's the kind of thing that seems both plausible and ridiculous. She climbs the stairs again.

She gets closer to Catherine's room and can hear the three

of them talking over the movie, lots of F-bombs being dropped about Ms. Hassoon, ranting about botany's impossible final project again.

"Goddamn it," Catherine says. "My whole planter looks like a dried herb. Like someone could grind it up and season their fucking turkey with it."

"I bet it would taste good," Julia says as if she's truly trying to be helpful.

"Fucking Hassoon!" Hannah cries.

Rejoining the room at this particular conversational juncture slows Shania's feet. She doesn't want to be the nerdy friend, the odd one out who likes the teacher they all hate. She inches along the hallway and notes that she's standing outside another door, only slightly ajar. The light from Catherine's room illuminates a sliver of it: a bed, neatly made, a lacrosse stick leaning against the headboard.

Prescott's room.

All the lights are off but it still somehow seems to emit a glow that lures her toward the cracked door. This is where he sleeps. Here at the center of this massive house is the place where the boy who pushed her hair behind her ear and kissed her lays his head. He dresses here. He texts her here. He's thought about her from here. This is where he might be most himself. She slips in through the crack, the sound of Catherine's laughter softening behind her.

The room isn't as big as Catherine's but it's still huge, bigger than the living room of Shania's apartment. It's cleaner than Catherine's: The floor glows up at her with the light that filters through the blinds of the panoramic window. She can't imagine being this rich, but right now more than that she's trying to imagine Prescott, how he must move around this space, how she thinks she can smell him even though his smell is something she only barely knows. It's this imagined smell that pulls her into the room. The ice cream sandwiches burn cold against her palms.

His bed is queen sized, a simple embroidered headboard crowning his pillows. The comforter is neatly made, the sheets tucked in. The blinds of the window are open and moonlight leaks onto the windowsill, illuminating a row of patches that one might sew onto a shirt or bag. His desk is long, everything on its surface squarely arranged. His walls are less cluttered than Catherine's: There are a few signed posters that appear to be from concerts, some unframed artwork with the corners pinned down, photos he's taken. Above his desk is a stark-white piece of paper with a quote on it, thick black letters glowing out in the moonlight:

*"It is the rare fortune of these days that one may think what one likes and say what one thinks."* —*Tacitus*

Shania drifts closer, shifting the ice cream bars into one hand and holding them against her stomach, ignoring the cold, the other hand reaching out to touch the bottom edge of the quote's paper. She doesn't know who Tacitus is, but she stares at the words, wondering what Prescott wishes he could say. She is witnessing the making of his frowns, the prison in his imagination that puts the furrow between his eyes. Closer to the desk now, something else catches her eye, whiter than both the paper and the moonlight.

Her face.

It's the photo he'd taken in the greenhouse the day Shania put her number in his phone. She barely remembers his camera being aimed, she'd been so fixated on his face. He'd raised it to snap a photo of the flowers and she hadn't noticed the tilt of the lens, the way he'd managed to include her in the corner, even paler in the thick light of the greenhouse, surrounded by blossoms. Her eyes are rounder than she typically thinks of them being, and focused on something to the right of the camera's eye—Prescott. He'd captured a look of awe, a pleased disbelief. She wonders if he knows the expression on her face was a result of his nearness. In the white edge that frames the photo, he'd written the word *Purity* in Sharpie as a title.

Her breath sounds loud in the silence of the room. Down the hall she hears Catherine yell, "GET OVER YOURSELF, JULIET!" They haven't noticed that she's been gone awhile— maybe they've forgotten she's here at all. Shania reaches out and touches the photo, her hand trembling a little. When she withdraws her fingers, her thumb brushes the mouse of his computer.

The screensaver is swallowed in a white blink, Prescott's computer suddenly wide awake. Shania gasps, but there's no one here to hear it. She's afraid iTunes will wake up, start blasting whatever band he was listening to before he went out of town. She snatches at the mouse, dropping two ice cream sandwiches. She bends down to grab them, nearly knocking her head on the desk. When she raises her eyes back to the screen, her heartbeat in her ears, she's looking at a long page of text in Google Chrome, many sections in bold, a string of animated ads stretching endlessly down the left-hand side. She doesn't recognize the URL but it appears to be a blog.

> One thing I remember more than anything is my
> grandfather's hands. He wasn't a big man, but he
> was strong, and although he died when I was nine, I

can still picture him sitting on the front porch of his house in Ohio, stuffing his pipe. That was his favorite place to be. He would have lived in that house until he died if he could have, but my grandmother was worried about the neighborhood getting too dangerous. I'm too young to remember myself, but my grandmother was always saying they would let anyone live there after a while.

Degeneracy is killing America. Sometimes the realization that no one cares about what this country is becoming fills me with a sadness so heavy I think the earth might swallow me up. This is our responsibility. America thinks it's changing, but it's all wrong. Tolerance does not equal love. Love does not equal progress. Progress means truth...and the people telling the truth are oppressed and persecuted. People want to feel high and mighty, but they're all hypocrites, and they complicate the issue. Truth is simple. Truth is white marble. It doesn't need paint and rainbows. The world they imagine isn't better. The truth is simple, and I won't apologize for that. We apologize for nothing.

At the bottom of the blog is an intricate graphic of a circle with jagged lines like lightning bolts inside, connected to a smaller circle. Inside the smaller circle are runes, all the lines thick and black. Everything else is colored with varying shades of deep red, splattering at the outer edges like someone opened a vein, puddled heavy and angry at the center. Something about it alongside the words above makes Shania feel uneasy. Her blood has transformed into crabs: skittering, pinching, hot on sand. A feeling of something inside her running away, too quick to catch. *A sadness so heavy I think the earth might swallow me up.* She knows that feeling.

"*Shaniaaaa*, are you somewhere dead in my house?" Catherine's shout comes down the hallway, and Shania jolts away from Prescott's desk, back toward the door. "Hath the Crime Snap killer cometh?"

Catherine is mercifully still in her room, so when Shania steps back out into the hall she thinks there's no one to see her, not even family portraits. But then there's a voice.

"Lost or found?" he says, and she doesn't know if she's relieved or disappointed to find Ben and not Prescott standing in the hallway by the stairs, watching.

"Neither," she says, trying not to look guilty.

He studies her like he's looking for clues. Shania thinks he looks sad.

"What's wrong?" she says when he only stares. She thinks of what she learned at the library and it makes her cringe under his gaze, as if he's seeing something clinging to her that her own eyes don't even pick up, like a black light.

"Have you talked to my brother today?" he says.

Her blush feels prickly, angry. She feels as if she is constantly being measured, or caught in the crossfire of something she can't see.

"No," she says, then demands, "why?"

"Just wondering."

"Wondering what?"

"About you."

He doesn't wait for a response. He disappears down the stairs, leaving her standing in the white light spilling from Prescott's door.

# CHAPTER 16

Prescott is back. Shania can feel it when she walks into school on Monday, his presence like a distant earthquake registering on the fragile scale of her heart. She doesn't see him until she's walking up to botany, when he appears before her looking a little pale, the fading lavender of lost sleep under his eyes. But the angles of his face are as pleasing as ever and the week and a half he's been away shrinks to a moment.

"I heard you were in my house," he says.

She freezes, thinking of standing in the hallway with Ben's eyes on hers.

"Catherine says you guys didn't even sleep. You wait until I leave to have a sleepover? What's up with that timing?"

"I have to be invited," she says, smiling, relieved.

He crosses his arms, and his camera swings on his shoulder. It reminds Shania of the portrait sitting on his desk and she has to look away to keep the blush from spreading.

"A sleepover with Catherine," he says, a shade of a joke in his voice. "Unexpected. I didn't really see you two being friends. Like, *friends* friends."

Her tongue goes to the tooth she's so good at hiding, slithering over its wrongness, the way it juts out from the gum, asking to be seen.

"Why not?"

He leans against the greenhouse's doorway.

"Catherine is a fucking mess," he laughs. "And you, you are not a mess."

"She's not a mess," Shania laughs. "I mean, her room is—"

"Exactly," he says, throwing one hand out for emphasis. "Her room is just like her. She's a zoo in human form."

"People like the zoo!"

"Only because everything is in cages. Put a zoo in any other scenario and see how people react. You've seen *Jumanji. Snakes on a Plane.*"

"Speaking of planes, are you jetlagged?"

He pauses, looking confused.

"Jetlagged?"

"You look tired. Did you fly back in with your dad last night or something?"

He studies her face, and for a moment there seems to be a zoo of its own pacing behind his eyes. But no beast springs out. Instead he adjusts the camera hanging from his shoulder and reaches for her hand.

"Yes," he says. "Come on, I want to show you something."

"I've got class!"

"I know," he says. His smile is all the convincing she needs.

With everyone else in class, wandering the school feels like being back in the museum: Bard is so small that instead of year-books, every graduating class poses for a group photo. The faces, which look stiffer the older the photos get, stretch down the hallways, the eyes like marble in the oldest ones. The trophies of past lacrosse teams are displayed like fossils. Something about walking the halls alone with Prescott makes her feel invincible.

He pushes carelessly through a door leading to the back stairs, part of the old building, which had been left mostly unrenovated for the sake of industrial charm, the smell of old stone hovering in the air with the vague scent of acrylic paint wafting down from the art studio. It gets stronger as they climb. They enter the studio, where Shania has never actually been. It's bright and empty. Shania pauses, gazing up at the skylights that bathe the classroom in sunshine. He smiles.

"We could just hang out and paint," he says. She gets a flash of something romantic in his voice and panics a little. Only two boys have ever seen her naked and never in light this bright.

"Are you a good artist?" she says, hoping he doesn't notice that she's embarrassed herself with a thought he can't even see. Surely he's talking about sex. She's already kissed him in the museum, but the stakes feel higher here. School. They could get caught. Prescott is invincible but is Shania if he removes his protective charm? This is how rumors are born, hatching like raptors and running up and down the halls.

"I'm great at stick men," he says. "I could draw a portrait of you but it would look like every other stick figure you've ever seen. Not exactly the MoMA here."

"I like your photos better," she says without thinking.

He looks at her, curious.

"Your sister showed me," she says quickly.

"Catherine's good for something sometimes," he says, and his smile doesn't seem quite genuine, but then he's turning away, crossing the art studio and approaching a door that bears a sign reading ALARM WILL SOUND.

He presses through it, her heart lurching, but there's no wail of an alarm. He pauses in the doorway, wind snaking in around him and rustling the chalky self-portraits tacked to the walls.

"Come on," he says.

She follows him, her pulse quick but her feet quicker.

They're on the roof.

Bard is five stories, and from here SoBR sprawls around them like a map of Camelot. That's what it feels like, she thinks, with Prescott standing so close she can smell his deodorant: like they're the king and queen of a magical land. His presence puts a hidden tiara on top of her head.

"I can see Paulie's from here," she says. She pulls her phone from her back pocket and takes a picture to post later.

"I won't actually believe you work there until I get free doughnuts," he says.

"Catherine saw me on the clock!" she laughs. "Isn't that proof enough?"

"Catherine's a liar," he says, showing his teeth, but the mirthless sound is back in his voice. Instead of responding, Shania looks back out over SoBR. *Liar.* It makes her think of Gram. She pushes this thought away, taking in the morning sun, coppery on the roof of the bank across the street. Farther away, where the real SoBR begins—coffee bars and T-shirt shops and Paulie's— she can make out the silhouette of a construction crane, arching up toward the frame of the building it's helping construct. She's walked past the site: a former soup kitchen being transformed into an artisan ice cream parlor—the sign says, BLUE ROCK CREAMERY AND BAKERY: BROUGHT TO YOU NEXT SUMMER BY THE SOBR REVITALIZATION COMMITTEE.

Next summer suddenly feels like a long way away: Shania can feel autumn in the air, tagging along behind the breeze that stirs the first dead leaves around their feet. She thinks of her grandmother, what fall had meant when she was alive. Pumpkin carving. Squash and the last of the summer melon in her garden. A few stubborn tomatoes. Without her, where will traditions take place? And do they really have traditions? This is what bothers Shania the most, sprung from the word *liars* on her grandmother's tongue. Just how big was that word, and what does it encompass? Shania imagines lies she can't see like a wet glass on a paper napkin, a spreading ring that obliterates the tissue holding her memories together. Green bean casserole at Thanksgiving. Stuffing scarecrows for porch decorations. This is what Shania thinks of when she hears *liar*. Her whole history unraveling, a square of cloth transforming into a pile of loose thread.

"There you go again," Prescott says gently. "What's on your mind?"

She shakes her head. She lies.

"Nothing. Is this where you come to think deep thoughts, Batman?"

"I wouldn't say *deep*," he says. "But I do come here to think."

"It's quiet," she says, but it's not really. The muted sound of traffic. The wind.

"Especially this time of day."

"Do you and the lacrosse guys come up here usually?"

"No. You're the only person I've brought up here."

"Everyone else thinks the alarm will go off," she says, laughing.

He grins. "Did you think it was going to go off?"

"I did at first, but I assumed if it was, you wouldn't actually open the door."

"So you trust me," he says.

"No," she says. She grins back, but keeps her mouth narrow to hide the tooth. "But I trust you're not an idiot."

"I'll take what I can get," he says and turns back to the city.

Shania moves a little closer.

"Blue Rock is really pretty," she says. "There's nothing like SoBR where I'm from."

"Morrisville," he says.

"How'd you know?"

"Catherine."

"Catherine lies," Shania teases and thankfully he smiles. It makes her feel more sure.

"About some stuff."

"Okay, well, yes, Morrisville. There's no views like this."

"I bet there's a lot about it that's better," he says, frowning.

"Like what?"

He points to two figures standing at the edge of the parking lot next door to Bard, a grocery cart between them. She can make out the yellow hat on one of their heads—it's a man who often sits at the bus stop when she gets off in the morning, panhandling with the hat as a bowl, a brown paper bag in the other hand.

"Homeless guys?" she says. "There's some in Morrisville. Not as many as here."

"That's because cities are full of degenerates," he says, and her

mind is drawn back to the night in his bedroom, the words illuminated on his computer screen. "It's like a magnet that draws all
the scum out of the gutters."

"Would you rather live in the country?" she asks, and now
she's thinking of her grandmother again, the way she had lived
her life avoiding the city. Supposedly. Shania keeps trying to
force her mind to wander away from the blue ink in the almanac,
but it always comes spiraling back, an itch not easily scratched. In
the pages is something about her grandmother that Shania doesn't
know, and she thought she knew everything. Charity worker.
Gardener. Lover of beagles and coffee cake. Sweet tea.

"I'd rather that cities were clean," Prescott is saying. "I want
to go to New York for college, but I think I'd drive myself crazy
surrounded by trash every day."

"*Trash* trash or . . . *people* trash?" she says.

"What's the difference?" he says, a laugh in his voice.

"Well, one is human, for starters," she says, laughing back.
She's trying very hard to be the girl who has crawled out of
her shell, the girl who grief stole breath from but now fills her
lungs with new air. She feels the pull of Hallie, Catherine, even
Willa—loud girls. Girls her grandmother would call "spunky."

"You know what I mean," he says, shrugging it off.

"Kind of?"

He glances at her then, and she knows he's heard the shade of
challenge in her voice. She hates conflict, and realizes in a rush
that she is not, in fact, Catherine Tane—not yet—and that her
hypothetical spunkiness can't steamroll dissent the way Catherine's does.

"I'm just saying," she says. "Maybe, you know, something
happened in their life."

"Like what?"

"Mommy and daddy were mean," she says. She hears her mother coming out of her mouth—it's the kind of thing she says: *Everyone has a sob story, Shania. Mommy and daddy being mean to you doesn't mean you're not responsible for your choices.* It always makes Shania cringe a little, but Prescott laughs. She knew he would. Perhaps this is why she said it.

"You're too nice," he says, but it doesn't sound like a real judgment.

"Not really."

"Nice is good. So many girls are bitches, you know? All that catty shit gets so fucking old."

The word *bitches* from Prescott is like a spark in her ear, unexpected and hot. But something in its venom is sweet, the realization that she is being set apart from the sleek militia of Bard girls with their rows of fangless teeth. She wants him to say "bitches" again, in front of his brother, so Ben can stop looking at her like she's on a scale and the numbers are wrong.

"I hate all the drama at Bard," she says instead. "Who did what and with who."

"I know you do," he says. His hands rest on the ledge separating the two of them from the air. "That's just one of a bunch of things that make you different. And you don't even know how different you are, do you?"

She shrugs, embarrassed, keeping her eyes fastened on the landscape of Blue Rock. She wants him to keep talking. His words feed her, fill the empty place. The allure of being like Catherine is strong but maybe Shania can be something else entirely.

"This world would be so much better if there were more

people like us," he says, and her heart leaps at the way "us" sounds coming out of his mouth with her on the other side of it.

From below rises the sound of the two men arguing in the parking lot. The one in the yellow hat pushes the grocery cart away; the sound of the rattling wheels bounces off Bard's brick.

"This city," Prescott says, disgusted. "Every time things get better they get worse."

"How?"

"They started cleaning up South Blue Rock and it started off great. It was cleaner and they started kicking out all the riffraff that lived in the projects around the expressway. They built a few cool restaurants. But now there's all these fucking bums. It's like they saw things getting cleaner and couldn't stand it."

"Where did the people in the projects go?" she asks.

"Who fucking cares," he says. He removes the gum from his mouth and launches it over the ledge. "Not our problem. Blue Rock has enough problems."

"The only problems Morrisville had was too many people doing oxy."

He chuckles.

"I'm kind of serious," she says. Cassie in Morrisville lost a brother to fentanyl, and she was never the same. There were a lot of Cassies. "Opioids are like...I dunno. A virus."

"No, I get it." He nods. "That's a problem in BR too from what I hear. Everybody's always acting like we should care about inner cities or the *hood* or whatever but what about us? Trust me, my uncle is chief of police and he sees some crazy shit."

She hears the *us* again, pinging in her ear like a needle falling on marble, but it's drawing a different circle this time. She's inside it, but it's wider.

192

"My mom works at the prison," she says. "The women's prison, I mean. She always has a wild story about what the prisoners do."

He turns to her with his eyes wide.

"Your mom works in Bonmeade? Holy shit, that's hardcore."

"She's been doing it for a long time. In Morrisville and now here."

"A good job to have," he says. "Working in a jail is like working as a doctor. You'll always have customers."

She laughs at this vision of his, the idea of prisoners as customers lining up with money in hand. He shakes his head, smiling, his hair gold in the sun and flopping down over his forehead. He's altogether golder than Ben. She tells herself that's better.

"Is your phone going off?" he says, nodding at the ledge where she'd placed it. She looks down to see its screen alight, a text from Catherine.

**CT: SOS. Emergency session tonight at 9+1. 7pm.**

"What's 9+1?" Shania says out loud, bewildered.

"Ten," Prescott says, straight-faced, and she gives him a look. He laughs then. "It's a bowling alley in SoBR."

"Guess I'm going bowling tonight," Shania says, staring at the text.

"She must be upset," he says. "She always goes there when she's upset."

"Any idea what about?" she says as she texts back a thumbs-up.

"Probably stressing about something that's already happened," he says, rolling his eyes. "Catherine spends about half her life living in the past."

Shania swallows, thinking about what she'd seen in the library. Would he laugh at her for the blistered feeling she carries in her chest? Is she living in the past? He squints down at the ground again. The two men have moved on, their argument disappearing with them up the street.

"I'd like to paint Blue Rock from up here one day," he says.

"What's stopping you?"

"Knowing how to paint, for one," he says. She catches the tail end of his smile. "But right now I think I just imagine it one way and it's not there yet. I'll paint it wrong because I envision it differently than it actually is."

"And you envision it how?"

"Clean," he says simply. Then, without looking at her, he reaches for her hand, taking it in his. His hands are soft, his thumb like the tongue of some velvet-mouthed animal as he rubs it across her knuckles. It's somehow unnerving, to feel this soft hand and hear these sharp words. She focuses instead on the world of SoBR stretching out before them. He imagines a better kingdom in the camera of his mind, but with his thumb stroking her skin she tells herself it doesn't matter. Whatever kingdom this is, he is king and she is queen. She enjoys the feeling of the crown.

# CHAPTER 17

Catherine has a nine-pound pink bowling ball with her initials lasered onto the surface, a matching pair of pink shoes. She's waiting for Shania at lane four, most of the bowling alley empty with the exception of a birthday party of shrieking ten-year-olds who bowl with the bumpers down. Catherine glances up as Shania approaches, and Shania sees immediately that she's been drinking. Her eyes are hazy and the smell of liquor wafts from her as she stands to offer a clumsy hug.

"You came," Catherine says. "What a champ."

Catherine holds her a little too long and Shania disentangles herself awkwardly.

"Where are Julia and Hannah?" she says, looking around.

"Just us tonight," Catherine slurs. "Just *usss*."

"Oh," Shania says, surprised. "I . . . oh."

"Julia is Julia. And, Hannah . . . well, Hannah Hughes is a fat nardshark bitch."

Shania looks away, embarrassed. She wonders what name she's been called when out of earshot. Her tongue slides over her tooth.

"I haven't bowled since I was ten," Shania says.

"Same."

"The same ball and shoes since you were ten?" Shania indicates the pink accessories.

"Oh, those are new," Catherine says. "When they opened up this place, I figured I'd get back in the game. You know— BOWLING."

She mimes rolling a strike and Shania laughs a little, nervous. There's a heaviness to Catherine's brow that tells Shania there's a reason she's been summoned here. Her mind immediately goes to Prescott, wondering if there's something Catherine has heard that she disapproves of. Or maybe she bears a message from Prescott that he can't deign to deliver himself. She imagines Ben telling his brother they've been texting, even if it's just dog pictures. The possibilities multiply in her mind like cartoon rabbits.

"I'm gonna bowl," Catherine says, picking up her ball. She hasn't put her shoes on yet and stands there in her socks. She marches toward the line.

"Catherine," Shania starts.

She squares up—Shania gets the feeling she used to be on a league—does a little shuffle, then throws the ball three feet through the air before it lands with a crack in the lane at the same time Catherine lands on the ground with a thud.

"Oh shit," Shania cries, scrambling forward. "Are you okay?"

Catherine looks stunned for a moment, her eyes wide and staring at the ceiling, which is coated with glow-in-the-dark glitter paint. Then she rolls sideways, burying her face in her hands and shrieking with laughter.

"Oh my God," she screams. "My ASS."

The chaperones for the birthday party scowl toward them

while Shania grabs Catherine's arm to help her up. Catherine yanks her down with her and Shania lands hard on one knee.

"Catherine, what the fuck!" Shania says, low.

"Everything floats down here, Shania!" she cackles, snorting, and Shania laughs too in spite of the scorch of alcohol wafting from the other girl's mouth.

"You need to eat," Shania says.

"Your MOM needs to eat," Catherine announces.

"Oh my God. Come on. They have nachos. I saw when I was walking in."

The college-aged guy working the counter of the small restaurant makes Catherine put on shoes before she's allowed to enter the concession area, so Shania helps her jam them onto her feet but doesn't bother to tie them. She leaves Catherine in a booth and orders a large nacho and a bottle of water. When she returns to the booth, Catherine is slumped against the wall staring at her phone.

"Boys fucking suck," she spits. "They fucking *suck*."

*Oh*, Shania thinks. This is about a boy. She relaxes and pops open the water. She'd meant it for Catherine but is so relieved she's not being told Prescott doesn't want to talk to her anymore that she takes a swig of it herself.

"Who are we talking about here?" Shania asks, replacing the cap, genuinely curious.

"My ex," Catherine says. "My fucking ex. What an... what an asshole. An *asshole*."

"Exes usually are."

"He's the biggest asshole, though," she says. "He hates me for no reason."

"Why did you guys break up?"

Catherine shrugs moodily, casting her eyes over the rest of the concession area. It's just the two of them, alone under the digital zig and zag of arcade screens.

"Do you still want to be with him or something?" Shania asks.

"No! I mean, not no but not yes. I just hate that he's probably telling people some bullshit. He hates me for no reason."

"Yeah, you said that. Why does he hate you?"

"I don't know!" she cries. "I didn't do anything!"

Talking to drunk people is like talking to drunk people, Shania decides.

"He's dating Michelle now," Catherine says after a long pause, the venom in her voice as sharp as the smell of booze.

"Michelle," Shania repeats. "Michelle who?"

"*Michelle.* Your little friend? The Black girl? Michelle."

Shania feels her forehead wrinkle.

"Michelle Broadus? In botany? *Michelle* Michelle?"

"Is there another Black Michelle, Shania?" Catherine says, grabbing a nacho and stuffing it angrily in her mouth.

"Michelle Obama," Shania offers.

"Oh, nice, Shania. *Nice.*"

"I didn't think Michelle's boyfriend went to Bard."

"He doesn't go to Bard. He *used* to go to Bard."

The pieces float slowly into place.

"Wait, Eric? You used to date the Eric guy?"

"Eric Young." Catherine nods.

"Oh," Shania says. "I mean...oh."

"Julia and Hannah are so over it," Catherine says, half wailing. "They just want me to act like I never met him. Especially Julia. Fucking Julia."

"Why Julia? Does she like him or something?"

Catherine squawks a laugh. "Ha! My parents were pissed I was dating a Black guy, but Julia's parents would literally kill her if she did."

"Wow." It's all Shania can think to say. Seeing Catherine like this is like looking at a photo on Instagram with no filter and in bad light. Everything is bumpy.

"My family's not racist, you know?" Catherine says suddenly, her mouth full of nachos. "It's not about that."

"What's not?"

"Any of it," she says, gesturing to nothing. The nachos aren't helping her drunkenness. Shania thinks she should have gotten her a pretzel instead.

"Here's the thing about Eric," Catherine goes on. She stares at her phone, black mirror, as if willing it to light up. "He didn't want to fit in. You have to fit in if you want it to work at Bard. It's a really old school, you know? Famous. It's part of history. There's some shit you just don't say."

Shania nods to mask her confusion. Her mother said something very similar.

"I've never actually met Eric," Shania says. "So..."

"I trust you, Shania," Catherine says. She finally looks up from her phone and stares at Shania, eyes bleary. "You know? I don't really know you yet. Whatever. But, like, I trust you. You seem like you get it. My brothers don't. But, like, you know I'm a good person, right?"

Even though it pisses her off, Shania can't help but hear Willa's voice in the back of her mind: *mythology.* But Catherine has been kind to Shania, in her way, even if in many ways she's still a creature of mystery. Shania knows Catherine volunteers at Planned

Parenthood. She knows she has a lot of friends. She knows she invited the new girl with the bad tooth to her party when she didn't have to. She reads poetry by Anne Stanton.

"Why did you invite me to your party?" she says instead of answering Catherine's question.

Catherine looks up, her eyes half sad the way drunk people's always seem to be.

"Because I'm nice," Catherine says. "And you were sitting alone."

Shania can't help but feel disappointed. She doesn't know what she wanted to hear, but something other than this. Something more like "I saw potential." Something like Prescott's rooftop declaration: "You're different from the other girls." Shania wants very much to be different but isn't sure what she wants to be different from.

"So, what, you were just taking pity on me?"

"I need new friends," Catherine says simply. "Mine are a bunch of nardsharks."

"Okay."

"And, okay, maybe I wanted a pet project? What's an American high school experience without a little makeover!"

"You think I need a makeover," Shania says flatly.

"Let's be honest," Catherine says, slurry. "The unicorn hair is...beneath you, babe. But behind the unicorn is a fucking Pegasus! Who wants a horn on their head when they can have *wings*! I just want to give you wings, Shania Twain." She sighs deeply, slowly, exhaling bravado. "I don't know. The new girl, sitting in the greenhouse, always watching people. You're, like, the quiet version of me. Maybe. Or something."

Catherine stares at her for a long moment of silence, and

Shania wonders if she's going to say something else, but instead she just laughs and eats more nachos.

"I'm a good person," she says to the plastic cheese. "I'm not a bad person. I'm good."

Shania wants to ask why she cares so much about being good anyway, she who seems to delight in badness. But then Catherine's phone is vibrating, and Catherine snatches it up, and Shania can only watch as Catherine swipes open the message that must have appeared, staring at it intently before the expression in her eyes goes blurry again.

"He hates me for no fucking reason," she moans. She shoves the basket of nachos away, almost sending them sailing to the floor. Shania catches them, surprised. "He can hate Prescott all he wants, but what the fuck does that have to do with me?"

"Why does he hate Prescott?" Shania asks, hoping her curiosity doesn't sound as intense as it feels, coiled in her gut.

"That's between them," Catherine says. She types something furiously and then slaps the phone back down. If it wasn't for the rubbery ladybug case the screen might have cracked. "I didn't *do* anything."

"What happened?"

"Boys will be boys," she says, rolling her eyes. She seems a little less drunk. The text and her anger have sobered her in some small way. Shania's own phone remains dark.

"Does your brother like me?" Shania asks suddenly. Catherine stares.

"What?"

"Sorry," Shania says. "I know you're upset. I just thought...I don't know."

"My *brothers* like you," Catherine says slowly. Her face looks pale.

"What do you mean brothers?"

"Ben keeps asking about you. And Prescott, well. You already kissed Prescott, so..."

Shania doesn't know what to say. She decides to ignore the comment about Ben. She has too many questions.

"I don't see Prescott very much. He doesn't text me...."

"It's not you," says Catherine. "That's just Prescott. Half the time I wonder if he likes girls at all because they just seem to piss him off. But I think he likes you. Why do you like him?"

"*Why* do I like him?"

"If he hardly ever texts you, I mean," Catherine says, staring at the table. "If you've only hung out a few times. Why? Why do you like him?"

Shania thinks the answer should be obvious. Prescott is the sun. He is the marble statue. She gropes for an answer but Catherine speaks again.

"Can you be yourself around him?"

*I don't know if I'm ever really myself around anyone*, Shania thinks. This is not what she says.

"I'm more myself around him than anyone else." This isn't true either—Ben and the tan hound, Michelle and the memory of manure. But what Prescott offers is more important than something as cliché as being herself, she thinks.

"Do you think he's himself around you?" Catherine says.

They stare at each other, then look down at the nacho basket. Something has changed. Here in the brightly lit concession area, the neon of the arcade falling across the table, Catherine's words could feel bright, an exchange between girlfriends. They are not. Shania understands then that she's being warned, but she doesn't know about what and she gazes down at the chips and wants to throw it all away.

"I saw Willa at the library earlier," Shania says, eager to change the subject, even if it's more of a subcategory than an entirely new one.

"Willa," Catherine says, her tongue sliding over each letter. "Quayloo, what a...what a waste of a scholarship. You two were just doing some studying? Spending some QT at the biblioteca?"

"No, she kind of just showed up," Shania says. "I was doing some research."

"Was Michelle with her? Were they gloating about stealing my boyfriend?"

"Um, no. Not that I saw."

"Eric never gave a fuck about plants and shit before," she says, massaging her entire face. "Now he starts dating Little Miss Beyoncé and suddenly humps ferns or whatever the fuck they do at that sad-ass garden in Western Pocket."

"I saw him at that event she was telling us about," Shania says, then regrets saying it. It's like dipping an already enraged cat into a bathtub.

"He was there?" Catherine groans. "Of fucking course he was. He was always so pissed at me for not coming to his house. Michelle's probably his goddamn neighbor."

"Why didn't you want to go to his house?"

"It's *Western fucking Pocket*, Shania."

"You shouldn't judge an entire neighborhood based on what you've heard," Shania says. It feels like the right thing to say. She savors the fleeting enjoyment of sitting astride a high horse, even if it makes her heart pound.

A long pause, the two girls staring at each other.

"I need to throw up," Catherine announces, then stands up and strides resolutely to the bathroom.

Shania is still staring at the pale food when Catherine's phone vibrates. Shania hadn't realized she left it, as it was concealed by the nacho basket. She scooches the basket sideways and peers at the glowing rectangle, then glances at the bathroom door. Using one finger, she touches the edge of Catherine's phone and rotates it around to face herself. She sees Catherine's last text first:

CT: It was just a white lie, Eric. Jesus.

EY: Keep telling yourself that. The photo is bad enough.
But the lies are worse. You're just as bad as him.
Delete the damn picture AND my number.

Shania swivels the phone back around and slides the nachos back in front of it, her pulse jumpy. The filterless photo of Catherine's life that she's getting a glimpse of suddenly looks like it might also be a mosaic and she's only seeing one little frame. She wonders what else exists beyond the edges of the view their fragile friendship provides. But it's the *him* that makes her heart beat faster, and whatever curiosity Shania has about what this *him* might have done retreats with the possibility of the *him* being Prescott. She finds herself at a fork in the trail of her mind, knowing and not knowing, and stands there uncertainly.

A moment later, Catherine sinks back down onto the bench, her eyes redder than before but looking more sober. The first thing she does is tap her phone to wake it up. She squints at the message. Shania studies her face, the way expectation wilts into disappointment, shrivels into blankness. Catherine gives a dry little laugh.

"Well, there goes the rest of tonight's plans," she says. "And I can't fucking drive."

"Still drunk?" Shania says, not knowing what else to say.

"Maybe I'll just total it!" she says. "Maybe that would be a good idea."

Shania stares at her, bewildered.

"You can drive me," Catherine says, and stands up. Shania follows her out of the concession area and outside, not bothering to tell her that she'd left her pink bowling ball behind. They'll keep it for her. Or she'll buy another one. Or both.

It's starting to get dark. The air is warmer than Shania thought it would be, summer hanging on for dear life. The girls both breathe it in, deep and slow, and Shania can tell they're deciding what they're going to take with them and what they're going to leave in the bowling alley. She can see Catherine's Mercedes parked across the street. Shania doesn't have a license and has only driven a few times, mostly her grandmother's old Buick. Now she pictures herself behind the wheel of Catherine's car, and though night approaches, she imagines herself in sunglasses. She imagines her hair blonde. She imagines her teeth straight and orderly as white tiles. No, marble pillars.

Beside her, Catherine fiddles with her keys, deciding something. She looks at her car too, and is no doubt picturing Shania inside it now. A chain reaction happens between her eyes and her brain: a series of dominoes falling, the first pushed by the vision of Shania driving her Mercedes. And like it was never gone, the golden Instagram filter slips back over her face, her life.

"I'm going to take a Lyft," she says, and even as she brings up the app on her phone, not looking at her, Shania can still feel her eyes, her whole body an eye, sizing her up. More sober than Catherine but somehow still lacking something essential. In the hidden cave of her mouth, Shania runs her tongue over the dagger of her tooth.

The silence while they stand waiting is dented by the people who mill down the sidewalk, calling across the traffic-filled street.

"Are you meeting us at Frog?" a guy shouts from just behind Shania, making her jump. Across the street, the intended recipient of this message waves, pointing the other direction.

"No, bro, Jessica was just there and she's grossed out—there was a dead cat or something out by the patio, so she's going to LNTRN instead."

"See you there!"

They move on, still yelling across the street, and Shania stares after them, the sinking feeling that has become familiar inside her melting down and dripping through each rib. She wonders if Catherine heard, what she would say if she told her about the cat curled into Earl's coat, how Shania wonders now if it was alive or dead.

"Find the break!" Catherine erupts, and Shania jumps again. The eyes of people on the sidewalk sweep in her direction, but never pause. Their gazes carry a list of parameters for identifying someone that is a "problem" and, while Catherine is obnoxious, nothing about her appearance triggers alarms. It takes Shania a moment to recognize the words she'd shouted.

"Anne Stanton," Shania says slowly. " 'The Bluff.' "

"Sometimes you just have to scream poetry into the night,

you know, Shania? 'AT THE EDGE WHERE THE WORLD FALLS AWAY, EVERYTHING BROKEN BUT BONE!' "

Shania doesn't know whether to laugh or flee. She stares at Catherine, who is breathing hard, openmouthed. Shania is a little scared of her and a little awestruck.

"You've got the poetry." Catherine grins, her teeth as bright as the storefronts lining the streets of SoBR. "Now you just need the pizazz. I won't give up on you, Shania Twain. Don't you give up on me either."

# CHAPTER 18

Neither Catherine nor Prescott are at school the next day. Shania texts Prescott once, when she's passing by the taco place. She sends a picture and nothing else. He responds, **eat one for me. Miss you**, but that's all, and the "miss you" is enough to sustain her until she hears from him again. At school she sits alone in the common room, flipping through his oldest Instagram posts and looking for the current Prescott in the lines of his sophomore year face. Michelle plops down across from her at the table.

Shania is immediately stiff. After talking to Catherine about Eric, any conversation with Michelle feels like approaching a box of wasps with a hole in the side. But Michelle's smile disarms her right away. The beauty queen beam is dazzling as she unfurls the wrinkled top of her McDonald's bag. Shania looks down at her own Tupperware bowl of soup, wondering what sparked Michelle's deviation from home-cooked.

"McDonald's today, huh?" Shania says, nodding at her bag.

Michelle glances down and the smile stretches a little wider. She withdraws a fry and tosses it into her mouth.

"Yeah, I guess so," she says. "Just felt like doing something different."

But there's a secret floating around her. The sparkle of it glints in her eye as she pulls out her little chest of chicken nuggets, and it glitters when she sucks on her straw. It's a milkshake. Michelle is the most frugal girl Shania has met besides herself. A milkshake on a Tuesday is significant. And then there's the way she casts her gaze around the common room, taking in the walls, the art, the occasional scuffs on the wall. Sizing it all up. Seeing it through a new lens.

"Something special about today?" Shania asks. To her own ears she sounds like her grandmother—wheedling.

"Not really," Michelle says, smiling close-lipped until her gaze eventually falls on Shania. Then her perfect teeth slip out again. "Maybe."

Shania smiles back, drawn in.

"What? What is it?"

Shania feels hungry, maybe for gossip. After yesterday's conversation with Catherine, an entire soap opera has been unveiled before her. Looking at Michelle now feels like actually seeing her for the first time. Man stealer? Heartbreaker?

"I got into Harvard," Michelle whispers. Her chicken nuggets are spread out before her like a court of knights. She hasn't eaten a single one. Shania gapes at her.

"What?"

Michelle glances around the common room again, making sure no one is close enough to overhear.

"Harvard special admission. I got in."

"Special adm—what? You're a junior, aren't you?"

She nods, and Shania can tell she's keeping her smile a

manageable size—that behind her composure is a display of fireworks.

"Kinda. I've been taking extra classes outside of school. Double APs and shit. I'm skipping my senior year. I'm going to Harvard. Next year."

She leans back in her chair, her arms hanging loose on either side of it. Shania is witnessing the sapling of her excitement becoming a tree.

"Harvard. Wow. I mean...wow. Congratulations."

"Thank you," Michelle says, looking her in the eye. Her eyelashes look like butterflies. "I'm mostly happy to be getting the fuck out of here. It's like getting early parole."

They both laugh but Shania can't help but keep staring at her.

"You're just...going?" she says. "Like that?"

"Yup. I've been working on a hydroponic program at my church. My dad's been documenting it for me. I think it was the video that did it. Well, and Mrs. Walker's recommendation. She's kind of considered a local celebrity because of everything she's accomplished in Blue Rock. We met this lady at a college fair over the summer..."

She stops and waves her hand, self-conscious. But her eyes glow. She sucks on her milkshake but still hasn't touched her food. She's somewhere else in her head, and looking at her, a green vine sprouts in Shania's stomach, winding its way up into her throat.

"Well, lucky you," Shania says, stirring her soup. "I bet you can't wait."

"Might be out of the frying pan and into the fire." Michelle shrugs, looking down. "Every year at Bard there's been somebody who makes affirmative action jokes. It's just going to be worse at Harvard."

"Nobody is going to say that," Shania says quickly, the vine tightening.

"Yes, they will," Michelle says calmly. The glow in her eyes is different now.

"You don't know that. If anything they'll treat you different because you're young. Not because..."

Shania trails off, and Michelle half smiles.

"Because I'm Black?"

"That's what *you're* saying," Shania says.

"Yeah."

"I don't know what you expect *me* to say."

Michelle looks at her with her eyebrows high in surprise.

"Expect *you* to say? I don't expect you to say anything."

"You're judging all those people before you even get there," Shania says. "That's not fair."

"You've never had a Black friend before, have you?" Michelle says, her mouth twitching like it hasn't decided yet between frown and smile.

Shania feels her chest bloom red.

"I actually have," she says. "My friend in Morrisville. Monica."

She doesn't say that the Monica she knew in Morrisville and the Monica in Hallie's photos feel like people on the opposite sides of a metamorphosis.

"Then I feel like you should understand what I'm trying to say," Michelle insists.

"Sometimes being white feels like walking through a mine field." Shania's stirring her soup faster now, creating a whirlpool in the broth. She feels suddenly fragile, a crack running through her. "Like one wrong step and *boom*."

211

Michelle's laugh jerks Shania's eyes up from her bowl. Michelle's leaned back in her chair again, her head tilted back and staring at the ceiling.

"And who do you think put those bombs there, Shania?" she says, and then to herself: "*Damn*, Harvard. Hurry up."

Shania's face burns, but she doesn't know how to apologize. Without meaning to, she's thinking of her great-grandfather, of his name glowing out of the screen at the library. She glances uneasily up at Michelle.

"I'm just having a bad day," she says, hoping her tone conveys an apology. "I'm just... I've got a lot of stuff on my mind."

"Like what?" Michelle says, not looking at her, studying her straw.

"I'm trying to figure out some stuff about my grandma. Like, remember the almanac thing I told you about? The address?"

"Oh, that's right," Michelle says, still looking annoyed, but now minorly intrigued. "What happened with that?"

"Well, the address was the Western Pocket Community Garden, remember?"

"Yeah. Which now you've seen. Thanks for coming, by the way."

"Sure," Shania says, blushing, wondering if Michelle noticed how she barely stayed a half hour. "But yeah, I mean... I did some research, and it turns out my great-grandfather—my grandma's dad—used to live in what's now Western Pocket."

"Oh, your people were white flighters, huh?" Michelle says, sucking her milkshake.

"You know about that?"

"Girl, everybody knows about that."

"Okay, well I'm not from Blue Rock."

"It's not just a Blue Rock thing. It happens everywhere."

Shania's tongue pokes her tooth. She's back in the minefield.

"*Sooo*, your grandma lived in Western Pocket?" Michelle prods, raising an eyebrow.

"Yeah. I mean, I think. I'm pretty sure, anyway. The address in her almanac is the same as the garden, and the article I found about my great-grandfather says he owned a block and then moved. He mentioned his wife and daughter. But she always said she'd never even been to Blue Rock. I don't know why she'd lie to me."

She stops then, because Gram *had* told her. *We're all what? Liars.* How big was that *we*?

Michelle shrugs. "Maybe she was a baby," she says, "and she didn't remember. Or maybe she was embarrassed, you know? Although, that said, not too many white folks her age seem embarrassed about that stuff. *That was just the way it was back then.* That old excuse."

"Ooh, are we talking about Shania's family tree?" Willa appears, plops down between them. Shania feels like a hermit crab curling back into its shell.

"White flighters." Michelle nods.

"Sounds like her granddad was a blockbuster too." Willa pulls a taco from a bag and takes a bite. "If my great-grandparents could have afforded to own land in Western Pocket back then, they probably would have been too."

"White people gonna white," Michelle says.

"It's as if entire systems were set up and maintained to make it possible!" Willa says with ironic awe.

"That's not what it's about," Shania says. "I mean, you said it like you were joking, but that *is* just how it was back then. Does that mean they were automatically bad people?"

"When you see racism as just a character defect and not a societal weapon," Willa says with her mouth full, "you fail to understand the problem. Remember what I said? Someone can be nice as hell and still be racist as hell. I know our history books say everybody from Columbus to Reagan were stellar dudes who petted bunnies and kissed babies, but all our textbooks are basically fan fiction."

Michelle shakes her head, but she's smiling, sucking the milkshake. Shania can feel the blush spreading down her neck. She feels the tug between who these girls are and who she's trying to be. But more than that, everything that she knew about her grandmother feels like it's being torn out of her grasping hands. *Liars.* If Gram had actually lived in Blue Rock, if Gram's father had been who the article at the library made him out to be, that made them something like strangers. And then what would she have left?

"If you'd met my grandmother," Shania says slowly, "you would know how ridiculous that sounds. She loved everyone. She was..."

She chokes a little, on the scream that never leaves and on the past itself. One by one her senses light up: She can smell Gram's hand soap. She can hear the clink of the spoon in her sweet tea. Shania breathes in deep. Her lungs feel cold with February. White marble. In her mind, she builds a church around her grandmother, walls that can't be shaken.

"I wonder if Mrs. Walker remembers her," Michelle says, changing tack. "She's lived in Pocket since she was our age."

Behind Michelle, Hannah and Julia enter with carryout bags from Rhino and pause at the entrance to the common room. The space has gradually filled up as Michelle and Shania talked, and now there are few unoccupied tables. Shania sees Julia see her. She and Hannah whisper a few words and then make their way over.

"Shania, why didn't you come to Rhino with us?" Hannah says, sitting down. Julia sits down beside Michelle but says nothing. Willa stiffens.

"I brought my food," Shania answers.

"*Laaame*," says Hannah.

The only conversation comes from the tables around theirs. There's something sitting at the table with them, a ghost from Michelle and Shania's conversation, and then some new ghost that Hannah and Julia have brought in with them. Hannah looks sideways at Michelle.

"You know McDonald's is the leading cause of obesity in America," she says.

"Yum," Michelle says. She picks up her first nugget and bites it decisively in half.

"How's Eric?" Hannah says, the words darting out of her mouth like squirrels.

Michelle puts the other half of the chicken nugget down.

"He's dope," she replies.

Hannah doesn't seem to have planned the conversation this far.

"Oh," she says. "Okay. How long have you been going out?"

"Couple months."

Hannah and Julia exchange a glance. The ghost they've brought to the table is Catherine, Shania finds. And something else. Boyfriends don't feel this heavy. Michelle's jaw has been transformed into iron.

"Did he tell you why he broke up with Catherine?" Julia says quickly. Hannah casts her a sharp glance.

"Yes." Michelle says.

"Look, she didn't know what else to do," Hannah says. "You need to—"

"Have you two checked lost and found lately?" Willa interrupts. She balls up the foil that had wrapped her taco.

"What?" Hannah says, her nose wrinkling.

"I think you lost something really important so you'd better go check." She stands up, tugging on Michelle. When neither of the girls reply, Willa rolls her eyes. "Your lives, you twats. You need to go get a life. Maybe you can get one on sale. I don't know. Why are people always ruining my jokes? Fuck off. Bye."

Michelle closes the lid to her nuggets, chucks them back in the bag. She and Willa depart, leaving Shania with Julia and Hannah and their coffee.

"Weird bitches," Hannah mutters. Julia stares, something behind her eyes ticking. The walls in Shania's head are still shaking. She feels the tug again.

"Why do you care if Michelle is dating Eric?" Shania says. With Catherine not present, she feels braver.

"We don't," snaps Hannah. Julia says nothing.

"If you don't care, then why ask her about it?" Shania says. She hates conflict and this feels like conflict but she resists the urge to shrink. Julia is still staring when Shania's phone buzzes. It's Catherine.

> **CT:** Are you going to community service day?
>
> **SH:** What's that?
>
> **CT:** Do you ever check the school calendar, woman? We do it every year. Go to different parks and do habitat restoration or something.

**SH:** When is it?

**CT:** Tomorrow!

**SH:** I guess I'm going then. My mom won't let me miss school.

**CT:** My parents don't give a shit. You can come over here! Hannah probably will too.

Shania wonders when the feeling of having friends will ever seem like something more than momentary luck. Her grandmother always said a good man was a church and a bad man was a casino. Every time Catherine texts Shania it's as if she's managed to spin three of the same picture on a slot machine. Shania wonders if that means she's a bad friend or just that Shania needs to win after so much loss.

**SH:** That would be fun.

She stops herself from asking if Prescott will skip too. All of her is thirsty.

Even with tomorrow's promise of hanging out at the Tanes', the conversation Shania had with Michelle about Gram itches like a bug bite, and she spends the rest of the day trying to sooth it—daydreaming in class, sneaking looks at her phone, hoping for a distraction from Prescott. By the time her free period comes around, the walls of the school feel claustrophobic, and she retreats to the greenhouse, praying it's empty.

It is. She slips in, looking for her grandmother. Something that doesn't whisper *liar* and *I'm sorry*. The added stress of Willa only makes everything worse, louder.

Ms. Hassoon's file cabinet is full of seeds, unlocked as always, and Shania stands in its open doors, flipping through packets and tiny containers. Everything is as meticulously labeled as everything else pertaining to Ms. Hassoon: Her handwriting is square and precise, and before too long Shania finds a little packet of seeds with LILAC: SYRINGA VULGARIS written on it. Shania takes it and returns to her workstation. It may be a different sort of lilac than the kind her grandmother so loved, but the name alone is enough to make her feel closer. She has a little room at the end of the planter.

She's just begun making little pockets in the soil when the suction of the greenhouse door opening stirs the air. She freezes, looking up. She doesn't think she's exactly breaking the rules by being in here, but Ms. Hassoon wouldn't like someone pawing through her system. It's Julia.

"Hi," Julia says. "What are you doing in here?"

"Working," Shania says. "What are you doing?"

"I . . ." Julia glances around and gives a half shrug. "I come in here sometimes. It's quiet. It smells nice."

Shania nods, continuing to watch her as she walks slowly down the line, letting her fingertips brush the tops of various sprouts in student projects.

"Have you talked to Catherine today?" Julia says.

Shania thinks of the text about community service day—Catherine hadn't mentioned Julia.

"No," she says.

"I just thought she'd be here today."

"Is she sick or something?" Shania asks, not knowing what else to offer.

"I don't think so. Just more family shit."

Shania puts down the packet of seeds. Julia pauses and smells one of Michelle's roses.

"What's up with their family?" Shania says, and realizes too late she's included Prescott—and maybe Ben too—in this question, but Julia doesn't seem to notice or care. She only shrugs.

"They've just got a lot of issues. They're all in therapy. Even Ben. Which, whatever. But I guess it's just been weird for them all since..."

She hesitates and her eyes flick in Shania's direction.

"Since what?"

"What do you guys talk about?" Julia says, ignoring the question.

"Huh?"

"You and Prescott."

"I don't know. Stuff. Movies. Music. College."

"Mmm."

"Why do you ask?"

"He just doesn't talk to many people outside his group of friends," Julia says. "And they all say he's been different lately too."

"Who says that?"

"JP and Adam keep saying he's changed."

"Since?" Shania says pointedly, feeling annoyed. "Is there something you're trying to tell me? Is that why you're actually in here?"

"Don't be weird," Julia says, scowling. "I told you I come in here all the time. I'm just talking, since we *both* happen to be in here."

"You're talking about *what*?" Shania snaps.

"Does Prescott talk about Eric?" Julia demands.

Shania realizes they have arrived very quickly at whatever landmine Julia has been dancing around. Something else about Julia's face has changed: The whisper of a smile that always hangs around her mouth, the thing that makes her face soft and friendly, is gone.

"Why would he talk about Eric?" Shania says, but she feels the looming worry, the ghostly outline of an iceberg floating somewhere ahead. And behind. Something she has seen and unseen a dozen times.

"Because," Julia says. "I don't know, because. Catherine still isn't over the whole thing, so I figured Prescott isn't either. Michelle added into the equation just makes things messier."

"So, what, the Tanes are heartbroken and mad about it? That's what you're trying to tell me? Catherine got her boyfriend stolen, and she and her brother are pissed? And Ben too? Did Prescott used to date Michelle or something?"

Julia yelps a laugh so sharp that it surprises them both. She puts her hand to her throat as if ensuring that another doesn't emerge.

"Prescott would never date Michelle," she says slowly.

"Then why is any of this relevant?" Shania demands, the seeds and their blossoms forgotten. Her heart is pounding. There is a thing floating near her ears, in front of her eyes, that she does not want to see or hear. "Why else would I give a shit about who Prescott and Catherine are mad at?"

"Because Prescott put Eric in the hospital," Julia says in a rush. "How do you not know that? Because Prescott got Eric kicked out of Bard. Doesn't that *bother* you?"

The words enter Shania's ear in knots before her brain slowly untangles them.

"What are you talking about?"

"You know Eric used to go to Bard," Julia says, her voice impatient. "Did you think he just *left*? He and Prescott got in a fight, and Eric had to have his jaw wired shut. Eric's parents talked about suing Bard. They *did* sue the Tanes. And won."

"No way," Shania says, feeling sick.

"Prescott didn't like that Eric was dating Catherine, but that was just part of it. It was all so fucked up. Ben doesn't even really speak to either of them anymore. Everyone was surprised that Eric was at that soccer game. I heard he wouldn't be able to play for a long time."

"He looked fine," Shania whispers, remembering.

"Yeah, well, he is now. But he got kicked out of Bard."

"*Eric* got kicked out?" Shania's mind is doing gymnastics, justifications crawling from the corners of her brain, pieces of what she's heard and seen and noticed latching onto other pieces. "What did Catherine do?"

At this Julia's eyes drop to the floor.

"She, um, Catherine...picked a side." She pauses. "So Prescott *didn't* tell you?"

Julia's eyes are empty and full all at once.

Shania doesn't want to say no. Saying no means there has been something looming beneath the surface of the water she's been swimming in with Prescott, a thing with scales that she might have noticed if she weren't so busy backstroking in the ocean of his eyes. She shakes her head. She thinks of the boy who bought her tacos. Who looked out over the city from Bard's rooftop with his hand on hers. The photo he took of her smile surrounded by green. Then she thinks of Eric at the garden, his smile rugged and his voice deep. Taller than Prescott? Maybe. In her head Eric becomes larger and larger, his features wilder and angrier. The real Eric is obscured by the beast her mind creates. Shania needs this beast. This is the logic that helps build a house around Prescott in her mind.

"Are you going to say something?" Julia says softly.

"I...I don't know what to..." Shania grapples for the right thing to say. She is always looking for the right thing to say. "I guess...I guess I need to hear both sides."

The blossom Julia's been fidgeting with comes off in her hand. She stares at it for what feels like a long while before speaking.

"I think there's only one side, Shania."

Julia lets the flower fall and yanks the door open. After she's gone, Shania goes on staring at the place where Julia had been, red petals dotting the floor like a blood trail. When the close green air becomes too much, Shania stands and picks them up, one by one by one.

# CHAPTER 19

On community service day, the bus that would take Shania to the Tanes' instead of school is nine minutes late, and therefore when her mother comes outside to go to work, Shania is still standing there at the stop.

"I had a feeling I'd run into you!" her mother calls, holding her coffee cup aloft. "Just heard about a bad accident in Northtown. You're going to be waiting awhile. C'mon, I'll give you a ride."

Shania stands there staring at her for what feels like a short eternity. Her mother has walked halfway to the parking lot before she notices.

"Shane?" she says. "Are you coming?"

"Uh…"

Her mother pauses.

"Shane, what the hell are you doing?"

Game over. Shania follows her mother, the promise of a day hanging out at Catherine's instead of doing community service fading. In the car, they sit in silence. The almanac is right there with them, tucked into Shania's backpack, the blue writing inside like a map to a destination she's unsure of. She thinks her mother must know—she had hidden the almanac, after all, and let all its secrets fester in a box under her bed. It makes Shania think of how Gram hid her doctor's notes, how she thought she could pretend her way into a future without pain. Is this what her mother was doing? Her mother was always talking about a fresh start—fresh implied a change from rotten, and Shania had always thought it was just about her father and the stench he seemed to have left over their lives, but now she's not so sure.

"You're quiet," her mother says. She looks at her sideways.

Instead of answering directly, Shania asks, "Picking up an extra shift?"

"Kind of. I wasn't going to tell you until I knew more, but I'm interviewing for a better position. Outside the prison."

Shania glances at her then, surprised. She hadn't even noticed her mother was dressed up. She's wearing a lavender-blue skirt, a white blouse tucked in. Shania can't see her shoes from where she sits but she knows which ones they are: The beige almost-flats, almost-heels that she wears whenever she has something important to do. They're just a little too shiny for almost any occasion but she's had them for years. She'll probably ask to be buried in them. Shania shoves this thought down.

"What job?"

"A supervisor thing at the Cradle of Mercy," she says.

"The baby jail."

"It's not baby jail. It's a home for troubled youth."

"At least there you'd be the same size as the prisoners," Shania says.

Her mother laughs and fake punches her arm.

"Hush your mouth, smart aleck. I'm small but I'll kick anyone's ass."

"I know. Those kids don't know what they're getting into."

Her mother laughs again but shakes her head.

"I'm hoping it will be different, Shane. I'm tired of—I don't know, tired of having to beat the shit out of everybody all the time."

"You don't really beat the shit out of anybody," Shania says, a half question.

Her mother doesn't respond.

"There's different ways to beat the shit out of people," she says eventually. Then she shoots Shania a look. "And don't say 'shit.'"

They drive in silence. The traffic gets thicker the closer they get to SoBR, but according to the low voice on the radio, the worst is on the other side of town.

"This traffic," her mother mutters. "This is why Gram hated the city."

The words seem to hang for a moment, thrumming like a hummingbird between them. All the things Shania wants to say, all the demands she wants to make, feel suddenly too thick in her throat. In the end, all she gets out is, "How'd she know she hated the city if she'd never been?"

Her mother pauses for just long enough to make Shania's stomach clench.

"How do you garden in a city?" she says a beat later. "You know Gram loved to garden."

"I actually know for a fact that people have gardens here," Shania says, swallows, and then adds, "and that's not an answer."

Her mother looks at her sharply now.

"What's your problem, Shania Marie? You have an attitude today."

"I *don't* have an attitude. I just—"

"I don't need negative energy before my interview," her mother says. "Jesus, I might as well have gone to work if I wanted to deal with nastiness."

Shania looks out the window.

"Not just anybody can deal with the dregs of society on a day-to-day basis," Shania says.

"The dregs of society," her mother repeats.

"That's what Prescott says."

"I see."

"Prescott says you're a badass," Shania says. The impulse to smooth over everything jagged between them feels as natural and necessary as drawing breath. "He says it all the time."

"A badass? I don't know about that."

But she smiles.

Shania gets out a block away from Bard so her mother doesn't have to get caught up in the traffic jam of teenagers driving luxury cars. As Shania walks past the bus stop, she begins to look for a sign of a transfer, the hope of still making it to Catherine's sprouting, but Mr. Foster has seen her from the front door and waves, standing and waiting with the door propped open. The hope deflates again, and she trudges toward him, firing off a quick text to Catherine.

Still, the school has the air of a field trip or a game day. Everyone is chatty and exuberant, anxious to miss classes even if it does mean community service.

## BT: Are you skipping like my sister?

Ben texts her as she's walking into the greenhouse. Every time she's expecting a text from one Tane, she gets one from another. She sends him a photo of her desk in reply.

**Good girl**, he answers, and it lands wrong. Her mother is lying to her. She hasn't heard from Prescott. Hearing from Ben is a drop of hot oil splashing from the pan.

**Save that for the dogs**, she types. She hits Send, then puts her phone away.

"It's a beautiful day to root out some invasive species," Ms. Hassoon says to Shania's class. They're all grouped in homerooms before the buses come to take them all to the park where they'll be doing the service.

"I just got a manicure," Julia complains.

"Me too," says JP, and his friends laugh. He looks around, bemused. "I'm serious!"

"Does anyone have any questions about their final projects before we go to the buses?" Ms. Hassoon calls. "I haven't been checking in with you on them. I hope you've been keeping track of things on your own."

"The leaves are supposed to be brown and crumbling, right?" Trevor says.

While they banter, Shania glances over at Michelle, who has her headphones in. She wonders if Michelle still cares about her final project now that she's going to Harvard, skipping her last year at Bard. Something tells Shania that Michelle would rather die than get less than an A in this class, Harvard or not.

Her phone vibrates in her pocket and she peeks at it while Ms.

Hassoon answers questions. She looks for Ben's comeback, but he hasn't replied. It's Catherine.

> **CT:** Where are you?
>
> **SH:** I texted you earlier. I can't come. My mom bogarted the mission.
>
> **CT:** Boo you whore
>
> **SH:** I know, I know. Trust me.
>
> **CT:** Enjoy your poison ivy, peasant. At least plan for girl's night on Thursday. It's the least you can do. Now I'm going to be alone with Hannah all day. You know how that goes.

Shania doesn't know how that goes, but she hesitates. In the end, she just types *good luck* as Ms. Hassoon herds them all toward the buses.

Garfield South Park isn't so much a park as it is a forest. There had been a playground at one point but it's overrun with weeds, the mulch barely visible beneath the wild. There's a gazebo and what might be a basketball court, but it needs to be repaved, every crack overflowing with moss and hosting plants as tall as a toddler. Wildflowers carpet the soccer field.

"It used to be beautiful," assures Mr. Johnson, the parks and rec employee who welcomed Bard off the buses with bins of work gloves and tools. "Before drugs hit this part of Blue Rock pretty hard. Folks are starting a community garden down that way." He gestures past the basketball court. "Inspired by Pocket. But we've got a long way to go. We're hoping to create some spaces where our unhoused neighbors can rest."

He pauses and frowns.

"It's always tough when it starts to get cold, and even tougher this year. A lot of fear in the air. In any case, we appreciate you all coming out to help."

Ms. Hassoon and Mr. Foster split the students into groups, assigning the appropriate tools to their particular task. Shania, Michelle, JP, and a few other people end up together, work gloves and loppers the only tools they're assigned.

"You're the loosestrife crew," Mr. Johnson says, chuckling. "Might be delaying the inevitable, but it's like those folks on that zombie show. You just have to beat back the horde while you can. They brought loosestrife over from Europe in the eighteen hundreds because they thought it was pretty, but it quickly did what loosestrife does."

"My students know all about invasive species," Ms. Hassoon says.

They do. Shania stares at the rolling purple, knowing that to the untrained eye, the flowers look beautiful. Almost like lupins from a distance, painting the playground in a swath of lavender and violet. But getting rid of this infestation will take more than a few high schoolers, she knows. Pulling these plants today is like paying off student loans a penny at a time. Purple loosestrife, allowed to spread, will do so with a vengeance, choking wetlands and crop fields out of existence. Shania has driven through parts of the state where it's overrun acres, crushing out birds and other less hardy plants. From the road driving by, it's beautiful. Until you know better.

Michelle and Shania are the only ones who seem to understand the task at hand. Everyone else seems merely glad to be out of school, and they yank plants slowly and flippantly, mostly goofing off until the occasion that Ms. Hassoon circles past, when suddenly everyone is very serious about weed-pulling. Michelle and Shania frown over their work, Michelle by the swings and Shania by the monkey bars. It's only ten o'clock and now officially autumn, but Shania is still sweating in no time, wiping her forehead with the back of her wrist, careful not to let the glove touch her skin. Her grandmother told Shania once that her mother got poison ivy all over her face like that when she was ten. The pile of loosestrife Shania makes grows bigger and bigger as she works her way down the line, and eventually she and Michelle are pulling stalks side by side.

Shania expects Michelle to speak, as she almost always does. Today she remains silent, the only sound her soft breaths as she yanks plants. Shania glances at her, finds a small frown on her mouth. Her mind arrows to yesterday in the common room, Hannah and Julia swooping in with their Rhino and their swarm of passive aggression. Inside Shania, a hive of anxiety begins to hum.

"Talk about pointless." Shania indicates the loosestrife, testing the waters.

"Some of these have already gone to seed," Michelle mutters, mostly to herself. "They should have had us come when it first flowered. But that would have been before school even started."

"Yeah. This stuff is mutant. I remember when one of my grandma's neighbors was showing her wildflower seeds she bought to plant. Gram took one look at the label, and it had loosestrife in there. She just took the packet right out of the lady's hand."

Michelle pauses, removing her gloves and running her bare hands over her hair, pulled back into a bun.

"Right." Michelle sighs. "Somebody probably planted it here thinking they were making it pretty." She still doesn't look at Shania, but Shania senses she's testing the waters too.

"Whole fields around my hometown were covered in it," Shania says. "Like an alien invasion."

"They don't call them invasive species for nothing." Michelle pulls her gloves back on, looking around. "I wonder if they're going to give us water."

"Or food."

"Community servicing us to death," Michelle says with a chuckle.

Shania smiles, the bees in her stomach quieting their buzz. She wonders if Michelle associates Hannah and Julia with her, if she thinks they're friends. On one hand the idea of it gives Shania a feeling of satisfaction, the idea of having people associated with her. On the other hand, she can't help but think of what Gram would say: *birds of a feather.* What kind of bird is she? Something tells her that joining one flock will keep her from the other. She steals a glance at Michelle, who's intent on the loosestrife, ripping out fistful after fistful. Shania has no idea how Michelle sees her. She doesn't know why she cares. She thinks of Prescott, his lofty apathy for popular consensus. She admires it. She's afraid of it.

"So, how's your final project going?" she says. "For Ms. Hassoon."

"Okay, I think," Michelle says. "The roots are healthy. The growth is strong. I'm even getting some new little buds."

"That's cool. I've got new shoots too. They're really tiny but we still have tons of time."

"Just don't let JP near your planter," Michelle says, grinning. "He'll kill them with one look."

Shania laughs, shaking her head. "What do you mean? He'd probably try to roll them up and smoke them."

Michelle throws back her head and laughs, and Shania feels a combination of pleasure at having made her laugh and envy of the teeth themselves: so white, seeming even whiter against her brown skin.

"Look, I'm sorry about lunch yesterday," Shania says, a blurt of words. "Hannah and Julia...I don't know. They're assholes sometimes."

Michelle doesn't look at her.

"Why didn't you say anything then?" Michelle says, studying the purple blooms. "You know, in front of them. It's easy to say sorry after the fact."

"You think this is easy?" Shania says, laughing a small, awkward laugh.

Michelle looks at her then.

"It should be. Why should apologizing be hard?"

"I...I don't know."

"You know why they hate me, right?" Michelle says, squinting.

"Because you're dating Eric," Shania says, and she has to drop her gaze then. This feels like tiptoeing through a minefield again, but this time the bombs are all ticking loudly.

Michelle shakes her head.

"That's only part of it. You know how Willa and Catherine used to be close?"

Shania scans the park until her eyes land on Willa. She's wearing a red tank top, an inch of her chubby belly exposed to the sunlight. She wipes her sweat, laughing loudly with the group she was assigned to. She looks beautiful, happy. Shania wishes she was her. She wonders why she's always wishing she were someone else.

"Catherine says she stole something from her." Shania shrugs.

"We didn't steal something. We took something back."

"What?"

"A photo," Michelle says. "We took a photo."

"Of what?"

"Oh, thanks for bringing me water, man. You're too kind,"

JP says, too loud. Shania looks up and finds Prescott approaching their work area, two bottles of water in his hands. She's so surprised to see him that she drops the loosestrife she's clutching. She's suddenly very aware of the sweat on her forehead, the smudges of dirt she knows must pattern her face. Her awareness of Michelle beside her is just as sharp.

"What are you doing here?" she asks as he extends one of the bottles of water to her.

"You're welcome." He grins. "What do you mean? It's a school day. I'm at school."

Shania glances around to make sure Ms. Hassoon or someone isn't nearby.

"I assumed you would skip," she says. "Catherine's not here."

"That's Catherine. Plants and dirt and shit? Seemed like the kind of thing you would like, so I pulled out my worst shorts and here I am."

"You shouldn't have worn shorts at all," she says, shaking her head. "You could get poison ivy. Or thorns. Snakes. Anything could be out here."

"But how else would I show off my legs to you?" he says, gesturing at his calves.

Nearby, two girls titter. Shania blushes, pleased. She takes a sip of cold water.

"You probably pull weeds like this every summer, huh, outdoor girl?"

"Not like this," she says. "Loosestrife is more than a weed. It's...dramatic."

"You're the only person I know who would describe a plant as dramatic."

He's taking her in, looking at her jeans, her plain white

T-shirt covered in smears of green. Somehow his smile knows everything, a dance behind his eyes that only she is invited to. But then the dance wanders, its sparkle moving sideways. It narrows. He's staring at Michelle, who has started to leave, walking in the direction of Willa, who Shania sees has paused her work and stands watching from across the park.

"Don't forget your do-rag," Prescott says, his teeth bared in a smile, pointing. It's the bandana Michelle has been using to wipe her sweat, fallen from her pocket onto the grass.

Michelle looks back, mutters something, and continues walking without the bandana.

"What did you say?" Prescott calls after her. Shania's heart has begun to pound, her grip on the water bottle tightening.

"I said fuck you," Michelle says over her shoulder.

"What?" Prescott demands. Michelle stops and turns slowly.

"I said: FUCK. YOU."

Shania stares at Prescott staring at Michelle. She sees the rawness of whatever he's feeling, bare and shining, an ember scattered from the fire. Shania says softly, "Prescott."

He ignores her.

"Do you think I give a shit about you?" he calls to Michelle, almost laughing. "Do you think I give a single fucking shit about you and what you have to say?"

"Maybe you should," Michelle fires back. Far across the park, Willa is a red storm cloud, rushing toward the scene.

"What does that mean?" he says, the smirk still on his lips. Shania can barely look at that smirk. She says his name again, but so quietly no one hears.

"I know about you and your psycho-ass family, okay, little boy?" Michelle shouts. "You think I don't know your sister is

234

as twisted as you are? How you lie for each other, protect each other's nasty little secrets? I see you. I see all of you."

Prescott goes motionless, his whole body transforming into a marble statue. Something about him is snakelike: the long, lethal muscle going still before a strike. Shania stands openmouthed, and so does everyone else, unsure what to do.

"You better watch your mouth," he says softly.

"Prescott," Shania says, louder.

"Yeah?" Michelle says. "You better watch your *back*."

"Or what?" he says, the smirk rising through the clouds of his face again. "Or your boyfriend is going to beat me up? I think we know how that would turn out."

Shania's body fills with weeds, masses of thick vines spreading outward from a single vibrating pod. Michelle snaps her mouth shut, her eyes bright and round, with tears or anger, Shania can't tell. Then Willa charges up.

"Michelle," she says. "I think Ms. Hassoon is looking for you."

Michelle doesn't answer; she's staring at Prescott. Their gazes are locked onto each other, invisible antlers intertwined, both sweating from the sun and the yelling. Michelle's skin has taken on a gleam like a polished violin. Shania can't stop staring at her, she can't make her own mouth speak, she can't find the string in her brain to pluck that will make her legs move.

Willa is leading Michelle away, an arm around her shoulders. Shania's pulse jumps. She waits for Prescott to speak again, to throw some word at their backs. He doesn't.

"Bitch is going to have a heat stroke," JP laughs, and then Prescott is laughing too. Willa and Michelle disappear behind a far-off gazebo. Shania turns to Prescott and her hands are on her hips.

"What the hell?" she says. "What was that all about?"

"Ask her," he says, glowering.

"Okay but I'm asking *you*," she says. "I'd rather hear both sides."

"There's nothing to hear," he scoffs. "She and her boyfriend are spreading all kinds of shit about me and my family and I guess they think no one is going to call them on it."

She hesitates. Her anger feels good—*pizzazz*, a voice in her head whispers—but Prescott stares her down, his eyes blue and unapologetic. Her anger falters. She feels the way she's felt so many times since coming to Bard: that she is on the outside of something peeking in and seeing only a corner. But more than this, she wants to be wrong. She has built a house around Prescott in the neighborhood of her mind. The walls are thick white marble and she wants them to stay that way.

"You don't have to talk to her like that," she says. "She's a girl."

His smile is warmer now, the blue of his eyes less icy. She sees herself at the pupil's center.

"Want me to apologize?" he says.

She crosses her arms.

"Yes."

And then he's down on his knees, his arms around her hips.

"I'm sorry!" he cries as his friends laugh, knowing the apology is to the wrong person. "Will you ever forgive me?"

She tries to pull away but can't and in the end she laughs at the absurdity of it while he kneels, looking up into her eyes. She's satisfied that she tried and tells herself she did the right thing. She doesn't pull any more loosestrife, and the sun goes on beating down.

# CHAPTER 20

Shania's mother wakes her by whipping her blanket off and flinging it into the air.

"Mom, what the hell?" she croaks, eyes barely open.

"What the *heck*," her mother corrects. "Get up."

"What time is it?" Shania reaches for her phone.

"Time to get up! You have a doctor appointment."

"I do?"

"Yes, Shane, get up! I already called school."

They take turns in the bathroom. For all her eagerness to get Shania out of bed, her mother doesn't seem to be in a rush. She's strange and leisurely as they eat cereal and she drinks coffee, sifting through bills. They don't talk much.

"What doctor appointment?" Shania asks when she's putting their bowls in the sink.

"Checkup," she says, looking at her watch. "It's almost ten. Get dressed."

The car smells like her grandmother. Something about autumn leaves and the too-warm smell of the car that still has Gram's

Troll keychain hanging from the rearview. Shania wonders if her mother is so used to it that she's stopped seeing it or if, like Shania, she can still hear Gram saying to rub his naked butt for good luck, the way some people pray before starting the engine.

Shania's mother is quiet as she steers the car out of the neighborhood. She's quiet as she gets on the expressway. She's quiet when she gets off in SoBR.

"I thought I had an appointment," Shania says, thinking she's taking her to Bard.

"We do," she says.

"We?"

"We both do."

They pass Paulie's. Shania peers in and catches a glimpse of Jai through the big shop window. They move on, passing the hidden entrance to the Sparkle Park. They pass El Jefe, where Prescott had taken her for their first date, and her heart skips a beat. Then the car is slowing down on Main, pulling off to the side. Shania peers through the passenger-side window.

"I didn't know there were doctors over here," she says.

"Not exactly."

"Huh?"

Shania looks around, uncomprehending. A flower shop. A coffee shop. A tattoo shop. A place that fixes bicycles. She raises her eyebrows at her mother, seeking an explanation. Her mother holds out a piece of paper.

It's a parental consent form with a notary stamp. The top of the page says *Squid 'n' Ink*. A tattoo shop. Shania raises her eyes to the place outside the car. Its window is dark glass with a big, white squid painted on, the creature squirting ink to spell SQUID 'N' INK. It slowly dawns on her.

"You're . . . you're letting me get a tattoo?"

"Yes. We're both getting them."

"Are you serious?"

"You still want one, right? Don't tell me you changed your damn mind. . . ."

"No! I mean, I didn't change my mind. You're serious?"

"I wouldn't pull you out of school if I wasn't serious! You've been so stressed, and I thought . . ." She trails off. "You seem like you need this, so I hope you're not going to chicken—"

Shania interrupts her with the force of the hug. She inhales deeply to keep from crying and smells the cucumber melon conditioner that her mother has used for as long as she can remember. For some reason it makes her want to cry even more. She doesn't know everything her grandmother knew, and she doesn't know everything her grandmother was. But she knows her mother smells like cucumber melon, and she knows her grandmother loved Trolls and used to drive the very car they're sitting in right now. Surely that's enough, she thinks. Surely.

"You're welcome," her mother says softly. "I understand."

Shania pulls away after a minute, swiping at her face.

"Did you say you're getting one too?"

She bites her lip.

"Yes. But you know I don't like needles, Shane."

"I don't think it even looks like a needle," Shania says, the excitement daring, now, to kindle. "What are you going to get? Where?"

"A pin oak leaf."

"Gram's favorite tree."

"Mm-hmm."

"That's great, Mom."

"I'm getting mine on my shoulder," her mother says. "But that brings me to the next part of the deal. You can get the tattoo but you can either get it on your shoulder or your foot. Nothing on your lower back, nothing on your bicep. No tramp stamps, okay?"

Shania rolls her eyes and laughs.

"People don't call them tramp stamps anymore," she says. "I don't even think people get tattoos there anymore either. Definitely not ones dedicated to their grandmothers."

Her mother stares at her, then brushes a strand of hair out of her face.

"You have your grandma's smile."

"So do you."

Shania is surprised by how busy the shop is on a Thursday morning. She'd pictured a tattoo parlor being the kind of place that's only occupied at night when drunken frat boys from the SoBR bars flood in to get ill-advised sports tattoos. But there's a college-aged girl getting her sleeve worked on and a burly white guy with a crew cut sitting with his shirt off, chatting with the artist who's working on his back. When Shania and her mother walk in, a white woman with very curly blonde hair pops up and walks over.

"Hi again," she says to Shania's mom. "You got the form! Was she surprised?"

They both smile at Shania.

"Very." Shania grins. "She told me I had a doctor appointment."

"Well, I have a PhD from before I was a tattoo artist, and technically this place is filled with needles. So it's not a lie. Come on back."

Her mother goes first, and Shania gets to watch her face go

increasingly pale as the shape of an oak leaf materializes on her shoulder. The tattoo artist, whose name is Linda, instructs Shania to buy a packet of Skittles from the vending machine, and she feeds them to her mother one by one, which helps return some color to her face.

"Have you decided where it's going, Shane?" her mom says when Linda is finishing up.

"My foot."

"I'll warn you," Linda says. "Foot tattoos don't always last as long as other locations. Not that it'll just disappear, but it may fade a bit. Something about the feet and hands. It's your call."

"I have one on my foot," the shirtless man calls from a few benches over. "And it's fine."

From the looks of him, he has a tattoo just about everywhere.

"Really?" Shania says, unsure.

"Yep. Just one foot. I was just telling Richie here that once I get the cover-up job he's working on now done, I'm going to get something new on the other foot."

"Like what?"

"I don't know. Maybe a hobbit or something."

"Oh. Okay."

In the end Shania decides upon the foot, reasoning that it will be easier to reach while it heals and requires care. She sits nervously while Linda runs a razor over her already hairless foot and cleans the entire area. The outline of the lilac Linda has drawn on Shania's skin is perfect but dull, and soon her grandmother's favorite flower will bloom bright and sunny. It makes her feel open, friendly, the way her grandmother had been.

"You said you're getting something covered up?" she asks the guy who had spoken to her.

"Yep. Hurts worse than the original tattoo for some reason. But it's worth it."

Behind him is a giant mirror tilted down over the tattoo bench. In its reflection Shania can see the guy's whole back, covered in a patchwork of tattoos, some big and some small, hardly any of them related to the others. As the tattoo gun begins to do its work on her foot, the pain like a burn and a bee sting all at once, she focuses on studying the man's tattoos, a mosaic of life decisions. They're all simple, but some are more detailed: a ship, the head of a deer, a grim reaper. Others just look like symbols. A red circle with a line through it. A stylized eight. It's not until Richie the tattoo artist gets up to get a bottle of water that Shania can see a piece of the tattoo the man is having covered up.

A swastika.

At first she thinks it's something else, since a piece of it has already been successfully covered by the lion head Richie is inking over top of it. But the brash lines are unmistakable. There is—or was—a black-and-red swastika on his back. She looks away just as the man sees her staring.

"It's okay," he says. "I'm ashamed, but not of getting it covered up."

Shania's mother has been using the mirror in Linda's booth to examine her new oak leaf. Shania watches her gaze lift to the guy's face, studying him. Her mother makes some mental calculation and then returns to looking in the mirror. If she doesn't sense a threat, then Shania decides he must be okay.

"A lion is a much better choice," Linda says mildly. She doesn't look up from her work. Her tools go over a tiny bone in Shania's foot—she winces.

"I might need a few more lions," the guy says, gazing down at his arms. Those are covered in ink too, mostly symbols, some of them faded and scratchy looking, like they were done by a shaky-handed toddler.

"I'll cover them all for you," Richie says. "We give a twenty-five percent discount for people covering up swastikas and stuff, so if you know anyone else..."

"Just me," says the guy, frowning. "I don't have too many friends these days."

"I'll be your friend," Richie says.

Linda shifts in her seat. "Why'd you get them to begin with?" she says. She's concentrating harder on Shania's tattoo now, her eyebrows furrowed.

"I was a different person then," he says. "The kind of person who thought he was going to be replaced in this world. Fear will make you do a lot of dumb shit."

Shania glances at her mother but she's flipping through Linda's portfolio binder and doesn't seem to hear.

"Replaced," Linda repeats. "Doesn't that kind of imply that you thought you owned the 'place' to begin with?"

The guy nods.

"Yep. Lot of arrogance in the world I came from."

"To say the least," she says.

"But you're different now," Richie interjects. "You've changed. That's what matters."

"Kind of," Linda mumbles.

"You can turn this one into something cool," Richie says, indicating the green triangle on the guy's upper bicep. It's a simple symbol and looks newer than the others: a triangle with the point aiming downward, three lines inside connecting at the center and moving outward to each interior point of the triangle.

Shania has seen it somewhere before, but she's not sure where. It looks almost like the logo for an expensive car brand.

"What does that one mean?" Shania says, pointing. "The green triangle."

He looks down, searching his body. He frowns when he finds it.

"Yeah, this one's gonna need a lion head or something too," he says.

"It looks newish."

"I got it in 2017," he says. "Funny. That was the same year I started getting my head out of my ass. Wish I had done it before I got this goddamn tattoo."

"What happened?" she says, trying to distract herself from the needling of her foot, but also fascinated by this living butterfly, a person metamorphosing right in front of her, it seems. "I mean, what made you decide to? To change, I mean."

His frown deepens, and he stares at the tattoo as if it's a vortex drawing him in.

"A girl died," he says simply.

The shop seems to have gone quiet. Linda is listening intently; Shania can tell by the way her movements have gotten slow and small. The only sound in the parlor is the low buzz of the guns.

"How...?"

"I went to a demonstration. I thought I was there for noble reasons." He gestures at his arms. "A lifetime of feeling lost. So many years of playing the victim. *Secure our border, secure our future.* All that bullshit. But then that girl died. And I saw it. And the way people talked about her—people who were in the same groups as me, on the same path as me—the way they spit on her name and her life...something shifted. I don't know. It took over a year, and I'm still fighting against myself. It's like an addiction, but this"—he points at the green triangle—"is an ugly thing. And I don't want my life to be filled with ugliness. I may have done and believed fucked-up shit. But I'm making a choice."

Shania glances down at Linda, whose brow remains furrowed. No one speaks. The guy doesn't seem to be looking for a response—he just stares down at the images covering his body. Shania wonders what other memories flow out of them, if there are more deaths hidden in the coils of the snake that curls by his wrist. She doesn't dare ask. The green triangle is familiar. It's all familiar. In her head, the stones of buildings tremble.

"What do your parents think?" Richie says. "I know when some people . . . change . . . they lose their parents too."

"I lost my dad," the guy says without hesitation. "I learned a lot of this from him. But the more I dug into my own beliefs, the more I uncovered about his. So many lies. Some big, some small. But lies nonetheless. I don't think he ever really believed the conspiracies he raised me and my brother on—it was just an excuse to be hateful."

"Were you aware of all that stuff?" Richie says. "Growing up?"

"That's the funny thing," the guy says. "So many things were a big secret. He would talk about white pride and all that bullshit. But in public it was all . . . coded? Does that make sense? He would just slap a thin-blue-line bumper sticker on his car and argue with people on the internet. But he had friends, military friends. Some of them went to jail for the assault on the Capitol. And, I mean, outside actual physical violence, he worked at a bank, you know? He decided who got a loan and who didn't." He shakes his head. "I love my dad. But I can only love part of him, you know? Maybe one day he'll make amends. On my part, it's a daily battle. It really is like an addiction, you know? You have to be conscious. Intentional. Every day."

"What do you think?" Linda says, swiping away blood and ink. Shania looks away from the green triangle and the half swastika and down at the lilac she knows so well. She can almost smell the flowers, hanging upside down in her grandmother's kitchen as they dried, where they would remain until Gram took them down and put them in vases around the house. They didn't retain their scent, but the sight of them was enough. A house full of sweetness. Goodness.

"Thank you," she says softly. She feels nauseated.

"I don't know if your grandmother would've loved it," her mother says, hovering. "But let's pretend."

"Yes," Shania says, staring. Something inside her feels upside down like those far-off flowers. "Let's pretend."

# CHAPTER 21

It's turning into boot weather but Shania wears sandals to let her tattoo heal. Her toes are cold on the bus to school, but she stares down at her nearly bare feet and thinks of Gram, feels the scream knitted in her throat, the hollowness in her body that she has come to associate with her grandmother's absence. She thought the tattoo would fill it, if only slightly. But she'd spent the night with the lilacs on her skin and woken up feeling worse. Something else has been planted along with the lilacs, and as the buildings the bus passes rise with the coming of SoBR and downtown, she takes out her phone, swipes down to Hallie's name.

**How's Morrisville?** she texts.

A few minutes later a reply comes through. Shania can picture Hallie slumped in the cab of her dad's green pickup, school bound.

**It's Morrisville ☹. No, it's fine. It feels different lately. Like things are changing. It's really subtle tho. What about Blue Rock? I saw there was a protest there last weekend.**

Shania blinks—it feels like they picked up in the middle of a conversation she didn't know they'd been having.

**There was?** she texts.

The typing bubbles appear, then stop. When they appear again, Hallie replies:

**lol Yeah, haven't you been paying attention?**

Shania stiffens in the cold blue seat of the BRTA bus. Ever since Prescott had talked about a time machine, she's been thinking of ways to time travel. She'd texted Hallie because she wanted to step into the past—pull the lever and rocket back to what felt safe and secure. Instead it's as if Gram's home shatters, wooden shards as sharp as teeth.

**It's not like I would really have a choice with you always talking about it**, Shania types angrily. **Just stick to doing theater, Hallie, Jesus**

She stares at her phone, waiting for the bubbles, for the reply. But there's nothing—Hallie leaves her on read, and in the city of Shania's mind, she relegates Hallie to another neighborhood. But she doesn't feel any better, and as she stares down at her fresh tattoo, the sharp pieces of her memories sharpen further into glass.

The bus passes the street that would take her back to the library, where she had uncovered her great-grandfather's words: *Daughter. His daughter. In Western Pocket.* By the time she nears Bard, the memories are needles. They dig into her the way the tattoo had. When the bus passes Bard, she lets it. She stays on past Thirteenth Street, past Twenty-Third. She could read the book of poems she carries in her bag, but she's too wired. Something about Hallie's text—*haven't you been paying attention?*—has ignited her, propels her. She *has* been paying attention. Blue ink. Green triangle. Newspaper. A shoebox full of secrets. The bus is carrying her forward and she thinks there's no going back now. She has only been on this road once, but her feet remember the path.

Mrs. Walker is in the garden as Shania knew she would be. The whole way up the block Shania had felt her there in the garden like the crater at the end of a comet's arc. She sees her before she's even crossed under the entry arch: a thin Black woman, her head bent against the sun, a hat wide and yellow like the halos painted on church ceilings. She must feel Shania coming the way Shania had felt her waiting: When Shania crosses under the arch, the old woman raises her face to take her in, studying her with a frown that's not unkind, but perplexed, trying to decide the purpose of a white girl with faded pink-and-blue hair in the Western Pocket Community Garden. She doesn't rise to meet her. She crouches by the neat rows of soil where she'd been preparing things for the colder months. When Shania approaches, Mrs. Walker removes her gloves.

"What can I do for you?" she says. Her voice is as soft as her wrists, peeking out of her long-sleeved white shirt.

"Um, hi," says Shania. "I was here recently. For the event. The fundraiser."

"Do you live in the area?" says Mrs. Walker, confused but too polite to say so.

"No," Shania says quickly. "No. I live...I don't know... I think the neighborhood is called Washburn. We just moved here."

"All right," Mrs. Walker says. Her eyes slide down Shania's arms to her hands, seeing if she's brought something, something that might explain what she's doing here.

"I...I go to school with Michelle," Shania says.

The eyes soften then, the folds on either side of her mouth lifting.

"Oh, you do, do you? Michelle Broadus? That's a good girl. That's a good, smart girl."

Shania nods.

"Yeah. Yeah, she's really cool. She's, um, really good with plants."

"She sure is. Better than I was at her age. I had a small garden myself when I was seventeen, but I didn't figure out the way things really grow until I was much older. Michelle has the touch."

Shania thinks of Michelle's jeweled roses, the way they command the light in the greenhouse. Shania wants to be that good, that effortless. Nothing ever feels effortless, she realizes. Like this conversation.

"When I came," Shania says, "to the fundraiser, I mean. I talked to someone, an older lady, who said this whole block used to be houses."

"Mm-hmm, it did." She nods. "The same kind you see all around you. Big, pretty houses. I lived in one of them for a long time. A different one now."

"You did?"

"Yes, I did."

She's staring at Shania curiously now, waiting for something. Shania is waiting too: for a signal, a sign, for Mrs. Walker to read her mind and just tell her what she wants to know. She doesn't want this work to fall to her—she wants someone else, anyone, to take it up.

"When?" she finally says, her tongue clumsy.

"When?" Mrs. Walker echoes.

"When . . . when did you live here?"

"I still live here," she says, a little stiffly. "But I moved onto this block in 1959."

"Nineteen fifty-nine," Shania whispers.

"Is something the matter with you?" Mrs. Walker says, none too gently. She's suspicious now and Shania can't blame her for it. She feels like a possum skulking around a lit porch, working up the nerve to enter the light.

"No. I mean, yes. I mean, no. I just... I'm trying to figure some things out. My... my grandmother died. And never said she lived in Blue Rock, never even said she visited, but..."

A long pause and then Mrs. Walker prods: "But?"

"But I think she did. I think... I think she lived here."

She points at the ground. At the garden. At this place.

Mrs. Walker raises her eyebrows, and Shania only then truly notices that she wears glasses, small gold-framed things that catch the sunlight peeking under the brim of her hat. Mrs. Walker stands up, slowly and carefully, each muscle being tested before being entrusted fully. Once standing, she bends to pick up her gloves, thoughtfully, one at a time.

"What was your grandmother's name?" she says eventually.

"Helen. Helen Rutherford."

Mrs. Walker stares at her through the small, glittery frames of her glasses. The softness left over from Michelle's name in her mouth has gone.

"I think I knew you were going to say that."

"You knew her?"

"We knew each other, you could say."

The breeze picks up and the plants around them shift.

"It's going to rain soon," Mrs. Walker says, not breaking her gaze on Shania. "Come sit."

She gestures behind her, where Shania sees the wooden gazebo. There's a picnic table inside it, where they must have served the cake at the event. She hadn't stayed long enough to see. Now she follows Mrs. Walker across the garden and a moment later they're sitting across from each other at the table. There's a wooden bowl between them, a few tomatoes and a cucumber clustered together in its bottom.

"So you're Helen Rutherford's granddaughter," she says. "And I suppose that makes you the great-granddaughter of William Rutherford II."

"Yes."

"How do you feel about that?"

Mrs. Walker pulls a round, yellow piece of candy from her pocket, slowly unwraps it. Shania gawks at her.

"How...how do I feel about it?"

Mrs. Walker nods.

"I don't...I don't know? I barely remember him. My mom loved him. I think I remember his voice? He was always laughing."

Mrs. Walker nods again.

"Yes, he was."

"So you knew him too?"

"He was my neighbor," Mrs. Walker says. "Your grandmother is—was, rest in peace—around the same age as me. They lived at twenty-three when we moved into twenty-one. Our backyards shared a fence. It was right about"—she pauses, squinting somewhere in the middle distance, then raises a finger to point—"right about there."

"Wait, so *here*?" Shania says, looking around. "The houses used to be right here?"

"That's right. You were told correctly: This whole block was houses until around the time my mama and daddy passed away. Nineteen ninety-eight—one after the other. June and July."

"How did it get turned into a garden?"

Mrs. Walker's mouth tightens, hiding some of her lips. She remains staring at the place the fence once was. She has the same look Shania's mother gets when she starts thinking about Gram, at the end of the day when there's no work and the dishes are done and the memories come sighing under the door.

"I'm surprised you don't know," Mrs. Walker says.

Shania thinks of all the things Michelle and Willa and everyone else seem to know about Blue Rock, its stories and its histories.

"I just got to Blue Rock," Shania says. "There's a lot of stuff I don't know, I guess."

"This has nothing to do with Blue Rock," Mrs. Walker says. "It's got to do with your great-grandfather."

Shania stares at her, her tongue motionless in her mouth. She thinks if she moves, even to touch the fang at the front of her jaw, something around her will break. Mrs. Walker stares back at her, perhaps waiting for that same breaking thing. Eventually she sighs.

"I'd better show you."

Mrs. Walker slides down the bench of the picnic table, reaching for a plastic Tupperware box. She drags it toward her, unlatches its lid, throws it back to reveal rows of manila folders and papers.

"All the information about the garden," Mrs. Walker says, mostly to herself. "Have to keep it on hand. Been caring for this land for twenty years and the police still stop by sometimes and ask for documentation. They want me to prove I have a right to dig around in this dirt. Well, I have the right and I have the proof. I keep it all right here."

She thumbs through the folders, peering over the top of the dainty gold glasses.

"Here it is. Take a look."

She holds the paper out to Shania and Shania stares at it, her heart thumping heavily in her head. She watches her hand reach out and accept the paper from Mrs. Walker.

"That's a record of sale," Mrs. Walker says as Shania's eyes pass over the words on the page. It's a copy, and even it is old: tattered, some words faded. But she sees *Mrs. Berniece Walker* written there as the buyer. And as she lets her eyes rove over the paper, she sees another name she knows, this time listed as the seller.

*Helen Rutherford.*

The garden around her goes blurry, a long, bending moment, before everything comes into focus again.

"You . . . you bought this land from my grandmother?"

Mrs. Walker nods, rubbing her chin with one knuckle, her gaze steady.

Shania peers at the paper.

"It says she sold it to you for a dollar."

"Yes, she did."

Shania looks around, taking in the long block, its rows that go on and on, the trees that shield it from the street.

"A dollar? In 1999? That seems—"

"Cheap," Mrs. Walker says, a ghost of a smile on her mouth. "Impossible. Dirt cheap. Your great-grandfather was madder than a cat on fire."

"Because my grandmother sold the land?"

"Sold it. Sold it to me. Ruined all his plans."

"What plans?"

Mrs. Walker does smile now, a slow-spreading thing, as if the memory is too sweet not to cherish.

"He'd already paid to have it cleared when he had a stroke. I don't think you were born yet. It was in all the papers. He'd owned the homes for a long time—renting to Black tenants for a profit—but eventually he kicked out all the tenants and had the houses demolished. Was going to build a couple liquor stores, a fast mart. That sort of thing."

Shania's stomach turns soft, a swamp hollowing out her gut. She remembers the newspaper clipping on the microfilm, Rutherford II's plans laid out for all to see. He followed through. Tried.

"That stroke had him on bedrest," Mrs. Walker went on. "He gave the land to his only child—your granny—and she came all the way back to Blue Rock from the country to oversee the development. But she did something unexpected. She sold it to me instead."

"Why? I mean, not that I'm not happy for you. Because now you have this garden. But why did she do that?"

"I'd say your granny thought she owed me. And maybe she was right."

"A lady at the garden fundraiser said you won the lottery," Shania says slowly.

Mrs. Walker looks down her nose.

"I didn't. But the odds were the same."

The smile is gone again. Mrs. Walker holds out her hand for the paper, and when she's stowed it back in its folder inside the box, she stands from the table.

"Walk with me."

Shania glances up at the sky, the gray moodier than ever, rain threatening the garden with its blessing. But Mrs. Walker has already left the gazebo, is moving down one of the rows. She carries the bowl of vegetables. Shania hurries to follow.

"I'll tell you something," Mrs. Walker says. "This place took a long time to become what it is. There was rubble. There was rock. There was glass. There were things from before stuck in the soil: nails and screws. No place for good things to take root. The same was true for me. Bad memories. Made me question whether I even wanted to stay in this place. I traveled a lot before I came back to Blue Rock in 1995. When I turned eighteen in 1961, I lit out of here like a bat out of hell. Your granny had a little to do with that."

The clouds far above move slowly across the sky. Here on the ground they seem to circle. Shania feels them wrapping around her, the story Mrs. Walker tells like a slow cyclone.

"What do you mean," Shania says, barely a question. She can feel it coming. Whatever it is. Fog has been gathering since she opened her grandmother's almanac from 1999. Now it shifts.

"I told you your grandmother was my neighbor," said Mrs. Walker. "When I first moved into Western Pocket with my family in 1959."

"Yes."

"This is where the fence was," Mrs. Walker says, sweeping her arm left to right. They're standing right at the line. It's a row of vegetables now, their stalks shrinking with the breath of fall.

"Did something happen?" Shania can hear her voice in her ears like a stranger's.

"Yes. Close your eyes and I'll tell you. Since Helen didn't."

Shania doesn't want to close her eyes. She just wants to look away. But Mrs. Walker is staring right at her and her only choice is to slowly let her eyelids down, leaving her in the dark as Mrs. Walker's voice swirls around her. Shania is rooted to the spot.

"I was planting our first vegetables. We'd lived on Chestnut for three weeks. I'd always liked to help things grow. I was crouched down over the soil when I heard the back door open across the fence. I looked up, and there on the back porch was your grandmother, Helen, and a few of her friends. One other girl and a few boys, all wearing the uniforms from their high school. Helen was smoking a cigarette."

Mrs. Walker's voice leads Shania through a tunnel into memory. Shania sees the version of her grandmother that her mother keeps a portrait of in the bedroom: young, narrow smile, eyes ocean-gray and sparkling. The tooth Shania inherited. Gram isn't Gram yet—she's Helen, a high schooler, stepping out with her friends into the sun, laughing. Her parents are out of town. It's a Friday: The friends are there for a small party, carrying booze they'd procured from older siblings. They approach Helen's garden, the one she'd started with her mother, and move among the plants. Helen has been gardening her whole life, her own mother plucked from the country when she married William Rutherford II. Helen has three tomato plants that are surviving. Cucumber. Beets. She and her friends have moved among the rows, the sound of their laughter cutting through the leaves, when they notice the Black girl who just moved in next door, frozen in her yard. Seeing them see her, she raises her hand to wave. She's wearing gardening gloves, the fabric bright white against her dark-brown skin. Helen and her friends stare. Western Pocket has always been theirs. A hello floats across the fence from the new neighbor's mouth. It's a small, gentle word but enters the pack of teenagers like a spark among dry brush. The boys mutter while Helen stares at her mother's vegetables. She picks the tomato she'd been stroking, its flesh red and round and falling into her hand. Her girlfriend whispers something, laughs. Helen laughs too. The laughter is a relief, a reminder. It feels as good as the beer. The white girls walk to the fence, cigarettes glowing like their eyes.

The Black girl across the fence—Berniece Walker, sixteen— lights up with hope for a moment. The fence is so short between them: waist high, more decor than barrier, small and painted so white. Words are exchanged. A question, another laugh. Shania sees it all.

She sees Helen Rutherford roll the tomato into the square of her palm. Shania feels her grandmother's muscles tense, feels the laugh like lightning through her jaw. She sees the hope freeze in Berniece Walker's face. Shania feels the tomato leave her own hand. She sees its slow, fast journey through space toward the Black girl carrying a basket in the sunshine. Shania hears the sound of it striking that girl's face, she hears the scream mag- netize the air, drawing Berniece Walker's parents out of their new home, into the backyard, where their daughter stands cry- ing. They think she's hurt, and she is. Her hurt will last decades. Across the fence, Helen Rutherford throws something else: a word. That word sails across the fence, heavier and sharper and redder than a tomato. It strikes them all. It leaves a mark.

Berniece Walker's parents have brought their child here in search of a future that shines. The tomato crumples it. They shout, and Helen feels a pale sort of fear beside a brighter sort of anger, and soon the boys from Helen's school are shouting too, alcohol and entitlement sending them leaping over the fence. Helen screams from her side as the boys in matching uniforms overturn the glass table in the backyard, sending shards into the grass. They tear the tomatoes off the Walkers' vines, throw them like grenades. They uproot everything with life. The boy who had been holding Helen's hand rushes back to the fence, he reaches for her cigarette. She sees what he intends to do and passes it over the fence.

The cigarette's trajectory is a neat red arc and is at first swallowed by the gray settling of dusk. The other boys go on flattening the garden while the Walkers' stand far away, Berniece crying behind the wall her parents build with their bodies. They don't call the police, only watch. Helen watches her cigarette, which coughs into the dry grass, then laughs outward toward the ruined rows of okra and everything else. And while the neighbor's yard burns, Helen Rutherford doesn't look away. She opens her mouth and the word that comes out is one last tomato, one last flaming thing.

The church that Shania has been building in her head loses its bricks. She opens her eyes, which are filled with tears. Berniece Walker is gazing into them.

"What did she call you?" Shania whispers to ensure she doesn't scream. She's asking from the future, standing in the past.

Berniece Walker sighs, and lifts her eyes to the gray sky, which will eventually weep. She reaches into the bowl and retrieves a tomato, and after staring at it for a moment, rolls it gently into Shania's hand.

"Honey," she says, "what do you think?"

# CHAPTER 22

Shania's mother calls her three times before she answers. When the text comes through—**Shane, I need to know that you're alive**—she finally steps out of the library, where she's been for the last four hours, and calls her back.

"Where the hell are you?" her mother says immediately. "School called me to say you didn't show up! I saw you get on the bus, where have you—"

"I'm at the library," Shania says.

"What? The *library*? You expect me to believe—"

"Gram was from Blue Rock, Mom. Did you know that?"

"Shane, what are you—"

"She was born in Blue Rock. She lived here. She went to school here. Great-Grandpa Bill was from here too. Your granddad. You had to have known this, right?"

She can feel her mother's rage fizzling, turning blue.

"I knew Grandpa Bill lived in the city up until his stroke," she says quickly. "But your grandmother spent so much of her life in Morrisville that I—"

"Never thought to ask?" Shania interrupts.

"I thought to ask, but you know how Gram was. She was private, Shania. She didn't like talking about her childhood. Her biological mother died when Gram was just ten or so. Grandpa Bill's second wife was a nutjob. It was hard. We just let the past be the past."

"But in 1999 it's not like you were a baby. Did she not tell you that she traveled to Blue Rock? When Great-Grandpa Bill had his stroke? That she sold his land?"

Silence. Then her mother's deep sigh.

"You start digging around in the past and all you get is dirty, Shania. Why does it matter? And more importantly: *Why aren't you in school?*"

"I just can't, Mom. I can't today. I'm trying to figure everything out."

"Figure what out? You 'just can't' go to school? What do you think this is, Shania Marie? You *have* to go to school!"

"I know, I just...I *can't* today!"

"So you've been, where, the *library* all day?"

Shania doesn't answer right away. She'd left the Western Pocket Community Garden in a hurry, Mrs. Walker staring after her. She'd gotten all the way to the bus stop before she realized she still carried the tomato Mrs. Walker had slipped into her hand. It's in her bag now, peeking out at her like a glowing, red secret.

"Yes," she says to her mother.

"Shane, I know you've been having a hard time. Gram's death was sudden. And your dad off being a piece of shit. I understand how it feels like everything is screwed up. Me and your dad... well, I know we weren't the easiest people to get along with while we were married. And Gram was your go-to. I try. I thought getting you into this school, starting over in a new city—"

"But it's not new, Mom," Shania says. "It's *not* new."

"It's new for *you*," her mother says, a little hard. "It's new for *us*."

Shania squeezes her eyes shut tight, thinking of the secret box under her mother's bed, her grandmother's wool and gardening gloves hidden away from light and eyes. This is a box within the box. Has her mother ever looked inside?

"I'm going to stay at the library and do some research before work," Shania says eventually.

Her mother hears research and thinks "school." She doesn't imagine her daughter peering at the blurry, shining screen of the microfilm, searching the lines of old text for her great-grandfather's name, for fire, for anything mentioning her grandmother and who she might have been in the years before she shed Blue Rock like an old skin.

"I'll see you tonight," her mother says. "We can talk then."

"Okay," Shania says. She knows they won't. It'll be avoided, all the sharp parts smoothed. All she can hear is Gram's voice: *Liars. Liars. Liars.* "See you later."

She hangs up and holds the phone to her face for a while, the warmth from its tiny battery almost like sunshine. When it vibrates against her cheekbone she yelps in surprise. It's Ben.

**BT: Sorry about "good girl." That was stupid.**

She glares at the screen, at this apology. She feels cheated in some absurd way she can't pinpoint, like biting a grape instead of an olive. She doesn't want sweet. At this moment she wants to taste acid.

**SH:** It took you this long to apologize?

**BT:** I had some denial at first. I was trying to justify the joke to myself and was convincing myself that you not liking it meant you didn't get it, but then I realized I was just being an asshole.

**SH:** Yes, you were.

She's mad, madder than she had been about the joke itself. She doesn't know where the red behind her eyes comes from. She's furious.

**BT:** I acknowledge that. Just saying sorry.

She's formulating a response when the shape of Willa Langford, dressed for work at the museum, passes across Shania's field of vision. Willa walks briskly, appearing and then disappearing across the length of sidewalk framed by the pillars at the bottom of the steps. Half a beat later, her head pops back from where it had disappeared, peering up at Shania.

"I thought that was you," she says. She doesn't move to climb the stairs.

Shania's still holding her phone. She just nods blankly, cursing her luck.

"Michelle said you weren't in class today. You skipped?"

"I guess so."

Willa steps fully back into the frame of the staircase.

"Not to be judgy about your truancy," she says, "but generally when you skip school, you go somewhere better than the library. At the very least you just stay home."

Shania rolls her eyes.

"Just saying." Willa moves to carry on down the sidewalk and then pauses again. "Are you, um, okay?"

"I'm fine."

Willa purses her lips.

"If you say so." She looks around. "Are you waiting for him to pick you up or something?"

"Who?"

"Prescott."

Shania's stomach sags a little at the mention of his name from Willa's mouth. The events in the park at community service day come rushing back. With her grandfather at her back and Willa at her front, Shania is a half-puffed hedgehog sensing a hand hovering near.

"No, he's not picking me up. I'm just sitting. Is that okay with you?"

"I would say it's a free country," Willa says, "but it's not. Still, you can feel free to sit your ass right there as long as you want. Nobody's stopping you."

Willa moves again to carry on, and her nonchalance grates Shania, pricks her like a hidden thorn piercing a gardening glove. She puts her phone and Ben away and grabs up this place to put her anger.

"Are you always such a bitch?" Shania calls, loud enough to catch Willa by the heel, which is all that's visible of her, walking away, by the time Shania finds her voice. Willa's head pops back in again, her expression smooth.

"Yes," she says. "Are you just now noticing?"

"I've definitely noticed," Shania snaps. "Same way I've noticed how desperate you are for approval."

"Whose?" says Willa, laughing. "Yours?"

"Michelle's," she says, her anger rising. "Tierra's. Like you want them to forget you used to be friends with Catherine Tane and Julia Hwang and all these other people that it's popular to hate."

"Popular to hate," Willa repeats, and there's mirth in her voice but she's not laughing. "You think Catherine Tane is a victim here, is that what you think? You see yourself as her bodyguard or something? You're protecting *Catherine*?"

"She's my friend," Shania says, shrugging. "So, yeah, you know, I'm going to stick up for my friend. All this bullshit between you and Michelle and the Tanes is he-said-she-said. It's from before I was"—she almost says *born*—"before I was at Bard."

Willa studies her, then climbs up one step. Shania tightens her fists.

"I don't expect anyone to forget me and Catherine were friends," she says. "I'll never not be embarrassed of that. But once I saw through her, there was no turning back. And Catherine hates me for it."

"Catherine doesn't give a shit about you fucking nardsharks," Shania says.

Willa stares at her for a long moment before she laughs, everything behind it sinking into them both. Shania's blush is deep and hot. The house that Prescott builds around Shania is gone when she's talking to Willa. She wonders what Ben builds before she can stop herself.

"Catherine wishes that was true," Willa says. "Catherine wishes she didn't give a shit about me. But deep down, Catherine knows that everything about her that makes people worship her—pretty, rich, white, smart, witty—is all a fucking farce. She knows I know the truth. And *that* is why Catherine hates me. Because I'm a mirror that doesn't lie."

"What was the photo that you and Michelle stole from her?"

Shania says. She doesn't know why she needs to know. But she does. The question shudders in her chest like an egg that could hatch either a chicken or a dragon. She doesn't know which she'd prefer.

"Ask your BFF," Willa says. She steps back down to the sidewalk. Her eyes suddenly seem very blue. "Do you think she'll tell you the truth?"

And then she's gone, and even when Shania calls her name twice, loud enough to be embarrassing to the other people walking past, Willa does not appear again.

# CHAPTER 23

When Shania walks through the door to Paulie's on Saturday, there's an older white woman she's never seen before wearing an apron. She tosses Shania one exactly like it and laughs a smoker's cackle.

"Aprons!" she says. "We all have to wear 'em now."

She has the same kind of skin as Shania's grandmother: sun worn and spotted with brown. Her hair is hidden underneath a Paulie's cap.

"Are we switching from visors to hats?" Shania asks.

"Nope, I've had this hat since my first week on the job," she says. "In 1995. They don't do caps anymore. But now we've got aprons."

"You've worked here for that long?"

"Yup. Other places too. I was a secretary at the hospital. Transcription at the police station. Bus driver for a while. But this is my longest gig."

"Oh!" Shania says, remembering. "You're Dorothy."

The woman cackles again.

"I must have a reputation."

"No. I mean, yes, but no. Jai was telling me you used to work in the police station, that's all."

"That Jai," she says fondly. She takes a coffee cup hidden beneath the counter and sips. "What a motormouth."

"Yeah," Shania laughs. "But he makes the time go by."

Time mercifully goes by with Dorothy too. Every time Shania starts to think of what Mrs. Walker had told her, Dorothy is providing commentary on the customer about to enter the shop.

"I can't remember a Saturday he didn't come in," she says after an old man in a leather-elbowed blazer leaves the shop. "Used to come in with his wife, and they'd each get a cinnamon bun. She passed a while back but he still gets two cinnamon buns, one for him and one for the birds."

A girl in head-to-toe pink spandex.

"She's always so matchy. Don't know how she does it. Only gets a cake doughnut. Disciplined."

A dark-skinned man buying a dozen.

"On his way to the Ethiopian Women's Society. Smart fella. Showing up to a women's meeting with chocolate."

On and on. It's noon before Shania knows it. One hour left and the traffic has slowed.

"It'll pick up again this evening," she says. "But we'll be well outta here by then, won't we? Night shift is Jai's problem."

Shania's pocket vibrates a text alert. Prescott. She hasn't heard from him in days, but her brain has been full of the Pocket garden, the land where her grandmother once lived, where beyond her fence a fire once burned. Prescott would be a welcome distraction if it weren't for what she knew about Eric. She stares down at the text for a moment before replying.

**PT:** Where are you?

**SH:** At work.

**PT:** Damn. I was hoping you were free.

**SH:** What's up?

**PT:** Just need to get out of the house.

**SH:** What's wrong?

**PT:** Family is pissing me off. Need a breather.

She hesitates. What Julia has told her is the buzz of a radio stuck between stations. She could tune it out. She wants to. Prescott reached out to her, after all, and her heart looks for a soft place for him to land. She needs a soft place too.

**SH:** I'm off in an hour...?

**PT:** You can't get off early?

Shania glances up. She thinks she could probably leave early but she's never worked with Dorothy before and doesn't like the idea of it getting back to Mr. Ahmed. He was annoyed enough when she switched her schedule to daytime.

She decides to reply with a sad panda GIF.

**PT:** Fine, fine. Pick you up in an hour.

She puts her phone away and looks up to find Dorothy watching her with a smirk.

"Boyfriend, huh? Or girlfriend, maybe. I don't know. Ain't bothering me."

"Not really a boyfriend," Shania mumbles.

"Well, why not?"

"I don't know, we're kind of just hanging out right now."

"Mm-hmm. Do your friends not approve?"

"Huh?"

"My first husband, Larry, I took forever to marry him because my friends hated him and said he was a pig. Honey, they were *right*."

Shania laughs. This sounds like something her mother would say, and it's the first time she's laughed about her parents' divorce. It almost feels wrong, but laughing is a salve.

"My dad was Mister Right for my mom at first," Shania says. "I think it would have been different if we lived somewhere like Blue Rock. We're from a small town and it's different there. Like, you have your high school sweetheart and you're just kind of expected to marry them."

"Ain't just small towns," Dorothy says. "Larry was my high school sweetheart, too, I just took my time about it. Blue Rock felt like a small town once upon a time."

"Have you always lived here?" Shania asks. Dorothy is younger, probably in her sixties, but Shania is thinking of Gram.

"I sure have. Went away for six months for a job in Iowa but couldn't stand it and came right back. Probably should've stayed."

"Have you ever heard of white flight?"

Dorothy glances at her, eyebrows at different angles.

"Well, sure. Happened a lot in Blue Rock. Still happening in some parts." She looks ahead, out the shop windows again at the people walking by. "SoBR is kind of the reverse now, ain't it? White folks running in and not out."

"Why does it always have to be *white*," Shania sighs. She wouldn't have said it to Jai, not after their last conversation. But she feels some kind of kinship with Dorothy: maybe because she reminds her of her grandmother. In the city of Shania's mind,

Dorothy is from the same neighborhood as her. Which is why when Dorothy cackles, Shania is surprised.

"You don't like thinking of yourself as a white or something?" Dorothy laughs, then takes a loud sip of coffee. "You think this is all something that doesn't have anything to do with you?"

Shania thinks of Prescott, standing on the roof with him, the breeze in their hair and him encircling her with the word *us*. He seemed angry about it then, but with some distance between that conversation and this one, the anger fades out of her mind and only the words are left. They make her feel better somehow, to have something to lean on in a conversation that makes her uncomfortable.

"I just don't see how it matters," Shania replies. "I mean, I know race exists. I'm not stupid. I just feel like people read into it more than necessary. Like what does SoBR have to do with race? Because the people who came in to clean it up happened to be white? Who cares, if they're trying to make it better?"

"You said you just moved to Blue Rock, didn't you?" Dorothy says.

"Yeah."

"So you never saw Southtown before it became SoBR."

"No."

"Then how do you know it's better, honey?"

The bell above the door rings, and they both turn back to the door, expecting a customer. Instead it's Earl, his orange jacket as filthy as ever, his hair matted. He shuffles up to the counter and Shania's fingers tighten.

"What'll it be, Earl?" Dorothy says, tapping a red oval nail on the counter.

"Coffee," he croaks, and starts to push change across the counter but Dorothy waves him away. She pours him a tall cup as black as what she's been drinking and passes it across the counter along with a cruller. He mumbles his thanks and retreats to the corner table he usually has staked out when Shania comes in at the end of the day.

"Jai said you used to work at the police station," Shania says.

"Mm–hmm."

"He also said you said there's a serial killer in Blue Rock."

Dorothy raises her eyebrows.

"What now?"

"You know, the homeless guys getting beat up? And the cats."

"Cats?"

"I found a dead cat, and Jai said you did too."

She frowns.

"Nobody told me there was another one."

"A couple more at least."

"Well," Dorothy says, pinching her ear. "It's the kinda thing I used to hear them talking about in the station. They call it escalation. Anybody who's seen an episode of *Law & Order* knows about that. You know. Starting with animals. Getting bolder. Madder."

Shania darts her eyes at Earl, imagining his orange jacket fleeing the scene of a crime.

"Somebody told me there's a lot more homeless people now that SoBR is getting built up."

"I'd say that's probably true," Dorothy says. "Reasons for that."

"So what if it's him." Shania nods a small nod in Earl's direction.

"Who?"

"Earl," she whispers.

Dorothy stares at her for what feels like a long time, then cackles her smoker's cackle again.

"You don't have to worry about him, honey," she says. "Especially with cats. Wouldn't hurt a fly."

"How do you know?"

"Same way I know this lady is the pickiest customer you'll ever meet," she says, nodding toward the door.

A woman clangs in, approaching the counter with small, hurried steps.

"Could I have one of those, please," she says, pointing. "Except could I have it without sprinkles? And one of those, but could you warm it up before putting it in the box? And…hmm…one of those, but do you have any without nuts? No? All right, then one of those. No, not that one. It's shaped funny. The other one. Thank you."

Dorothy rings her up with a smile and waves her out the door. When she's gone, Dorothy fixes that smile back on Shania.

"I know all these folks, honey," she says. "That's what comes when you actually live in the community where you make your living, and have for a long time. Earl's been coming here for years, and he's a lamb, not a wolf."

"Some wolves wear sheep's clothes," Shania replies. It's something Gram used to say. Saying it feels like slipping on a hand-knit sweater.

"Sure, honey," Dorothy says, sipping her coffee. "But some people see fangs in a lamb's mouth that don't actually exist." She pauses, then points. "I think somebody's looking for you."

Shania jerks her head up, following Dorothy's finger. Prescott stands outside the window holding a paper bag, cupping his free hand around his eyes to peer through the glass.

He is the physical rebuttal of all Shania's lonely thoughts.

"Get out of here," Dorothy says, shooing her with the corner of her apron. "You're not bothering me."

Prescott drives toward Klondike Park, which Shania has never heard of and he's never been to. He intermittently peers at his phone for directions, and she uses the opportunity to sneak looks at him. He's wearing a white T-shirt as usual, but the onset of fall has put a gray hoodie on top. He smiles when he catches her looking.

"Are you hungry?" he says as the car climbs the last hill.

"I wasn't until I saw the tacos," she says.

"Tacos have that effect on people."

"Thanks for picking me up."

"Don't thank me. You're doing me the favor, letting me take a break from my family. You could have been doing anything after you got off work but you're with me instead."

She smiles but he doesn't look at her to catch it. He squints at the road ahead as if something might jump in front of the car.

"Are you going to tell me what's happening with your parents?" she asks.

"They're complete hypocrites," he says. "We'll just leave it at that."

"About what?"

"Everything. They think they're so much better than everyone because they donate money to charity and sponsor scholarships at Bard and all that crap. But they're pieces of shit."

"What about your sister?"

He rolls his eyes as he pulls into a parking inlet.

"Catherine is just as bad," he says, and Shania can't help but think that this is the second time someone has said this about Catherine. "I'm sorry, I know you're friends. But her little pro-choice protests are such horseshit—she just likes being different. She wants to wear her pink pussy hat and stand outside without a bra on. My dad hates that shit. At least we have that in common."

"And Ben?"

"Ben, I don't even know. We used to be really close. Now he's so fucking uptight."

"He seems really moody," she says. "Like he's one way one day, another the next day."

"He can never decide if he wants to save people or write them off," Prescott scowls. "He thinks he has all this conviction, but he can never actually commit. Like, if you're going to judge people, fucking do it, man. Don't just be on a high fucking horse." His voice has risen, he's almost yelling. "All of them are like that. They're all just trying to hide what they really are and we can't get away from that!"

His voice makes her skin ripple. He takes a deep breath.

"Sorry."

"You don't have to be sorry. My family sucks too."

"They can't be that bad. They made you," he says, attempting a smile.

"Please. My dad is a dick and my mom is like a robot half the time. I might as well be adopted. Sometimes I wonder if they found me in a well."

"In a ... well," he repeats, straight-faced.

She shoves his shoulder, laughing.

"A river or something. A doorstep."

"Like Moses."

"Oh, hush! You know what I meant!"

"I do," he says, finally laughing. "I really do. You were close with your grandma, though?"

She had thought they were. She thought she knew her grandmother's life inside and out: Morrisville born and raised. Church. Gardening. Secretary at the elementary school. Overseeing the Christmas pageant. Blue Rock and Western Pocket were never part of the life her grandmother shared with Shania.

"Yes," Shania says.

"I'm sorry."

"I...me too."

She can feel the tears stinging and she looks quickly out the window.

"It's okay," he says. "It's really okay."

"It's just..." She sucks in breath. "She was the only person that made me feel like...like I'm real. She knew everything. Recipes. Dates. What flowers need how much sun and how much water. Birthdays. She knew everybody's birthday, you know? The names of trees. Different birds. Which bugs were good for your garden and which you need to kill. How am I supposed to know which ones to kill?"

Then she's actually crying. The moment before the tears feels like that teetering second at the top of a roller coaster. She's too high to go back, but plunging forward feels like certain death— and at some point the decision is made for her. She's over the edge now and sits in his front seat with her hands over her face.

"She made you feel like you know who you are," he says quietly.

That just makes her cry harder because she thinks that after all these months of missing her, this is the first time she's understood why the hole in her life feels so jagged. Something vital has been ripped. For months, when she closed her eyes, she could only see Gram's garden, the brittle tomato plants in February. Now when she closes her eyes, she's in another garden. Mrs. Walker's.

"It's okay," he says again.

"Let's get out," she sniffs, shaking her head. The car suddenly feels too small, like her tears might fill it up and drown them both.

"Okay."

They walk, quiet for a while, the bag of tacos swinging from his hand.

"You've never been here before?" she asks.

"Nope."

"Why did you want to come?"

"I wanted to be somewhere beautiful with someone beautiful."

She laughs a little, shaking her head. The version of him Julia painted in the greenhouse feels fuzzy and far away. Julia must be wrong. Jealous, maybe. A piece of the drama Prescott has complained about despising so much.

"I'm serious. Plus I know you like trees and flowers. This place is supposed to have a good view. It should be up here somewhere."

He pauses to consult a wooden sign that bears the markings and routes for different trails.

"I didn't even know this place existed," she says.

"Even better."

She follows him down the trail until the path opens up ahead, the trees folding back like the edges of an oyster, the sky a blue pearl growing larger and larger. When they leave the shelter of the trees, they find themselves by a bench situated on the ledge of a modest cliff, below which rolls a steep green hill blanketed in white and purple flowers. She wants to say something about how beautiful it is but all she can do is exhale.

"Yeah, me too," he says.

They sit on the bench, their legs almost touching.

"Do you know what those flowers are?" he says, pointing down the cliff.

"Blue-eyed Marys," she says. "And purple loosestrife."

Community service day comes swarming back through her mind. Julia's words in the greenhouse. It all creeps to the edge of that house she's built around Prescott. She turns to him before she can change her mind.

"What happened with Eric?" she says.

He looks at her in surprise, the tacos forgotten.

"What *happened*?" he says. "What happened is that guy is an asshole. I'm assuming Catherine has at least told you that."

"I mean, kinda," she says. Now that she's opened the can she's embarrassed of the worms. They both fidget, the sun beating down. He shrugs off his hoodie, squinting in the brightness.

"Where is this coming from?" he says.

"I mean, I've been hearing bits and pieces of stuff ever since I started at Bard. I just figured I'd ask you."

"I kicked his ass," he says, hard and flat. "I didn't like him dating Catherine. Any big brother would have done the same thing."

"Did he cheat on her or something?"

"He would have. They always do."

*They* is like a stone. She doesn't say anything. She built a house around Prescott, but she doesn't know how big it is. How much can its roof cover?

"There's something on your mind," he says. "Something else."

She says nothing, and he presses forward.

"Are you still thinking about your grandma?" he says. "She would be really proud of you, you know that right? You may not think you know everything she knew, but that's because she had a whole lifetime to gather all that knowledge. You will too. And you'll pass it down like she did. I think it's awesome that you're so proud of your family and your history."

"I feel like that's changing, though," she blurts. "I feel like I used to know who my grandma was, and my great-grandpa too. Like, you love your family because they're your family, you know?

My great-grandpa died when I was five or something but you grow up remembering their voice and seeing pictures of them smiling and their story just gets built up in your head as one thing. And then maybe there's more to it than that, and nobody told you...."

Gazing down the hill at the loosestrife, she closes her mouth around the ramble. He frowns at her.

"What's going on, Shania?" he says. "You seem like you're carrying a lot, but I can't really help if you don't tell me."

She feels the prick of tears again. It's the kind of thing her mother might have said before Gram died, but now the words are too soft and her mother can't say soft things anymore, not without crumbling. At one point she might have told her mother what she'd found in the library, what she'd heard from Mrs. Walker's mouth— but it's the opposite of soft: too hard might make her crumble too. But Prescott is stronger than her mother, and Shania finds the words tumbling out of her mouth, telling him what she'd seen, what she'd learned. Her great-grandfather's name and then her grandmother's. White fence. Red tomato. Flames leaping red. Prescott listens intently, his eyes fixed on the ground ahead of them.

"I just feel like I don't know who anybody is anymore," she says when she finishes. "Or how I got here. I thought Morrisville was home, but in a way Blue Rock is since my family was here first? And I didn't even know about it. My grandmother died so suddenly. And now it's like she's really gone. Farther. Like the only option is forgetting her entirely. Letting her disappear."

"What makes you say that?"

She glances at him, remembering the conversation she'd had first with Willa, then with Willa and Michelle. They hadn't said anything about disappearing—just suggested that Shania look and not look away. But she doesn't think she can do that either.

"Well, according to Willa," she says, returning her eyes to the flowers, "I just need to accept that my family was racist and move on."

"*Willa*," he snorts. "Should've known she would have something to say. She loves to make people feel guilty about shit like this. But let me be the one to tell you: You shouldn't feel guilty. Why feel bad for what they said or did? Your great-grandfather was trying to protect his family. He was doing what he thought was best. I mean, if you were going to feel bad about anything, it's that your grandma gave the land away! I mean, do you know how much *money* she could have made if she hadn't done that?"

He offers these words to her with silver cutlery, but she looks away, her tongue seeming to shrivel in her mouth. Gram had driven the Buick for Shania's entire life, and that was fine. It was fine with Gram and fine with Shania. *Do better, Shania.* Shania doesn't think that's what Gram meant.

"She was good to *you*, right?" Prescott goes on. "She loved you! That's all that matters. I think it's amazing that you're proud of your family, okay? So many people feel like they're not allowed to be. And you should be."

She looks back at him then—she feels the distance between herself and the past stretch and pull, lengthening, building a wall between what's been done and what she's responsible for. It feels like falling into a feather bed, or polishing grime from a statue. She thinks maybe this is how to patch the hole in her heart—fill it with marble. It's easier to look at marble than at the truth, red as blood and split tomatoes.

"Do you not feel like you're allowed to be proud?" she says to distract herself.

"It's bigger than me," he says. "My family may be shit but I'm part of something bigger. My heritage is powerful and I'm proud of that."

There's something in it that sounds off, like a statement being read from a script before news cameras. It sounds like something he's read—something devout—and then swallowed, consumed, before spitting it back out again as canon. But the words shine. They draw her in.

"Your grandmother is so much more than this shit," he says, and shifts forward on the bench, elbows on knees. With the hoodie off, she can see the faint outline of his tattoo through the white cotton. A green triangle. She can't take her eyes away from it, remembering. The lilacs on her foot prickle. But there are other flowers in his words—he plants in her the feeling of a shared something, a shared shedding of the things that seek to weigh them down.

"Don't let them take your family from you," he says.

She stands up, electric, and walks to the edge of the hill, where the ground flattens for the last time before rolling down into the floral crush. Her fingernails bite into her palms as her teeth bite into her bottom lip. She has walked away from the bench but she's not sure what she's walking toward.

"You feel it," he says, and she's not sure what he means, but she does feel something.

It's been clawing at her insides since February, a fanged tumor. The grass is too green and the flowers too purple and the sky too empty. Somewhere a dog howls. And then she can't bite it back any longer—she stands at the edge of emptiness and the sound that comes galloping from her mouth is hound, marble, almanac, garden. The scream empties every shoebox and uproots every tree. She screams until every neighborhood in her head has turned off the lights.

She stands there near the sky panting, throat like a skinned knee. She wants to close her eyes but doesn't—if she still sees Mrs. Walker's garden behind her eyelids she might collapse. Instead she turns back to Prescott.

"There is so much about you that people don't see," he says, gazing at her in wonder.

She stares back at him, at the way the afternoon sun paints stripes of gold across his nose and jaw. Sitting here at the edge of the world, she gets the sense that she's sitting at another edge with him as well, on the border of something. He opens the bag and takes out a taco, and for a moment she's not sure she's even hungry anymore. But when he extends the food to her, his eyes the same frail blue as a robin's egg, she takes it, and she eats.

Shania's halfway home, the sky dark, when she realizes she left her keys at Paulie's. Prescott swings his car around slowly in the middle of the street, ignoring honks from other drivers.

"No biggie," he says. "Let's go pick them up."

But when his car pulls up outside, the line for doughnuts is out the door.

"Just drop me off," she says. "It's going to take forever to get in there and find them. I'll take a Lyft home."

He takes some convincing, but after she promises to text him when she gets home, he finally lets her off, leaving a kiss like rose petals on her lips. She watches the Audi be swallowed by SoBR traffic, her heart thumping. She's almost relieved to be alone. Her throat is scratchy from the escaped scream. She's eager to get inside and find her keys. Until she sees Jai behind the counter.

He's working with the new night shift worker, a short girl with deep-brown skin and pink braids who Shania has heard is named Tanji. Crowded on the street with the SoBR bargoers jostling in line for doughnuts, Shania watches Jai and Tanji take orders, box dozens. They talk while they work, Jai's face lighting up over and over with hilarity while Tanji claps her hands in front of her face, laughing. They move the line fast, tongs snapping, and Shania suddenly feels absolutely unable to enter the shop. Jai is ordinarily surly, and now the shop seems brighter than usual. Tanji fills boxes without looking, grinning over her shoulder at something Jai said.

Shania turns away, marching down the street against the prickly wind. She doesn't care that her mother will probably be calling soon, wondering where she is. Her mind is full of loose-strife and she isn't sure if she wants to cut it back or let it go wild. She's almost surprised when she finds herself at the Sparkle Park, the lights glittering like glowworms. She lets it swallow her.

Unlike when she came with Catherine and the girls, the park is empty, the benches bare. She doesn't go to the benches, though— this time she wanders to the fountain, as dry as ever. The fairy lights make her feel like she's dreaming, the shreds of the scream from the cliff still in her throat. *Don't let them take your family from you.* Prescott's words feel like a golden ticket somehow—passage across the river of grief that had begun to flow that day in her grandmother's garden, and whose current has grown only stronger since she found the almanac. *Liars.*

Shania yanks open her bag, stuffing her hand in for the almanac. She needs to see it. She snatches it out into the sparkling lights, the cover barely hanging on since the day on the bus. She can see the words without even opening the cover. *Do better, Shania.*

*Don't let them take your family from you.*

*Do better, Shania.*

She can feel the scream again, but there's the sound of voices from nearby, a crowd of people on the sidewalk through the perimeter of the park. Still, her body vibrates, a rubber band strung between two distant pegs. Her teeth chatter, the almanac gripped hard in her hands, bending under the pressure.

And then, as if forced from a geyser, she throws it, launching the yellowed book into the dark bin of the dry fountain. She hears the dry clatter of it landing somewhere in a heap of shadows. Her hands are empty. She realizes she's gasping for breath, as if she just came up from under water.

"I have signs and whistles for whoever needs them!" calls a voice. One of the crowd that Shania could hear through the Sparkle Park's trees, louder and clearer than before. "Turn right! Yes, into the park. We'll get everybody sorted out before we march."

Shania spins around, the fountain pressed hard and cold against her back. She still hasn't caught her breath, and tears run freely— the sudden realization that other humans still exist sends a jolt through her bones. Without thinking, Shania runs. She goes to the first bench she sees, situated to the right of the entrance. She ducks behind it just as the group of people flood into the park.

They're gearing up for a protest, she realizes, glimpsing signs between the slats: UNHOUSED NEIGHBORS ARE STILL NEIGHBORS and GET SOBER, SOBR. The people carrying them wear black shirts with words written in phosphorescent paint: SHINE A LIGHT ON SOUTHTOWN. Two Black women carry megaphones and give direction, divvying up signs, passing out whistles and instructions. A white boy in a black hoodie stands passing out glow-in-the-dark paint. His chest is illuminated with the words PEOPLE USED TO LIVE HERE.

It's Benjamin Tane.

Shania shrinks deeper into the shadow behind the bench, her heart thrumming. In her bag—the bag that no longer carries Gram's almanac—she feels her phone vibrating. She doesn't dare reach for it. She feels inexplicably hunted—the idea of Ben seeing her here, of asking her why she's hiding, why she's here at all, would she like to join...she still can't catch her breath. So she watches as the crowd grows, as Ben passes out more paint and waves people in who are coming from outside. How his grin widens when two girls enter the park, black hoodies already painted. One tall and Black, one short and white with fire-engine hair. Willa and Michelle.

Beside Shania in the shadows, a leaf crackles, something moves close. She almost shrieks, but her throat is too tight, and she jerks away from whatever or whoever it is.

It's a cat. Almost invisible in the dark, its body striped in layers of brown. The cat's eyes are as luminous as the paint on the black shirts, and it stares at her from the leaves of the bush it's made its cave. They peer at each other, girl and cat, two crouching things, and she feels suddenly huge, like Alice eating the strange bread in Wonderland, growing and growing until the bench no longer conceals her. A balloon of panic inflates in her body, and when the next group of people enter the Sparkle Park, she pulls her pink hoodie up over her hair and allows the balloon to bear her up and away from the fairy lights, out onto the street, where people not wearing black shirts move, laughing and oblivious, from bar to bar.

# CHAPTER 24

Morning, and the bonfire smell of her mother's coffee. Morning, and Shania brushes her teeth alongside her in the bathroom, both studying their own reflections and avoiding each other's eyes. Shania eats cereal while her mother eats toast—they talk about what might be needed at the grocery store. They say many versions of nothing on their separate ways out the door. A few days ago, all the nothing would have felt like a rash. But today, after last night, Shania is grateful for it. She has made a decision, and her mother's embrace of silence is a balm on everything red and angry. The nothing enfolds her on her way to the bus, and all the way to school. It still envelopes her as she sits alone in the greenhouse, until Ms. Hassoon stops by her workstation in the last few minutes before class begins.

"Your shoots are looking very healthy," she says. "You have a delicacy that botany requires. You've heard people say a green thumb? It's more like a green fingerprint. Light. Barely touched at all but leaving the mark."

"Thank you," Shania says softly, surprised. "My grandma

always called it the green eye. So much of it is about, you know . . . watching."

"Yes." Ms. Hassoon nods. "Watching and waiting and remembering is so important." She taps the table for emphasis, one long unpolished finger. The elegant crescent is black with soil. This is how Shania's fingers always looked after gardening until Gram taught her to scratch a bar of soap before working with the soil. The memory is like a blow. Shania practices not flinching.

The rest of the class is arriving and Ms. Hassoon gives Shania one more nod before moving to the front of the room. Beside her, Michelle's seat is empty. Ms. Hassoon clears her throat and after JP and the lacrosse guys settle down she brings her palms gently together.

"Today may be one of the last warm days of the year," she says.

"It's not even warm," Catherine complains. She rolls her eyes conspiratorially at Shania. It's her first time in class in days. Her planter looks how Shania feels, but Catherine's attention is like water.

"There are still green things out there, so it's not winter *yet*," Ms. Hassoon says, her voice crisp. "So I am sending you outside the classroom today. Urban plant specimen collection."

The entire class perks up.

"You two, and you two, and you two," Ms. Hassoon says, pointing, going around the room pairing them. With Michelle gone, the numbers are odd and Shania is left unpaired. Ms. Hassoon consults her attendance book.

"The office has sent word that Michelle will be a few minutes late to school," she says. "Shania, start your foraging at Fountain Circle and I'll have her join you when she arrives. Everyone get your jackets. Stay within a three-square-block radius of the school. Find me three unique plant specimens and then bring them back here."

They stampede out, except Shania, who plods to the front door without her coat. She tells herself she wants to feel the wind, but when she steps out she finds that it's colder than it was this morning. It feels like rain, and between that and the granite sky, the world looks as if it belongs in a Netflix detective show. She waits for first one crosswalk and then another. Across the street, a homeless man drifts along, limping. When he glances at her, it's with one eye open—the other is swollen shut, a purple mound. Her breath catches in her throat in the long second he seems to stare before going about his business. She has the sudden urge to run after him, to ask who did it, but fear keeps her still. She isn't sure what she's actually afraid of—him, or what he might say. He disappears around the corner and Shania keeps watching for a moment before slowly making her way over the crosswalk to Fountain Circle.

In Fountain Circle, a sort of courtyard, balconies of a hotel on three sides, there are four benches and an empty birdbath and quite a bit of trash. Everything is overgrown, long spidery fronds along the edges that might have been on purpose at one point—maybe some kind of hosta. Clover-like weeds ring the base of the birdbath, and then there's the ivy that climbs the three walls, its sights set on the balconies above, every arrow-like leaf a sign detailing its plans. Shania uses the scissors from her collection kit to snip a leaf of the ivy, hoping it counts. She's eyeing a dried patch of clover when her pocket vibrates.

**Do you ever feel like you took the wrong pill?** the words on the screen read. They're from Prescott.

**I'm assuming you mean like The Matrix and not that you're confusing your prescriptions,** she types back.

**Very funny,** he says. **Yeah. What they don't tell you about the red pill is that it gets lonely being the only one who sees the world as it truly is.**

She thinks about the way she sees the world and how it's changed so drastically just in the last weeks. She hadn't asked for the red pill, but it had made its way into her bloodstream anyway. She's tired of feeling sad. She's tired of feeling torn. Her grandmother had left her entire life behind in Blue Rock—and for what? Because of guilt? Then why leave the almanac in her drawer, Shania's name on the first page like a rusty chain dragging her back into the past? She tells herself she's glad she got rid of it. Her grief for Gram has turned into a chain itself, braided with a new red thread of anger. Prescott's electricity transforms it into a wire. She replies:

**I see the world as it is too. And it sucks. Maybe we can find a new pill.**

She's satisfied with this message, and when he sends back a heart emoji, the snakes that have been hissing inside her quiet their tongues. She puts her phone away and gazes up at the sky. Cold blue. Summer is truly over.

"SHANIA."

She jerks her head up at the sound of someone shouting her name. She wonders if she's lost track of time, if someone has been sent from the greenhouse to collect her. She's forgotten all about Michelle, and is half surprised when she sees her across the street, pacing at the crosswalk, waiting for the walk sign. Shania can tell immediately something is wrong. Even from where she is, she can see that every muscle in the other girl's body is steel, coiled like a spring in a too-small box. When the walk sign dings white, Michelle marches toward Fountain Circle. Shania doesn't know what to do but stand there and wait for her, bewildered, the hurricane of her classmate surging toward where she stands by the rusty bench.

"Michelle?" she says when Michelle closes in. In one hand Michelle carries a book, and the other hand's index finger is raised, straight out ahead like a sword aimed for Shania's heart. Her face is full of fury. Shania takes a step back.

"You better get your little boyfriend, Shania," Michelle says, eyes burning. The finger connects with Shania's chest, and Shania gasps. "You better GET HIM."

"What? What? What?" Shania says it three times because she doesn't know what else to say. All of her self-satisfaction from a moment before has melted away.

"Prescott fucking Tane, Shania," Michelle says, her voice grating. "You better check him, because if you don't, I don't know what to tell you. GET YOUR LI'L PSYCHO-ASS BOYFRIEND, SHANIA."

"What are you talking about?" Shania demands, stepping back again to get the steel feeling of Michelle's finger off her chest. Her heart patters, quick rain.

Michelle takes a deep breath, one hand rising to her own cheek, where it curls into a fist, reining in the storm. She squeezes her eyes shut for a moment, and when they open again they pierce into Shania's.

"This morning I went by the garden in Pocket, like I do every morning on the way to the bus. Mrs. Walker wasn't there yet, and thank God, because she didn't need to see that shit. She been through enough to have to see that shit."

"See *what*?"

"A dead cat, Shania. A dead fucking cat, hanging from its tail at the gates of the garden."

"You...what...a cat...a dead..."

"You heard me. A dead cat. That's why I'm late to school. I had to get rid of that shit before Mrs. Walker got there. Everything she been through, to have to come to the garden she started from rubble and see that shit."

"I...I..."

"Prescott did it," Michelle says, her voice rising again. Tears glisten in her eyes now. "You know it and I know it. He was pissed after I called him on his shit at community service day and he did this shit. To try to scare me."

"He...he wouldn't."

"Oh, please," Michelle rages. "Don't give me that shit. You're not fucking stupid, no matter what people say."

"People *what*?"

Michelle clasps her empty hand over her face, shaking her head.

"Prescott did this," she says again. "He did this shit and I'm telling you that you better check him. You need to do something."

"Me? Why me?"

"That's your boyfriend, ain't it?"

"No, I—"

"He might as well be," Michelle shouts. "Whatever he is, I don't care! CHECK. HIM. Catherine ain't gonna do it. Bard 'In the Pocket of the Tanes' Academy sure as fuck ain't gonna do it. They didn't give a shit about him attacking Eric, so they're not going to do shit about this."

"You don't know that it was him," Shania says.

"Yes, I *do*."

Shania's fear and anger smash together, yellow and green combining to create a heavy blue smear. *You're not stupid, no matter what people say*. She feels herself transported to the edge of something, to the edge of everything. Rootless.

"And I'm supposed to just believe you?" Shania says. "How do I know you're not trying to get him in trouble? Or Catherine? You and Willa hate them. I'm supposed to just *believe* you?"

"Are you serious right now?" Michelle says, dropping her chin. "Are you...are you serious?"

"You and me aren't even real friends," Shania says, the words bubbling up from somewhere red and raw. "You and Willa have made sure of that. And now you sit here and tell me people have been calling me stupid. For all I know, you're one of them. So why should I believe you?"

Michelle stares at her, her expression flat, her eyes narrowed.

"Did you...did you just take everything I said and make it about you and your feelings? You're ignoring all the violent shit Prescott has done because you feel *left out*?"

"That's not what I'm doing, I—"

"That's exactly what you're doing."

"You're telling me I'm responsible for Prescott," Shania shouts. "What if I don't want to be? What if I just want to be responsible for myself?"

"You're not even doing that!" Michelle fires back.

Laughter rings from across the street. They both look. Catherine and Hannah are circling the block, carrying cups from Rhino. Hannah doesn't take botany, so she must be cutting to hang out with Catherine, who doesn't even carry her botany kit. When the girls aren't sipping coffee, their mouths move at gossip-speed. Catherine's gaze flicks across the street and over toward the courtyard, and she notices them. Her eyes settle on Michelle and Shania like the laser scope of a high-powered rifle. If Shania were a plant, she would wither. She feels her leaves curling. Catherine and Hannah move off, not looking back. Something tight and nervous grows wings deep in Shania's belly. It clatters against her ribs and she thinks Michelle must be able to hear it too, because she stares at her as if just realizing she's been sitting next to a vampire in botany all year.

"They really got to you," Michelle says, almost in wonder. "Willa called it. I didn't want to believe it, but I guess I shouldn't be surprised. Why would you even know what to do with your first Black friend—"

"You're *not* my first Black friend!" Shania interrupts. "I told you that."

"You ever been to that girl's house?" Michelle says, almost mocking. "Did she ever tell you about people being racist to her in a town like Morrisville? Cuz I bet it happened a lot. Hell, you were probably one of the people doing it. And that's how I know she wasn't your friend—she didn't trust you enough to say any of this to you."

Shania just gapes at her.

"Same old shit," Michelle says, shaking her head.

Michelle looks down at her hands, as if only just remembering the book she carries. She holds it up for Shania to see. Yellow cover, fading letters.

Gram's almanac. A tremor makes its way coldly up Shania's spine.

"How did you—"

"I found it at the Sparkle Park. Thought you must have lost it and would like to have it back."

She all but flings the book at her, and Shania fumbles it, wanting to embrace it, also wanting to heave it away.

"I bet she'd be real proud of you," Michelle says.

She turns on her heel and Shania is left alone once more.

# CHAPTER 25

Neither Catherine nor Prescott have answered Shania's texts in two days. She doesn't bother texting Ben. She sits in Pre-Cal on Thursday afternoon, three days since she'd stood in the courtyard with Michelle, English ivy between her fingers. Mr. Alden's voice has become a buzz in her ear: She sits in the back row with her phone out under the desk, staring at Hallie's Instagram, which is filled with pictures of her and Monica. Monica smiles and smiles, her cheek pressed close to Hallie's. Monica is out of her shell, and so is Hallie, when Shania thinks about it. She hadn't imagined there was more to her than theater. But there they are, both knowing more about each other than Shania ever will. She wonders what Monica trusts Hallie enough to tell her.

She moves on to the feeds of Prescott and Catherine, of Michelle, of Willa. The deeper Shania dives into their accounts the deeper the pit in her stomach spirals. Prescott rarely posts—the last thing he'd put in his story was a video of him walking along the river, his knuckles flashing silver, maybe a bracelet. He'd been alone, but now she imagines Prescott's feed filling with images of a new girl, hair blonder, teeth whiter. Shania curses the tooth at the front of her mouth. She imagines Catherine's future posts: pictures with Hannah, girls' nights, Cheetos, inside jokes. Ben with dogs, and then a girl. Everyone leaving her behind. Even Michelle: her adventures at Harvard, in fancy botany labs, in a real city, Willa and Eric visiting her and getting the tour of her sparkling new life. Shania has been jealous before but not like this.

To escape the feeling, she navigates out of Michelle's page and back over to Catherine's, looking at the same photos she's looked at a dozen times since she met her. Shania envies her in a different way than what she feels looking at Michelle. There's something unattainable and unreachable in the photo of Michelle on a family cruise, her hair braided in designs along her scalp. It's a club Shania can't even find the door for, and the feeling of imagined rejection hits her so hard she feels it in her ribs. But Catherine is a club she could be a member of if she tithes just right. She wonders about the price.

"Miss Hester? Miss Hester? Shania?"

Shania's head jerks up from her lap, the filtered clouds that have been floating in front of her eyes evaporating in an instant.

"There you are," Mr. Alden says, annoyed. He points at the door.

Mrs. Floyd, the school secretary, is standing in the doorway.

"Shania? Ms. Green would like to speak with you for a few minutes."

Shania has never even seen Ms. Green, the guidance counselor, except passing by her doorway, where she is always hunched over her desk flipping through folders with a light frown. She's fortyish, younger than many of the teachers at Bard, with an actual hairstyle that she hides in a ponytail: natural makeup, stylish shoes. She always has her head down. Shania figures that with as many alcoholics that Bard houses under its vaulted ceilings,

Ms. Green keeps pretty busy. But not with Shania. She rises hesitantly.

"You can leave your things," Mrs. Floyd says, nodding at her books. Shania moves slowly to the door. Her first thought is that something has happened to her mother, and fear grips her knees in a sudden embrace of cold. But Mrs. Floyd doesn't wear the kind of frown that tells a girl her mother is dead. She just looks tired.

Mrs. Floyd walks with a slight limp, and so Shania walks in slow hobbled steps beside her as she's chaperoned to Ms. Green's office. Shania remembers the day Prescott had walked her through the silent halls, the way no open door actually exposed them. Now it feels like every inch of corridor has eyes, and she imagines whispers every time she passes a classroom. Even the class photos of long-graduated Bardians, 1990, 1980, 1970, seem to murmur after her.

Mrs. Floyd closes Shania into the counselor's office, where she sits fidgeting until Ms. Green finally looks up from the manila folder on her desk, fingers steepled under her chin. She's wearing glasses, the cute kind, and Shania somehow can't remember if she's always worn them or if they're new, and rather than looking into her eyes, Shania studies the rims of the glasses and hopes it looks like eye contact.

"Miss Hester," Ms. Green says. "Are you happy here?"

Shania's stomach immediately stirs, a jellyfish of emotions shifting its tentacles. Shania thinks lying to counselors is a teenage instinct. Back in Morrisville, Dana Cochran confided in her school counselor that she thought she might be pregnant because she felt sick for two mornings in a row—she was in the alternative school two weeks later. Ms. Green has the concerned face down pat: eyes drooping a little at the outer corners but still bright with interest. Her mouth frowning and smiling at the same time. It must take years of practice; it must be a resume requirement.

"What do you mean?" Shania replies.

"You're a new student," she says, "and we're past the point of start-of-the-year jitters. So this feels like a good time for a check-in. Just to see how you're settling in."

"I think I've settled in okay. My grades are okay. I know some people. I think I'm okay."

"Okay," Ms. Green repeats. "Is okay *okay*? What's keeping 'okay' from being great?"

"Um…"

"Do you understand what I mean? Is something standing in the way of Bard really feeling like a place where you can be happy and successful?"

"I don't know. I'm fine," Shania says again, not quite sure what the woman is after.

"Your high school years are some of the most important of your life," Ms. Green says. "I wouldn't want you to look back and think of your experience at Bard with regret, or wishing that you had made different decisions. Sometimes the only thing standing between us and the life we should be leading is one decision. One day… one friend."

Her voice shifts when she says these last two words, her eyebrows lifting just a fraction of an inch. Shania realizes very slowly that she's here for a reason, and that reason is somewhere inside Ms. Green's mouth, hiding behind her neat rows of somewhat small teeth.

"I have friends," Shania says, and suddenly wonders if she has come up in faculty meetings, banter between teachers. *Shania. You know, the one with the tooth and the cheap clothes. Always sits alone in class. Brings her lunch. Doesn't drink coffee. Oh, her, yes, Shania. Yes, I'm worried about her. Doesn't quite fit in.*

"That's good, Shania," Ms. Green says. "Having friends is good. Sometimes when we start at a new school, we make initial friendships as we start to get comfortable, but sometimes those friendships don't serve us. Do you understand?"

"Um…"

Ms. Green sighs patiently and removes the glasses Shania has been trying hard to focus on.

"It's easy to fall in with a person because their friendship is convenient," she says. "Or maybe because it makes you feel like you belong somewhere. But sometimes that person can keep you from getting closer to the friendships that will actually serve you in the long run."

"I'm confused, Ms. Green," Shania says, her voice wobbling a little. "Am I in trouble?"

Ms. Green looks at her, evaluative, gently swinging her glasses back and forth by one of their arms. Then she folds them and places them neatly on her desk.

"A concerned citizen," she says. "Completely anonymous, before you ask. It was a note slipped under my door. Someone expressed worry about a person you've been spending some time with. Concerned that they may lead you down a path that may not be best for your continued success at Bard."

A miniature storm whips through the enclosed landscape of Shania's skull, stirring up flashbacks and replays. The thunder cracks and when the lightning flashes, a single scene glares at her, white hot: standing in the courtyard while Michelle shouts at her, the laser of Catherine's eyes finding Shania's face from across the street. One moment everything feels blurry, and the next everything has snapped into focus. She can still feel the burn of being in Catherine's crosshairs and now, Ms. Green staring at her like a second sniper, Shania realizes she's being given an opportunity. Catherine is here in the words coming out of Ms. Green's mouth, telling her to make a choice.

The realization settles into her lap like a house cat. Shania looks at Ms. Green and wonders if the relief shows on her face. She's being given permission, she thinks.

"I might know what you're talking about," Shania says.

It's Ms. Green's turn to look relieved. She puts her glasses back on.

"It sounds like there's someone who cares about you at Bard," she says, a soft smile replacing the wavering line of the concerned mouth. She can't know that these words, conjuring Catherine and Prescott, fuel something marbled and hungry in Shania.

"Yeah, it sounds like it," Shania says quietly, and the hope that this is true bypasses hope and becomes certainty.

"Now," Ms. Green says, steepling her fingers once more. "This is the part I hate to do, but it's my job to ask. You seem like you're a good kid, Shania. But is there anything you want to tell me? Anything about who you're hanging out with that made this anonymous party concerned?"

Shania's heartbeat surges. She feels the words in her mouth before she actually says them, rolling around under her tongue like a jagged rock. She pictures Michelle at the garden in Pocket, her hair curly and free and her accent changing before Shania's eyes like the tilt of a raven's feather. She pictures Willa, vomiting guilt onto Shania for things she can't control. In the city of her head, she sees Michelle walking down the sidewalk and is suddenly angry at the space she takes up. She remembers her voice rising higher and higher at Fountain Circle. "I think they—this concerned citizen—is talking about Michelle."

"Michelle Broadus?" Ms. Green says. The frown is back.

Yesterday Shania might have winced hearing her name, but today she doesn't. Today something has been confirmed. The door to the club is open and Shania need only walk through.

"Yes," she says. "I've hung out with her a couple times. But she seems to really hate Bard. Like, she's always complaining about people here."

"I see," Ms. Green says.

"Yeah. And she basically attacked me this week." Ms. Green raises her eyebrows and Shania presses on quickly. "I mean, not physically. But she ran up to me and started yelling at me, cussing me out. Literally."

"Why would she do that?" Ms. Green says, looking concerned. "Where did this happen?"

"In Fountain Circle. I don't know why she was mad. She doesn't like that I'm dating Prescott Tane. I . . . I don't know why."

She has to squeeze these last few words from her mouth. It's like wrapping a thread around and around her finger, watching the flesh go pale.

Ms. Green takes a few notes on the paper in front of her, then pushes back from her desk.

"Thank you for coming in, Shania," she says. "This has been . . . enlightening."

Shania walks back out into the hall. She still feels inflated, light-headed. She stares up at the impossibly high ceilings, the morning light from the center where the greenhouse lives filled with the promise of sunshine. She imagines her light-headedness carrying her all the way to the top, where she can see the view that Prescott had shown her from the roof, the kingdom sprawling below.

# CHAPTER 26

When Shania walks into Paulie's on Saturday morning wearing her apron, Dorothy doesn't smile. She doesn't even look up. She stands behind the counter staring up at the TV that is kept on mute in the corner of the shop. But today the made-up faces of the local anchors actually have voices, and Dorothy stands rapt.

"What's going on?" Shania says as she moves behind the counter to join her.

"Shh," she says. "They're about to recap everything."

"South Blue Rock is tense this morning after a man was beaten to death under the overpass bordering the east end of the up-and-coming neighborhood. The overpass is a known place where the Blue Rock's homeless congregate and the victim is believed to have been homeless himself."

"Someone died?" Shania breathes.

"Shh," Dorothy says.

"Due to recent attacks on other members of Blue Rock's homeless population, police are not ruling out a serial offender at this time," the woman onscreen says, somber. "The assailant was originally believed to have been homeless himself, but witnesses to today's killing report otherwise. The assailant was described as a young white male wearing a gray hoodie, and was seen approaching the encampment under I-72 and then fleeing shortly after in a gray car. The victim, Earl Hutchins Jr., is said to have died from burns and blunt force trauma. W5BR learned that Hutchins Jr. was known as the Cat Man in the areas of Blue Rock he frequented. A local animal rescue has stepped forward to bring the animals Hutchins Jr. cared for into the shelter."

A face appears onscreen.

The face has deep brown skin and a shy smile, a scruffy beard at his chin. Shania barely recognizes him without his highlighter-orange jacket, without the tangled, flopping locs. The face belongs to Earl. The man who sits in Paulie's every Saturday night with a coffee and a stale doughnut is Earl Hutchins Jr., and the people on the television screen are telling Shania he is dead.

"Wait, no. Seriously?" Shania says. "Is that—"

"Yes," Dorothy says. She clutches the counter. "That's Earl."

"Someone killed him?"

"That's what they're saying," Dorothy says. She shakes her head slowly. "They're saying someone set him on fire."

Shania stares at the TV in silent shock as the newscasters wrap up the story.

"The victim's family has asked that anyone with information about the circumstances of his attack please come forward. The tip line onscreen is available twenty-four hours a day and may be phoned with anonymous information."

They move on.

"His family?" Shania says, confused. "Wasn't he homeless?"

"Homeless doesn't mean someone doesn't have family," Dorothy says sharply.

"I mean, couldn't he have stayed with one of them? If he had family?"

"There's a lot in life more complicated than that," Dorothy says, still staring at the screen even after the photo of Earl has faded. Her eyes are far away. "A whole lot."

The news doesn't say how old Earl was: The photo they showed of him, minus the beard and hair, made him look not much older than Shania. She wonders for the first time where he was from—if he was from Blue Rock, or if, like the weightless eyelashes of a dandelion, he detached from somewhere else and floated here. She feels a bit like that herself, then thinks of the almanac in her bag, returned to her by Michelle. Shania may have drifted here, but this is where her roots are. She had tried to throw them away, but they came drifting back like a determined ghost.

"I don't know what's happening here," Dorothy says. She moves to wipe down the counters, shaking her head. "Blue Rock has always had its issues but nothing like this. Everyone's lost their damn minds."

Shania swallows. Somewhere in her vision floats a glowing red tomato. Without meaning to, she imagines her grandmother's arm cocked back, the catapult that sends Blue Rock into chaos.

"What happened?" Shania says.

"I don't know." Dorothy sighs. "A little bit of a lot of things. Maybe a lot of a few things. Whatever it is, it's only getting worse. This country is a goddamn circus."

The door jingles and a gaggle of young white women in jeans and boots enters.

"Fifty-five-minute wait!" one wails. "We should have made a reservation."

"Toast doesn't even take reservations," another says. "We can wait. We'll just get doughnuts so we don't starve to death."

"Calories on fleek," the third one says and they all trill slightly different versions of the same laugh. "Can we get a half dozen?"

Dorothy rings them up while Shania plucks out their order, her eyes wandering over the counter to the street outside. A Black man across the street wears a baggy gray shirt and moves slowly down the sidewalk. He pauses to light a cigarette and a young white couple moves hastily around him, giving him a wide berth. Behind this little scene is the dark window of the hat shop. Shania remembers, almost with a start, the morning she'd walked through SoBR, her paycheck clutched in her hand, oblivious to the dotted trail of cat blood along the sidewalk. It had started at the hat shop's door. Now the storefront beyond the glass is empty, the raucous hats with their pastel feathers gone, replaced with dust. The blood has been washed away. On the window is a new sign: COMING SOON: SOGGY PAWS PET BOUTIQUE.

As the brunch girls leave the shop, Shania's phone vibrates. She withdraws it and sees Catherine has started a group text with her and Hannah—Julia notably excluded.

> **CT:** Girls night tonight! My parents have a thing they're going to (what's new) so we can smoke wherever we want.
>
> **HJ:** I'll bring the weeeeeeed
>
> **CT:** Don't say "weed." Shania might try to uproot you.

Catherine is speaking to her again. Neither she nor Prescott had been at school, and Prescott still hasn't answered Shania's texts. She wonders if he'll be home tonight, imagines leaning against the desk in his room and telling him what she'd heard about Earl, how she'd been building a story for him in her head that now feels crooked and wrong. Does she have to imagine what Prescott will think? She remembers the breeze in her hair as they'd looked down at SoBR from the roof of Bard. She remembers standing at the edge of a cliff with him while he built a house around her, bricks of *us* and *we*. She realizes that when she builds a house around him, it shelters her too, and she does it now to keep out the cold that began stalking the edge of her heart the moment she saw Earl's face on TV. Maybe, she thinks, looking down at Catherine's name, she just needs a distraction. She thinks of what Prescott had said at the edge of the cliff—*you're carrying a lot*. Maybe she can just put it down. She types back:

**Count me in.**

When Shania gets off at one o'clock, she sets off down the main drag that makes up SoBR, thinking. Being invited to Catherine's sans Julia feels significant somehow—Julia has been removed from the fold. *There can only be three musketeers*, Shania thinks, and is pleased because it sounds like something Catherine would say, and she feels even more like Catherine wandering confidently through SoBR. She takes her time moving down the sidewalk, weaving between people at bars with sidewalk spillover and the long lines that form outside brunch places like Toast and Jelly. She knows these places now. The newscasters had mentioned SoBR being tense after the attack this morning, but if SoBRers had been, they're not anymore, the tension drowned by mimosas and iced coffee. It's the sunny kind of fall day where the air is as orange and crisp as the leaves. She checks her phone.

**PT:** Hey. Sorry I've been MIA. Can we talk later? I really
need to talk to you.

**SH:** Sure. Of course. Is everything okay?

**PT:** It will be once I talk to you.

She feels her heart swell, and when she looks up she's approaching El Jefe. Transparent plastic curtains have been strung up around the eating area with the heat lamps to keep the warmth in, and she feels an idea forming. She'll surprise him with tacos, as he had surprised her.

She gets in line. Prescott had ordered for them the last time, and the menu seems overwhelming now as she waits alone. She's almost annoyed with herself for feeling intimidated—with Prescott she had felt that same kind of invincible as she had walking the halls of Bard with him. The way he drives: unapologetic and unconcerned. She can be that, she thinks. She can not give a fuck.

"Two number twos," she says when she gets to the register. A Latina girl around Shania's age is taking orders, long hair and bright-blue earrings. She's wearing makeup, the kind of thick flawless application that Shania has never quite been able to pull off. Her lips are painted bright red, not a fleck of it to be seen on her straight white teeth. Shania looks away, down at the menu, feeling small and plain, the order she'd been so sure of a moment before evaporating in her mind. "And um, I guess, one number four, please. And, um...chips and guacamole?"

The girl nods, tap-tapping the order into the iPad. She takes Shania's debit card and flashes her a smile as she spins the screen around for Shania to sign. Shania fumbles the card back into her wallet. There are a few other people waiting for their orders, and

Shania steps closer to them while the girl goes back to chatting with her coworker. Shania wonders what her own lips would look like in lipstick that red.

"I wish they'd stop talking and make my order," a white woman beside Shania grumbles. The woman glares down at her receipt, talking to herself but speaking loud enough for those around her to hear, hoping someone chimes in. Shania darts her eyes at the employees to see if they heard—the two girls taking orders aren't actually responsible for making the food. From where Shania stands she can see the cooks in back wearing white aprons, putting orders together in stacks of Styrofoam containers.

"I've been waiting forever," the woman says, louder this time, her receipt crumpling in her hand. Around her, people look at her sideways, one or two shifting impatiently in agreement. It's the thing people do when faced with inconvenient customer service scenarios: Shania has been on the receiving end at Paulie's when they're out of fresh glazed. Shania is torn between having been on the other end of this group sigh and the careless red smile of the girl at the register. The girl hasn't looked up, and something about her—her flashing eyes, the flip of her long black hair—is like a pebble in Shania's shoe.

"Excuse me," the woman says to the girls, the politeness wrung out of the words. "There's a lot of people waiting?"

"I've already taken everyone's order," the girl says, turning halfway to face the woman addressing her, her eyebrows quirked in confusion.

"Isn't there something else you can be doing to make this go a little faster? I've been waiting for ten minutes."

The girl focuses on the woman now, studying her. Something in the lens of her eyes adjusts.

"I'm sorry, ma'am," she says. "It should be ready soon."

"Should? Shouldn't you at least go *check*?"

The girl starts to reply then exchanges a look with her coworker. Then she takes a step to the right and leans back into the kitchen.

"Leo," she says, and one of the cooks looks up. She says something to him in Spanish. Leo turns his head to study the screen situated above the prep line, squinting. He says a few words in response then returns to preparing the tacos in front of him.

"Two minutes, ma'am," the girl says, "and it will be ready."

"Two minutes," the woman says. Her fist now encompasses the receipt. "How do I know that's what he said? Why can't you speak English?"

"I am speaking English," the girl says through a frown.

"You work for English-speaking people," the woman says. "So you need to speak English."

"I *am* speaking English," the girl insists. "Leo's isn't very good, so I speak to him in Spanish."

"Then maybe he shouldn't work here!" The woman's voice has risen and Shania feels her eyes ping-ponging back and forth between the two of them.

"Ma'am, your food will be ready in a minute," the girl says. "You don't have to be rude."

Shania flinches. The girl's tone is metal, her eyes shiny like she might cry, but Shania can tell she's angry, and for some reason it makes Shania angry too. Shania looks at her phone, at the time. She told Catherine she'd be over at three, and it's now two thirty. By the time she catches her bus, she'll be late. She's been waiting for six minutes, and it's suddenly been forever.

"You watch your tone," the woman says, still loud. "You think I won't call your manager? Are you even licensed to work here?"

Shania's fingers tap. She wants to say something—she doesn't know what. Or to whom.

"Hey, is that really necessary?" says a voice. Two young white men who look like frat boys are waiting for their food and have moved a little closer. The one wearing glasses is addressing the angry woman.

"Is it necessary that I should wait this long for two fucking tacos? *No*," the woman says.

"She said it was almost ready. Relax," says the guy. His voice is unsteady and has a laugh behind it, like he's nervous about speaking at all.

"Mind your own fucking business," the woman says. "I'm trying to speed up the process for everyone."

"Okay, well, you can be impatient, but what is yelling at her going to do? She said it's almost ready," he repeats.

"I don't care what she said," the woman says. Everyone's voices are getting louder and Shania feels herself shrink inside. "People like her are the problem with this country. If he doesn't speak English then he doesn't need to be working here!"

"Sooo you having to wait two minutes for two tacos is ruining America," he says, deadpanning. His friend laughs, and so does someone else. Shania finds herself glaring at him.

"Ironic as fuck," his friend says, softer but still loud enough to be heard. "Saying all that shit and then ordering *tacos*. Maybe get a good ole American heart-stopping burger."

A few other people laugh. Shania says nothing. But she finds herself looking at the woman, hoping her own silence says enough, hoping her refusal to laugh is a code that the woman can break.

"Order number 265," the red-lipped girl says, a white bag in her hand. The woman charges the counter and grabs the bag. She says a few more curse words and then shoves past the two guys. The one with glasses calls "have a good night" after her.

The girl behind the counter flashes a smile at the two guys and eventually the orders roll out one by one. She puts free guacamole on the guys' tray and they leave her a twenty-dollar bill in the tip jar. Shania feels a little like she's sitting in the middle of a highway, and moving either forward or backward will put her in the path of a semi. She's the last one to get her order, and when the girl calls number 271, Shania takes the bag without looking at her, without saying anything at all.

As she turns away from the counter, she inexplicably hears Catherine's voice in her head, screaming poetry. *"At the edge where the world falls away, / everything broken but bone!"* The past few days are a blur in Shania's veins, and she's angry. She imagines that she has a right to the anger that swims in her blood. It carries her forward, her feet fast. She passes by the table where the two white guys have settled with their food. She walks close, her heart hammering, and she mutters, soft but not soft: "Assholes."

And then she trips.

She saves the tacos, but her shoulder bag spins onto the floor, its contents spilling out. One of the guys begins to rise, a strange expression on his face.

"Are you, um, okay?" he asks. He's not asking about the fact that she'd almost fallen. He's asking about her curse, about her step too close to his table, which is how she fell in the first place, her foot catching on its leg. But then his eyes flick down to the ground.

"Is that—is that a tomato?" he says, pointing with his gaze.

Amid the ChapStick and receipts and her wallet and loose change sits the half-smashed, slightly wet tomato from Mrs. Walker's garden. Shania stares at it in horror, the way it fooled her into forgetting it existed, the way it hid inside her purse only to leap out now, spilling its red juice onto the floor, with so many eyes around to see.

"I—" she starts.

But she can't speak. She snatches up her wallet, shoulders her bag, and shoves past strangers on her way to the gap in the plastic curtain. She leaves the tomato, the change, the trash, everything. She pushes out into the chill.

# CHAPTER 27

Benjamin Tane answers the door, a piece of pizza drooping from his hand. He stands in the doorway staring at Shania for a full five seconds before either of them speak.

"You okay?" he says eventually after his eyes have roamed her face.

"Jesus, Ben, let her in!" Catherine yells from somewhere in the house. "You're the worst butler ever!"

He stands to the side, wordless, and she steps in. It feels like her first time ever coming here, and she wonders if one ever gets used to living in a house this big.

"She's in the kitchen," Ben says, and she's afraid he'll disappear but also afraid that he'll stay. He follows her, chewing.

"What's in the bag?" Catherine says from the fridge.

"I brought Prescott some tacos," Shania says, and realizes she's done something stupid. "And I brought you guacamole."

"From El Jefe?" Catherine says, perking up. "They have the best fucking guac, oh em gee."

"I haven't had it yet," Shania says, withdrawing it from the bag. She's relieved by her save, willing to sacrifice the guacamole she'd gotten for Prescott to rescue this situation.

"Bust it out," Catherine says. "We might as well eat his tacos too. Pres just left a little bit ago. I don't think he's coming back."

"Oh," Shania says, trying hard not to sound disappointed. "He said he wanted to talk."

Catherine sighs dramatically as she crosses the kitchen to scoop guacamole onto a chip.

"Quayloo, I don't know what the fuck is going on with him," she says. "He's being even murkier than usual. He went apeshit on our parents earlier."

"Why?" Shania says, and glances at Ben, who has finished his pizza and merely stares steadily at her.

"Who knows? Because my mom was about to go in there and vacuum. He's so weird about his room. I wonder if other dudes are as fucking anal as he is."

"Probably has porn in there," Hannah says from the other side of the massive couch she sits on. Shania had forgotten she was here and glances in her direction. She can only see the top of her head. She's flipping through Netflix.

Catherine glances at Shania.

"Definitely," she says apologetically.

Shania shrugs. "All guys look at porn."

"Girls too," Catherine protests. "Just not the weird shit guys look at."

Shania decides to taste the guacamole, thinking of her first date with Prescott. The texture isn't what she anticipated but it's good.

"Kind of spicy," she says.

"Spicy porn?" Hannah calls.

"No, idiot, we're eating guacamole," Catherine says.

"So," Ben says. "Girls' night?"

"You could say that," Catherine says. "What are you doing tonight, dear brother? With our parents absent?"

"Going out," he says.

"I don't know what you and Prescott have against staying home. Fucking roaming wolves. I myself am a hibernator, Shania. A den creature. Just feed me guac and let me nap. Maybe that can be my excuse for skipping school. *Catherine Tane is hibernating. She'll be back next season. Maybe.*"

"Why *do* you skip so much?" Shania says, curious. "Prescott told me you're a genius or something, so it can't be that the work is too hard."

Catherine stops laughing and peers at her.

"Prescott said that?"

"Kinda. He said you skipped two grades and have a ridiculous IQ or something."

"Well," Catherine says, staring at the chip in her hand. "I'm not a genius. But I did skip a grade. And preschool, but that doesn't count. I'm smart, I guess. I don't know. I just get bored."

"With school?" Shania asks. She scoops more guacamole, getting used to it. She wants Ben to speak, to make this all comfortable. She's here in the house of the Tanes, the lights bright and the huge windows filled with fall trees. She wants to eat this food and the Tanes' presence and feel full on both.

"With everything," Catherine says. "I just want to get the fuck out of here."

"And what, go to college?"

"Sure," she says, shrugging. "Or wherever."

"You kinda need to go to class if you want to go to college, right?" Shania laughs, chewing.

Catherine smiles a half smile.

"They'll give her As either way," Ben adds. Catherine's smile fades, staring at him. He stares back.

"Didn't you say you were going out?" she says.

"Yep."

"Run along," she snarls. She shoves another chip in her mouth then heads for the couch.

Shania turns to follow, but Ben catches her, saying her name.

"What?" she says.

"Can I ask you something?"

She feels like a mouse caught out on open ground, and glances toward the couch where Catherine and Hannah sit.

"Sure, I guess."

"Why are you here?" he says.

"What?"

"What are you doing here?"

"Girls' night," she says, pointing at Catherine, hoping this is answer enough, hoping he doesn't see the way his question prods the desperate core of her, pours gasoline on its thirst.

"I thought you were friends with Willa," he says. "And Michelle."

He seems genuinely confused, and she feels that he is suddenly walking the streets inside her mind, looking at the way she has arranged everyone into neighborhoods. The way Willa is a neighbor with a red X on her door, the way Shania evicted Michelle from one house and shoved her into another.

"I can't be friends with both?" she says, her throat dry, knowing they're not friends.

"No," he says plainly. "I don't think you can."

"Shania Twain! Bring forth the guac!" Catherine calls, and Shania does, turning away from Ben fast and eager as if it might

315

also put distance between herself and the conversation. It doesn't. She sinks down on the couch and the next time she glances at the kitchen, Ben is gone.

"Finally," Hannah says and digs into the bag. Onscreen a bunch of people wear crowns and argue in false British accents. "I would like to have lived back then," Hannah says. "I'd wear a fucking corset if I could look like that."

"Or you could just stop eating chips," Catherine says, crunching.

"Or I could just wear a corset," Hannah says.

"As a good feminist I'm supposed to say that living in those times would be oppressive," Catherine announces, "but I'd be willing to makes sacrifices if it meant I could wear that dress."

"Or just be a princess," Shania adds, to add something.

"Catherine's already a princess," Hannah says with a snort, and Catherine slaps her thigh. "Ow! It's true. I mean your bedroom has a view of SoBR. It's like your little kingdom."

"Speaking of which," Shania says. "Did you hear someone got killed in SoBR this morning?"

"What?" Hannah snaps her head away from the screen.

"Yeah, like really early this morning. Before dawn."

"Holy shit, who?" she says, her eyes huge.

"A homeless guy. Someone set him on fire."

"Oh," Hannah says, visibly relaxing. "I thought you were going to say, like, somebody who goes to Bard or something."

"Oh. No. A guy named Earl."

"You know his name?"

"He used to sit in Paulie's all the time."

"Oh. Well, holy shit. What happened? A bum fight?" Hannah has gone back to watching the crowns arguing. Catherine is still looking at Shania.

"*A bum fight?*" Shania says. "Someone died."

Hannah looks at her sideways.

"Don't dehumanize the dead," Catherine says in that announcer's voice she does sometimes when she's half serious but half mocking. Shania never knows exactly what she's mocking.

"They're saying somebody attacked him," Shania says.

"You know," Hannah says. "You're always talking about somebody getting killed. Cats, rats, whatever. Now this."

Shania blushes, embarrassed into quiet. She is the tooth that doesn't fit in the mouth. Catherine and Hannah sit watching crowns atop blonde hair. Shania fiddles with her split ends, the unicorn dye almost faded. *Beneath you*, she remembers Catherine saying.

"I'm going to the bathroom," Shania says and stands quickly. Catherine salutes.

The hallway is just as quiet as it was the last time she was there. It's easy to imagine that Catherine lives here by herself, that her parents are names on a scrolling cast list and not actual humans on this movie set of a house. She tries to imagine Prescott going apeshit on them here just a few hours ago, but she can't. She finds herself angry at them, without ever having seen their faces. She imagines herself coming to Prescott's aid, intervening on his behalf. Catherine has said he doesn't like anyone but Shania— obscure, angry...all these words to describe him, but he's rarely these things with her. He makes heavy things light. Before she knows it, she's passing the downstairs bathroom and climbing the stairs, running her fingers along the wall where family photos should be, rising to the second floor and moving down the landing toward Prescott's room. She wonders if Ben will be there to stop her, to question her, but the hall is empty.

The door is closed and she turns the knob silently. Not a

squeak. She half expects to find Prescott inside, hiding from his family and the world. But his bed is neatly made and empty, his desk square and black and empty. The ceilings are high and silent. The walls are empty too.

It's empty.

It takes her a moment to realize it. Not just empty of Prescott, but bare. All the posters and graphics and books that had littered the top of his desk and spanned the walls are gone. A single thumbtack remains to the right of the window. It looks like the scene in a movie where the character has left town, but his computer is still here, his shoes outside the closet. His phone charger plugged in by his bed. The patches that had sat on the windowsill are gone, dust in their place.

Shania taps the spacebar on his laptop. When the screen comes to life, there's no window left open for her to see. She stares at his desktop, empty of folders or links. Just the background photo, an American flag waving over rolling green hills.

"Where'd you go?" she whispers.

"Pining, are we?" Catherine says from the doorway, and Shania screams—she can't help it. Surprise and embarrassment wring the sound from her mouth. She spins around and finds Catherine leaning against the doorframe, studying her with an expression Shania hasn't seen before.

"I was...I was just..."

"Pining," Catherine says. "Although I don't know why."

Shania just stares at her for a long moment. Then she says, "He's been weird lately. Distant."

"Welcome to the land of Prescott, my lady," Catherine says, and gives a stiff little curtsy.

"Do you even *like* your brother?"

"Is that a requirement of having a brother? Pretty sure you're supposed to hate your siblings until you're at least thirty, when lived experience allows you to acknowledge each other's humanity and forgive past mistakes. Or maybe that's your parents. I don't know. Whichever."

Shania doesn't say anything, and Catherine continues studying her until it's as if a dam in her wells with the flood, and she sighs.

"Shania, come on. Do *you* even like Prescott? You barely know him."

"I know him."

"*I* barely know him," Catherine insists. "Why do you like him? Why are you here?"

It's like pressing a bruise, hearing these words first from Ben and now from Catherine.

"There's something about him, I don't know. He makes me feel...better."

"Better than who?"

"That's not what I meant. But better than myself. Like I'm not being judged. It's like he's invincible."

"You sure you're not trying to save him?" Catherine says, dropping her chin. "Save the bad boy? The troubled youth with the stormy brow?"

"Oh, please."

"I'm serious. You wouldn't be the first."

"He doesn't need saving."

"Yes, he does."

It's the first time Shania sees the mask slip while Catherine is sober—she gets a glimpse of something naked and cringing in her eyes, something that shrinks away from the light. Catherine feels it too. Her jaw tightens and her arms, which had been hanging loosely, now encircle her waist.

"Do you think you're a good person?" Catherine says.

"What?"

"What I said. Do you think you're a good person?"

"I mean, I guess. I don't think I'm a bad person," Shania says.

"Who would have to tell you you're a bad person in order for you to believe it?"

"Who—"

"Like, would you believe just a rando on the street if they walked up and said, 'Hey, you, you're a bad person'? Or would it need to be someone whose opinion you trust? Somebody you love?"

"I mean, yeah, it would have to be, I guess." *Do better, Shania.* Shania pushes it away. "If my mom told me that, I would believe her. That would suck, though."

"What if it was your best friend? Would you take it to heart?"

"Yeah, I guess so."

"What if it was *two* of your best friends?"

"Two? I mean...yeah," Shania says.

"What if it was three?" Catherine says. She's gazing at Shania, and that same cringing something behind her eyes looks hollow now, scooped out.

Shania stares back, looking for a path through the cities in her head, the streets rotating, the routes shifting.

"I don't have three best friends," Shania says finally.

"I do," Catherine says. "Did."

They're silent again until Catherine's hand rises, pointing at Prescott's bed.

"He told me you were researching your family," she says.

A fire in Shania's cheeks burns to life.

"Why did he tell you that?"

Catherine shrugs.

"He's my brother. Your great-granddad was William Ruther-ford II. Isn't there a street named after him downtown?"

Shania looks at the floor. Yes, there is. She'd seen a newspaper article at the library the day she'd left Mrs. Walker's garden with a tomato in her purse. Rutherford Court, a dead-end street in the financial district. He'd not only been in Blue Rock—he had been *someone*. Prescott had been so thrilled about this, had been aston-ished by her reluctance.

"What did you find out about your grandmother?" Catherine asks.

Shania makes herself look at Catherine. She wants to lie. The urge to shore up the shelter around her grandmother is even deeper, more powerful, than with Prescott. Her grandmother is a tower made of lilacs, a sacred site. But there is something new and raw in the way Catherine looks at her. It's a wide-open door that is usually either cracked or closed.

"Something . . . something terrible," Shania croaks.

"How terrible?" Catherine says.

"She . . . she did something. A long time ago. Something I would never have thought she could do. . . ."

She stops. She feels out of breath, as if she's been climbing. It feels more like descending. She's standing in Mrs. Walker's gar-den again, but when she blinks too slowly, Earl is there with her. She shoves the image of his orange coat down and back.

"And you're wondering where to go from here," Catherine says. "You're wondering if you're still allowed to love her."

"Yes."

"You're wondering if you're able to love all of her or just a piece of her," Catherine says.

It feels too close, all of it. It's like ghostly hands tightening around Shania's neck.

"Why do you care?" Shania says quickly.

"Because I know how it feels to be confused as fuck about your family. And for... for them to be confused about you."

"Hey, bitches," calls Hannah, her voice echoing off the bare walls of the hallways into the bare walls of Prescott's room. Shania and Catherine both jump. "Someone's at the door!"

The doorbell rings.

"See!" Hannah shouts.

Catherine stares at Shania a breath longer, and then pushes off the doorjamb, retreating out of Prescott's room and back down the hall, toward the stairs. She's already halfway down by the time Shania catches up. Shania's on the landing when Catherine opens the door.

It's Willa.

"What the fuck are you doing here?" Catherine says, a laugh tacked on at the end, genuine surprise.

Willa holds up a phone.

"Not that you need this," she says. "But I'm bringing you your phone back."

Catherine doesn't reach for the phone. She leans against the doorframe, hooking one leg behind the other.

"Oh, wow, that's a nice surprise," she drawls. "Hello, little phone, I haven't seen you since you were kidnapped from your bed! Have they been feeding you?"

Willa doesn't blink.

"We wouldn't have had to take it if you had done the right thing from the beginning, Cat."

"Don't fucking call me Cat, Willa," she snaps. "We're not friends. Not anymore."

"Oh, trust me, I'm fully aware. I can't be friends with someone who can't see why keeping someone's nudes without their consent is a fucking problem."

"For fuck's sake," Catherine cries, throwing her hands up. "It was a dick pic. Eric's face wasn't even in it. Why did he send it if—"

"Some fucking feminist," Willa says, loud to drown her out. *"Some. Fucking. Feminist."*

Shania is still watching the scene from the middle of the stairs, feeling dizzy, when Hannah makes her entrance.

"Willa, I get why you're mad, but what the fuck," Hannah says. "Sneaking in to Catherine's party to steal her phone is like the tackiest thing ever."

"I didn't sneak in," Willa says. "I showed up. Just like everybody else."

"I would have kicked you out if I had known why you came," Catherine says. "When you showed up with Michelle, I was like, okay, weird, since we hadn't been hanging out. But I was willing to give you the benefit of the doubt. I thought you were making an effort. I know you're a psycho bitch, but I didn't think you'd go full-on headcase and steal my shit."

"It wasn't yours."

"Really? Because that *truly* looks like my phone."

"You know what the fuck I mean, Cat. Catherine."

"Does your little sidekick know you're here? Michelle?"

"I told her I was coming, yes."

"She turned you into such an asshole," Hannah says. She's drinking Sprite, standing a little behind Catherine. "You used to be fun, you know? A couple years ago you would have laughed about the picture."

"A couple years ago I was a piece of shit," Willa says. Shania can see her blush from the stairs.

"Maybe you're a piece of shit *now*," Catherine says coolly. She holds her hand out for the phone. A second later Willa plops it into her palm.

"I already bought another one," Catherine says, studying it. "But whatever. Thanks for bringing my shit back, you little thief. You're lucky I didn't tell Ms. Green or the headmaster. They would have kicked your povertous ass out on the street."

"Tell them," Willa says. "Then I can tell them about the photo and everything else I found in your phone."

From where Shania stands on the stairs, she can only see the back of Catherine, her golden shoulders, her bundle of blonde dreadlocks obscuring most of her slender neck. But the shoulders stiffen, the neck goes rigid.

"What the fuck are you talking about?"

"Your texts. You probably went and deleted them on your laptop, huh? As soon as you realized your phone was gone. But that's not how it works, dumbass. With your ridiculous IQ, I figured you'd at least know that. You can't delete from the cloud what's saved on the phone itself. So I had plenty of time to read everything. And I've been reading everything since I took the phone too. It's like being back in the group chat: The messages get sent through Wi-Fi, so as long as I was connected, it was like I was still there chatting it up with you and Hannah and Julia. Interesting you took Julia out this week. What happened? Did she get sick of your model-minority bullshit? Or did she violate the rules of White Club now too? First rule of White

Club: Don't talk about White Club. Second rule of White Club: Don't—"

"Fuck off, Langford. You're full of shit," Catherine says. The tremble in her voice unnerves Shania. It's like seeing the Sphinx twitch.

"I'm not, and you know it. Last year when I told Bard why Prescott attacked Eric, they didn't believe me. But now I have proof."

Catherine takes a step out the front door, a single staggering step. Willa leans backward but her feet stay planted.

"You told them Eric started it," Willa says calmly. "You lied. And you admitted that was a lie in your texts to Prescott. I saw where you told your brother not to worry, that you told the headmaster Eric threatened to hit you so it would look like Prescott was just protecting his sister from the big scary Black guy. Real nice, Catherine."

"Prescott is just—" Catherine begins, but Willa cuts her off.

"A racist," she says calmly. "Prescott is a racist. Before you make any excuses for him or, God forbid, try to make him the victim. Your brother is a white supremacist, Catherine, and it's weird that you and your family are always trying to hide it, because Prescott is really proud of it."

"You fucking fat bitch," Catherine says, and goes on cursing, but all the other names she spits at Willa blur in Shania's ears. She's only hearing two words, the ones Willa had spoken: *white supremacist*. For a moment she's no longer standing in Catherine Tane's house—she's standing outside Gram's hospital room, listening to the sound of doctors murmuring. Gram had tried to pretend her heart was fine, and so Shania pretended too, ignored every time her grandmother paled and had to sit. But Gram had still died. Now Shania is remembering every time Prescott has said "we" and "us," Shania hearing the words but letting them, like stones, sink beneath the blue of his eyes. She'd never heard Gram say "we" and "us." Had she left words like that behind the way she did Blue Rock?

"So, what, you're going to tell Bard?" Catherine is snapping. "You think they give a shit? You think they care about Eric or you or Michelle at Bard?"

"I *know* they don't," Willa says calmly. "But that's not the point. I'm going to show them, and I'm going to tell them everything I know about Catherine Tane and Prescott Tane and at least I will have done that."

"My dad will kick you out," Catherine spits.

"Willa, are you serious?" Hannah cries, stepping closer to the door. "It's all just jokes, oh my God. Why are you so serious all the time now?"

"Eric was in the hospital. That's not a joke. Catherine keeping a naked picture of him when he asked you to delete it is not a joke. Showing them to people at parties is not a fucking joke. You don't even see him as a person, Cat."

"I loved him," Catherine says, her voice rising. "I fucking loved him, Willa."

"No you didn't," Willa says, shaking her head. "You fetishized him. And then you threw him under the fucking bus with that *poor little white girl* act when it mattered the most."

"You and Michelle and this bullshit," Hannah says, loud. "You think you're this fucking saint now, Willa? You think you're perfect now that you've learned some crap?"

"It has nothing to do with Michelle," Willa says. "And I don't think I'm perfect. It's not what I've learned—it's what I've unlearned. Maybe one day you'll understand that."

"You're still white, you nardshark," Hannah scoffs.

"Yeah. I know."

She turns to leave. Shania can't see if she drove or walked or got dropped off, and descends a few more stairs to see. Her breath catches when she sees Ben behind the wheel of a car she's never seen—a beat-up Mazda 3. He's been watching the scene impassively and starts the engine when Willa approaches. She's halfway to the car when Catherine throws the phone.

It strikes Willa in the back of the head, makes a sound like a hockey puck striking a tree. Willa cries out, staggers. Hannah stands with both hands over her mouth.

"What the fuck, Cathy," Ben shouts, half getting out of the car.

Catherine is poised on her front porch, one foot on a step and the other on the ground. Willa raises her hand to Ben, then turns slowly.

"Nice, Cat," she says. She almost sounds disappointed. Then her eyes raise to the doorway behind her, glancing at Hannah before landing on Shania. She registers her presence with a blink, then a small shake of her head. "And I guess I should've figured you'd be here. Good luck."

"Fuck you, Willa," Catherine stammers. "Fuck you—you—you—"

"Catherine, be quiet," Shania says from inside the house. She doesn't want to hear. She's afraid someone else will.

Willa picks up the phone and tosses it back to Catherine, where it lands with a clatter at her feet. Shania can see that the screen is shattered. She guesses it doesn't matter, for either of them. Willa turns and walks away, climbs in the car with Ben. The park lights blink out and they make their way down the hill that the Tane house sits on like a lord. Catherine screams curses after them until her breath, and Willa, is gone.

# CHAPTER 28

Shania stares at Eric's face on the bus to school. She's studying Michelle's Instagram, to which Catherine had directed her the night before in a thread of drunken misspellings. She'd rage-texted Shania until she'd fallen asleep.

**Duckin hitch**

**Who thee duck does dhe thank dhe us**

Two photos were posted on Saturday afternoon from Michelle's account, one of her standing in a pumpkin patch, the sky wide above her. She stands with her back to the camera, the sunrise ahead, her arms overhead and her fingers outstretched. Her head is angled just slightly sideways, enough to where Shania can see from her cheekbone that she's smiling. She looks like she might fly. The other photo is a selfie in profile, her nose smashed against the cheek of a boy, the boy Shania had seen at the Pocket garden. Eric Young. Shania's first time actually getting a good look at him.

She studies him again now, his face broad, a small gap between his teeth, large eyes with eyelashes almost as long as Michelle's.

His hair is curly but short. They grin at the camera together, him squinting a little and her eyes filled with sunshine.

Shania can see why it set Catherine off.

She studies his jaw. Julia said it had been wired shut after his fight with Prescott. Willa had said "attacked." The city in Shania's head shifts and turns like a Rubik's Cube. Everything she's seen, everything she's been told, are like dots of ink waiting to be connected; but whenever she begins, the inkpot spills, the impulse to build a shelter around Prescott like a spreading puddle. Gram died with secrets on her tongue—Prescott swallows his. The spilled ink of Prescott leaks over the memory of her grandmother, making them part of the same indistinguishable mess. She wonders why she has to be the one to clean it up, and the indignation feels good, is a distraction sturdy enough to lean on.

She pulls the cord and a moment later is off the bus, walking toward Bard. She's early. The line of Jaguars and BMWs is just beginning, which means the school will be mostly empty, the brief slice of time when she is able to walk the halls and not compare herself to anything except the silence opening before her like a wound.

The heat in the greenhouse should feel pleasant. But today Shania feels a shiver leftover from the outdoors. More than summer finally giving up, something inside her feels as if it has curled in toward itself. As she makes her way toward her planter, her mind wanders down the rows of other gardens: her grandmother's, the short, neat rows of Morrisville; then the Pocket garden of Mrs. Walker, her cucumbers and her corn. Her tomatoes.

Shania sees the lilac first when she reaches her planter. Tiny shoots, but the sharp, fresh green of newborn things—for a moment it's the only memory she has. She touches the shoots lightly with her fingertips and swears she feels her tattoo tingle under her sock, a shiver from root to petal. Fresh starts. She wonders if she should try getting rid of the almanac again, or if, like a bad penny, it'll keep turning up, a paperback haunting. And then there's Prescott's theory—that a ghost can't haunt you if you hug it tightly enough.

She reaches for Anne Stanton's poems instead and draws the book out, thinking of Catherine. She doesn't feel like shouting poetry, but she does whisper:

> *And I am as the land, splitting*
> *at seams hidden by soil:*
> *the stone of me ready for water*
> *to change what looks unchangeable,*
> *to find each crack and slowly rend*
> *me open.*

This had been Gram's favorite, and Mr. Foster had rolled his eyes about this poem—"Anne Stanton had some pretty words, but overall, a throw-pillow poet." And it was true, Gram *had* crocheted a few lines of "Watching Horses." But how can Shania be ashamed after watching her grandmother's fingers work so carefully with the hook and yarn? She closes her eyes and sees a tomato spinning through space. Is there anything she can keep? No, Gram hadn't hugged her ghosts. She had come back and laid them to rest when she gave Mrs. Walker the land. But was that enough? Burying a ghost feels incomplete, Shania thinks, when you don't tell your granddaughter about the skeletons.

Her phone vibrates against the metal table and she jumps, bumping the table, sending it spinning to the floor. When she picks it up it's still vibrating. Not a text: a phone call. Prescott. At the sight of his name, her stomach drops. What can she even say to him? After she'd left the Tanes' house yesterday, she'd texted him three times—*I need to talk to you*—but he never responded. They've never talked on the phone, only texted, and when she answers, she fully expects to hear nothing but the rustled static of a pocket.

"Hello?"

But instead she hears Prescott's voice, sharp and direct.

"Shania? Where are you?"

"Where? I'm at school."

"*Where* at school?" he demands.

"The...the greenhouse. Why?"

"Stay there," he says, and then the call ends, the phone silent against her ear. She holds it away and stares at it, dumbfounded. Her first thought is a school shooting and her heart begins to hammer, calculating the likelihood of this happening at Bard. She stares at the screen, considering calling 911, when the door sighs open.

"Prescott," she says, breathless. "What's happening? Is—"

"I need your help," he says. His face is paler than usual, the whites of his eyes red in the corners. This plus the lavender half-moons under his eyes give him the look of a werewolf watching the moon rise.

"What's wrong?" she says.

"You understand me," he says. He pauses a few feet away. "You know how I feel about you. You know that, right?"

"I... what? I mean... yes? What...?"

"You understand me," he repeats. "I feel like you get it. You get *me*. You understand."

"Understand what?"

"You may *not* understand," he says then. He shoves his fists against his eyes, rubbing. "Fuck. You might not. But it's all for a reason, okay? I think you'll understand when I have a chance to explain it."

"Explain what?"

"I can't right now. Right now I just need your help, okay? Can you help me, Shania?"

"I . . . yes. But with what? What do you need? Is everything okay?"

"It will be," he says. "I need you to do something for me."

He comes closer now, reaching his hand into his pocket. He glances toward the door and then comes even closer. He withdraws an object from his pocket.

"I already cleaned it."

It's metal, a silver glint catching the light and throwing it up toward the ceiling. He presses it into her hands, and she stares down at it.

Brass knuckles. Except not brass, but silver, the ridge for each knuckle like the curving back of a Harley Davidson. She studies the rings, each one like the mouth of a miniature exhaust pipe, smudged with fingerprints, before she looks up into his eyes.

"What is this?"

"I need you to hide it," he says. His eyes are wider than she's ever seen them, the red at the corners creeping out closer to the pupil. He looks like he hasn't slept in days.

"Hide it?"

"Yes. Please, Shania. Shania, please. They're coming to the school and I know they're going to search all the trash cans and all that shit and I just really need you to hide it, okay?"

"Prescott, what?"

"You're a girl," he says. "They won't search you. They won't even look at you. Can you help me? I really need your help on this."

He's staring so deeply into her eyes that she feels it in her stomach. All her questions are answered there in his gaze: the wildflowers growing on the hill; crying in his front seat; standing on the roof with his hand in her hand and the wind in her hair, the world their kingdom. She's seen the way he sees her, the photo that makes her a queen. The hate like a house cat on her lap. She thinks of the words Willa had said in Catherine's driveway: *attacked, proof, racist.* What Michelle had said about the cat hanging from its tail. Shania can almost hear the sound of its fur rustling against the metal of the gate. She shrinks from it. But then she's remembering the houses she's been building: her great-grandfather, her grand-mother, everything transforming into flawless, shining marble...

Her fingers embrace the silver, encircling it, just as the doors to the greenhouse open and Ms. Hassoon enters, followed by Catherine and Adam and everyone else. Prescott gives her one last look, squeezes her clasped hands, and leaves. Catherine looks at them the way only Catherine does: both bored and interested, like a cat eyeing a bird through glass.

Shania stares down at what she's been given, what she accepted. This metal was made for violence. Shania blinks and she's standing in Gram's garden, watching her relocate slugs. *Killing is ugly, and God don't like ugly,* she always said, but she said so many things, and Shania has other words in her head now too, spiky green shoots, fresh and new. She wants to believe these new words—maybe they're easier to carry than what's in the almanac, even if they stick in her throat. She squeezes the knuckles tight in her palm and tells herself this isn't the same thing as killing.

She slides her hand over the top of her planter, slowly pushes the metal down between the lilacs and the hollyhock, deeper and deeper, until her knuckle meets the surface of the dirt and the silver flash is far out of sight, buried in cool, dark soil.

# CHAPTER 29

Shania can hear the howling. She stands outside B-Rock Dog Rescue Association, working up the nerve to go in. She's supposed to be at Paulie's, is even wearing her polo shirt. But when she'd left Bard and checked her phone, there had been a text waiting for her from Ben, simple words: **We need to talk.** And she could have merely texted back. But her feet had taken her to the opposite side of the street, onto the 13 bus, the business card Ben had given her at the farmers' market clutched in her hand. She watches two women walk inside with their children, the volume of barking rising for the moment the doors are open before falling again. She hasn't yet decided if she's going in. She doesn't even know why she has come. All she knows is that when Prescott stood in the greenhouse, his wide eyes took her in and were certain of her being on his side. And when she squeezes her eyes shut, standing outside the rescue, she can see Ben's eyes in his house that night: *Wondering. About you.* In that moment, Ben had seen her too. Ben, who had smiled at her on the bus and said, *Good people tend to gravitate toward each other.* She thinks of the magnetism that had pulled her to Prescott, how she had become a willing moon, revolving. She can feel the weight of the metal transferring from his fingers to hers. The howls rising from the shelter could be coming from her own throat. She climbs the stairs, grips the door, and pulls.

The animal smell washes over her as she steps into a large, bright room—one whole wall is a glass observation window into the room where all the dogs are kept, rows of steel cages where staff in matching polos tend to various big-eyed prisoners, cleaning cages, scratching ears. One of those people is Ben Tane, his unmistakable broad shoulders and hair the color of shining wet wood. Watching him through the glass, the floor feels tilted. Shania doesn't have a plan. She's realizing that the best thing to do is leave, when he looks up while lifting a grizzled cocker spaniel from its cage and sees her.

He freezes, the dog cradled in his arms, his eyes sizing her up, scanning the reception area to see if she's alone. She usually only thinks of her tooth when she smiles, but in this moment every inch of her feels wrong, sharp, treacherous. They stand staring like this for what feels like too long until he finally untangles one hand from the dog and lifts his index finger. *Wait.*

She does, lurking near the door. She avoids looking at the dogs. She feels as if all the threads of her are hanging loose, frayed, and that pulling any single one might undo her. When Ben emerges from the holding room, he has three dogs on leashes. The tan hound from the market, Sunny. The cocker spaniel. A black, vaguely pit bullish dog that rescues seem to overflow with. Ben moves toward a door she hadn't noticed and motions with his head.

They step out into an exercise yard, high fences and AstroTurf.

There's a kiddie pool that the pit bull runs for and leaps into with a happy tail. The other two slowly patrol the edges of the yard. Ben stands watching, not looking at Shania.

"What are you doing here?" he says.

"I don't know," she says. Honesty feels easy right now. All her wounds feel open—words just fall out. "I got your text saying you needed to talk to me."

"You could have just texted me back, or called," he says. She knows this.

"Why do you like me?" she says, then blinks hard. "Not *like* me, like me. I'm not saying you do. I mean...tolerate me. Why do you even talk to me?"

"I tolerate everyone," he says. "Unless they give me a reason not to. I try to look for friends in unexpected places."

"And that was me...."

"A girl who goes to Bard, with pink-and-blue hair, who actually has a job...was unexpected."

"But?"

"But then you did the expected. So." He shrugs, not looking at her. It's his nonchalance that stings the most. She knows what his voice sounds like when it's warm. Now he doesn't care enough to be cold. The truth is she doesn't know him at all, and she sees that the opportunity has been lost.

"Do you think I'm a bad person?" she says, but the words aren't even out of her mouth before she regrets them, before Ben groans.

"This isn't what I wanted to talk to you about," he says, shaking his head.

"What is?"

"I think you can probably guess," he says.

336

"What happened with Willa and Catherine."

"That's part of it."

"Your brother—" she begins.

"Is a piece of shit," he says quickly. "And you know that."

"He—"

"Is a piece of shit," he says again, harder this time.

The cocker spaniel ventures toward the pool, and the pit bull wiggles its butt in the air.

"I'm just trying to do the right thing," Shania says quietly. It sounds too much like a whine. And that's when she realizes why she'd come. She wants someone to tell her what the right thing is. But more so, she wants to be told she's already doing it. "Your brother is just—"

"That's for you," Ben interrupts. "Why are you telling *me*? Like I don't know? I know who he is. I know what he's like. And *that's* what I wanted to talk to you about. If you want to date my brother and be friends with Catherine, fine. Whatever. But you need to leave Michelle the fuck alone. Never talk to her again. And I'm serious. You're just lying to yourself pretending to be friends with everybody, knowing good and well—"

Her temper flares then, and she cuts him off.

"So, wait, you said we needed to talk, but what you really mean is you wanted to lecture me. About how I'm lying to myself? You're one to talk, Ben. What, you think because you choose to drive a goddamn Mazda instead of a BMW that you're somehow *better* or like on the moral high ground? Because you take the bus? Because you go to protests?"

She's gratified by the flush across his cheeks, but she also wishes she could put her hands on either side of his face and hold him until it fades.

"I'm not perfect," he says. "I know that. But I'm trying to be different from my family."

"For who?" Shania sneers. "Michelle? Willa? Because as far as I can tell, they're the only ones who know you think Prescott is a piece of shit. What, you're making some big passive statement going to public school? Big whoop. It just looks like you're running away, and hoping somebody else does the hard part."

"Which is what?" he snaps. "What is the hard part?"

Shania is transported to her grandmother's garden, her earliest memories; Gram with her trowel, digging out the rotted roots of planted carrots. *Root rot will spread*, she'd said, sweating under her sunhat. *The only thing you can do is dig it right out.* But to Ben, Shania only says:

"You're the one who knows everything. You tell me."

He sighs and runs a hand through his hair.

"I just want everybody to stop lying, Shania," he says. He sounds tired. "There's like this whole quilt of white lies holding everything together—all the lies we tell each other and ourselves and about ourselves—and it's not even keeping us warm."

She stares at him, hating that she wants to cry, hating the thread she can see laced through every square of her life.

"You think I'm just this stupid girl who is lying to herself, but maybe *you're* the one who's not being honest," she says. "You said if I 'want to date Prescott, fine.' Why is that *fine*? If he's so bad? Because then you can feel good about yourself, telling yourself you drew a line in the sand?"

"Maybe so," he says, shaking his head. "Or maybe because when I met you I thought you seemed like the kind of person who would make her own choices and choose her own path."

Her stomach clenches—she has made choices. She thinks of what she'd told Ms. Green about Michelle. She thinks of the taco truck. She thinks of standing behind Catherine, watching Willa turning away. Staying silent had been a choice too. *Do better, Shania.* Do better than what?

"You said a quilt made of white lies," she says. It might be all she has left. "But white lies don't hurt anybody, Ben. That's why they call them that."

"Maybe we actually call them that because they're hidden," he says, frowning. "White ends up invisible. Unless you really, really look. And when you really, really look, you see this huge web of them. And the truth is, you can't build anything on spiderwebs. Nothing that lasts. And it keeps us all stuck."

They pause, staring at each other.

"You're so worried about being good," he says quietly. "Maybe you should focus more on doing good."

The door opens and the tattooed girl from the farmers' market emerges, letting a small shaggy mutt out into the yard who immediately starts tearing around in zealous circles. The girl laughs and then puts up a hand to block the sun, looking at Shania.

"I think I remember you." She smiles. "Come to volunteer?"

Shania's phone vibrates and she glances at it. Catherine.

**CT: Guess who's picking you up for school tomorrow? ME.**

"Something like that," Shania mumbles. "Just trying to help."

**SH: Do you even know where I live?**
**CT: I am all-knowing, Shania Twain.**

The tattooed girl is actually remembering now, staring at Shania.

"Wait, I do remember you! You're the girl who found one of the cats! In SoBR. Did you hear? About the guy who got killed? What the cops are saying?"

Ben says, "What?" but Shania just stares, walls in her head shifting, looking for purchase.

"It started with the cats," the girl says. "Can you believe it?"

"What are you saying?" Ben says.

"Cops say they have a lead on who did it. The radio was talking about surveillance tape. They don't have him on tape with the homeless guy, but they have him with the cats. White guy in a gray hoodie."

Shania looks down at her shoes, the same ones she'd been wearing the day she saw the blood. When she blinks up at the sun, she can still see the outline of her feet against her eyelids, a snap of red. She turns away from Ben, toward the door. The tan hound walks along the edge of the yard, sniffing the brick, and the call of his gentle ears, his fawn eyes, is too much. Before she reaches the exit, Shania squats down, hand outstretched, cooing for him in the voice she'd use for Simon.

The dog doesn't move, the smile of his teeth hidden by wet black lips. He gazes through her as if she's air.

**CT: See you at 7:30. Cock-a-doodle-doo.**

# CHAPTER 30

Shania is brushing her teeth when her mother comes in and opens the closet, withdrawing her striped bag of makeup. She hasn't had more than a few sips of coffee yet, so she doesn't speak, dipping the wand into the mascara and swiping it over her eyelashes in long, slow strokes. Shania watches her in the mirror, her own eyes tired. She hadn't slept. She feels shaky and doesn't understand how her mother's hands can be so still. By the time her mother begins to apply foundation, Shania feels she's watching the pieces of a costume slide into place. Her mouth is full of toothpaste when the words pop out:

"What else have you lied to me about?"

The hand with its beige-tipped fingers freezes.

"Excuse me, what?" her mother says.

"Why are we here?" Shania says. "We both know Gram was from Blue Rock, but you're still always talking about how this is a fresh start. Either way, why are we here?"

"We have history here," her mother says.

"*Bad* history!" Shania snaps.

"Oh, please! All history has bad and good! It's what we make of it!"

"So, you *do* know," Shania hears herself croak. "What happened. What Gram did."

She and Shania stare at each other in the mirror, frozen. When her mother moves, it's to adjust the watch on her wrist, a thick gold thing. It was Gram's watch and it only just occurs to Shania that it was probably her Great-Grandpa Bill's and Gram wore it after he died, transferred from wrist to wrist after funerals and funerals. The thought of it suddenly fills Shania with dread. She thinks of her grandmother's house, the way, together, she and her mother boxed things after Gram died. Shania had been reeling from the funeral. What happened to Gram's sun hat? What happened to her glass figurines? How did a watch become the thing that they inherit? What else do they pass on? She leans to spit toothpaste into the sink, feeling rabid.

"The past is the past," her mother says. She's left a smear of foundation across the watch's face. "Your grandmother made amends and moved on. We all did."

"How is it making amends if I didn't know?" Shania says. "What amends did Great-Grandpa Bill make?"

"He's dead, Shania," her mother says, blinking. She pulls open the bathroom door, looking like she wants to escape. "What can a dead man do?"

"But *we're* alive," she says. There's still toothpaste in her mouth, but it's joined by a sourness. "And I've lived my whole life thinking my grandma was this perfect person, and all I knew about Grandpa was his laugh...."

She trails off, floundering.

"It's not a bad thing to remember the best parts of someone," her mother says, wavering in the doorway.

Shania doesn't know how to tell her own mother that she sounds childish, that she's admitting to telling herself a bedtime story. Shania thinks this is how myths are made, and her face burns. What if Cinderella's carriage wasn't a pumpkin, but a rotten tomato? What if Shania's been carrying it in an invisible purse?

From outside the apartment comes a flurry of honks, and hearing it, Shania's mother goes to the window, frowning. Shania follows her into the hall, mouth still ringed with foam, and watches her peer through the blinds.

"I think one of your friends is here," she says, and moves toward the kitchen. "A girl."

Catherine. She'd spent all night thinking about Prescott, about what he'd given her. What she'd taken. She's forgotten all about his sister.

"I need to—" she begins.

"Go to school," her mother interrupts. "And I need to get ready for work. We can talk later."

Shania imagines a quilt sewn with spiderwebs cascading over their apartment in a pale wave.

Catherine shoves coffee in Shania's face the moment she opens the car door.

"Rise and shine, butterball," she beams.

"Butterball?" Shania has barely buckled her seat belt when Catherine is rocketing out of the apartment's side street and onto the main road. The coffee is so hot Shania has to keep switching hands: Catherine's cup holders are full of candy wrappers and receipts.

"Butterball—I don't know. It's the first thing I thought of. This was not a veiled fat-shaming attempt."

"Okay," Shania says. "That's comforting, I guess."

"I'd tell you if you were fat, dear Shania. And then I'd tell you that you're perfect just the way you are."

"Oh. Okay."

Catherine seems wired. Not just the coffee: Something is blazing at her center, bright and electric, something that makes her screech through yellow lights and barely pause at stop signs. Every action is illuminated. It takes Shania a while to realize she drives a stick shift.

"You drive a stick," Shania says.

"You bet your tits I do," she says. She passes a cop on Broadway and waves cheerily at him as she goes by. "That way no one can drive my car if I don't want them to. Nobody really drives a stick anymore, you know. It used to be a 'girls don't drive sticks' kind of thing, but now it's a 'nobody drives a stick' thing."

Shania immediately thinks back to the night outside the bowling alley.

"Is this why you didn't want me to drive your car?"

"When?" she says.

"At the bowling alley. When you were drunk."

"Yes," Catherine says. Shania can never tell when she's lying. She blows through another yellow light. Shania wonders if this is what it's like to be Catherine Tane: always being almost caught but never really stopped. In another life she might have been a bank robber. Shania thinks it would suit her.

"How's the coffee?" Catherine asks.

"Hot."

"Do you even drink coffee?" She slides Shania a look.

"Sometimes."

"Liar," she says.

Shania sips the coffee in defiance, burning her tongue.

"So here's the thing, Shania Twain," Catherine says. "Prescott is gone."

"What?"

"Prescott is gone. He's on a trip with our dad."

"Again."

"Again," she says, bitterly, and a red light finally brings their careening progress to a halt. The cop she'd passed a while back is behind them, talking on the phone and smiling.

"Where did they go?" Shania asks. She keeps her eyes fastened on the road ahead. If she looks at Catherine she thinks the feeling that's building inside her will overflow, disappointment and confusion crashing together and making a mess of everything. She might cry. Not because he's gone. She doesn't know why, but she might cry. She thought the scream was gone, ripped out over loosestrife. But her throat is tight with it now, newer and sharper.

"The same place they always go," Catherine says, but shakes her head as if she immediately regrets saying it. "Toledo. They're in Toledo."

"Toledo?"

"Fucking Toledo."

The light turns green and she stomps the gas. Shania glances over at her and it suddenly hits her how angry Catherine is. Shania doesn't know how she didn't see it before: Catherine is absolutely furious. The bright wire of her energy is rage, so hot it's almost smoking. When she gets up to 55 in a 35, it's rage that fuels the car, not gasoline.

"Are you okay?" Shania asks after a moment. They're entering SoBR.

"I think I'm great," Catherine says. "Don't you think I'm great?"

"Honestly you sound a little insane," Shania says before she can stop herself and Catherine snaps her head to look. She stares for a second before turning her eyes back to the road and laughing, long and loud and hard.

"Shania," she says. "You're a fucking keeper, that's for sure."

Shania doesn't know how to reply to that so she doesn't. Catherine turns onto Jarvis and Shania glances at her.

"What way are you taking?"

"The scenic route," she says.

"You're not taking me somewhere to murder me, are you?"

"No," she says. "I wouldn't do that."

They pass Paulie's and Shania can see Dorothy inside in her apron, drinking the coffee that Shania knows is black, looking up at the TV. Shania wonders if it's still unmuted from last week, if the shop is filled with the sound of newscasters saying Earl's name.

"Have you heard anything else about the guy you say got killed?" Catherine says, as if reading her mind.

Shania clenches the hot cup tighter, until it hurts.

"No. Just that the tip line is still up."

"They don't know anything," Catherine says, half question.

Shania can't make herself answer. A white guy in a gray hoodie. It's not the hoodie that burns in her mind—it's what might be under it. A white T-shirt? A green triangle? She has almost googled the symbol a dozen times, her courage always failing. And just like that she steps into a time machine, hurtling back to the day her grandmother died, the words before *liars*.

Gram had said, *I don't think I can keep it up*, and now Shania knows exactly what she meant.

Catherine turns onto Garden, which leads down to the river.

"We're going to be late," Shania says. Catherine's breakneck speed has dragged slower and slower and here her Mercedes crawls around each curve in the road. The lakefront area where the city hosts concerts and festivals is bare now in the colder weather, only a few joggers and their dogs dotting the scene. The overpass looms ahead, packed with rush hour traffic, the cement dark in the morning gloom.

"That's where they said he lived," Catherine says, slowing down even more.

"Earl," Shania says. His name feels like peanut butter in her mouth. An elephant squeezes into the backseat—she thinks it might've been there all along.

Catherine nods. She slows even more, the car barely moving. Beyond the window Shania can make out a few shabby tents, sheets of plastic lashed to shopping carts, a makeshift city. A few figures mill about in the shadow of the overpass, faceless phantoms, none of them wearing a neon orange coat. The elephant presses its knees into Shania's back.

"What are you thinking about?" Catherine says.

"I'm wondering what we're doing over here," Shania says.

"You're not stupid, Shania," she says. Catherine throws the car into park, barely pulling out of the lane. She turns, jerking against her seat belt to face Shania in the front seat. "You're not fucking stupid so don't pretend you are."

So close to what Michelle had said in Fountain Circle, the words feel like a punch. Shania stares at her for as long as she can, Catherine's eyes bluer than her brother's, her blonde dreadlocks tied at her neck except for one or two that hang like fuzzy vines around her face. Shania has the sudden desire to cut them off. She imagines herself with a huge pair of cartoon shears like the ones her grandmother used to trim back the lilacs, taking each golden rope one by one and lopping it off at the root. Shania turns away. There are phantom cats coming out of every corner of the car.

"Willa is full of shit, you know," Catherine says when they're silent for a long time.

"About what exactly?"

"About everything. The phone. Michelle. Eric. Prescott. She's a bitter bitch. I hope you didn't believe any of the shit she said at my house."

"I don't know what to believe, honestly," Shania says. She feels as if she's being squeezed.

"You believe *me*," Catherine barks, an order.

"I don't know what to believe," Shania repeats.

"You think we're all crazy, don't you," Catherine says, almost laughing. "You think you stepped through the mirror into Wonderland and we're all having tea with a fucking rabbit, don't you?"

Shania just stares at her. The time machine Prescott had asked her about feels large enough to encircle the whole city, the whole country. Morrisville and Blue Rock melt into each other, and Shania remembers how it felt to be a swaying daisy onstage in first grade. Her grandmother was alive and Shania was safe in her shell and all the lies were coiled neatly in their boxes. She would give anything to go back. But it would be stepping into a bedtime story.

"You can't say anything," Catherine says after a long moment. "My dad took him to get help. You can't say anything or you'll just make it worse."

"Prescott?" Shania says. "I thought you said he was in Toledo."

Catherine blinks at her.

"Quayloo, Shania. Yeah. Toledo. The mental hospital. What-ever you want to call it."

"Your dad took him to a *mental hospital*?"

"He needs help, Shania."

"What, like he's crazy? Prescott's not crazy."

Catherine squints her eyes, and Shania can't tell what she sees.

"He needs help," Catherine says again. "You don't think he needs help?"

"He's not crazy," Shania snarls.

"Why not?"

"Because! I've talked to him! I know him! He knows what he's doing—"

"What he's doing," Catherine repeats softly. "So you know."

Around Shania, a bigger picture floats: flowers, cats, tacos, tomatoes, newspapers, rows and rows of garden. There are a thousand glimmering pieces and she thinks if she lets them drift closer, knitting, the picture will be too terrible for her eyes. Blinding white marble. She closes them.

"You can't say anything, Shania," Catherine says.

"Why not?"

Catherine stares at her hands on the steering wheel.

"He's my brother."

They sit there by the overpass, watching the traffic crawl over-head. Red car. Blue car. Black car. Blue car. A river of steel and noise that Shania can barely hear through the window. In the city beneath the overpass, more figures stir. Someone wearing a red sweatshirt emerges from the encampment and wanders toward Catherine's car. Before Shania can even say anything, the sound of the locks clicking makes her jump. The sound becomes part of the static in her brain; her mind has become a loop of surveillance tape. She sees Earl in grainy gray and white. She remembers staring over the counter at him, watching his hands, half imagining warm fur squirming in his grip. Now when she closes her eyes he has the whiskers of a cat. She wants to claw her own face.

"I wish I had never come to your party," she says softly.

"My party?" Catherine says, her voice rising in surprise. "What?"

"I wish I had never gone," Shania says to the window. "I could have avoided him, I could have avoided you. I could have avoided... this."

"You think any of this was something you could just steer around?" Catherine snaps. "You on your lonely little boat, just paddling out to sea and avoiding the big storm? Fuck you, Shania. That's not how this works! You're one of *us*."

"I am *not* one of you," Shania cries, finally turning away from the window. "You think you own everyone and you think you can just move people around like fucking dolls in a dollhouse. Your weird made-up words and your pink bowling ball and your house! You're a... you're a rich bitch who thinks the whole city is your playground!"

Catherine's face is a dish of spilled milk.

"Don't try to go all Willa on me," Catherine says. "Don't try to act like you're different from us now. You know what?"

She yanks on the stick, throws the car into drive, and casts Shania a poisonous look, made terrifying by her almost-smile.

"You know what?" she says again. "I'll fucking show you."

The Mercedes meanders back to Bard; the hot rage that had sent Catherine rocketing through SoBR leaked out of the tank somewhere on the road behind them. She obeys traffic signals. She comes to a complete stop at each red octagon. By the time they reach Bard, the line of cars leading up the ramp has dwindled to nothing. They don't even have to wait.

"Perks of being a lateflower," Catherine says as she maneuvers them toward her parking spot. She gets out, slams her door, strides on. Shania follows as if in a trance.

First period is upstairs for them both, but Catherine leads her downward. They descend toward the common room, past trophy cases and storage closets and the athletic director's office, always closed. Catherine marches on, a gravitational field pulsing around her like a black hole, towing Shania past the event horizon and into whatever awaits beyond. They pass the class photos of the decades of previous Bard graduates, her fingernail tapping the glass frame of each as they pass. It sounds like slow hail in the empty hallway.

"1966, 1965, 1964, 1963...Whew, the uniforms were ugly that year.... 1962, 1961, 1960...Ahh, here we are. 1959."

She stops, and so does Shania.

"Hello, Gramps," she says brightly, and the tapping fingernail zeroes in on a face in the frame, tapping twice more. "Look at that crease. That guy meant business, even at seventeen."

Shania stands at her shoulder, peering silently at the class photo. Twentyish faces stare back, mostly smiling, all suited smartly in the school uniforms that Bard gave up on two decades ago, ushering in more casual generations. They're all white. They wear neckties and skirts. They all look vaguely strange, the way people from old photos always do.

"George Tane," Catherine says, and Shania glances at her, something in her stomach unfolding. She's already widening the scope of her vision when Catherine's manicured finger slides over two faces to the left, quickly, brutally. "Oh, and who is this? Gasp! Why, I think I know who! It's—let's take a peek at that caption—ahh, yes, Helen Rutherford! Nineteen fifty-nine graduate of Bard Academy. Well, I'll be!"

If Catherine keeps talking, Shania doesn't hear her. Her ears echo. She stares at her grandmother, the smile there an exact copy of the photo her mother keeps in the bedroom of their tiny apartment. The dimple on one side. The squint of her left eye. The tooth that doesn't quite line up with its neighbors. Shania's tooth.

"It hit me last week," Catherine says. "After Prescott told me you were researching your family. I was down here looking at this and then I saw her name. You don't need my IQ to put it together. You wonder why you're here, Shania Twain? It's not a scholarship. It's because you're legacy. Just like me, bitch. I looked in my dad's files."

A goldfish removed from water flops and gasps. Shania is a whale, slid up onto sand, lungs huge and empty.

"This doesn't mean anything," she says eventually. Her voice sounds hollow.

"Of course it doesn't," Catherine snaps. "Bard means nothing. It's a fucking school that just happened to throw us together. But you think because I'm rich that you can turn me into the supervillain in some sad-ass story where you get to play the victim? I think the fuck not, Shania Twain." She jabs her finger at Helen Rutherford and Shania's whole skeleton flinches. "She was *here*. She walked these halls. She walked this city. That's your blood. I don't know if she was rich. I don't know if she was poor. You said she did something terrible—I don't know what. I don't give a shit. That's your problem. The point is, rich or poor, she was here. And so are you."

"What about Ben?" Shania demands. "He's your brother but his face isn't in this fucking hallway, is it?"

She doesn't know what point she's making—only that she sees an exit sign. Catherine glares at her. The bell rings, a shrill dirge. Shania jumps but Catherine doesn't move a muscle. She gazes into Shania's eyes, the hallway lights straight above her. She casts no shadow.

"You're in this shit with us, whether you like it or not. The point is, what the fuck are you going to do about it?"

Then she turns, taking in the hallway, which stretches on to more hallway, which gives way to the stairs, the glass-cased common room. It's all hers. Shania just stares. It's like watching an actor prepare for the stage: no makeup, but layers of something else being applied to her face and eyes on the short walk inside. By the time she looks back at Shania, she's a new person, weightless and sparkling.

"Just in time for second period," Catherine beams. Then Shania is alone.

She can't look at the photo again. She stands with her back to it, her throat full and tight. Her breath shudders out. She's been wondering why they're here, and now she knows. A circular puzzle—it leads back to her. She moves away, up toward the buzz of students. She's late. Everyone is late. Mr. Foster is standing in the hallway looking tired, looking like he's considering switching careers. Shania avoids his eyes and moves toward English. She has an essay about *The Great Gatsby* in her bag, stuffed into the book's pages. She hasn't actually read the book. Shania passes Ms. Green's office, which is closed and dark, but something on the door catches her eye. A flyer. Michelle's face. Shania retreats a step and looks again.

CONGRATULATIONS, MICHELLE BROADUS! HARVARD IS LUCKY AND BARD IS PROUD.

Shania stares at the poster for a long moment, a flurry of emotions scrambling across the screen of her being like code she can't decipher, the static that has filled her head growing louder. She reads every single word on the flyer three times, takes in the photo of Michelle at the center. It looks like it might have been a yearbook photo from Bard from last year. Michelle is skipping her senior year—she won't be present for the group photo that Bard has made tradition for the graduating class, the photo that Shania's own grandmother posed for in 1959. That Shania will pose for next year, her face in these halls with Gram forever. Meanwhile, Michelle will be at Harvard, the memories of Bard evaporating while Bard goes on remembering. Shania is a whale again, sand against her shoulder. She turns abruptly away.

She runs right into Michelle.

"Watch out now," Michelle says, sidestepping her neatly. "Gotta be careful. You never know, I might get *ghetto* on you or something. Might get *aggressive*."

Shania is airless.

"Yeah, you thought that shit was cute, didn't you?" Michelle says. She's smiling but the smile is a tightrope, and she places one foot resolutely in front of the other. "Thought you would find a speeding bus and just toss my ass underneath as you ran by, huh? Too bad Ms. Green has been my counselor since I was at Bard Middle. I've been talking to her about people like you for *years*."

"I...I didn't..."

"Yes the fuck you did," Michelle says patiently. "Just stop. You're such a liar. At least be honest with yourself, if nobody else."

The word *liar* seeps into Shania's pores. It would be easier, Shania thinks, if Michelle were angry. Then the people who are walking by them on their way to class would stop, notice, maybe intervene. Instead they pass by, oblivious. Someone gives Michelle a light punch on the shoulder and interrupts as they pass: "Michelle! Congrats!" She beams a smile of thanks, then turns the headlights of that smile back onto Shania.

"You know what's sad?" she says, lowering her voice. "The sad shit is that I tried to help your dumb ass." She laughs, mirthless. "Ms. Green called you in to talk about an anonymous concern, right? Somebody said they were worried about you?"

"Catherine—" Shania starts.

"*Me*, fool," Michelle snaps, almost whispering. "Me. I wrote a note saying I was worried about you because you've been hanging around Prescott fucking Tane and I don't even think you knew what a violent piece of shit he is. But now I feel pretty damn dumb because you *do* know, don't you?"

"I don't know what Ms. Green told you," Shania says, scrabbling for a hold in this conversation.

"She didn't have to say your name," Michelle says, shaking her head. "I knew it was you. Wolf in sheep's clothing, aren't you? I saw you sitting alone in the cafeteria, in the greenhouse, and you looked like a little lost lamb and I tried to be nice. Look how far that got me. Well, guess what, li'l girl? You're not going to stop me. None of y'all are going to stop me. I'm going to Harvard, and next year Eric will too, and we'll forget all about your miserable asses."

She takes a breath, as if deciding something.

"Mrs. Walker told me about your granny," she says, so softly, and Shania's heart seizes. "I know what she did. I know what you're from. But you want to know the worst part? The worst part is, your racist-ass grandmother figured out a way to move what she did toward right. She tried to repair it. Only for her spineless fucking granddaughter to just do it all over again. You and her and Prescott are all from the same cloth. And your granny at least *tried* to cut herself out of the fabric. But you?" She sighs. "People like you and Prescott and Catherine and Hannah? You think you're invisible. Colorless. Prescott hurts people and they check him into some fancy hotel disguised as a hospital and wait out the storm behind closed doors. No real proof, so no real justice. The world makes excuses for it all. You think everything you do is hidden. But I see it. I see *you*. And one day, everybody will."

Shania wants so badly to breathe. She wants so badly to say something. The city of spite and anger that's been building in her head collapses brick by brick, just like that. She feels her eyes prickling.

"Don't you dare," Michelle says. It's the first time she's actually looked angry. "Don't you even dare. You don't deserve to cry. *I* deserve to cry. But I won't. Not for you."

"Tink!" Tierra cries from two floors up. She stands looking down between the staircases from above. Michelle looks up and the smile that spreads across her face is sunlight. She doesn't give Shania another look. She turns away. She ascends. Shania watches her until she's out of sight. When Shania lowers her eyes again, Mrs. Floyd is walking toward her, beckoning. She pauses halfway down the hall and calls.

"Shania," she says, an omen on her face. "I need you to come with me. Someone is here who needs to speak with you."

# CHAPTER 31

S hania sees her mother first.

She's sitting by Bard's front door near a conference room looking small and confused, her uniform shirt creased at the elbows where her arms wrap around herself. Beside her are two other people: One is a brown-skinned woman wearing a hijab, khaki pants, and a blazer. The other is a white woman wearing a blue police uniform. Shania's mother appears to know the woman in blues. The woman in khaki pants locks onto Shania with her eyes, and with a start Shania realizes she's seen her before. On TV, being bombarded by reporters after the first attack in SoBR.

"She just needs to ask Shania some questions, Pam," the white woman is saying to Shania's mother. "I think she'll be okay. Rana will take it easy on her."

"You must be Shania," the other woman says, unblinking. "I'm Detective Rana Omar."

"Hi," Shania says. Her mother is searching her daughter's face for the answers to the questions she hasn't been asked yet. Shania stares back at her, wishing they were alone. This is Gram's school and they're both standing in it.

"Step into the conference room," Detective Omar says. "I'd like us all to have a conversation."

The conference room is glass-walled but there's a curtain, which Shania is thankful for as Detective Omar slides it around them. The curtain doesn't cover the door. As students go about their business in the hallways of Bard, more than a few cast curious glances at the conference room, at Shania, some seeing her for the first time. The detective stands just outside, exchanging a few other words with the woman cop.

"Shania, what the hell is going on?" her mother whispers while they're alone.

Shania turns on her, feeling both sodden and ablaze.

"Legacy scholarship," Shania hisses back, and part of her enjoys the realization that spreads across her mother's face like wind over wheat. "When were you going to tell me about *that*? You said Dad's wife was paying for Bard. Gram's picture is in a hallway downstairs!"

Her mother's eyes dart to the door, then back.

"It's complicated, Shane—" she starts.

"You lied!"

"It wasn't a lie!" She pauses, chewing her lip. "That woman paid for your textbooks and enrollment fees. But this isn't the time for this conversation."

"It never is," Shania snaps. "And the lies just go on and on. I have her almanac, Mom. You lied to me. You hid it. You both hid everything. If she hadn't written in the almanac, I wouldn't have known. She never told me—"

"I told her not to," her mother hisses. "I told her there was no reason to ruin the version of her and your great-grandpa you have in your head—"

"Mythology," Shania says. She sucks in a sharp breath, hating that she's repeating Willa, then wondering why she hates it.

"*What?*" her mother says, baffled.

Detective Omar's voice yanks them back into the room. She's closing the door softly.

"You're new to Blue Rock," she says.

"Yes," Shania's mother says.

"No," says Shania. "My grandmother was from here."

"Okay," Detective Omar says, and nods patiently.

"We just moved here," Shania says.

"But I understand you've made some friends. Friends from school?"

Shania swallows again, the conversation with Ms. Green like a picked scab. She had lied to Ms. Green, and the truth had slithered its way to Michelle's ears like a poison snake. Detective Omar doesn't seem like the kind of woman who can be lied to. Her eyes are still pools focused on Shania, a small notebook in her hand with a black pen poised to scribble.

"Yes," Shania says.

"What's this about, Detective?" her mother interrupts. "What do you think my daughter has done? You said you had questions about the SoBR attacks. Is this because Shania works at that doughnut shop? You think she saw something?"

Detective Omar blinks slowly away from Shania and rests her eyes on Shania's mother.

"Shania works in Southtown?" she says.

"Yes. Paula's. *Paulie's*. The doughnut shop."

"How long have you worked there, Shania?" Detective Omar asks.

"All summer until now," Shania says. Her head is buzzing. Behind the detective, the hallways of Bard are buzzing too. She can feel the energy like a swarm of mosquitoes. Mr. Foster appears, loitering by the front desk. His eyes wander to the room, curious. Word is getting around. She wonders if it's reached Prescott, wherever he is. He'd been right—they came to school.

"You have certainly heard about the violence that has taken place in that area lately." The eyes lower to the notebook.

"The cats."

The eyes snap up to Shania's face.

"So you're aware of the cats?"

Shania's lips move but don't make sound, her tongue dry. She hadn't meant to say it. But the cats had sprung into her mouth from the part of her brain where she'd been keeping them caged. She thinks of Mrs. Walker's garden, a soft body hanging like a pendulum.

"Yes," Shania finally says. "Someone has been killing cats. This woman I work with at Paulie's says that's how serial killers start."

Detective Omar is quiet for a moment and then leans forward slightly with an expression of frankness.

"A serial killer is a scary notion," she says. "But the truth is almost worse. You might have seen on the news that someone named Earl Hutchins Jr. was attacked?" She waits while Shania nods. "You might have also seen that he was known locally as the Cat Man. They called him that because he took care of a half dozen stray cats. Would buy little tins of tuna and feed them under the overpass."

Shania doesn't admit that she had spent weeks thinking Earl had killed them, only now to learn that he had loved them. Her cheeks burn, feeling the story she's told herself shrivel. Detective Omar goes on.

"We have learned," she says slowly, "from witnesses and security footage, that the same person who attacked Mr. Hutchins also attacked his cats. Killed them. Sought Earl out and hurt the animals that Earl took care of."

Beside Shania, her mother gasps.

"How could anyone do that?" she says. "It's so cruel."

"The cruelty is the point," the detective answers, but she keeps her eyes on Shania. "This wasn't a serial killer from a late-night movie, Miss Hester. It's a young man in Blue Rock who stalked and harassed a man experiencing homelessness, and then eventually attacked the man himself."

"And now he's dead," Shania chokes out.

Detective Omar's mouth twists to the side, thinking. She decides something and then says, "Actually, Earl Hutchins Jr. is not dead."

"He's not?" Shania says. Her bones feel loose.

"No, despite the fact that someone worked very hard for the opposite. We're not releasing this to the public yet, but Mr. Hutchins is alive. He spent a few days in a coma. But now he's awake. And I am going to do everything in my power and the BRPD's to make sure that he receives justice for what's been done to him."

"Earl used to come into Paulie's," Shania says quietly. "He always said hello to me."

"Right now we're assessing his condition," Detective Omar says, eyeing her. "Seeing how his brain function will recover. But soon we're going to start asking him about what he remembers. And when we do—" She pauses for what feels like a long, long time. "What do you think he'll say?"

Shania has been building houses in her mind, neighborhoods where certain thoughts live, some with basements where she keeps the things she would rather not see. Things have been growing: Some are seeds she planted herself, some by other hands, some by Prescott. The walls are tall and marbled. Under Detective Omar's eyes, the foundations begin to shake.

"I don't know," Shania says.

Detective Omar keeps staring, a frown deepening on her mouth. She opens the notebook a little wider and fishes between a few of the pages, withdrawing a loose piece of paper. She unfolds it and pushes it across the conference table. She rotates it so it's facing Shania.

"Do you know what this is?" she says.

Shania looks down. On the piece of paper is a green triangle, pointing downward, bordered and intersected by white lines.

"No," she says shakily. A half lie.

"But you have seen it before?" Detective Omar says, not quite a question.

"I . . . yes."

"This is the symbol of a hate group," the detective says. Her eyes do not leave Shania's face. "An organization that advocates for white supremacy and white separatism. Did you know that?"

Detective Omar continues when Shania says nothing.

"Do you know what I mean when I say online radicalization? It's generally a term people use when they're talking about Islam after an act of violence has been committed. The sort of terrorism everyone is comfortable calling terrorism. They say, *So-and-so was radicalized online by ISIS*, or *an Islamic State group radicalized Americans online*. But one thing we don't hear as often—although we're starting to more lately—is about how young white people, particularly young white men, are being drawn in and radicalized by white supremacist and neo-Nazi organizations. Often it begins as humor. Memes, GIFs with funny captions, jokes. This is how a sense of community is created for young people who feel left behind or disillusioned. Then, when the stakes raise, everything can be dismissed as 'just jokes.' But humor is merely the jumping off point."

"What does this have to do with my daughter?" Shania's mother butts in. "You think she's, what? A neo-Nazi? Is that what you think, Detective?"

"She could be," Detective Omar says flatly, and Shania is too shocked to react. "White supremacy is certainly not limited to men. White women's violence just flies further under the radar. But in this case, I think Shania is pre-radicalization. I think she is nearing the point on her path where she will make a decision of who and what she wants to be."

"None of this makes sense," Shania's mother snaps. "And you haven't told me what Shania has done!"

Detective Omar ignores her, fixes her gaze on Shania.

"We understand you've been spending time with Prescott Tane. Is that true?"

Shania glances at her mother, whose eyes have narrowed into wet slits.

"Y-yes," Shania says.

Detective Omar picks up the piece of paper that had been left on the table between them, studying its green triangle for a moment. Then she turns it to face Shania again.

"Do you know why Prescott Tane would have a patch depicting this symbol?"

Shania's head is full of clamor, houses falling down and being built up. She finds she doesn't quite hear the detective, that she can barely hear herself.

"Do you mean his tattoo?"

Detective Omar raises an eyebrow.

"Prescott Tane has this symbol tattooed on his body?"

"You said...I mean..."

"Prescott Tane has this symbol tattooed on his body?" Detective Omar repeats.

"I need...I need...," Shania says, her mouth still too dry for words. She stands shakily.

"Shania?" her mother says, half rising.

"Shania, please sit down," Detective Omar says.

Shania pushes away from the table. She takes a few steps toward the door.

"Shania," Detective Omar says, her tone turning orange with warning.

Shania runs.

She stumbles out into the hallway, ignoring the glances of Bard's student body. Her veins are full of loosestrife. She needs the green air and the warm breath of plants. She needs lilac. Keeping her head down, she rushes through the halls toward the heart of Bard where the greenhouse is nestled, expecting someone to stop her. No one does. She thinks maybe Prescott's cloak of invisibility remains on her like a skunk's spray. She pushes through the sealed door and into the greenhouse, and only when it closes behind her does she breathe.

Empty. She thanks God, inhaling the thick air, letting it coat her skin. She drifts down the aisles of the greenhouse, eyeing the various shoots and sprouts. JP's planter is populated with varying heights of brittle brown, Michelle's roses climbing the planter in vibrant towers of scarlet. Shania averts her eyes, skipping Michelle's workstation for the one she knows to be her own.

She almost passes it. She's looking for something green, the hint of purple lilac, and her eyes don't find it. She has to double back, looking at the plastic folder beside the planter with her name on it. Shania Hester. It's hers.

It's all dead.

Almost all. The plants along one edge remain—their green is somewhat muted but holding onto life. It's the lilacs and the sprouts that hug them that have wilted. Her heart is a ball of lead in her chest, trying to make sense of it.

Everything had been alive. She had watered it, trimmed the few drooping blooms, checked the soil, added some fertilizer. The green had been strong and lively, the leaves shining.

Then her eyes find the place in the soil where her fingers had sunk, bearing metal. She had brushed a thin layer over top of the knuckles' hiding place, but the indentation stands out to her eyes like a fang. A grave. A pocket of poison. Her nostrils fill with the scent of invisible tomatoes.

She doesn't think.

She picks up the entire planter and is moving toward the door, ignoring its weight. Her arms are aching by the time she makes it halfway down the hall. By the time she gets to the door she's spilling dirt. She passes by Mr. Foster's class and hears her name being called. She carries on. She pauses at the stairs. If she goes down, she will come face-to-face with her grandmother, although they're already eye-to-eye. She goes up. She makes it up one flight. Then two.

Three. Splashes of dark soil trail her up to the fourth floor and then the half flight of stairs that leads to the art studio, which she knows will be empty. She shoves open the door with her shoulder and nearly drops the planter again, staggering through the bright space of the studio and its poorly drawn self-portraits. She faces down the door and its warning: ALARM WILL SOUND. She pushes through. October is at her cheeks immediately, at her neck, through her shirt. The wind tries to blow her back, but she braces herself, uses the weight of the planter to bull forward. In the sunlight her careful little garden looks even paler, its bones more brittle. Somewhere inside is the metal corpse that had poisoned the roots.

She wants to dig it all up.

Below her is Blue Rock, gray and small. It felt so big when she first moved from Morrisville; the traffic loud and the streets wide. From here she smells exhaust. From here she can see the crane in the heart of SoBR bending its neck to build something else glossy and empty. She tries to see it the way Prescott had painted it the day he had stood above the sky with her, holding her hand, but everything looks blurry.

When she pushes the planter up onto the ledge, the plastic makes a scraping sound against the stone. For the briefest moment, that scrape sounds like her shovel, digging Simon's grave.

"Shania," says a voice.

Shania gasps, jerking her chin to her shoulder to see who has followed. It's Detective Omar, breathing a little quickly, one hand outstretched cautiously as if to pet a tiger.

"Hey," the detective says. "Whatever you think you're doing, let's talk about it first."

"He's not crazy," Shania says, her voice thick with tears she didn't know were falling.

"No. No, I don't think he is."

"I can do better," Shania says, and Detective Omar, despite her effort to remain relaxed, looks baffled. But in Shania's head it's all connected. She can see the whole city in her head now: the way she and Prescott and Gram have all been walking on the same marble streets all along. Their paths wind and twist around each other. With Michelle's words in her ears, she suddenly feels as if she's watching her grandmother veer off along another street. Shania feels more alone than ever.

She turns back to her dead garden. She imagines tipping it over the edge, the silver knuckles careening out into space, lost forever. Even if found, no one could prove they were his. She is inventing an alibi for him without acknowledging what he has done. The act is a secret she keeps from herself. But what about the lilacs?

"Did he ask you to do something for him?" Detective Omar says softly. She's closer now, feet light as a cat's. But not close enough to reach, not yet. "Did he ask you to hide something? Don't do it, Shania. You're not a person to him either."

Shania stares down at the dead plants, wondering if that's why she's here. To hide the metal? Or is it because she can't bear to look at what she's done?

"Oh my God!" Shania hears her mother's voice, and she jerks, but doesn't look. "Shane, get away from the edge! What are you doing?"

The uniformed police officer says something Shania can't hear, and then her mother's voice lunges across the roof again.

"She's going to jump!"

"She's not going to jump," Detective Omar says, almost impatient. She keeps her eyes on Shania. Shania looks back.

"I don't know what to do," Shania says. "I don't know what it takes to be a good person."

"That's not what I'm interested in," the detective says. "When we focus on whether someone is good, we lose sight of the harm that is done. I'm interested in what Prescott has *done*. The people he's hurt. Now you need to make a choice. Are you going to protect him—Prescott Tane, and everything he stands for? Or are you going to protect the people he has hurt?"

"Everything he stands for?" Shania says, almost panting. The house she's built around him is on fire. She doesn't need to ask.

"I think by now you know that Prescott Tane is a white supremacist," Detective Omar says, her voice flat. "He was radicalized online and has been planning acts of violence in Blue Rock for eleven months."

Shania can't look at her. She stares instead at the planter that rests there at the edge of the sky, the crumpled brown leaves like fists.

"You need to make a choice," Detective Omar repeats herself, but also Willa, also Catherine, Ben. "I'm going to take you into custody either way, for concealing evidence. I already have Prescott's sister in custody as we learn more about another assault Prescott committed. The way it looks now, you and Catherine Tane are both accomplices. But you still have the opportunity to make a choice in your own heart. What's it going to be?"

The paths are before her as they have always been. She's afraid of them both. Prescott beckons from one, a lump of marble that fills the hole in her chest, a sweeping arm that lifts guilt and uncertainty away, replaces the fragile trembling with something like power. Down the other is something that scares her even more, something that looks like truth, white marble cracking.

Pressing the planter against her body, Shania frees one hand and touches one finger to the soil inside, is surprised by how cold it feels. She takes one of those crumpled leaves and holds it in her palm, wondering which path will let things grow.

The breeze has just picked up when she turns to face Detective Omar, slowly, slowly extending the planter out into the void between them. In Shania's head, cities fall. She wants to build them up, presses her tongue against her tooth to stop herself. The only quilt left is the one wrapping a dog's bones in Morrisville, and Gram wanders somewhere beyond its yarn, a web of threads between them. Shania imagines what it would take to hold a blade firmly, and slice.

# ACKNOWLEDGMENTS

I hardly know where to begin. I firmly believe that no book comes to life without the breath of many lungs, but this book in particular would not exist if not for the love and labor of a great many people. I'll try not to forget anyone. If I do, please charge it to the brain of a mom with a toddler and not to my heart.

I'll try to start at the beginning, because I feel like I've been writing this book for a long, long time, or maybe it's been writing me. My eternal gratitude—and I mean *eternal*—to the faculty of the 2005 Kentucky Governor's School for the Arts: Kelly Norman Ellis, Mitchell Douglas, Ellen Hagan, and Frank X. Walker. I don't know what would have become of me if I hadn't met you that summer, when you showed me what Kentucky writers can do and be. Special thanks also to Shayla Lawson, who called me fierce when I didn't feel fierce, and who eventually led me back to GSA to teach, where I have found renewed purpose in what I do and how I do it.

In my time studying race and racism, I have learned that there are exit ramps out of the racist thinking that permeates white America—inciting incidents that serve as a sort of "wake-up moment" for white people. Sometimes it's a conversation; sometimes it's an event, a film, a moment. Often it takes a few of them. By the time I reached middle school, I'd experienced several of these moments but had not yet put them together into a coherent analysis of our world. But in tenth grade, my geometry teacher,

Jason Bell, heard me say something about "reverse racism." He was the first person to tell me I was wrong, the first adult to tell me racism was about power. At the time, I thought I had none. I was wrong. Thank you, Jason, for telling one of your favorite students she was a young fool. In that vein, thank you to Nicole Garneau for watching my development with critical eyes while I sorted through denial and accountability and what it means to seek absolution for what we cannot be absolved for. If it wasn't for your class, I might have ended up a Rachel Dolezal. I've been so lucky with the educators the universe has placed in my path: Sheila Baldwin, Cia White, Kristin Dennis, Theresa Pfister, John Murillo, Prexy Nesbitt, Robbie Q. Telfer, Kris Erickson, Kevin Coval, and so many others who guided my steps, sometimes purposefully and sometimes by happenstance, a side effect of their own brilliance. I am so grateful to have been a byproduct of you all speaking your truth—especially the times when I wasn't ready to learn the lessons but stored them in the back of my brain. I've heard that sometimes the way out of whiteness "only takes one person" to shake the foundations of an existence not socialized to question the systems from which we (white people) benefit, but my, if the process isn't smoother when instead of one, there are many.

Dr. Jenn Jackson, I thank you for your years of love and friendship. Thank you for brunch and laughs and for coming to my very first "real" book launch (even when you didn't like the book). Thank you for holding my daughter. And for being the first person who made me realize, "Hey, Olivia, you don't always need to be the one talking." I learn from you every day, about community and love and imagination. Thank you always for challenging me—you have made me wiser and kinder.

Special thanks must go to Zoé Samudzi and Kush Thompson,

who, in 2016, read a draft of what this book began as and had the courage, wisdom, and kindness to say, "This isn't what you're trying to do. You're not doing what you think you're doing." And it wasn't. I wasn't. Thank you, Kush, for poeting the ways this story wasn't walking the path it needed to walk. Thank you, Zoé, for telling me what I knew deep down: that I had written a white-savior narrative, and that I hadn't yet let go of the desire for White Girl Absolution and Heroism. It would fall away in the years and drafts that followed, and I am so grateful to you for instigating that shedding.

I would not have been able to take up that "shedding" had it not been for the words and wisdom of Black women writers and scholars, some still on this earth and some who have moved on. Audre Lorde, Toni Morrison, Lucille Clifton, and Octavia Butler have left this world, but their legacies endure, and I could not be doing the writing I'm doing without theirs. I'm grateful also to bell hooks, Kimberlé Crenshaw, Trudy, Mikki Kendall, and Layla F. Saad, whose work and words I return to again and again, and will always return to again and again. There are so many people whose words have watered me: Kiese Laymon, Jason Reynolds, Jesmyn Ward, Mab Segrest, Jacqueline Woodson. Thank you for being.

Writing this book made me question myself time and time again, and so often I wanted to give up, knowing it would be easier to put this book in a drawer than face the inevitable unease that would come with finishing and publishing it. Asha French, I also met you in 2005, and I'm grateful to the universe for thinking it right to keep our paths close to each other. When I am at my lowest, you don't pick me up—you give me the tools and memories to pick myself up. Your gifts are many, and tenderness is one of them. God, I love you. I'm grateful, also, for the tenderness of my writing community—Lucie Brooks, Minda Honey, and Kaitlyn Soligan Owens. Thank you for always being a soft place to land. Thank you to Regina Brooks for finding this book a home and not letting me quit. Thank you to Jocquelle S. Caiby for not being quite convinced—this book still had a long way to go even when it had already come so far. Thank you to Ben Rosenthal, for trying. Thank you also to Viveca Shearin, for reading this book with Black readers in mind and helping me keep them safe. Thank you.

I certainly would not have reached this place had it not been for the generosity of spirit of so many Black women in publishing. Ashley Woodfolk, who has gone from "book friend" to "book and mom friend" to one of the best friends I've ever had. Truly. Tiffany Jackson, we were tossed together, but I'm so glad we stuck. I am inspired by you all the time. (All. The. Time!) Thank you to Dhonielle Clayton (my Wife-from-Another-Life) for reminding me—often—that patience and pettiness must be my fuel. Thank you to Nic Stone for the phone calls you didn't have to take and the texts you didn't have to answer. Thank you to Angie Thomas for *The Hate U Give* and for telling the truth about Hailey—whenever I felt like I should bury this book, your work reminded me that I couldn't. Thank you to L. L. McKinney for your pursuit of justice: You have often reignited me in the moments I start to feel tired. Thank you to my agent, Patrice Caldwell, for tapping in so fast to everything I'm trying to build. I can't wait to keep going. Thank you to Daniel José Older, for everything. You've been so kind for so long, and sometimes I don't know why, because I am very annoying. But I am grateful. Thank you, Eric Smith, for your (truly) undying enthusiasm. I can't wait for our kids to have a playdate.

I worked on this book in three states but published it in one: Kentucky. I came back in 2017 after ten years away, and I barely recognized Louisville when I got here, have been slowly catching up with the history that was made while I was gone. And so I must also thank Attica Scott, Ashanti Scott, Hannah Drake, Nubia Bennett, and Shauntrice Martin, whose leadership and thirst for justice have illuminated this whole city and all of us in it, and have thus illuminated this story.

Every time I think this book is complete, there is more that I want to say, more that needs to be said. But I am full of gratitude for my editor, Alexandra Hightower, for grounding this book when it was doing too much, for recognizing the times when I was letting Shania off the hook, for understanding that I was interested in looking at roots, not just flowers. You reined this book in but also helped it run. When it came to your desk, I thought it was close. But we have come so far. Thank you also to stellar copy editors Jake Regier and Caroline Clouse for your sharp eyes and soft hearts.

Finally, thank you to my husband for your unwavering support, and for furnishing our home with our daughter's signature giggle while I slammed my head on the keyboard behind a closed door. I couldn't have done this—*gestures at my life, our child, all my most joyful things* *any* of this—without you. I love you.

The word *acknowledgments* has come to mean "people to whom we are indebted" when it comes to publishing books. Yes. I am. Deeply. It also means a sort of acceptance of truth, and the truth is that the folks I have thanked here are the ones I remember, but there are countless people who, by living their lives and speaking their truth, by their lives brushing against mine, by our heads striking skull against skull, led me to the writing of this book. I am grateful for you all. I will not forget it.

# OLIVIA A. COLE

is a writer from Louisville, Kentucky. Her essays, which often focus on race and womanhood, have been published by *Bitch Media*, *Real Simple*, the *Los Angeles Times*, HuffPost, *Teen Vogue*, Gay Mag, and more. She teaches creative writing at the Kentucky Governor's School for the Arts, where she guides her students through poetry and fiction but also considerations of the world and who they are within it. She is the author of several books for children and adults. Olivia invites you to learn more about her and her work at oliviaacole.com and to follow her on Twitter @RantingOwl.